MOONEY IN FLIGHT

A NOVEL BY BRUCE DUCKER

MacAdam/Cage Publishing
155 Sansome Street, Suite 550
San Francisco, CA 94104
www.macadamcage.com

Library of Congress Cataloging-in-Publication Data

Ducker, Bruce.
Mooney in flight / by Bruce Ducker.
p. cm.
ISBN 1-931561-52-4 (hardcover : alk. paper)
1.Islands–Fiction. 2. Solitude–Fiction. 3. Midlife crisis—Fiction. 4. Middle aged men—Fiction. 5. Bahamas—Fiction. I. Title.

PS3554.U267M66 2003

2003014112

Manufactured in the United States of America.
10 9 8 7 6 5 4 3 2 1

Book and jacket design by Dorothy Carico Smith.
Cover painting by (to come).

MOONEY IN FLIGHT

A NOVEL BY BRUCE DUCKER

MacAdam/Cage

To Jaren, with love

Man has places in his heart that do not yet exist,
and into them enters suffering,
in order that they may have existence.
—Léon Bloy

CHAPTER 1.

What the ocean offered was nothing, no people, no Stace or Tommy, no home, no kid named Dog.

And all you felt, as the speeding dinghy slipped the surface on every wave, your insides ballooning out ahead and your weight rising to hammer height and then—bam—back to the seat on your sit bones, all you felt was terror and a sore butt.

Each leg of the trip got worse. It would make a cartoon, the centipede complaining to the chiropodist, each leg is worse than the last. I started by airplane from my hometown in the middle of the country, changed for the Bahamas to a plane the size of an elevator, engines that gagged like they ran on unfiltered Camels. First stop Nassau, then on to Providenciales, they call it Provo, the capital of these islands, then to sea. I traded my fear of heights for a fear of spaces. By launch over a washboard chop to the last inhabited key, and finally this, a rowboat twelve feet dent to dent, my worldly possessions sloshing in two inches of cloudy bilge.

Two inches and rising.

The sulky black man I hired to ferry me over stood in the stern and took his hand from the outboard's handle only to light a cigarette or flick one overboard. Once to tuck another roll in his trouser legs, a sign I took to mean we'd be taking on more water.

Pills for motion sickness had made me drowsy. In the patches where the water flattened out, my head flopped to my chest. The drone of the engine, the clop-clop of the waves, the clammy air. Then we would hit a speed bump that God had forgotten in the middle of the sea, and my neck would snap. The boatman kept squinting into the glare, a look of doubt on his face like he was sailing with Columbus and had forgotten the location of the hospital corner where the earth ended.

I must have been dozing when the island, my island, came on us. The outboard slowed to a grind, the forward shift of my body startled me awake and my grip tightened on the rail. When I looked up the bow was pointing at a scruffy line of sand broken by mangrove and stunted pine.

A floating dock jutted out from the beach. Isaac—he had told me his name, said I might need it—tied us fast to a rusty cleat. I sat useless while he heaved my bags onto the dock. The two canvas duffels held a toilet kit, a few books, the three-ring binders that were my stamp albums, and all my clothes. Plastic sacks full of canned goods, mostly soups and meats and a case of creamed corn. Two weeks' supply of fresh produce, okra, lettuce, blotchy yellow tomatoes. An open carton the butcher in Provo had begrudged me to carry meat that had been sliced and decked into white paper packets, neatly bundled for freezing.

Should he tote them in? The way he asked, he wanted me to understand he thought me a loony, a misplaced white man who didn't belong here and who wouldn't last long.

He asked a second time. "You want I carry the shit in, man?" He wasn't black, any more than I was white, but the colors of eggplant and motor oil.

"No need."

There were few enough chores, nothing other than settling in, storing gear, putting things in their place. I sat in the middle of the boat—he had scolded me about where to sit to keep from upsetting things. Now I stuck like a dog to the curb, and when he realized I needed a command to move, he flapped his hand to release me. I stood unsteadily and climbed out.

Isaac hopped between dock and boat, swinging the packages up. His sleek seal color reached down to just above the soles of his feet, and there like the rim on a pair of sneakers it turned into a gummy pink fringe. Days of standing in the bilge had washed out the browns and purples.

He was lining up the bags in neat rows. The afternoon wind had come up strong ahead of a front, Isaac agreed to ferry me so long as he could be back before the front blew in. Wavelets popped against the sides of his metal dinghy, and against the hull of a second boat, a Boston Whaler that came with the house. It was moored fast on the far side of the dilapidated boards. I recognized it from the estate agent's pictures, and even there it looked sorry, its motor pulled clear of the water and covered in torn orange jacket. The Whaler too had taken on water, and I peered in to see a plastic margarine tub floated about. I don't like boats. For that matter, movement.

Perfect weather for my adopted life. Gray mournful clouds bunted across a gray sky. Far out in crusted seas, a sun lighted pools of blues and blacks, a sun miles away shining on somebody else's planet. Not the Caribbean of the back-cover ads where tanned people in pastels chat and drink highballs, here skies were fat with moisture and the air smelled of dead fish and rain.

"We get a second wet season now," the estate agent in Provo had said. "You will find it quite short, quite refreshing. Rain and sand fleas through June, then heat and sand fleas to the autumn, then hurricane and sand fleas. The winter is pleasant, Mr. Mooney, our loveliest season. Merely sand fleas. That is your selling time. If you desire to try to live on Penniel Key for a little while, Mr. Mooney, that is fine. But if you desire to introduce this house into the marketplace, don't miss your selling time. The Hofstadter House is not a property that will easily gain access into the marketplace."

Not my concern. I reached into my pocket and fingered the two keys she had given me. Identical, tied by white twine to a paper disc on which "Hofstadter House" was neatly printed. When I'm gone will she, I wondered, buy a new disc? Will it become the Mooney House? Paid her past due invoices for plumbing, propane delivery, and security. And so bought a double-slice of time, extra cheese. Time and solitude, both as useless as the cement-foam water around me.

I could hear Hofstadter: Don't get mad and don't even get even. Just get out.

Isaac swung the last sack to the boards and stared at me. One of his eyes, the right, showed a color you didn't want to look at. Red the meat of a clam. It pushed out the white. He balanced himself in the boat, silent, waiting for me to understand he was through. I opened my wallet so he could see in. Watched him watch my thumb graze over the blue and purple Bahamian dollars. He breathed through his nose, you could hear it. Behind those exotic bills, a smaller, neat file, I riffled the green U. S. currency. Slid out two twenties and handed them over. Thirty-five dollars had been quoted. He rubbed his dangerous eye over me and made no move toward change.

"What if I want you?" The extra five bought me a dumb question.

"You got no radio here. You can't call."

We studied each other. I wondered if his eye was sick, maybe in Provo he could have it examined.

"Hoist sometin'." He said at last and nodded toward the house. "A towel in the window. I pass by every week to Mayaguana. If I see a towel or sometin' I stop. You leave a note, I bring you shit."

Isaac stepped over the broken plank serving for the stern seat, put his foot on the engine housing, his first two toes around the starter cord. He yanked and the motor fired. He walked forward and loosed the line from its cleat, jumped in. He steered slowly around the floating debris that was the dock. When he was clear he looked over his shoulder—a last chance? Maybe the lunatic will come to his senses—and wrenched the throttle. The boat carved through the water.

I watched the dot disappear into bands of color. You would have thought the sounds would leave, too, but after the rattling tin boat was swallowed up there was no quiet. The static of the water, the rasp of the sand, the wind that flapped against my trouser leg. At my feet lay bags of provisions in rows. They were the army of enemy. I picked out the first carton box, Carnation condensed milk—why the hell had I bought that? I don't drink milk—hefted it to my hip, and began the walk.

The dock went halfway up the beach to account for tides. Its boards, doused in salt and dried by the sun, had been nailed to a frame and the frame set on caulked oilcans. An anchor rope pointed the walkway into the sea, and the oilcans buoyed the whole assembly. It shook and slid around when I walked over it to the beach.

A sand path ran through the yellow sea grasses of the dunes. A hundred yards up sat the house. I realized I was standing on the spot where the agent shot the file photo, from the start of the dock, to catch the dunes and the house at its best, its elevation, a clear sky. The photograph was honest, showing a dilapidated cottage, unpainted shingles grayed near to silver from neglect. A dozen blown-down shingles lay where they fell. A few were replaced, I could see the catalogue-brown stain on the new wood, they looked like missing teeth. A double window sat in the front dormer of a partial second story. Penniel Key it was called, although it couldn't be the key to anything. Penniel Lost in the Ocean, Penniel Birdshit-on-the-rocks.

I went up the three outside steps. Once the porch was screened in, but the occasional guest, maybe even Hofstadter, had clipped random squares so there was more air than mesh. The door to the porch lolled open on its hinges. I set down the carton of cans, grasped the handle to the inner door and gave a twist. The tongue engaged the gears, the latch gave, if you take care of moving parts they don't let you down, and I went in.

Where the heart is. Home sweet home, ever so humble. Inside, on either side of the door sat two chrome straight chairs with seats of flecked red plastic. A daybed sofa, a half-upholstered easy chair, and across on the long wall to my right a small fireplace. Where to find wood on this smear of land? But a hearth nonetheless.

I am a sucker for fireplaces, for all sites romantic. Even the two women I married would have admitted that. When Alice and I decided to wed, her first time not counting an annulment and about four thousand live-ins and my second, resolving that our pasts were just that, past, to be blazed to ashes, we commited an eternal and romantic act. It was my suggestion, right after I proposed or she did, I never really understood how it came about, we were finishing a bottle of red wine after a spaghetti supper, so we took pens and wrote on a pad of slate blue paper, hidden from the other, the names of every lover we could remember. Wrote out our lists and crumpled the pages into a ball. And I, her eyes aglimmer in the light, her face beaming with just the expression of devotion you'd want if you were directing a school play, then I tossed both balls of paper onto the logs and we watched our new life flare up in the flames. Very effective, very eternal.

Perhaps I would have a fire. Perhaps there was a grove of hardwood behind the house, and perhaps there was more on this tiny fishhook of an island than the estate agent had let on. The agent was angry with me. When she heard of Hofstadter's death, she went to the expense of preparing a brochure to sell the property. It looked to be an easy commission. But Hofstadter tricked her by leaving the house and island to some Statie, some inland, pallid crackpot who showed up in Provo and declared he was going to move in. "People vacation there," the agent told me over the phone and again in person, in that particular blend of Bahamian courtesy and disdain. "We get a few rentals in season, Mr. Mooney, though not many. It's too remote. You must understand, there is no source of supply, your only electricity is from a generator. You will be quite alone. Propane lamps, a two-hour open-boat ride to the nearest inhabited island. People simply don't live there."

I banged through the first floor. Behind the main room connected by a pantry were a 1940s kitchen, gas burners and electric refrigerator. The cabinets at eye level had what I'd need. Jam-jar glasses, chipped china. One setting would do. Above all sorts of crap to make it a cutesy home, straw place mats, candles, a hardwood salad bowl. Uncharacteristic of Hofstadter—they must have been spoils from a former owner.

The rest of the first floor consisted of a small room with a dilapidated double bed, iron headboard painted white. A bathroom where the toilet and sink functioned despite the rust scars. The medicine cabinet over the sink had a mirror facing out. I looked at its sorry view, wished it wasn't there. I checked the closet: old, gray linens, and on the top shelves games for a rainy day. Upstairs the one room, windowed on three sides, and a single army bed tented between the eaves. The mattress was ancient, the cover lined in blue ticking. Someone had folded linens and an unraveling wool blanket and piled them on the dresser. Welcome home.

I suppose, to give Alice her due, we had no real chance. You need a certain momentum to get on with life, like leaping across a stream. It's harder to do from a standing start, and when we married I had no momentum. I tried to gather some speed—why else that evening of movie drama, the list, the crumpled ball, the names of past loves firing up the chimney? Of course I started and ended my list with Reba. If we had thought to set out rules for the exercise, we'd have excluded departed spouses. But I thought this was the right way, I wanted to list them all, I'd made my list before, and lovers—love—always started and ended with Reba.

I finished my tour. Behind the house a healthy sedge grew over the sands, marking the boundaries, I only later realized, of the leaching field for the septic tank. At the far edge a knobbled, pygmy pine. Attached to the back of the house and coming up by the kitchen window was a metal locker that housed the tools I might need to get on here. A fishing rod, a spade and pitchfork, various rakes. A scythe, of all things. Maybe I'd give a costume party, I'd wear the scythe and the sheets from the bed and come as the Grim Reaper. Several sizes of linoleum cutters. Boxes of spare shingles, a stack of flagstone, though I hadn't seen any installed, piping joints, wires, small jars of nuts and fasteners and eyelets. I was not interested in maintenance. Does the condemned man shine his shoes?

Against the back wall of the house, by a rear door that wouldn't latch, a small pile of wood. Nothing more than the cuttings of old bush, each branch the diameter of a woman's wrist. I brought an armful inside and arranged it to the side of the fireplace.

Then I went about my task of stocking the house. Don't some birds store gorge in their gullet and just cough it up for their young? I made several trips. The place was what I anticipated, just rummier.

The stand-up freezer swallowed my supply without a burp. On the porch I watched darkness seep into the horizon. There was nothing else in it, just dark and water. The rains started, only a spit but sweet-smelling and soft. I went indoors. Checked to make sure the flue was open and stacked a few logs in a square, like building a model outpost on some frontier. Paper would be at a premium—why hadn't I thought to ask for paper sacks? I unwrapped a tin of Norwegian sardines and used the label. It was enough and the sticks caught fire. They burned in blue and yellow flames, colors of the chemicals of the sea.

Seven, eight trips down the path in a light drizzle. Monotonous. Again I stowed the food that needed putting away. The crabs, Mr. Mooney, the agent said. If you leave the bread out the crabs will come through the walls and take the bread. Then I sat down and watched the fire. It burned too quickly to enjoy. I was alone at last, and, now two hours into my exile, I was lonely. Two hours into my plan of giving up a life that had nothing in it, I was bored.

When I left Alice that last day, after we talked about my departure like our lives were different movies, we are deciding which channel to watch, we discussed who kept what. There was no argument. I told her to tag whatever she wanted and sell the rest. Hofstadter's house came furnished. Besides I wanted to leave all that stuff behind. Even though I hadn't seen the house I was hoping that it was beyond the reach of her magazine racks and potholders in the shape of kittens. Before I left, I set the ball of paper on the mantel. Of course I had palmed her list of lovers, stuck it in my pocket and threw into the fire a blank page I had in my hand. So I placed her list on the mantel. Not that I'm proud of this, I know it is cranky and cloddish, but there are times, and birth and death are among them and maybe this one too, a man and a woman leaving their marriage, that cranky doesn't count. I smoothed it out and centered it on the mantel. With a black ballpoint pen that bears an unfurling U.S. flag and the name and telephone number of Alice's real estate company, Miramonte Farms, I printed clearly across the top, ONE TOO MANY.

CHAPTER 2.

Hofstadter informed me he is in an argument over life itself. After Hofstadter grew too ill to drive, I took him on the weekly route, first the shrink at the fancy end of Sycamore, sometimes laundry and grocery shopping. He didn't like to stop. I could sense his right foot jamming the floorboard, overriding my accelerator. Each traffic light we made he uttered a tiny, satisfied grunt.

"It is," he croaked, "the single question. Unless you can answer yes, and no thinking person can," he waved a hand to supply the missing words, "no other issues."

Hofstadter spoke through a mechanical larynx. His own had been removed in an operation. They didn't mean to do it, they were radiating his throat for the cancer that spotted his body like—his words—ketchup spotting a bun, and they accidentally burned out his larynx. His new voice was weird and aluminum, they stuck in the voice of the villain from a science fiction movie. Every so often he removed the apparatus that hooked his mechanical box to the muscles in his throat, exposing the dressed O in his neck, and plugged in a cigarette. That way he could smoke through the hole at the base of his throat. It avoids, he said with a leer, staining your teeth.

When he first got his mechanical larynx I had to lean forward and place my ear by his chest to understand him. I can't say I liked it. But I got used to him. The sound came out hollow, metallic and hollow. You heard blades turning slowly in a giant silo, and the broadcast came at you with that wah-wah voweling that dance-band trombones make. No one else, he told me, has the patience to listen. The words came out slowly, he skipped verbs, and you got the point long before he finished. No one else has the patience, except the checkout counter lady at the supermarket. But if there was any kind of line, Hofstadter wouldn't wait, so that left only me.

"They talk about…reason to live," he wah-wahed. "They don't understand…Faulty…If no reason," he shrugged, waved, panted for his energy to return, "premise fails."

Sycamore was a residential street of large, overstuffed houses where doctors and dentists kept ground-floor offices. We stopped in front of an orange brick building. Stone lions guarded the front stairs and a white-pillared porch. I would pick Hofstadter up in forty-five minutes.

"Bible…fifty minutes to the hour," he told me. "Father Sigmund himself. New breed…cutting corners…screwing the nutcakes." He shrugged to show he couldn't fight them. "Then again…Freud didn't play golf…Bastards."

At least I thought he said bastards. On the last words he opened the car door and the traffic noise stepped on his voice. Hofstadter walked with weariness, he trudged off to join another battle. Before his climb he rested his hand on the head of the lion, patted its brow.

I took an early lunch at a Woolworth's counter. Today's Special, touted by a color photo on my menu, was spaghetti with one meat ball. Woolworth was holding the line, resisting the march of time. F. W. and I oppose change. I ordered a fried egg sandwich and a vanilla shake. You should be allowed to find a place where time is not in control, where you can revisit your mistakes. Like fantasy baseball camps, men going away to Arizona to pretend they have made the Cardinals, fresh out of insurance companies and law firms they have had a tryout and they've made the farm system, even if only for a week and four thousand dollars. It's a great concept, they should have more variety for the rest of us. Fantasy baseball camps, fantasy military camps—kill Gooks, win the war, ten days in Scottsdale—fantasy sex and parenting. Go away for a week and have your kid elected to Boys' Nation. Don't let the past come out wrong. That's what Woolworth should serve with its Tuesday special, choice of twelve-ounce soft drink included.

A fried egg sandwich takes no time to eat, and I was early to retrieve Hofstadter from his session. I watched him fight against the glass storm door of the shrink's house, push it open, take the stairs like an invalid. On the concrete balustrades at the top were two enormous pots where geranium plants bloomed orange and green. Hofstadter looked weakened by them, their vividness, what I thought I could smell even from my distance to be their lewd odor. I admired Hofstadter, how he decided to go over. Not just his illness. Early on you collect things, materials, food, touch. Everyone is pressuring you to stay, to stay in the game. All the ads, your doctor, every religionist. Once you go over you lose interest in those things, give away possessions. Lose the color in your hair, your skin turns to paper. Hofstadter had gone over.

On the drive back we talked about Reba. Or rather I talked. His session had tired him, and he slumped against the door. I stopped at a drugstore and shopped a short list. I renewed a prescription and signed his name. It was a comforting feeling to deal for him. I had become a substitute for Hofstadter, I had a second life, but without people. All I had to do was furnish it, keep it in stock, and it would soon be over. I didn't even bear the pain. This day I chose brands of razor blades and shaving cream.

"If I had only had some warning," I told him back in the car, not for the first time. "For her to be taken away, it was so sudden. I feel like the man on the sidewalk when the guns started going off. What's the newspaper phrase, an innocent bystander? I had no idea there was a bank robbery in progress." He sat silently, withholding his sympathy. He looked like the puppet when the puppeteer was on break, and I took his slump for assent. So I went on.

"But maybe it wasn't that. Maybe it was just the times."

In many ways Reba and I had the perfect marriage. People often told us that. I pulled up in front of Hofstadter's house. It was a brick bungalow on a block of identical bungalows. His was the only lawn in need of cutting. I asked him if he wanted a quick game—we'd invented a variation of chess we called Ssech. He shook his head. It's just as well, I told him, I needed to get back, which was true. He looked at me. Somehow it was the melancholy expression Reba would have used. He was tired of talking, I could tell the words would hurt him to say.

"You had warning," he croaked. Then he got out carrying his drugstore bag between one finger and thumb, dainty, and I drove back to work.

Hofstadter had been on the faculty, I knew, for many years at an obscure college. He'd let it slip once, never referred to it, it was yesterday's weather. He never mentioned his subject or where it was, but from the soiled regimental ties he used to wear and the several melanoma, Cheerio-size and brown, that dotted his temples, I guessed, or rather I put in my mind, that it was at a small private school somewhere with good skiing. He had a peculiar way of speaking. The way some people avoid religion and politics, he avoided the past and the future.

At my desk I considered his words. My work allowed me time to think. I worked for the Clerk of the Municipal Court. On the days that I ran errands for Hofstadter, I took a longish lunch hour. Mentioned it to the Clerk, the gracious way of asking permission without asking, and made sure I put in equal time while others take their lunch. The Clerk was lenient about a seventy-minute hour because she respected my professionalism, because I was diligent about the job while I was there and, just as likely, because there was often nothing for me to do.

Maybe Hofstadter was right. Maybe I had early

indications but what of it? I didn't see them, and if I had, I didn't do anything about them. There were too many contingencies: one, are there warnings? two, do I see them? three, do I understand them? four, do I know what to do? and last, do I do it? Would that have satisfied Hofstadter? What is he trying to tell me?

At the Office of the Clerk of the Municipal Court, most of my energy went into a private and unspoken feud with a co-worker named Canges. He seemed to share my meanness of spirit, and it made him a worthy adversary. He also understood that in the Office of the Clerk one was safe doing nothing. Mistakes occurred only in action, and they occurred daily. When they did, Canges's genius lay in slipping some trace of them under my blotter. His title was dockets clerk, and mine was assistant to the Clerk. Who was superior, Canges or Mooney, was uncertain. We both worked for the Clerk. She was in charge of the entire bureau, and it was clear that neither Canges nor I could order about the other. That, his inclination to bully, mine to be bullied, and our dislike of each other, bound us together. It made the office less lonely.

When I returned from lunch my task was to discover what files Canges had routed my way. New lawsuits came to me first, I stamped them in, registered the docket fee, created mailing labels. Canges got them next in case they needed some special attention. Like a temporary restraining order, with its threat of imminent harm. That is, harm to the combatants—we in the Clerk's office were safe. The task took no exercise of judgment—the pleadings always used the frozen, identical words. If there was no overt and imminent danger, one of the key phrases, I got them back, logged them in, and assigned them to a judge.

It was the hidden danger I looked for. Canges might have set a hearing for a restraining order without telling me, leaving me to blunder by assigning it to a second judge, only to be ridiculed when number one judge discovered he was not alone. Every file Canges sent me had a lethal potential, somewhere in the innocent and tedious papers there might be a small sliver of bamboo spread with excrement. My task was to find the traps and disarm them. When I'd first met Canges I had liked his black humor, I had thought we would become pals and conspirators. I let him in on my little ironies, how I would assign to the racist judge the lawsuit between black and white, to the alcoholic judge the DWIs. I tried to spread the malice around. Together we could have had some laughs, but Canges didn't care for pranks without an audience. Everyone said about him he's a great kidder, as if that was something to be proud of.

The day ended. I packed up to go home. Since I lost Reba, each day was a wall to be painted. I remembered putting in a new garage door, a satin surface that I stained in rhythmic, even strokes. A thin coat each day against the weather. And each day, by the time the sun lit the afternoon clouds, that surface was blistered with bubbles.

I said goodbye to my office workers and left. Twice a day I had something to say to them. On the way home I considered whether to have a glass of gin or a glass of bourbon.

Alice and I dined on a pork loin she baked. She was a good cook, and she clipped recipes from the newspaper, put them by my place for approval and stuck them with magnets to the refrigerator, little plastic bananas, watermelons, onions. She had square, rubbery magnets, too, from trips we'd taken to destination resorts, Atlantic City, Disney World, that she used to hold postcards sent her by friends in the real estate business. This week the refrigerator displayed pictures of Catalina Island and Independence Hall. By my plate she arranged scraps of paper she collected during the day so that we could discuss them. Not only recipes. Invitations to some benefit for a skin disease, a newspaper article about stamps from Cameroon, a coupon for flower seeds that had been hung on our door. She'd retrieved a list I did for myself of household chores. The chores were undone. Did you mean to throw this away? she asked as I carved the roast. Alice was a trash detective.

The pork loin was delicious, she served it with a tiny cored apple sliced into coils. Buttered asparagus, Minute Rice. The vegetables were as colorful as the ones on the refrigerator. I downed my dinner with a second bourbon and water, no need of water since the ice cubes had melted a little. Afterward I retreated to my room under the basement stairs. We called it my study, although I didn't study anything. I contemplated furniture I'd make if I had the tools, and I pasted stamps, none collectible, into my collection. I imagined myself in a vast basement shop, making fine cabinetry. Planing valuable and exotic woods, aromatic curls coming off evenly and falling to my feet. I stood ankle-deep among shavings of sandalwood and ebony. Soon the wood had been planed away. I didn't have a shop, didn't want one. I had this room, Reba had used it for storage and I left her bracketed shelves in place. I bought a child's desk at a garage sale, and I sat at it under a bare bulb pasting in stamps from Sri Lanka, Nicaragua, the Seychelles Islands.

Alice took comfort in being present. When I read a book she read a book, and when I chose a sofa she sat next to me. The principal function of my study was escape—the stamps were something I took up after Reba, thinking, I don't know what. Now I heard Alice at the top of the cellar stairs, her weight cautiously testing the steps, her feet inches from my head. Soon she tapped on the beveled door. It was my early warning system. She called, Lennie, as if I might be dead. She opened the door and smiled bashfully, said, I just wanted to make sure everything was all right. That was my signal. I closed my albums, pulled the light chain, and withdrew. Time for bed. Once a week we had sex. Usually on Wednesday, following her favorite shows on the television. Alice had a good heart and a great eye for decorating, and believed ours a successful marriage. I was lucky to find her the second time around, her friends from her office often told me, and it was so. She dressed well, earned a considerable income, more than I did, selling real estate. She gardened, she worked on the annual food drive at her church, and except about colors that are not complementary she never complained. She was cheerful and optimistic, she did aerobics to keep herself fit, gynecological exercises to keep herself sexy, read summaries of the national and world news in *USA Today* to keep herself interesting, and, I can't explain it, she had a way of moving, chatting, placing a cup of coffee on the table by my elbow, that drove me mad.

* *

I lay in the metal bed upstairs, tracing spider cracks in the ceiling to see where they led. What in hell had I done? The stupidity of the island, the loneliness and stupidity of it all shuddered through me, a small delight like the passing of gas.

I dressed in long khaki pants and an army shirt. I laced my new black boots to the shin and struck out for the morning's exploration. The estate agent's sketch showed the island as J-shaped, with the letter reversed so the short arm stuck east into the Atlantic. The house built on the long arm just above the bend. The builder had chosen the site with the bay for an anchorage, I'm sure he had figured to sell to some stockbroking mariner, moored out the window a boat full of brightwork, flying one of those jokey flags with a cocktail glass. He'd used the island as a windbreak. Dawn from the front porch, in the evening, you could set up a lawn chair out back and watch the sun set over the septic tank and the thin pine forest beyond it. He hadn't counted on Hofstadter and me.

I ate a quick meal, coffee, toast and apricot jam. The fresh fruit was ticking away, but it looked too healthy.

I finished my coffee on the porch. The length of the island ran off to my left, no more than a mile. To the right was the curve of the bay, and the scruffy point sat across from me. The growth looked impenetrable. I chose that way.

The day was summery, fresh with rain. The hardened sand supported my weight until I took a second step, then it broke under the ball of my foot. As I went deeper into the crotch of the J, red mangrove spread down to the bay's edge, and I went to the higher ground and blazed my own path. It was slow going. Mangrove roots knit themselves together like God's own chain link. Farther from the shoreline the mangrove gave out, replaced by a sorry brush and scrub pine. As I bushwhacked the woods kept out the breezes so the air was locked into its space. Sand fleas clouded on my covered arms and legs and nipped through the cloth.

I spent the morning fighting my way to the hook end of the island. Beyond was only water. The bear went over the mountain. My shirt was sweat-black and heavy. I made it back, frustrated and itching. Little red welts covered my legs to the top of the boot, my arms to my wrist, and where the buttoned cuff opened, the buggers had bitten the bites.

My view of bravery came from those war movies where the G.I. gets tortured by the Nazis. Decide when you're going to break. My threshold was maybe the enlistment office. Once you break, there's no sense taking the first hot poker—save yourself the trouble and the potassium picrate.

On the way back, mostly I thought about the family—Stace and Tommy and Reeb. Tommy had a dog named Swami and a friend named Dog. The family was together in those white evenings, all four of us in the present tense. Tense was a good word for it. We'd scattered since. Or they scattered, I didn't scatter, I stayed on, like the clinker in the bottom of the popcorn pan.

Somewhere along midday—my watch had given in to the moisture and clung to 12:17—I sat at the Formica table watching the dunes out the dirty window, a sandwich in front of me. The saw grasses bent in a new breeze. An unlatched screen flapped in the wind. All I could think of was the solitude. It sounds absent-minded, but I hadn't focused on its connection to being alone. Would solitude drive me mad? Would I become one of those loonies who talk to clouds and, when the season dried and they didn't appear, to pebbles on the beach?

All I needed was to persevere. Everyone's crazy, Hofstadter says. Eventually you come out the other side. I would burrow in like a worm into an apple and pop out fat and gasping through the skin. I took a slice of white bread from the plastic sleeve, tore it up and tossed the pieces out the window. Then I balled a second slice into a gunky mass and placed it on the sill.

In minutes there was a clatter at the window like old St. Nick and I looked up to see a crab at the sill. He had climbed up the strut that supported the outside shed, across its roof and now stood at the screen as the breeze pushed it out, deciding on his entrance. You see them in a restaurant aquarium or even on their own beaches and they seem just what God intended. But at the threshold of a desolate house, he might be a special effect in the highlights film of your life, the part about sins. Pink and cream on his back, arms unbalanced and quirky as a robot, tiny maraschino eyes stuck on his head. Every time he moves and sometimes when he doesn't there is a clacking. We watched each other for a mistrustful moment. The screen swung—the breeze pulled it out two or three inches, then let up so it fell again. The crab, the size of the ball of bread he was after, froze and watched. In that buckled brain was he solving the puzzle? Wind, bread, distance. He lunged, the ball in his pincers when the screen shut behind him. At the next swing of the frame, he side-winded out and disappeared. I checked the sill for loss of limb. He'd got away clean.

In the afternoon, I made myself a drink, white rum and grapefruit juice, and sat on the screened porch to read a book. It was a paperback, with an orange cover. The day was hot and close. I stripped off my clothes and carried the chaise lounge to the crest of the dunes where the path led. Every so often a cloud passed and stained the sand. The sun was steady and blue, and I thought it might be pleasant to sit in its company.

It was a mistake. The sand on the surface had formed into a clumpy crust, and it gave off a damp odor, the smell of decay. Dried bits of seaweed blew about like cigarette papers, and quick flies darted around my legs.

I had no sooner set down the lounger and adjusted its back than the flies found me out. Not sand fleas, these were visible, bottle green with a white after-body, as if they might be diseased. They circled my feet and for the briefest pause lit upon my bone-white shins and the tops of my feet. It might have been a tickle, if you could overlook that they were flies. I waved them off, they came back. I swatted at them, but they were too fast. The more I swung, the easier they seemed to get away. I ran back to the house and searched the kitchen drawers. In the back of an eye-level cabinet, behind the soup bowls, I found a pamphlet. It described the workings of some household appliance that wasn't there. The rear cover had a drawing that showed some sixty-eight replaceable parts, an order form, and a list of dealers worldwide. I rolled it into a stick and went back armed to the beach chair.

The club increased my speed, but still I was missing.

Suddenly, with one swipe, my luck changed. Maybe skill. Splat, and I left a smeared corpse on my left instep. I was on target. I squashed a dozen of them, and I quit before they did. I went back inside. The pamphlet was permanently rolled and stained with blood. My legs, otherwise wedding-cake white, were spotted with the satisfying blotches of success. I poured a second drink. The first had made my eyelids heavy, and I took my hope for a breeze upstairs and lay on the bed, listening to the cotton curtains whisper against themselves. I dozed.

In the heat sleep didn't refresh me. I awoke parched and anxious. The north leg of the island would be my afternoon's work.

* *

I never got to it that day. Or the next, or the next weeks. Middays I napped. In the afternoons, chores. Upstairs I pinned a shutter back to its brackets and from atop a stepladder tacked loosened shingles to the side. Each task that called for minutes sucked up hours.

Most evenings I built myself a fire. Sat on the sofa with a last drink and watched the colors jump. When the woodpile was spent, I gathered branches from the pines. I had no good splitting tool, but they were easily broken into regular lengths. One of the things I used to do with the kids was split wood. I'd use the wedge and hammer and Tommy, and later Stace, would pick up the pie-shaped pieces and stack them. I would split the logs small enough so the kids could lift them, and keep a mindful eye all the while that they not get too close to the stump. I always worried they'd get too close to the stump. The sledgehammer would come down on the steel wedge with a great clank, the log would split in a single stroke usually clean, but sometimes, especially with the softer woods, splinters would fly. I wore safety glasses, but you couldn't get the kids to keep them on. So I'd have to keep an eye.

What holds a family together? Less than you think. It's a stack of split wood, irregular shapes that hang together without any glue. The odd gnarls and knots and elbows. You take away a log at the corner and the whole thing comes chock-a-block tumbling.

In the cabinet where I'd discovered my flyswatter was a palm-sized spiral notebook. One of those grammar school things. On the top of the first page I wrote "Isaac" so I wouldn't forget his name and jotted down my needs. Hofstadter's notes were on the last page, lettered in that exact hand, it reminded me of when I used to shop for him. I could read in his printing how he'd pressed on the pencil, how he'd bend over to write and knit his brow. Peanut butter, he had printed. Half-inch brads. Soldering wire, Mazola oil, electric tape.

Hofstadter was dead only months and sitting there I couldn't bring back his face. I wanted to see his expression as he wrote out his needs, but I couldn't bring back his face. Would that be embarrassing if you went wherever we go, the afterlife, and at you came all these people whose names you couldn't remember? There would be your own son, your wife, running toward you in slow motion and you couldn't think who it was. Maybe they use subtitles. That's not as weird as it sounds, if it's truly heaven and they're looking after you, they would do that.

Once I told Hofstadter about Heaven and Hell. He liked it. How when I was a kid and believed in them, I always saw two opposing teams. The Fallen Angels were playing God's Pals.

"The names gave me the clue, Heaven and Hell. Goal posts with the two big H's."

"Makes sense to me. I hope you didn't try that on the priest."

"On a Sister. Sisters taught Bible."

"And?"

"She came unglued. 'Mooney, you're either a heathen or an indolent lout.'

"That got a great laugh. 'Which is it?'"

"Which did you choose?"

"I had no idea what the words meant. No one did, but it gave the kids high sport for a year. 'Mooney,' they would call, 'you're either a heathen or an indolent lout.'"

* *

I had time cornered. Stored in the crawl space, maybe eighteen inches deep, under the joists that supported the house so you could get at the pipes. The hell with tasks. I opened my second bottle of white rum—I'd brought a case of twelve with me, it had seemed ample at the time, but now that the first bottle was spent I grew concerned—poured a dose and stirred in an equal measure of orange juice. I opened my note pad and printed the word Rum. It looked odd by itself, so I printed words to keep it company.

RUM
BUM
BUT
BAT
BAR
FAR.

My unreliable watch said 12:17, maybe the same 12:17 I'd set six days ago. The north end could wait.

CHAPTER 3.

Alice brought me the news of Hofstadter's death with the morning paper. I was not surprised. Most days she fetched the newspaper from the front steps while I fixed the coffee, and on her walk back to the kitchen she peeked inside to find a tidbit to start our breakfast conversation. Or rather hers. Her favorite crib notes were death notices and white sales, she'd often begin our day with the market price of percale sheets. This morning it was the one-inch obit of my friend.

"'Donations may be made,'" she chirped, "'to the Bide-a-Wee Home for Animals.' I didn't know he was a dog lover."

"He wasn't," I told her and took the sections of paper she offered me.

"Cats?" she asked hopefully. The story tells me nothing new. Hofstadter had been born in Pittsfield, Massachusetts, and had been hospitalized with illness for a month. He was a retired college professor. No survivors were named.

The service took place at a funeral parlor, part of a national chain, that shared a block with a Subaru dealership and a chicken franchise. The day was bright and pleasant, a breeze cool for the season jiggled the white blossoms of spirea that bordered the property. At the entrance to the lot, a sign in Gothic font directed mourners in case of overflow to park in the street rather than risk towing at the take-out restaurant. We did not need to confront the risk. There were only a handful of cars in the funeral home spaces, and only one besides ours turned out to belong to mourners. Maybe the undertaker had a big staff, or maybe cars had spilled across from Dandy Andy Fried Chicken. I was a mourner, and Alice and I followed the next Gothic sign pointing us to the entryway.

We found in the sanitized chapel only one other couple. They had chosen to sit at the far edge of a front pew. We took the same seats in the parallel pew. There are times when people seek space from each other, sick people in waiting rooms, men at urinals, and this was one. Hofstadter lay in a metallic coffin that could do for intergalactic flight. It had polished rails running its length, and a propped lid in the shape of an airfoil. I glanced over to see if I knew the other mourners, and stealing my look they nodded sympathetically. A frail-looking fellow about my age and his puffy wife. They both wore black. It was summer, I was in a tan poplin suit with a striped tie and Alice wore the aqua jacket and skirt she had on when I met her. We nodded back, the same solemn gesture in tandem as if we'd rehearsed it, and stared ahead quietly.

I would have said meditatively, but the fact was, I

was not meditating. Twenty feet away was old Hofstadter. Satin pillows bolstered his head so his face, side-view and noticeably waxy, poked above the coffin's rim. Other than that he was looking about as healthy as I'd seen him in months. They'd done his hair, which was either graying or gray, hard to say, in some sort of rinse that gave it a strawberry tint, and the result was becoming. He might have been a punk rocker or a drag queen. For once the hair was well groomed, combed straight back off his face—they probably had no one to tell them how he'd worn it, and even if they had, they couldn't teach his egg-beater look in mortician's school. I whispered my insight to Alice, they ought to name the shade Hofstadter pink, and Alice, who'd never met him but had assumed a serious bearing, even tragic, elbowed me in the ribs.

Someone, I made him to be with the funeral parlor rather than an organized church, said a few words and read two of the Psalms. Then he talked about David, the Psalmist, whom he clearly knew better than the Deceased. That was how he referred to Hofstadter. He announced that we would hear musical selections specified by the Deceased and, pleased with himself, sat on one of the two high-backed chairs on the podium. The audio system was engaged with a loud click, and we sat through a marching band's rendition of "The Marine Corps Hymn," elevator strings playing "Moon River," and "Get Me to the Church on Time," from the original cast recording. The place had great acoustics, paneled walls and hardwood pews. For a funeral with a lot of moaning and grieving, which ours was not, this would be a good venue.

"Was your friend in the Marines?" Alice whispered as we filed by the coffin. Ambled really, there being only four of us and hard to make a file.

"No," I whispered back. I was pretty sure I was right.

"Why the Halls of Montezuma, then?"

It was at this moment I decided that I had to lose either my life as I was living it or my senses.

"He must have liked it," I told her. I got a firm grip, thumb and two fingers, on the fleshy part of her arm and steered her into the sunshine. We stood in the parking lot waiting for our next instruction. It seemed too early to go back, I to the courthouse and Alice to Sundance Ridge. The other couple approached. Their costumes were perfect, so morbid I decided they too were with the funeral parlor, they must get dressed like this on days when management needed to paper the house.

I was wrong. He introduced himself, then his wife. We shook hands around. He said something sympathetic that I missed and then, "Too bad" and we agreed. I didn't know him well enough to disagree.

"You are Leonard Mooney," he said. He'd picked up the same solemn cadence the guys from the funeral home used.

"I am."

He told me his name a second time, expecting it would mean something, and then, having prepared himself for the act, plucked a business card from the handkerchief pocket of his black summer weight. A magician. Held it by two fingers and handed it to me. "I was Mr. Hofstadter's lawyer," he told us. You could hear pride in his words and I wondered if he'd lost his only client. "You might stop in to see me next week."

"How about tomorrow?" but I was just being difficult, seeing as how tomorrow was Saturday.

"Sure." He looked at me funny. "Sure, that would be fine." I dealt with lawyers all the time and you needed to establish beachheads. He and his wife retreated, got in their late-model wagon, and drove off.

We had come in Alice's car. It was leased by the company, the people who gave you Miramonte Homes, and so long as she was one of the top three producers she got the use of an Acura. She moved it out with some pace, wanted to be at the show home for the noon hour when on a bright summer Friday you might just get a lucky drive-by. I checked the time. The funeral started at 11:30, it's ten of twelve. No sense going back now. I walked next door to Dandy Andy's and ordered the special platter, a large Sprite, and for twenty-five cents an extra cup, the size of a shot glass, of cranberry jelly. I sat, their first customer of the day, in the glistening room while MSG softened up the chicken and the fryer popped like static over the rap music. I went through the thigh and drumstick, mashed potatoes, brown gravy and salad. The funeral had given me a keen appetite. It was my private sacrament. Hofstadter, I remembered from buying his frozen dinners, ten at a shot, was a dark-meat man.

Saturday I woke early and studied my wife in the coming light. Her thick and amplified brown hair spilled across the sheets. Her nightgown had ridden up to her thighs. The flesh was creamy and marbled as an expensive Gorgonzola. She surprised me looking at her and mistook my thoughts. I knew this from the smile, the feline smile. It is ardor. You could look into the yellow heat of it and see below the surface. Used to be I wasn't sure I liked what I saw but I couldn't pull away. Now pulling away was easy. That's the trouble with those volcanic feelings. When the magma dries the landscape you're standing on is dry and nasty.

"Why would he want to see you?" she asked over raisin bran and coffee, then gave me her theories. She dismissed a legacy since she never liked what she'd heard about Hofstadter and believed that he lived and died indigent.

"If he's named you as executor, you decline," she instructed me. "Unless they'll pay for it. I'm betting the lawyer wants you to cover the funeral costs. I'm betting that atheist didn't put enough aside for his own Irish funeral."

Alice believed whenever Hofstadter and I were alone we were plotting against her. She didn't like the funeral service, she was still troubled by the musical selections, and I early learned not to puncture the pontoons she inflated to ford life's waters. Alice's vocabulary was regularly filled to overflowing with thoughts she got from daytime talk shows. She would threaten me with Do unto others. I won't be happy until you're happy, that was another of her favorites. Where would we be if everyone took that position? A stalemate.

I decided against a coat and tie (this was, after all, not my appointment but the lawyer's) and headed out. She told me it was to be another hot and dry day and asked me to water the wheelbarrow. In our front yard sat a wheelbarrow and a Dutch windmill that Alice built herself. Traced them from patterns you get from a women's magazine. She was quite handy. For the first spring I peed nightly into its plantings, but they survived. Petunias, I think. The blooms were long gone and the vine that now crept over the red lacquered sides was robust, clearly beyond any damage from my kidneys. Blossoms in several pastels looked up at me without malice. I poured a full watering can into the wheelbarrow's bottomless pots and walked to catch the bus.

The lawyer's office was a twenty-minute ride, not far from the courthouse. Alice offered to drop me off. Saturdays are a good day at Sundance Ridge and she would open the sales office by nine. But I liked the time to myself. The bus route was my usual commute. The half-empty bus rolled by the house of an acquaintance of mine, someone I knew from the courts, where at a Christmas party I first meet Hofstadter.

A Christmas party ten years ago. Reba was somewhere with the kids, she hadn't come and I'd planned not to stay. I was trading gripes with this man I didn't know, a wiry, nervous man, pulling his Luckies down to a lint-size scrap and every so often inspecting the butt between pinched fingers. For most of the party he and I stood by the bar, only it wasn't really a bar but a card table, checked cloth cover, on which sat bowls of mushroom-colored dips, mixers, bottles of BYO brands, and two large boxes of wine, one white the other a pretty, mineral pink. We were to get out and socialize, our hostess had threatened us, Hofstadter was an eligible male and she invited eligible females. I judged Hofstadter to be fifteen years my senior, his voice had that woody timbre of good newscasters. He told me he was there at the suggestion of his analyst, who instructed him he needed a series of trivial relationships.

"Why are you in analysis?" He ignored the question.

"I should have told him I'd go if he would. Next time your doctor tells you to take an enema, tell him to go first."

I had not BYO'd, I'd arrived empty-handed. Hofstadter offered me Scotch which I ordinarily did not drink and when I nodded he filled an iceless and plastic glass an inch from the brim.

I'd found a friend.

I pointed out to him that he and I were not decorated. Everyone else who came to the bar had pinned on some emblem of the season, the men wore ties of reindeers and snowmen, plaid vests, some of the women tree ornaments. Hofstadter said he *was* in season, he was carrying a stone in his pocket. I began to wonder whether the whiskey was too high a price to pay. I asked him whether analysis works.

He looked off for a long minute, I wasn't sure he'd heard me.

I started to ask something else. "It is a curious thing," he said. "There is nothing in my life I can complain about, nothing I would change. And yet I am utterly depressed by it. For one thing, it is ending. Isn't that odd? Why do I dislike this pudding? One, it tastes awful. Two, there's so little of it.

"And I move about so badly. Worse each day. A rotator cuff, bursitis, perhaps they'll fuse that disk. Glasses for movies, glasses for driving. Everywhere about me, firm flesh, the leer of youth. I tell you Mooney, it is Mooney, isn't it?, I tell you my depression isn't in my mind. It's real."

Hofstadter and I took in a few movies together.

Sometimes we met for dinner at a bar where on Tuesday nights they made a passable meatloaf. He was good company, except when his health weighed on him. Then being with him was a strain. He wouldn't put up with the news of the day or my struggles for position and favor at the Court of the Clerk. It was like being in a room with your emotions. Or your children. I told him this and he insisted the problem was not health but mortality.

Only six weeks after the party I was visiting him in the hospital. He was being prepared for the operation on his larynx. He'd made a conquest of the nurses with his vile manners and Walter Cronkite locutions. I was pressed down by the smells of the place—strong disinfectant, tomato sauce, urine. Not Hofstadter—he found it all interesting, he might have been at a ball game.

"Next door," he boasted, "is a man whose jaw they took. Smokeless tobacco. We're all cancer cuts, the whole floor, oncology, all of us here are being sliced up so many carcasses to a blind butcher. It's like those doll hospitals, Santa's workshop, you know? Except in reverse."

I asked about pain and he waved me off with that vexed impatience, a backward slap with his hand flapping loosely. I said something dumb, told him nothing is good or bad but thinking makes it so. "Well done, Mooney. Said like a man who has never had a hangnail," he replied, "let alone a kidney stone."

He insisted on taking me for a walk through the corridors. His hairy ass peeked out of the dressing gown they put him in. Why he couldn't wear pajamas or overalls or whatever the hell he pleased I didn't understand, and I threatened to raise the point with the staff.

He told me not to bother. They do it, he said, to put dignity in its rightful place, which is somewhere east of here.

"I have discovered," he lectured me, his broadcaster's voice stopping orderlies in their deliveries, the last time I heard it before they burned it out, "I have discovered the ultimate fantasy for a dying and impotent man. I use it in place of their little pills to fall asleep. Do you want to hear? I meet a stranger on a boat. It is a long cruise and we have no apparent destination. Each day that we meet he carries a different shoebox. He tucks it under his arm. Each day I ask him to see the contents. He declines. Finally he says to me, 'Look. We are within sight of our destination.' Sure enough off the bow of the ship I see a little line of land.

"When I turn back he has opened the box. Inside are photographs. I look over his shoulder. They are photographs of *me*, my life. They are in no particular order, and I've never seen any of them. They were taken without my knowing. In this box, I am young and strong. Here I am as a five-year-old with my parents at a lake. My father wears a woolen bathing suit with a sleeveless top and a webbed belt. My mother is beautiful and smiling. Here I am floating a leaf down a stream in the park, prodding it with a forked stick. I am eleven. Most of the pictures have water.

"I look around. He has brought up to the deck several other boxes. I race through. Each picture forces new tears to my eyes. I have to blink, rub the back of my hands to wipe the tears or I shall miss what he shows me. In the next box I am making love to my wife. I am holding my child by the hand, he looks up at me. I am riding a train into a distant city. What does it mean? The whistle of the ship blows. We are coming into port. I have looked only at two of the boxes, he has ten, a hundred. I cannot stay my sobs."

Nurses and orderlies scurried out of our way and looked around surreptitiously, I couldn't tell whether they were scared by his voice or his story. I returned to the room with him. They served lunch on a tray and all Hofstadter would eat was the lime Jell-O, to which he was partial. I went next door, the man without a jaw who was napping, and stole the dessert from his tray for my friend.

He was in the process of scraping the specks of green from the sides of the bowl when he spun on me. "Isn't it true the Church thinks God does not attend the death of an unbeliever?"

I wasn't prepared for it. "How would I know? I don't know anything about that."

"But you were taught. You got instruction."

I didn't want to talk about it. I was an impostor. "I suppose any God would be there when anyone dies. I mean, if there's a God, He can't be taking coffee breaks or playing favorites."

"But don't they teach that unbelievers are doomed, that they can't make it into Heaven?"

"No, no." I lied. What the hell did I know about it? Besides Hofstadter wasn't on some quest for truth.

Before I left I wished him good luck. He backhanded another stupidity out of the room, scoring it down the line, and announced in his theatrical voice, "Semper afflatus." His goodbye.

After they took his voice he stopped driving. He said it was part of the process of reversion. Ashes to ashes, pedestrian to pedestrian, he croaked through his metal tube. Drooler to drooler. I ran errands for him. I didn't mind the errands, but I could have done without the intimacy—knowledge of his bowels, the cost and names of his several prescriptions, what brand of mouthwash he preferred.

Then of course he needed driving to his therapist. He raged each time about their cutting the classical fifty minutes to forty-five, it seemed desperately important to him, like in those last seconds he might finally break through. I argued it was economic. Hofstadter said no, it was clinical. They decided how long for small talk, and just as it ends, so does the session. Of his times with the shrink, Dr. Litvak—whom Hofstadter called Dr. Lithium—he told me little.

"I make up symptoms," he blurted out once, we were stopped for a light. "It seems to me fair game. My dreams are so dreary they get dreary responses. So I give him better ones. Most are plots from old movies in the *Halliwell's Film Guide*. It is working. Dr. Lithium has become interested in my case. He has medical journals in his waiting room, also *Vanity Fair*, and he thinks I may be the case that gets him written up."

He lost his larynx, other parts, I lost my wife. We are both, he wah-wahed to me, scolding, careless with important things. I asked him whether he wanted me to check with Lost and Found, and he laughed, a dry wind. Only it's poorly named—the stuff that's found gets to leave.

In my bachelor years, between marriages, he cooked me dinner and I kept his house alive. I did little plumbing tasks, repaired a cracked pane, replaced a shorted thermostat.

I told him I'd met a woman. I didn't spill the details —they might be too vivid, and besides, the workings of the flesh had lost interest for him. He listened, smiled.

"I'm thinking about marriage. Or really she is."

Hofstadter looked me straight in the eye. It was a trick of his, and I was on to it. After several seconds I looked away.

* *

No one was around in the office building. The lawyer heard the elevator open and met me in the hall. Instead of the black suit he dressed in a sky blue knit shirt and lemon slacks.

"He was a good friend?" We moved into his office, papers were shuffled in a weave across his desk. Behind his chair were terraced books that look unread. "Yes," I told him. Should I be careful of what I say?

"Must have been," he said and I gathered from his tone, the way the words come out through the nose, that he was wary of me. Making the other fellow wary gave me a warm feeling, superior elevation, no wonder lawyers liked it.

"Why do you say that?"

He picked up a typed document. Read in secret while I sit.

"Leonard, you are a devisee. Mr. Hofstadter has named you in a specific bequest. Left you a house in the Caribbean."

I assumed he was joking. "He had no house in the Caribbean."

"Oh yes he did. And now you have it. It's on a tiny spit of coral, part of the Turks and Caicos Islands. Do you know where that is? Well, you might find out. Mr.

Hofstadter bought it years ago for appreciation, against my advice. I gather it didn't turn out too well. This may turn out to be a mixed blessing, what with the taxes and the repairs."

You could tell he was pleased about the investment having gone sour. He handed me a thick folder. Correspondence from an estate agent in some place called Providenciales, monthly maintenance, an income and expense ledger showing a trickle of rental revenue but mostly deficits. Not large, though. Nothing I wouldn't be able to handle if I didn't have my house, insurance, the newspaper subscription.

"That's it? That's what you need me for?"

"That, and this receipt and release. We'll have the deed issue out of the estate, so there's nothing really left for you to do. Buy yourself some suntan oil."

He put a paper in front of me and I signed. Before I got out the door he was on the phone telling the pro shop he was on his way.

I returned on the bus. Why was Hofstadter leaving me this? Did he hint on my last visit? No, we talked of nothing. Less than nothing. Hofstadter was heavily morphed, a viscous clear liquid in the IV dripping into his arm, and strapped to the headboard was a little plastic button he could push to boost the dose. A two-fisted invalid, he wah-wahed, when he showed me the painkiller button and his magic talking wand. In the morphine sleep his voice came in and out. When he came in so did the pain, a short visit, and he buttoned out. He barely had the strength to force air through the wand, his voice was ethereal and reedy. I leaned to hear him, placed two fingers and the thumb of each hand on the sheet and leaned. My weight dented into the mattress and Hofstadter, down to the weight of a bag of dog food, family size, started to slide into the crevasse. The room smells were dark and molasses, medicinal but not healing. I swallowed the gorge in my throat. Hofstadter slid into the canyon, the stirring wakened him and his eyes opened. He put his wand to the hole where his larynx used to be, in his chest collected air.

"The invoice," he croaked.

I looked down at him. I must have misheard.

"The invoice," came the sound again, unintelligible, unmistakable.

Was there some bill that needed paying? Did Hofstadter need help?

I looked down again, frowned to show I didn't understand. No explanation. Exhausted from the effort Hofstadter settled back into his pillow. His eyes closed, opened once to glare, and closed in sleep. I left knowing I wouldn't see him again.

CHAPTER 4.

In the afternoons, bugs and heat drove me to the metal bed upstairs, each time after a taller highball for a deeper nap. By night, I found less and less sleep. One evening as I walked to the pier to pin my first message for Isaac I realized how much I had gone over to the dark. The stars were beginning their turns and I was waking. I ripped pages from the notebook, stuffed them into an envelope with four fifty-dollar bills, and nailed the packet to the pier's farthest stanchion. I was down to the last few bottles of white rum, not urgent yet but I wasn't sure how reliable he was.

I looked back. A towel hung from the front dormer window like a tongue, except they'd better send the doc, the way it gleamed bony white in the shine of the humpbacked moon. The flag of V-M Day, Mooney surrenders.

Days later, maybe a week, on the dock sat three cardboard boxes. In the same envelope were all the receipts and my change less twenty bucks. Each item had been lined through in black ink. There was no other sign of him.

I carried the cartons back up the path and decided on an outing. I mixed myself a tall rum and juice and stacked wood for a fire. I found one of my stamp books, loose-leaf pages printed by country and denomination. Two sheets of commemoratives from Brazil started the flame nicely. The stamps still carried traces of glue on them, and as each one caught it gave off a quiet pop. I had yet to explore the north end and tonight I would make the journey.

The winds fell off. In their place bubbled up sounds of the ocean, sounds squashed in the day for the noise of the sun. Gurglings and sputters, dribbles and tiny sucking gulps. It is almost a language, if you're alone with it long enough you think it is, you wait to hear a word you recognize.

I watched the fire peak and built another drink. All the while working a word ladder. Words weigh you down, just when you think maybe you're only an idea in your own mind, you can think on words and they give you weight. I turned HERE to LOST in six steps, though not on the first try:

HERE
MERE
MORE
LORE
LOSE
LOST.

The supplies stowed, I opened a fresh package of sliced balloon white and ate a piece. Balled up a doughy wad for the crab and measured off where to put it on the counter. Each feeding I moved his treat farther from the window. He was a day feeder. Now that I was all but reversed, I might not see him again.

An upper cabinet held dozens of jars and screw tops. I poured rum halfway up a mayonnaise jar, topped it off with grapefruit juice. I folded up some yellow cheese squares into the fresh sliced white, tucked them in my shirt pocket, tied up my boots and, grabbing the plastic flashlight, set out to see my property.

Out the back door, light from that lopsided moon and from a zillion stars lit the sands and water bright as fake day. I set the flashlight down on the back steps. A twisted scrub pine marked the far end of the property. Some oddity had bent its trunk at a right angle, with a knot at the elbow. From my angle the bend showed a human profile that looked like C. Aubrey Smith. From the movies. It wasn't much of a stretch, you could see the chin, the nose, the forehead. Even, at exactly the right level, a protuberance to sex it as male. As I passed I said hello.

The air was absolutely still. Only the surf was alive, the surf, the chunking of the breakfast bottle in my hand, my breath. Footfalls gave the whole place a pulse. A world's record sky, my own island and a brand new supply of rum. And my overriding sense was disappointment. It was an old story. At the very time I should be up, the serenity of the place, the victory of self-sufficiency over solitude, I began to panic. The beauty didn't interest me, only the pain of an airless life.

To the interior, the footing became easier. There, away from the mangrove by the shore, pine trees grew spare from an easy fern floor. Every so often there would be a patch of dense bush sprouting gray berries. The fruit had no taste, and the patch was impenetrable for its density and thorns, but it was easy enough to detour and find a route that would pass. I was never far from the beach and as I walked I watched the ocean, shuffling and dealing.

Half an hour out I came upon a clearing. It was a stretch of moss the size of a double bed, slightly raised and soft underfoot. I sat down for my meal, put the three bread shells on the ground and rationed the drink so it would last. Afterward, warmed by the rum, I lay down and watched the stars, daring them to move. I may have slept.

* *

If we hadn't lost Tommy, would it all have been different? When Tommy was born, I went into the labor room with Reba. That's what we had planned to do, it was in vogue. Reba had taken all those classes—Reba was a great one for classes—she was ready for it. I wasn't.

At the first pangs she was brave and breathing, and I stood at my post. But it went on. Try mopping your wife's brow for three hours while she's going through torments.

"God damn it to hell," Reba yelled. Next time louder. On and on, you start timing the pains and you know they're coming so you can't relax in between.

"Damn it to hell. Damn this baby, Leonard. Leonard I don't want this baby."

I ran to get the nurse. If she doesn't want it she shouldn't have it. The nurse had no interest. You can't pay them any mind, she told me, as if Reba was hallucinating, as if she was making up the pain. You can't listen to what they say.

The nurse was an old-timer, two sets of glasses on a bead chain. Even for that she put up a hell of a fight when I dragged her in. I never would have gotten her moving except for the surprise. They sent an orderly to see if she needed help, the nurse, not Reeb, but by then she was sort of an ally and sent him away. Tended to Reba and sent me out of the room.

"You can go back in there now. And pay no attention to what they say, they don't mean it."

She'd given Reba something, I could tell from the eyes. But the pain went on. I was going mad. You love this person, she's in pain, and you can't just say I'm sorry, I figure I'll get a doughnut. You're responsible, and you're there. Then I found a trick to rise above it. All I needed to do was pretend I was watching a movie, I wasn't really in the scene. There was an actor playing me, he was saying soothing, considerate things and holding a washcloth to her brow. My brain got a seat in the audience. Knocking down Junior Mints, some you crunch with your tongue others you suck all the chocolate off first. In the audience watching. That was it. And the pain went away. It didn't for Reba, of course, but it did for me.

It was a slick little trick, you could plug it in when you needed it and the unpleasant stuff disappeared. Like swallowing in an airplane.

He was born, Thomas A. Mooney, heir to the line. You took him home and if you were not struck with the horror of what you'd done, you were not paying attention. This tiny abandoned thing, helpless as a boast, and all you needed to do was make sure for about eighteen years or until common sense kicks in, maybe double that time, make sure he's breathing, not under a truck tire, not sticking a paper clip into the electrical outlet.

From the start, Tommy was tough on parents. Not acting up or anything, he was the kid whose heart cannot abide what he sees, how people treat each other. When he was six, Reba just home from the hospital with Stace, I wanted to do something special so I took Tommy and his friends to the circus. Everything was fine until the clowns. A lot of that clown stuff is sad, outright meanness, and they try to cover it by wearing a red nose. This one clown lost his spotted dog, and when the others loaded into the VW bug, he stayed behind, looking everywhere. The audience was charmed. They laughed. I glanced over. Tommy's two friends were laughing. Glistening wet stripes were running from Tommy's eyes to his chin. The man was abandoned, his pal had disappeared, and it was breaking up everyone but Tommy. And, I suppose, me, since I was watching my son, not the show. Finally the clown looked under the elephant's diamonded stand, and sure enough, the spotted dog leaped into the clown's vest and they ran off.

Reba said not to worry about it, the world will teach him soon enough. I was perplexed. I didn't want the world teaching my kid what it had to teach. Had she noticed the curriculum? Of course what I wanted didn't matter. Reba was comforting, sympathetic and comforting. It's all part of growing up, she told me, you have to get used to it. It'll get better.

She was wrong. It didn't. It festered and grew and when it bulged to the surface in his teens, it had taken a different shape but it didn't get better.

The next year his grammar school took a field trip to the main police building, downtown, in the middle of skid row. They listened to the radio dispatcher, got a ride in a squad car, got locked in a cell, all fun. Reboarded the bus, they were waiting for the rest of the class. Tommy was the kid who stepped off the bus to listen to the panhandler. Heard him out and got his name, he was the kid who packed up a paper sack of food—English wafers, cocktail oysters, Campbell's cream of mushroom soup, baking soda—and set off on his bicycle to find the drunk. We only knew about it because he came home after dark. He'd placed the sack on the steps of the precinct house and found a patrolman who promised to keep an eye out.

* *

I left the almost-empty bottle on the mossy site and went on. The soil underfoot turned stony, and the brush grew thick and brittle. I was nearing the northern point, bushwhacking and short of breath. Deadish stick poked at my face. Where my wrists and hands had been scratched the sweat stung through. I sank to all fours. The stones of the floor were smooth and rounded. I passed under the growth more easily than through it, but it hemmed in like a tunnel. Suddenly, the land sloped off, the elevation gave out. I stood, went down a gully and crossed a bed moist from receding seas. On the far side stood a maze of mangrove that made a small subisland, attached to mine at low tide. Passage looked hopeless, the mangrove grew thick together and I tripped and skinned the heel of my hand on broken shell. I had come far enough, I didn't need to clamber up on this last jot of land. I wished to hell I'd brought the rest of the rum, there was just enough for a good swallow and I'd never find it now. I took a last step as the resolution to continue left me, and cleared the patch of mangrove.

And what I saw stuck me fast. There, not twenty yards away on the little dot at the top of the island, was a shed. No bigger than a single room, but a shed. And shining in the window was a light. There was someone here.

I had no breath. My chest couldn't move, it was stuck in dry ice. I could feel the top of my stomach sucking against collapsed lungs as I ran, scrambled, tripped through the mangrove thicket and back up the main islet. My gut cramped first and then, for lack of air, my legs. Twice more I fell, ripping the knee of my khakis, fought to my feet and through branches that scratched my forehead. I reached the back steps of my house and sat in terror. What could this possibly be? Who was it? Can he have been here all the while, keeping himself hidden? My ribs forced themselves out and air juddered in. He must know of the house, the pier, me. My skin was slick all over like a fish, a slick warm from the run and cold with fear. In the metal locker behind the house Hofstadter had stored a few tools. I opened its tongue latch and banged through what was there. Something to use? Paint rollers, a push broom, mops, I managed to tangle them in each others' shafts. Toward the back were gardening tools. A pitchfork. I drove it into the ground at my feet. Its tines thunked in. I pulled it out. The four holes it had punched into the earth were calming, though not enough, and I went into the house. I took a swig of rum from the bottle, but it about came back on me and I choked down the burn. It was an hour before dawn. Upstairs, I lay on the bed in terror, the pitchfork tucked against my side.

CHAPTER 5.

It was a fateful day at work, for which I brought the car. Not out of any premonition, seeing as how I am not given to visions of the future except bad ones, and those aren't premonitions but simply understanding the way the world works. The car was a strategy, part of my war with Canges. The way Rommel used tanks. Today the Clerk would be presented with a request, unknown to Canges but processed yesterday by me, that eight storage boxes be moved to Monroe County Court. Monroe is a neighboring county where farms are being eaten alive by frame houses. We would mail a single jacket and ask the sheriff to deliver a single storage box, but eight boxes made for a hefty load. The Clerk would assign a deputy clerk to shuttle them. In the absence of my strategy, that would be Canges. He'd make a day out of it—lunch in the topless bar along the highway, flirting with the staff at the court house, back at four-thirty with a mileage chit that he'd put under my nose to sign.

But I had a plan to beat him to the punch. I drove

in and parked, bold as a soldier, in the Spot. The Clerk had a designated parking slot outside the courthouse, just down from the judges' slots, and she never drove. Her name was stenciled on the yellow bumper, and low as it was, it stood as her monument. The paint was freshened twice a year, she had the prisoners' work detail do it. Every so often, she allowed her minions to park there, but only on official business. God's Spot, Canges named it, the G-Spot. I pulled my Plymouth into it careful not to mar the bumper, and popped the trunk.

I had logged the order that granted the change of venue, so as I walked into the office, only I knew that these files were to be moved. Jiggling keys around a finger, I delivered the order to Canges without a word, so he could enter docket info. He regarded me suspiciously. Usually I rode the bus to work and the clink of the keys must have sounded to him like the robin's chipper song sounds to the worm.

I knocked on the frosted glass door and the Clerk looked up as I entered. Our offices were housed in the basement of the court building—it was originally to have been a garage but courts and clerks, prisoners, sheriffs and bailiffs prospered, the spaces were too small before the building was completed, and we occupied the whole floor—and her corner office had two rare windows. They looked out eye level to the sidewalk, and through one, I glimpsed the neat tread of my tires.

"I've brought my car today," I ventured.

"So I see. It *does* look like rain, Mooney, but that's hardly justification."

The Clerk was a woman born shortly after menopause who since had been aging without grace. Once a chief judge of the higher court tried to oust her. He spent the rest of his shortened career in an interior courtroom that vented into the drunk tank. The smell of vomit drove him back to private practice, where he ended his career defending insurance companies whose doctors were regularly amputating the wrong limb.

"No, Ma'am. I noticed the volume of files Canges is packing on a change of venue. I thought it would be easier if I ran them down to Monroe. Save us from asking a favor of the sheriff."

She peered through my eye sockets at the place where my spine entered the cranium. She was not a fan of favors, from either side. "How many boxes?"

"Eight, packed to the gills."

She nodded her head back and forth quickly. Not a Yes, it could mean anything. She could be limbering up to strike.

"O.K. But not until lunch, Mooney. And then straight back. You're supposed to be working here."

As I passed Canges I mentioned we have a large change of venue coming up. Also that as soon as he assembled the files, he ought to load up my Plymouth. Can't be too efficient.

It was a spring day dark and green. All our rain falls in May and June, farmers get flooded out one year in four, and this morning thunderheads were piling up thick as diesel. On the drive out only a few drops, caught by the winds at the edge of the front, splattered the windshield. Fruited rain, drops the size of plum pits. Monroe County used to be truck farms and trailer parks, the city pushed people out and they took refuge everywhere. Some dumb bunny bought a line of sugar beet dumping stations smack by the tracks, converted one to a clubhouse, built a subdivision around it and called it Sugar City. And what do you think? Another bunch of dumb bunnies bought the houses. I had to laugh driving out how people get taken.

My work at Monroe was over lickety-split. There was a good-looking clerk out there I liked to joke with, although she was married and at the time I wasn't, this was right after Reba, but I joked around. She had long legs and green eyes, my favorite, and she was a great toucher. Nothing serious, fingers on the back of your hand or touching your arm. When you're single again you can go a long time without someone touching you. I stopped wearing a wedding band a year after Reba, I thought that was a respectful period and I took it off on the anniversary, she was the first to notice. Today she was busy so she had me stack the boxes and signed the receipts. "Say hi to Canges," she called, and I figured that's her way of kidding back.

The clouds had ganged up. I turned the car north on the Interstate and it was as if I had punctured a tunnel. Water cascaded down. In front of me, I saw muddled red lights where the traffic braked to a halt. I did the same, sat on the shoulder for five minutes watching nothing and listening to the radio where someone with a crushed nose was singing about the ache in his heart. I did a quick word ladder:

LOVE
LONE
DONE
DONT

WONT
WANT
WAIT
WHIT
SHIT

If anything the rain was getting worse. The Clerk herself clocked me out and unless I called I'd catch hell. Acts of God didn't count unless the Clerk was in on the act. I pulled out and crept beyond the slurry lights and stranded cars. Most drivers had snugged in and looked happy, most everybody wanted to be somewhere else, and they were. We recognized each other as I passed. You could tell they thought me nuts. Why leave?—this was perfect, alone, dry, out of reach. One guy in a pick-up gave me a fighter pilot thumbs-up as I splashed by.

I was in my own LST, it planed up the highway curling a wake. In a few miles there was an exit and I took it. I was now in the boonies, that no-man's land where city and burb have yet to meet, 7-Eleven has yet to convenience, nothing but a few land-poor farmers, watching the water drown their beet seed and waiting for the phone to ring. I drove east hoping for a commercial zone. Down a freshly paved road, the bladers at rest on the cut and soaking earth, stood giant sign for a new residential development. Miramonte Farms. On the sign a formless lady in a fifties bathing suit dove into a pool while her neighbors waved. Its parking lot, the real life one, not the one on the billboard, was awash to the hubcaps, nobody figured on the drainage problem, but there were strings of yellow and red pennants on the sign and a single car was parked outside the model townhouse. I pulled in. Covering my head with the newspaper, I made a run for the oak-stained door.

I skipped the brass knocker and pushed in. My entry made a lot of noise, but the woman seated at the desk inside had her face buried in a paperback. Brown hair, no memorable shade, but highlighted (that's what they call it she told me later) in yellows. Hair piled up in swirls, confectionery as spun sugar. I closed the door and she looked up.

"Hi." Her hi hit several notes, all in the baritone. I liked the voice, a sales voice, eager to please. It made you ready to please back.

"Hi. Can I use your phone?"

She opened her hand palm up, showed the white and gold phone on her desk. I took the receiver off the hook and dialed the numbers. My finger stuck in the holes and I had to redial.

"Hard to use."

"French Provincial." Outside the thunder started, not quite overhead but close by. A dagger of pink lightning pointed at the ground a few miles out the window.

"Wow," she said, and I said it too.

I asked for one of the underlings and they put me on hold. It was a favorite game at the Clerk's Office—see how long people will stay on hold. They called with the dumbest questions—where is the zoo? my ex is on his way over here to beat me with a broom handle, what do I do? as if I knew—and we put them on hold. All the while I was watching this woman watch the same page in her book. She had on an aqua summer suit, a white blouse open to Uruguay, and under that a black bra. Pinned to the jacket of her suit was a name card for

Miramonte Farms that said her name is Hello Alice.

She caught me catching the cleavage.

"Why Miramonte?" I kept my eyes fixed.

"What do you mean?"

"Miramonte Farms. Mountain view. There are no mountains around here."

She shrugged. Her great chest heaved and the rounded flesh at the border rippled.

"No one's ever asked."

"Of course," I pointed out, "there are no farms either."

She perked with a little chuckle. Easily. Let you know she's a giver.

I held my eyes there and realized she liked it. Usually I'm not this way, what used to be called a masher, on the make, but the thunder was growing louder, it was night dark outside, and I had nowhere to be. I hadn't had a woman in my life since Reba. I guess I didn't need excuses, and whatever the reason, I kept looking.

"Nice blouse."

She looked up. Brown eyes, my favorite. "Thanks," and put in the bookmark. Slow, as if she had something in mind, and pulled her finger from the book. It was one of those thick romances, the first part fanned out where she'd read it, and on the cover was a brunette in a low-cut peasant dress wrestling over a sword with a Moor in a studded leather vest.

I pointed to it. "Looks like you."

"Thanks again," she said. "But I don't like the darkies."

Somewhere a clock was ticking and water was rushing against the window. She followed my eyes again.

"Is that what they call a bustier?"

"Yes," she said and laughed. Of all times, just as she was going to say something else and I figured that will lead to something else that I'd say, they picked up my call. I didn't ask for the Clerk—that's inviting disaster. Besides, I'd prefer not to grovel at this particular moment. I told the secretary I'm stuck out in the boonies and can't get back until after the storm. From our end of the conversation it could be I'm in charge.

I hung up. A phony antique telephone, and I had trouble fitting the handset into the wire cradle. I was still thinking about the bustier but I was out of comments.

Hello Alice moved her eyes around the room. "Would you like to see it?" she asked.

"See what?"

She laughed. "The model, of course. Most people stop here for a viewing, to see the townhouse."

"Oh, sure. Yes, I would."

"What did you think I meant?" and, I swear, she put her finger to the top closed button of her blouse, then went one higher and buttoned it. I was having trouble breathing. The tip of her tongue sat on her lower incisors. It's a funny place to rest your tongue, unless you're intending to spit. You can't start a word from there, I've tried it.

We started in the kitchen. She described the cabinet hinges and the range hood. I told her my name. "Do you prefer Len or Leonard?"

"Neither, really."

"I'll call you Lennie," which I like least, and she closed the 17.2 cubic foot GE refrigerator with external icemaker and ice water tap. She asked me where I live and I gave her the address, like a school kid answering his teacher. She knew the neighborhood, told me it's split level single-family homes built in the Fifties. Mostly brick with all-weather roofs.

"You got it."

We went to the family room, perfect for informal gatherings and easy entertaining. The faux hearth and the terrazzo floors are both options, she let me know, and I wondered what the other options are.

"What is faux?"

"It doesn't work." The first negative words she'd spoken.

"Do you have one, Lennie?"

"A family room? No, actually I don't."

"No, silly. A family."

We laughed again, though I wasn't sure why. I liked to see her laugh. She had a big, pneumatic-looking body, she could be in that Thanksgiving parade, and when she laughed you thought you'd set the moving parts moving. A hell of a body given the afternoon, though maybe her skirt was too tight across the stomach. And thick ankles, which I didn't notice at the time.

"No, no. I lost my family."

"Oh," she said and her eyes went dewy. One thing about Alice, ample sympathy. She cried at those long-distance ads on television. "How tragic. There were children?"

"Two." She took my arm and turned me to view the main-level laundry and attached powder room. We were standing close, as you can only be in a powder room, the toilet before us, when tenpins of thunder split overhead.

We both jumped and her breast pressed into my ribs. Landed from above against my ribs and leaned against me so I could weigh its plumpness. I immediately became aroused, and I realized she sensed my cock against her hip. And what's more, she didn't move. Me, I couldn't move. I'm frozen in the headlights.

"We're in the Primrose," she said softly. "In the Sunflower this is a full bath with shower, and in the Morning Glory you can make this a hall closet or a mud room. But a powder room is so sensible. That's why the Primrose is my favorite."

"Me too. I could use a powder room in my house. I have a lot of powder." I was now at full staff.

"Is yours very large?"

I could not think of an answer.

"Your house?" Was she teasing me? She smelled of soap and hair spray and I guessed she'd had tuna fish for lunch. If I could have just stuck my head outside in the rain to moisten my mouth.

"It's manageable," I finally stuttered out. "It works for me."

At the base of her neck was a birthmark, brown-egg brown and the size of a dime. Right above it through a little macaroni of a vein clicked her pulse. She walked away from me and, distanced, I grew embarrassed about my state. She rummaged about her to find pricing sheets. Somehow I found my voice.

"Upstairs?" I pointed a weak arm at the banister.

"Yes," she said, and I felt a perfect idiot, but Alice was sincere. She is a professional, she told me later, and always tries to put the client at ease.

"That's upstairs. Would you like a viewing?"

"Please."

She went first. It was an exposed minute, it could have been awkward and I became doubtful whether anything was going on. Alice talked as she climbed. I admired that at the time, the way she could rattle, and it didn't occur to me it might come to be nettlesome. On the stairs I noticed the ankles, but I was prepared to overlook small flaws. Also large ones. We did the linen closet.

"The master bedroom is the clincher. People just go ape. We'll find that it's enhanced with lots of windows, a volume ceiling, and a walk-in closet. And the master bath? Makeup mirror, floodlights, and dual basin vanity."

"Big enough for two."

"Big enough for two."

In the master bedroom she stepped back with pride for me to view. The moment seemed to have passed, though not my readiness for it. The thunder had moved off down the unbuilt block, it now sounded like a neighbor's party, and I feared my chances had blown out with it.

"What do you think?" she asked brightly. "Couldn't you just move in?" I walked over to her, where she was demonstrating the curtain pull.

"Does it come furnished like this?"

"We have four decorator packages. This is Highland Heather. Homeowners who select Highland Heather have a choice of four different color bases to choose from. This is Beaujolais."

"No, I mean all this stuff. The bed."

"The bed?"

"The bed. Or is it faux?"

She smiled. "Feel free to try it out."

I never found out if it was a come-on. I never asked. I dove for the dime birthmark right above the collarbone, and she leaned her chin back so her throat grew and stiffened. I'd hit the right spot because she was moaning and tearing off clothes and her perfect fingernails, which I'd vaguely noted from the phone call, were under my jacket then under my shirt. My hands were all over her and we were stripping back the Highland Heather bedspread—no sheets, just a mattress—shedding the last scraps of cloth, my hands all over, a thumb deep in her slick and mothering as a bubble bath. God, she was saying. God, God, God, and I had all I could do not to look over my shoulder in case He'd shown up for a two-thirty viewing.

Suddenly she pulled away.

"I'm sorry. I have to inspect you."

I was sitting, a single black anklet sock to go. She pushed against my shoulder with an easy force and I went flat. She slithered down and had my cock in hand, not an unpleasant experience, and whatever test she was giving, I was desperate to pass. Then, to leave no doubt, sort of my graduation, she swallowed me. I gasped. If I thought of anything it's when I had my last EKG, but I couldn't swear that's what I had in mind, and when she came up again, wrapped in the bed spread and smiling, she explained.

"Sorry. You can't be too careful. There's a lot of stuff going around. A lot of guys out there with herpes."

I caught my breath. "I know. Their names are lesion."

With that she laughed, her body full in motion, the great balloon body inflating and rising over me, over me, I was hoping those Macy's people were holding fast to the ropes, and laughing too I entered her.

* *

After the fun we turn the mattress over, a four-handed job, and get back under the bedspread. It occurs to me to check for other pecker tracks, but I don't see anything and I'm not especially choosy. This beats an afternoon with Canges. We get back in and wrap the bedspread around us. I pull it up over our heads. We're in a tepee, she says. She's very playful. Alice has her assets. Sympathetic and sincere and very playful. A great body, except for the ankles. She could have lost ten pounds but who couldn't, and I wouldn't have minded if she'd worn clothes that fit.

We're in this tepee, and she's telling me how her one marriage didn't work and thank God—there he is again—there were no kids, because she's self-supporting and always wants to be that and nothing more. Her nails are going lightly over my stomach, which as it happens I don't like, and she's telling me about working for Miramonte, really the developer behind it, she's been in the top sales circle on two of their projects before and next she'll move to Sundance Ridge, but she really likes the product so she can sell the shit out of it—just what she says—'cause she believes in it. Her nails are perfect, they're polished bright red and cut so the arc of the nail matches the arc of the cuticle. I turn over and she uses them on my back, which I do like.

I tell her she has great nails. "You're full of compliments," she says, and takes my hand to examine mine. "A man's nails are important. Ragged, he's a bum. A man with long nails is a fighter, but a man with short ones," and she rubs mine against the palm of her hand, "he's a lover." The rain is pattering on, the sound is a record you just let run and run and run. She cuddles up and says, Purr purr. The first time I hear that, I think it's cute. Dumb, maybe, but cute. Water pitters on the windows like static. Her leg is over mine, and I feel her thigh, hot and chromium, against the back of my knee. It's cozy and I think, maybe I'll just buy this, the Primrose model in the Heather Highland Beaujolais package, I can probably afford it if I unload my house, and I'll move right in and keep her in this bed. We'd need sheets. When she showed the house she'd just have to explain, that's Lennie on the can, don't mind him. He came one day and he just went ape over the cedar-lined closet in the master bedroom and the six-setting shower head. Then in quiet times, when there were no showings, she could come upstairs and we'd screw.

Pretty soon we're ready for another inning, this one slow and easy. Not the same intensity, although she does a lot of moaning, it's her sincerity. Afterward, I need to get back, I start to think of the office and Canges, and so we dress but there's no embarrassment. I leave, race through the lingering rain and realize on the drive we never exchanged last names. But as I was going out the door, she gave me the Miramonte Farms information packet, including architectural covenants. I look to see it on the passenger seat: stapled to the cover is her card.

I showed up at the end of the day—that office was locked and secured at 4:30 on the dot—and took a lot of kidding. I'd checked myself in the rearview for lipstick or fingernail scars, still I was nervous. It helped to devote myself to figuring out what went wrong while I was out. Canges had doubtless retaliated for my victory at the Battle of the Eight Boxes. I was right. For one thing, there was a pile of new cases. I swear Canges kept the oddball ones in a bottom drawer until I was out. I sorted through them. One guy had paid his filing fee in pennies and they need counting. Someone else had mailed back an order for past due child support and included a desiccated dog turd. Canges stacked this stuff on my desk, and I knew he was watching me go through it. Also he'd changed the nameplate again. We had these cheap holders on the desks that spell out your name in plastic tiles. L. Mooney. Canges liked to rearrange mine when I'm gone, so it read M. Looney. All in all, nothing new. Nothing I wouldn't have endured for the afternoon's adventure.

CHAPTER 6.

I awoke convinced the shed was a dream, but the pitchfork handle inches from my nose put a stop to that. Living alone you get to ignore the world of science. There being no movie theater on the island, dreams are the best part of your day. You can always separate out what happened if you're motivated. Mostly I'm not. What happened always wins, fact triumphs over fiction, no matter which is true.

So the handle, ash and speckled like a Louisville Slugger, let me know about real life. Light was seeping through the evening sky where God had forgotten to pull the clouds all the way down. I stirred and grabbed the pitchfork neck. Strode down the stairs as if I was unafraid while clumps of dirt dropped from the tines.

What could the shed mean? A house for a watchman? To watch what? A hermit, a fugitive? Whoever was there didn't want to be bothered, wanted to live and let live. That shed had been here since before I came, he must have known of my arrival. He was trying not to be discovered. What did he do for fresh water, and how did he supply that bulb with juice? He could certainly have had his own well. Maybe he came in under the cover of day and ran my pump. For power, he could have been bleeding a wire off my generator. But any wire would run a short mile, I'd have noticed it. A clever fellow might rig a solar panel and a storage battery.

And his attitudes. Did he get along well with others, as the Sisters used to say? He'd let me be for a month, never announcing himself or bothering me. Then again, he *was* a trespasser. I had deeds and surveys, I could prove title. In the Clerk's office, he'd be toast. He was an outlaw, which made him a threat. Sooner or later, he would decide that my presence infringed on his.

By now I'd eaten and cleared breakfast, and dark settled across the sky. I resolved to make a second visit, this time having prepared to scout. Or fight. I took up the fork and flashlight and retraced my path. Gauzy clouds covered the sky, you could sweep them away with a long broom. It was impossibly black. I reached the little moss clearing. There waiting for me was my almost empty bottle, not a step too early. I finished it off and waited for starlight to break through. Better to do this when you can see the enemy. Of all things it grew darker, and I retreated. Why strike the first blow? Or worse, the second.

I spent the rest of the night pacing the crescent beach by my house, gathering wood and debris that had drifted in. Two-by-twos spotted with gunky tar. Once driftwood dried it fired well in the hearth, full of color, and I was short of fuel. The day opened pearly and timid. I heated a can of soup and ate it, and all the while the pitchfork lay across the table.

It wasn't so bad, living with the fear that your neighbor might come over and do you in while you slept. The thought was grisly, but chewing on it had a nostalgic tang. Dread mixes in with desire, soon the two are one solution, bourbon and water. I thawed a small loaf of ashcake from the freezer and ate the entire round.

* *

"Why" Hofstadter asked when I told him Alice and I were getting married. "Why would you want to do that?"

I hadn't prepared for the question. "It's getting harder and harder to have a good beat-off."

He put the wand to his throat. "A poet's gift."

"It's true. The memories I have of real women are filled with unhappiness. Or something like it, something gritty like sand. And I don't know any imaginary women." We were in his bungalow.

"That's your reason? Masturbation?"

I nodded. In a funny way it's great to have a friend who is dying. It's like meeting someone on a train. "When I finish it seems sterile. Uncomplicated but sterile. I talk tender to the Kleenex, will you be the mother of my child?"

Hofstadter snorted. Filtered through the equipment his laughter came out the same as disgust. That was true when he had his vocal cords, he'd never give you a clear sign. He lit up a Camel, stuck it in the slot, inhaled. Smoke dragoned out his nostrils. He rehooked and came back at me.

"Lonely? You talk…to yourself?"

"No," I told him, not entirely untrue. "Not much."

"That's because…you don't have much to say." He rested from the effort, saved up for the next speech.

"Marriage…a juggler's trick. Some learn how…some…." And here he shook his head. "Juggle three objects. Irregular. Don't balance. Love…obligation…resentment. Delicate equilibrium." At the missing words he wagged his hand.

I was replacing light bulbs in the overhead fixtures. He'd grown too weak to climb a ladder, so I had pressed myself on him after I'd come in one evening and thrown switches to no effect. Pressed despite his swearing and despite my fear of heights. He called me melodramatic, a few steps up a ladder is hardly a height, and I didn't argue the point. I was making the house cheerful. In the bedroom, three sixty-watts, all dead, while he continued to carp.

"House…a retreat. Silent…dark. Now…lit up…hamburger franchise." For reasons I didn't question, he had no floor lamps.

"Tell me," he rasped. He was holding the stepladder and I was detaching a milk-glass globe filled with the corpses of moths. "Your dreams…Sexual?"

I handed him the globe.

"I buy a rifle." I didn't have to ponder the answer.

"Long distance, like Lee Harvey Oswald. I adjust the range finder, one of those telescopic things, and I teach myself how to use it. Over time I become proficient. Bullets thump into cantaloupes at three hundred yards. I'm after someone specific, someone nobody will miss. When my training is over, I visit the packing house viaduct." Hofstadter knew the site. The remains of a deserted overpass ran by the packing house. The highway it carried dead-ended on both sides of a littered couloir, masonry pillars blackened with rainwater, concrete crumbling like a hunk of old cheese. Underneath the viaduct the city's homeless assembled, with their own kitchens, box houses, fires in fifty-five-gallon drums.

"I roam the arches at night, looking for this one guy among the drifters. I never see his face—I know him from his build. He's my height, only shorter. Kind of starved-out, shriveled. It's easy pickings. The next night I go gunning for him again. Nobody looks for me, I'm never caught."

Hofstadter was listening carefully. He noticed the globe in his hand. Dumped the dried carcasses into a wastebasket and swirled his handkerchief around the insides. Raised it up to me. "You are a man," he said out of nowhere, slyly, as if giving me the answer to a test in advance, "you are a man who needs to find pleasure in loving." For these words his sentences were complete and uninterrupted. His speech took a long time. "I chose not to love, but you love excessively, and it gives you only pain. The prospect of spending a week alone with your lover at some cabin by a lake would crush you."

"I have no lover," I answered. I was tightening the last of the set screws.

"I am speaking...," he said archly, you couldn't hear it in his voice it was always the same metal pitch but you could tell from his eyes. He tired before the sentence could end and began again.

"I am speaking hypothetically."

* *

After dinner I walked on the beach. I took a boning knife in my rear pocket—perhaps the watchman watches. A clump of mussels the size of a fist had washed up. I pulled one free of the kelp and pried it open. Its meat was the pink of some inner organ. The shell was black, spilled ink and white, where does this mussel come off doing so much art? Maybe it kept him entertained, maybe while he sat on the ocean floor huddled inside his shell, mollusking in water from one side and spitting it out the other, he decorated his walls. Was what Hofstadter charged me with true? It didn't make sense, for me love left the game early and cashed in. Excessively, and with only pain? I thought on Reba and could not imagine what she looked like. I saw her in two photos of a folding silver frame, but no face. In one she's pleased with me and in the other, she is angry, I have done something wrong. Our lot in life, she would say. This is not our lot in life.

Whose lot was it? Reba was one of those Sixties kids, came out of her youth thinking we could change things. She and I. We set out to have the perfect marriage, a boy and a girl who had a boy and a girl, a Kodak ad with vivid colors. Live by our wits, candles and incense to make love. I started off serving subpoenas, five dollars apiece plus mileage. Then I ran cases, it was my own invention, but she never much liked it. It's that old kid's trick. A fork and a spoon, linked tine to bowl, balanced on the edge of the glass? That was us, we hung our lives by a single toothpick. What happened?

Hofstadter argued that I had warning. True, she once told me we were growing apart. Was that what he meant? You'd have to know Reba to understand that was only talk, and he didn't. When she said that I asked for an example and she said, Just look at our dreams. Our dreams used to be like a good double feature movie. I figured she was joking around or nuts, either way I ignored it. I called her on it—we match dreams. In mine I am running a case from one side of the city to the other. I settle it and both sides give me a party with champagne. In hers she flies around the countryside on the back of a black leopard. People speak words that rise in cartoon balloons, white and soft as marshmallows. She flies high above the city eating the words.

Did she have a point? And could I be blamed for my dreams? She never thought the job I invented honorable. I had a son to feed and she was dealing honor. What I did was, at four every afternoon I went to the courthouse and looked up the new personal injury cases. Brown hit Smith in a rear-ender, and Smith figures to get rich. The car, the medical bills, the pain and suffering. I watched the file for Brown's answer, someone to start spending money on the case, and then snuggled myself into the middle.

—Hello, Smith Lawyer? I see you represent Smith in Smith versus Brown. A number six vertebra, no permanents, one five in specials. Am I right? You're asking fifty grand, what do you want for a quick settlement? No work no nothing. Twenty? I'll get back to you, but you better start to think realistic. The name is Mooney.

—Hello, Brown Lawyer? You've got Brown in Smith versus Brown. I can get rid of this for you for twenty-five grand. You got problems in this one, Smith's a sweetie and he's fractured a number six vertebra. Keep him out of church. No more than eight? Are you kidding?

—Smith Lawyer? I can get you a sure five grand in Smith versus Brown. Check will be there tomorrow.

That suit you? Fifteen but only by the end of the month? Be back to you.

We're off and running. Some lawyers tell me to take a leap, but most times they're busy, angry, lazy, any one of those will do, and I'm snuggled in, lubricating the deal. Whenever there's a gap, it's mine. If Brown pays eleven and Smith takes ten and a quarter, I pocket seven fifty.

It's a start, I told Reba, and I was right. Hanging around the courthouse, I met the players. Lawyers, adjusters, investigators. They did this in bulk, they were happy to have someone lighten the load. Everyone at the Clerk's office got to know me. Someone asked if I wanted to work on the Clerk's next campaign, so I did. I raised money from players, the Clerk got reelected, I got offered a job. At first I was answering crank calls and starting file jackets. Three years of nuts and white paste and I was promoted to deputy. Reba couldn't see that it was just a start, she thought it wouldn't amount to anything.

If we had a perfect marriage at first, we had it later on. But something went wrong. For one thing, I was introduced to Tommy's view of the world. He had, after all, the right view. He thought someone should help the clown find that dog, it was not funny just because it was supposed to be. It tore me up to see Tommy take it so hard, the dog, kids born with a shriveled hand, those stories where the hunter shot the elephant. He took it hard, beyond where we could comfort him. Comfort is overrated, I told Reeb. Like prayer.

Reba was troubled by all this too, but in a different way. She was bothered by my reaction to parenting. She thought I saw it as useless and left the job to her, which wasn't the case. The case was it hurt too much. She told me, Leonard, this is not my lot in life, and she joined a book discussion group. If you ask me, that was the beginning. Tuesday mornings, neighbor women rotate from house to house and serve coffee. At first, it seemed to help, she felt stronger. But in a short time, I didn't see strong, all I saw was angry. The movement, she began to call it. At dinner I found myself discussing her oppression, how my world was empowered and conspired to keep the power in the hands of a select few. I was happy to discuss this, knowing I had no part of it. I've never joined so much as a record club.

When we lost Tommy, she joined a second group. Someone in the first group recommended it, though it had squat-all to do with Tommy. It had to do with how I'd sold out, and with my drinking, which I admit was getting pretty wound up, and with how I was part of the problem, not the solution. I love Reba and mostly I agreed with her, and that just made her angrier. She began to leave the beds unmade. Daily. The linens became her declaration of independence. Steinem's glasses, Angela's Afro, Bella's hats. My Reba had blankets. I was at the same time proud—she sees herself, she told me, as part of a historical imperative, and for that I was proud—and uncomfortable. When we had visitors, no matter how casual, I made up the beds lest we be caught with our sheets exposed.

* *

I washed and set out a wad of bread for the crab. He was by now risking the entire length of the kitchen counter for his meal. I had lulled him away from a sense of peril. Out the front porch I surprised dawn leaking into the east. The sky was a not-color, if wrong answers didn't count against you I'd call it gray. The gray of vacuum-cleaner bag dirt, the gray that is a collection of nothing. A God on the job would have made dirt magenta, say, or the yellow of warblers. No wonder so many people get depressed. This was as gray as gray, and the entire construction hung rim to rim without any dimension. Below it a sea the same color.

Scuttling came from the kitchen. The crab was racing across the counter to the hinged screen, bread-ball held high. This was an all-star crab, ready to spike his ball in the end zone. Only then did the purpose of the trick occur to me. I took my pitchfork in hand and trudged up the stairs to bed. Tomorrow, perhaps, the night sky would be bright and I would confront my jailer. My fears and I had joined against a common enemy. Since I can remember, I had been nagged by a sense of dread that tailed me like a movie detective. For once, with the nonappearance of the man in the shed, it had an object.

Was it the very next new moon or the month after that? Days and nights passed very much the same. One evening there came to me the resolution to sneak up on my captor. If he hadn't yet challenged me, he must be more afraid than I was. It was a brainteaser: two people meet on a bridge, a prisoner and a jailer, but neither one knows his role. They're not allowed to speak. How do they find out? I invented a puzzle, but it seems to have some flaw. Warmed by a wake-up rum, I hadn't the focus to track it down.

I packed for my crusade and set off. Boning knife in belt, buccaneer style. No moon, but a spill of stars whose pooled light made the going easy. My eyes quickly adjusted. I stopped on the back steps and went over my plan with C. Aubrey Smith. I had taken to confiding in the tree, on whose probity I had come to depend.

I moved slowly. The more I dawdled, the more likely he was to be asleep. Glittery silica bits made the soil snowy and brown in the night's shine. I stopped again at the spread of moss to rest and to swig from the juice bottle. I could hear my breath. I stood up and went north. By now the path was familiar, and the entire journey, house to gully, took less than an hour. I climbed carefully down the depression, holding the flashlight beam close to the ground to light up chunks of coral to hold my weight. Now that I knew them, the mangroves were an easy fence to cross. This way, careful and slow from step to step, avoiding shell and loose stone, I made my way up the slope to the spot where I had first come upon the hermit's house.

I peered into the near distance. The shed stood in precisely the same spot. Smaller than I remembered. And no light in the window. He's asleep. I had thought this through. I'd decided to rush the door flashlight blazing and fork at the shoulder, screaming like a John Wayne Sioux. It no longer seemed a good idea. For one thing I had no voice, and I was discomfited by a full bladder. I approached carefully, listening to my pulse and to the sand squeak against the Vibran of my bootsoles. Now I was ten feet from his little house and I could make it out clearly.

An astonishment—the window had vanished. The wall was solid. Confused and no less afraid, I pushed the flashlight button and shone its beam ahead. Nothing. A blank wall. Only a circle of light on aluminum and a ghostly, ribbed reflection at my feet.

How can a window disappear? I backed up, and retreated down the gully. Got all the way back to the moss before I dared to piss.

Where is the answer of the missing window? Could he have replaced a wall? I wrestled long with the problem before it struck me. Perhaps *I* was mistaken. Perhaps I hadn't seen a window. But I had. The difference? Of course. On the first night, the moon had been rising low to the south and east. What I had taken as a reading light from inside was the moon's reflection.

Made bold by this bit of deduction and by the last five fingers of the night's rum, I retraced my steps. Up the gully and out into the clearing to face the shed.

"Hallo," I cried, and the sound bounced off the metal wall. As soon as it was out I regretted it, tensed my hand on the pitchfork. What if I was wrong? I moved quickly now, circling to the right. A ten-foot margin in the brush surrounded the shed, and I circled full around. At the front, facing the surf, twin doors like those of a barn, slightly ajar. No latch, no handle. I shone in my beam and called again. My voice was unused, and it creaked and trembled. Only the most timid of watchmen would respond to it. I tried again, this time making my call deeper.

But there was no one. No one.

Against the black velvet of the silence my breath sounded in Dolby, you could see audio guys scrambling to push levers back to soften it. I squeezed closed my eyes. No one. Kept them closed for the entire fall back into the pit, until I had fallen all the way and landed back into the cellar of alone. In my ears I sounded like I had my head in a tin can.

I peered inside. There sat a complicated piece of metal, enamel yellow and fronted by a rectangular, rust-colored blade. Gears and track, blade and spindle staring at me. It was a bulldozer, perhaps four feet in height, at least that wide and twice as long. Ready for action. I aimed my beam to the sand and realized that the clearing around the shed bore the treadprint of this very machine. Someone had ridden it to push back the growth to make room for the shed. In the far corners were drums of diesel fuel, gallon cans of motor oil, scrap wood. An empty can of Hires Root Beer. Three sawhorses and some tubing. On preset hooks on the rear wall hung what I guessed to be spare fan belts and half a dozen soiled rags.

The seat of the dozer was a steel thing with round holes punched through to form a pattern under your butt. Heart-shaped, a valentine. I put a foot on the rubberized step and swung myself into it. No steering wheel, instead two levers sticking up from the floor. The key sat in the ignition. I turned it to the right and heard the brushes spin. On the dash left of the steering column was a button and I thumbed it. Sure enough, the engine gave a single cough and died. On the second try, only the whine of the alternators. The battery had given out.

I sat panting in disappointment. There was no watchman watching over. Apprehension leaked off me, drained off with my sweat. The mad exile had been my companion, friend or enemy didn't seem to matter. I wished to hell I'd let him be.

I kicked at the corrugated wall and it gave up a dent.

Rang back at me. Kicked again and a seam yielded, starlight snuck into the corner.

Hofstadter, I knew, had been stockpiling. That day I helped him change lightbulbs. I was replacing a broken hinge on the bathroom cabinet and came across his stash. Thirty or forty Phenobarbital—little football jobbies, looked like they came from some kid's game—stored in a pint-size plastic jug. He used a cork for a stopper, and on the side he'd written in that professorial scrawl, "Sugar Substitute."

"Don't be a child," he'd croaked when I challenged him. "Not...your business. Have to muck...our own stables."

That's what I thought about the move to the island. I mucked out my stable and thought I'd be done with all the choices. Instead I'd been left nose to nose with Hofstadter's single question, the only one you can count on. Meeting my watchman would have been a time-out. Once you've taken all your time-outs, you can't stop the clock and the game ends. Hofstadter's stash was now sitting in my kitchen, upper cabinet on the left.

The shed held a supply of discarded tools, some were scattered on the floor some hung from spot-soldered hooks. I picked out three fitted wrenches and worked the battery free from its mounting. It weighed a good fifteen pounds and electrolyte had caked around its terminals. I shone the beam to see its innards. Except for corrosion, the worse for the sea air but easily cleaned up, it ought to hold a charge. I cradled the battery in my arms and began the trek back. I would put life into it.

CHAPTER 7.

My alliance with Alice, soon to be a marriage, had me in an optimistic mood. I wore a clean shirt every day, I put the right amount of money in the parking box. For a brief time, I revived my interest in sex, mostly to keep up with her. She had a healthy capacity. You would think jizzem were water from the River Jordan and she one of the children of Israel, the way Alice took to dick.

Having an outside interest, we are told by the advice columns in the daily paper, will beneficially affect your work, and I approached what little work I had with new zeal. The Clerk noticed. One morning Alice had an early showing and dropped me off an hour early. Like the troll under the bridge, the Clerk was always there. She came out to the bullpen.

"What has gotten into you, Mooney?"

"Ma'am?"

"You seem different. Almost ambitious. What has gotten into you?" I thought to wisecrack, it's the other way around, but wisecracks were not the Clerk's meat. Years of administering the squabbles of others and the squabbles of the squabblers' lawyers made her indifferent to jokes. Besides, I wasn't sure she means her words as a compliment.

Still. My appearance of industry—there was nothing for me actually to do that early—was rewarded. A bailiff for a sitting judge took sick and the Clerk tapped me to fill in. It was a welcome change. Attend the courtroom, sit in front of the judge's bench at a special table to track and relay exhibits as they are offered from the floor to the judge above. You were a part of celestial workings, people waited on line for you to process them, they showed up early, refrained from smoking. Maybe Reba was right about the power structure. It was fun, this nudging people's lives ever so slightly, especially if, as was the case for my week's assignment, your judge had a flair for ceremony and humiliation.

We had set down the criminal trial of a man, Pederson, accused under city ordinances of being a scofflaw. Municipal Court is the court of lowest jurisdiction, so we didn't see rapists or murderers or any dispute where real money's at issue. But we did box office all the same.

Pederson had no lawyer, he appeared on his own behalf. He described himself as a contractor, but really he was a handyman, he operated off a pickup and did odd jobs. He was maybe seventy years old, dressed in a flannel shirt and jeans, his white hair was turning shades again, this time to an inconsistent yellow, the color of a nicotine stain. He'd asked for a jury trial, and in Municipal Court you got a jury of six. My judge was annoyed. He was missing out on a conference of judges in Southern California because this guy insisted on his constitutional at-bats.

We got started, and the assistant city attorney was loaded for bear. She put the jury into the box one-two-three, and when the judge asked Pederson if he had any questions, he sidled up to the front bar and began murmuring to the six selects.

"Mr. Pederson, what are you doing?"

"I'm asking questions, your Honor."

"You have to ask them out loud, Mr. Pederson. So we all can hear them."

"They're of a personal nature."

"No matter," said the judge, and winked at the prosecutor. "Please stand at the lectern and ask your questions from there."

Pederson obliged. One by one, he asked each juror how they like the mayor, what they think of the income tax, isn't it a shame about O. J. being set free. People were enjoying themselves, except maybe the judge who was musing about the sun on Mission Bay. After half an hour or so, Pederson thanked everyone and sat down.

Then a funny thing happened. There were a handful of spectators in the room, a few for matters to be called but mostly old people and vagabonds with nothing else to do. A woman in the very back of the spectator seats stood up and said can she speak. About this case? the judge asked. She said no. She was maybe forty, dressed in black, Hispanic—or do you say Chicano? City employees are supposed to know—and very handsome. Strong face and fierce black eyes, and a chin that she stuck out and you knew it took some real bravery. The judge was about to tell her to shut up and sit down, when he noticed her eyes. They were shining, even from where I sat you could see it, and she was about to cry or maybe she was planning on being martyred. He told her to come forward.

Her name is Isabel Segura, she says, and she has this paper from the court and it is about her refrigerator from Sofaworld, and she doesn't mean any trouble. When these people showed up in the Clerk's office it was our job, Canges and me, to attend to them, that they don't wander about, and for sure that they don't find their way into the courtroom. I was sitting there figuring how I could duck the blame for this one and have it land on Canges, but the judge wasn't getting out the hook. He invited her through the gate, I took the summons from her and passed it up. He explained what she had to do and how long she had to answer and where to get the forms. He did a nice job, and you could see the jury thought so too. When he was through he asked if she understood and she said yes, but what does his honor think about the credenza. What credenza? he asked her, and she told him she'd like to keep the credenza because it's full with her mother's dishes that have made the journey all the way from Matamoros. You'd have to have witnessed it, but this woman was beautiful, the way she stood taking on the room. Everyone, the court reporter, the city attorney, was watching her. She was shaking just a little, the paper in her hands trembled when she held it out, but her voice was steady as pudding.

The judge explained it a second time, then he said this man will show her where to go, and the deputy sheriff got out of his chair and led her out of the courtroom. Pederson might as well begin serving his time, he was as good as convicted. I couldn't tell you why, but everyone in that courtroom was thinking about Mrs. Segura. The city attorney delivered an opening statement and put into evidence ten tickets for no inspection sticker. Pederson took the stand and made a speech. The law was unfair and all he was trying to do was make a living. The jury was nodding, but they'd just seen the law in action. At the end the judge asked does he want to change his plea to guilty with an explanation. The judge told him he'd admitted the charge and hadn't put in any defense, so the logical thing to do was to change his plea, but Pederson said no, let the jury decide. It was too late to hold them over. The judge dismissed everyone for the day.

Next day, they came back, deliberated for ten minutes, and found Pederson guilty. The judge told him to pay the fines and stop screwing around.

The quick verdict set the docket free, and you could see in the judge's frown he was thinking he could still catch the last of the week in the sun. He polished off some minor stuff and was out the door by ten. He heard a couple of domestics, entered a dozen, maybe fifteen defaults for a single collection company, and sentenced five misdemeanors. It is a marvelous system. No relationship stuff, no justification or revenge, just a good dollop of impersonal punishment. You take the rest of the week too, the judge told me, sliding papers he wasn't going to read into a briefcase. I can hear Hofstadter, Don't get mad and don't get even. Get out. It's not all one way. The defendants do it back. Like pro tennis players on the tour. We'll see each other again, maybe on clay or in the rain, I'll get you on your off-day. The good ones take the shit with a classy sullenness to let you know that while they do your bidding, they are thinking exactly the opposite. They're telling you how pointless and petty your efforts are, how they won't be on the street a day before they break into that vending machine or piss in the gutter again. A great system, people sell it short.

I had Thursday and Friday off. The judge neglected to report his leave-taking to the Clerk because otherwise she would have assigned him a new case, and so he flew off business class only two rounds behind the pack to the La Costa Golf Resort. Me, I simply disappeared.

Alice was happy to have me home. These were her off-days, the weekends being when Miramonte did serious business, and there was shopping to do. She had a Wal-Mart list and a fabric shop list. Alice had moved into my house, I can't remember quite how that came down, and she was quickly rooting out its defects, noting them on a Miramonte pad and lining through them as they were cured. No bolsters on the couches, an undersupply of throw pillows, curtain-rod hardware that no longer pulls. A window shade, and oh yes, the light in your little room, Lennie, under the stairs for your little stamps? That is ruining your eyes—you need one of those high intensity lamps you just plug in and hang from a nail.

How had she managed this foothold? Alice would have been a secret weapon in World War Two. Send her into Guam before the Marines. She'd have done curtains for Jap kitchens in a spring floral print and those little toilet roll covers, and pretty soon, boom, up would go the Stars and Stripes. We'd had maybe four dates since our romp in the Primrose, date is a lost generation's word I'm sure, my generation, and before I knew it her curlers were tumbling off my dresser and in the cabinet my dental floss was tucked in behind her paregoric. It wasn't the sex. By the time she planted the flag the only notable thing about the sex was that, afterward, I was home in my own bed.

How did she manage it? I pondered the question as we drove off.

"I said to her," she was chirping, "there is a difference between tinting and frosting and streaking, and any good hairdresser knows it. If I have to tell her, I should be the hairdresser, not the client. What do you think, was that too forward?"

Client was one of Alice's words. No one, her real estate firm, the plumber, had customers. They were all clients. "Among," I suggested. In her world, cops arrest clients for speeding.

"What?"

"*Among* tinting and frosting and streaking."

Alice regarded me. I could feel her look without taking my eyes from the road. It said, somewhere out there is a village in desperate need of an idiot and if I can collar this man I knock down an easy commish.

She continued. "But you'll never find a manicurist like Gloria. Never. You can't just patronize a beauty shop for the manicurist. I'll tell you this, Lennie, in all seriousness. If Gloria would leave, I'd be gone in a shot."

We drove to the fabric shop tickety-boo. I offered to wait in the car but she said, no, you're needed, this is after all your house, which I took to be rubbing it in, but I accompanied her and watched as mattress ruffles were cut. For the window shade Alice chose a pattern of a little boy and girl with oversize, alien eyes holding hands. To cover the half-frosted glass in the upstairs bath. Reba always wanted a bath in the open air. She had a vision of it. An old-fashioned, iron tub, with feet that looked like claws, sitting on a platform, surrounded by birch trees. You hang your towel and scrub brush from a branch.

We were back in the car headed for Wal-Mart. Myself, I never go there. Large stores fill me with fear, malls too, I get an urge to leap into their Grand Canyons, their shoppers' rest pits, whether it's the space or the cheer or the constant dance tempo of the music. I once chanced Sears to find a one-eighth drill bit and spent half an hour wandering, dazed as a shipwrecked sailor, until a saleswoman helped me to the exit, empty-handed.

So I was walking the aisles and concentrating on breathing steady. It forestalled the panic. Alice was describing what is sensible and what is not in the world of room fresheners.

"There's a consistency. If you're done in pastels or warm colors, then you're toward the red end of the spectrum, and juniper makes no sense. It just smells out of place." Her unconditional good nature thwarted my anger at every turn. She was like Joseph Smith and the Mormons, she followed a private set of rules and knew a reward waited at the end. I had none of her energy. Would people, I wondered, follow her across deserts on the promise of a coordinated kitchen? I listened after a fashion, heard mostly the tone of the voice, not necessarily what it was saying. The way when you spin the dial you can tell in a flash if you'll like the music.

We went through the Wal-Mart list fast. We were satisfied with everything except the choice of welcome mats, for which Alice had her heart set on an Old English scene. The clerk was not helpful in recommending alternatives. He did produce a Yellow Pages and we jotted down names of other stores. I was doing my rhythmic breathing. "I did not do well in marriage," Hofstadter told me. It was all he ever said of family. "Much of my time I spent recalling problems from seventh-grade algebra and computing them in my head."

We made the checkout counter at last. Fourth in line behind a one-item Nike sweatshirt, a heaping basket of groceries and a kid with electronics. The groceries got logged in and out, the kid was up, and I realized with a sinking feeling he had a third-party check. I despair at being in the wrong line, although I almost always am and the truth is I have nowhere else to go. The person behind me touched my shoulder, a familiarity I was sure was accidental, so I ignored it. It happened again, this time no mistake, the fingertips gave a tug.

"Leonard?"

I knew the voice at once. I didn't have to look. Alice had not yet realized that I'd been engaged. The wait was too long, the manager had been summoned to approve the check, we would not escape by a call to the register.

"Leonard?"

I turned. I couldn't repress a silly grin, as if I'd been caught shoplifting.

"Hello, Reba."

"Leonard, how *are* you?"

"I'm fine." Like a goon, I neglected to ask how she

was, but I could see. Terrific. She had a scarf around her neck, her black hair was cut short in an Audrey Hepburn, her eyes jiggled up and made you think she was about to ask for your life.

"How is everything?" I finally managed. "Derek?"

"Oh, fine. Derek is just fine. This is the crunch season, of course. SATs, everyone pumping hard. Hormones and parents."

Reba is short, shorter than I and I'm short, and she had this way of getting close and looking up at you. It really worked. I disengaged and thought to remark on her shopping cart. She was buying contact paper. Magic Markers in six colors. A humongous box of Tide. The third-party check had cleared—how I knew this I couldn't say, but the line moved up one, Alice looked around to find me with the basket, and stepped back to join the conversation.

"Lennie?" she said.

I introduced them. Alice, Reba. Reba, Alice.

"You're…?" Reba asked, and Alice knew just what she meant.

"Lennie's girlfriend," she said like it was a top diplomatic post. "And you're?"

"Me? I'm married to a high school principal. We live on the other side of town. You haven't moved, have you Leonard?"

"No," wondering how long those groceries will take.

"I'm Leonard's ex-wife," Reba said.

"You're *that* Reba?"

"I'm that Reba."

I needed to get in here. "Stacey," I said. "What do you hear?"

"Still in Medford. Still in nursing and living with her carpenter and sounds happy. She doesn't write much."

"No. Me either. She doesn't write to me either. Have you visited?"

"Just at Christmas. It's expensive. And you? She'd love to see you, Leonard."

"Maybe someday. It's expensive for me, too." I didn't mention Tommy, but I thought of him, and I could see in her eyes she knew that's what I was thinking and how that made her feel. The same feeling at the same time, like a flashbulb popping and I sensed it off to the side and in her wince and I saw the reflection on her face at the same time, and she me.

"You should get out to see her. She asks about you when we talk. She'd love to hear from you. And to have a visit."

"Sure," I said. "I know. You too," I assured her. And then like an idiot, "vice versa."

We were at the register, Alice paid with a charge card, signed the slip. She hurriedly packed the bags into the wire cart.

"Nice meeting you," Alice called over her shoulder. I reached over and touched the back of Reba's hand. She has the softest hands.

"Listen, I have to go."

"Of course. Leonard, take care of yourself."

"Yes," I agreed, easy to say but it was a promise I wouldn't keep. I thought to kiss her but instead I touched my fingers first to my lips then to hers. Pushed the handle of the cart. Alice was ten yards ahead and I caught up in the parking lot. She jammed in behind the wheel and sprang the trunk. I packed away the stuff.

"I'm going on home," she said. "We can look for the mat some other day. Or maybe you don't even want it."

This was dandy with me, since the welcome mats at the house Reba had macraméed fifteen years ago from some kit, and as far as I was concerned they were just fine. A little tatty, the way Reba's stuff looked even when it was new, like her flapper dresses and the bead necklaces she would string, but fine. That the mats were not the agenda was made clear to me as the Acura squealed TV-cop style around the corner and gunned down Elm.

"I've never been so mortified," Alice told the windshield, accelerating to fifty. "Never."

"Why is that?"

"Why *is* that? Reba, that's why. I thought she was dead! You led me to believe she was dead!"

I shrugged, kept my eyes on the road hoping she'd do the same. "I don't know where you got that idea," I said. "She's not."

"You led me to believe she was dead. I almost said that to her. Can you imagine? Can you i*ma*gine? Oh, Reba. I thought you were dead."

"Well," I tried to bolster her up. "You didn't say it. What you said was just fine."

"Thanks. Thanks for nothing."

"I just mean there's no need for you to be mortified. You didn't say it."

"And Stacey is your daughter? She's alive."

"Oh, yes. She's alive. She's in nursing."

"Both alive? I can't believe what I'm hearing. Who am I sleeping with? It's as if you're a stranger."

"Both." I answered the easier question. Truth be told

Alice and I hadn't known each other very long, and our courtship had not exactly been marked by long soliloquies, as she well knew. But I decided not to split hairs.

"I don't understand it. And I don't understand you, Leonard Mooney. That's your ex-wife and she's married to some high school teacher and you don't mention a thing?"

"Principal, actually. Derek's a principal. At Benjamin Harrison."

"Principal and you don't mention a thing. I almost made a real fool of myself. I'm supposed to be living with you."

It was one of those inevitable storms in relationships and my practice was you batten down to wait it out and it blows over. I really didn't understand this one, so anything I do would be wrong. Alice had seen the one picture in my room under the stairs. It's the only picture I had out of Stacey and Tommy, a picture of when they were kids. Though I could hardly bear to look at. They were maybe eleven and five, and Reba had taken them to this kids' shoe store that had a special on family pictures and there's Stace and Tommy and Tommy's spaniel—he loved that spaniel, went everywhere with him, I used to tease he was teaching him to read—the spaniel is sitting up like a show dog. You knew Reba was behind the cameraman calling their names. Look up, Stacey. Tommy don't push. The dog didn't need instructions. You could almost hear her voice when you looked close. In the picture the kids seem just like you'd hope, like there was no evil or danger or drugs in the world and in the background were these painted trees, the kind from New Orleans? with the droopy branches?

these droopy painted trees and the kids were looking out into the camera full of hope. I have that picture still in the silvered cardboard frame that it came in, on the back stamped, Stanley's Shoes. Cure the Blues. Men Women Children. And I can hardly look at it, it breaks my heart.

So I lay low, battened down, and by the time we unpacked the car and put up the Ross traverse rods and hung the window shade in the upstairs bath, Alice calmed down. She wanted to know more about Reba, you could just tell, but she was waiting till the temperature cooled to ask, and that was just fine with me.

The next day, we went to the new mall in the western suburbs to look for welcome mats. She found just the mats she was looking for, they had a pack of foxhounds grouped around the master of the hunt. By this time the crisis had passed, she was back to normal.

* *

It's odd, how I came together with Alice. In that brief courtship, it lasted maybe until we got upstairs at the Miramonte, she was a strong sexual fantasy. The available, full-blooded woman. Someone you just happen on, all you know is what's written on her name tag, Hello Alice. Soon into the relationship I realized I'd begun to fantasize that she herself was someone else. Anyone else. So I traded her from the fantasy team, whose ranks by that time were slimming to an exotic few, to the reality team, where she had a steady position but no future.

Shortly after the skirmish at Wal-Mart, Alice took an interest in my psyche. It was a scrutiny I could do without. One night we were reading in bed, she asked out of the clear blue about my potential. She was taking a test in a magazine about realizing your potential. Alice was a sucker for any magazine featuring an eighty-pound woman on the cover and a lead story on improving the uterus.

I went along—she asked me questions like what I did when I arrive at a new city. I had her dead to rights, because I don't arrive at new cities. At the end she told me we were opposites. She scored second highest, Doing More than Enough. Alice didn't take it as a criticism. I got an SQ, a squanderer, the lowest. That's me, the Happy Squanderer. There was no category for Humbug or Lout.

* *

Late Friday, after the shades and valences were hung and the bolsters set, I stopped by the office. I pulled out Mrs. Segura's file, read the papers, and called her. I told her my name, that I was calling from the Clerk of the Municipal Court, and I wanted to make sure everything is all right. She was surprised, maybe a little scared. There's good news, I told her. The credenza is not part of the case. They're just after the refrigerator.

"Yes?"

"And if you can make the back payments, they'll let you keep that. Often, you can compromise. Offer them less?"

"Yes?"

"Do you think you know what to do?" I just want to make sure, I told her, you know what to do about your refrigerator. Oh, yes, she said. The judge has splained to me. She had this thick accent, you could tell she was confused. Well, OK, I said. But if you need help, you call me. I gave her my name and number, slowly, but I was betting to myself that she didn't write it down.

CHAPTER 8.

It was a simple thing to hook the battery to the generator for a charge. I found electrical wire and alligator clips in the storage locker to connect the poles and ground the current.

In the kitchen at the weak first light, I set bread for the crab three feet from the sill, a new Olympic record. Then printed out a shopping list. Foodstuffs, rice, cabbages, vinegar. Vinegar taken a teaspoon to a glass of water chastened me, and rubbed on relieved the sandflea bites. Three cases of rum, the Dominican turned out to be cheaper than the Puerto Rican and of no less effect, and one of juice. A nail clipper. Several books. I found I preferred ones in the orange covers, but also, I wrote down for Isaac, to help him choose, blue or white.

I stuck the list and some bills in an envelope and placed it in a crack on the farthest stanchion on the pier. On it always perched a tern. A cartoon: a bedraggled bird in court, explaining to the judge. "Your honor, somewhere in my youth I took the wrong tern." Back at the house, I hung a fresh white towel out the dormer window to signal Isaac. As I entered the kitchen with the old towel, the crab was making his getaway. I took aim and tossed. The towel splatted on the counter in front of the crab and swept him to the floor. He dropped the bread and scurried frantically about the baseboards. Gotcha, you bastard. You are sprung to a new dimension. How will your priest explain this one? My laugh came out cracked and phlegmy. My house was his prison. Or is it vice versa? I wanted a hostage, not a pet. I'd use him to negotiate, in case God turned out to be a crab.

I was discussing this silently at the bathroom mirror when I tired of the company. I picked up a hairbrush, a Christmas gift from Reba—wood handle, real bristles—and popped the mirror. It broke like confetti.

Several nights later I looked again to the pier. The moon had been halved by a dull knife, whoever got the other piece had been shorted. On the regular boards were four open cardboard crates. They bobbed as the low surf moved under the dock. On top of an open box sat a white envelope with receipts, thirty-six dollars, and some coins. I licked the flap closed and slipped the envelope with its paper and metal through a crack in the planks.

New provisions. None, not even the two-pound Cadbury's milk chocolate bar with filberts, none was the treat of the nail clippers. That night I sat out on the back stair talking to C. Aubrey. First the fingers, then in the glow of the threatening day, toenails. My toes belonged to some reptile, yellow and stone-broken, they could rip open shells. Then the cutting, concentration and a click. It is a private release, the monk's version of great sex, a secret place opens to the air.

I told C. Aubrey about the crab. How would a dumb being react to a life of confinement? Nothing cruel, I guaranteed him safety, diplomatic immunity, and good treatment. I undertook to set out food and a dish of water. Just no hope of crabdom again. All because he couldn't grasp the idea of up. If he could only imagine height, he could retake the counter and be gone. What would he do? Would he renounce crabkind? Would he become like a crustacean saint, like Father Damien, sanctified by isolation? Would he choose to end his clacky, bug-eyed days?

C. Aubrey was a good listener. He had fewer ego needs than most conversational partners. For one thing, he had no parents that he could remember. I admired that, it made him stoic. He'd developed the knack of staring day and night at a single scene and the tedium, instead of driving him crazy, he'd learned to thrive on it. Still, he wasn't happy. He could see beyond the horizon, far off he could see people eating in cafés, drinking coffee, talking with each other. Even as I talked to him he could see a couple, they were lovers. They were sitting in a park, on soft grass. It was their last day together, they read poems to each other, she had the sniffles, he saw the man reach across and push back a lock of hair from her forehead. Watching didn't hurt, he watched every day. True, in the deepest part of night, when he couldn't see for the dark, a sadness overcame him and he would want to cry. But of course, pulp and bark, stuck as he was in a limestone reef, he could not. He wanted to shriek, to protest, to scream I hate this, I hate being frozen on the edge of this shore. But of course, being a tree, he couldn't.

Lately I'd been sleeping less, or maybe not at all. I think it was the disappointment over the madman of the shed, and besides until this last delivery of Isaac's I had been rationing the rum, and the measuring was worrisome. I walked on the beach where the receding tide had left the shoreline foamy. I picked up a clump of kelp, the bubbly kind, pale brown with hollow leaves that if you let dry snapped when you pinched them.

Never look at those things too close, nature. You never know what you'll see. The kelp was covered with a cherry-red roe. I squeezed off enough to fill a palm, and downed them. That was my first food of the day, and the salt and the taste of raw sea helped. Grains of caviar, grains of sand. Grain, train, twain, swain, swaim, swarm, swamp, stamp, stomp, stoma, stope, stops. Sand is simply life that has come to rest—didn't I read that?—sand used to be little coral creatures and once they're gone their bones break up in the waves. Bone-sand-dust. Just words.

People like words because they have them. If you ask a cheetah what's important, he'll say speed. Take your average toaster. It gets on fine without speech. How do words help? Nothing hatches from words except more words. Egg, ego, ago, age, are, art, ant, and, end. Egg to end.

* *

Hofstadter's unmistakable squawk came over the telephone. "Shopping," he said, and I was made to understand that I was to pick him up. It was a first lovely Saturday of May, only a week before he went to the hospital for the last time. He'd drawn a map of the city that he kept on his lap, and after every stop, explaining nothing, he called out the next address. We were touring garage sales from that morning's classified ads.

Each time I pulled up he said, dismissively, "Won't be long." In five minutes he returned. He bought nothing, what was he looking for? At the next stop I followed him up the lawn. A mock orange was in bloom and I walked through its spongy scent. I watched him dwell on a set of nesting kitchen canisters. At fifty cents each I'd buy them for Alice if only they were Dutch Colonial, my kitchen was becoming Dutch Colonial, but he'd moved on, disappeared. I asked the proprietor. Dressed in a chocolate angora sweater, short-sleeved, and beige slacks. She sat inspecting a discolored mark by her elbow. Her hair was dyed to match her sweater.

"Have you seen the man I came with? On the cane?"

"He asked to use the lavatory." The wattles on her throat shook. She had set up a beach umbrella, and on her card table was an open cash box.

"I've sold the house," she volunteered. I nodded, looking for Hofstadter's return. "My husband up and left." I grew increasingly anxious. Maybe I'd buy the canisters anyway, there were six of them and they fit together like those Russian stacking dolls. "He left me for digitized TV. Can you believe it? After forty-one years."

A young boy, maybe ten, helped Hofstadter down the stairs. He rasped to me it was time to go.

We drove in silence until he spoke. "Thinking. About your mother." I had told Hofstadter how my mother died when I was eleven. Tuberculosis. The Sister told me I was wrong, nobody dies of TB anymore. Hofstadter had asked how I felt, and I'd said lousy.

"Should I be grateful?"

"In my experience," he didn't answer the question. That was Hofstadter for you. "Children. Who lose. Mothers Young age. Different."

"Different how?"

"They are taken," he took a deep breath. "With a durable." He kept his eye on the sentence while he rested. "Melancholy."

"And it changes them?"

"They don't believe. Life works. They believe. Life abandons you."

"So?" I asked. I didn't see this getting anywhere. "Where would you say they've gone wrong?"

The next stop was an open house at a ranch-style home, the real estate agent was showing it to four earnest couples at once. Hofstadter and I wandered along behind the tour. Was he after canisters or a house to put them in? We finished the circuit and thanked the sales lady. Despite her sneer (people tend not to like a man with a hole in his throat), Hofstadter asked to use the toilet. He now used a cane with a tripod leg, and that and his space-man voice made him repulsive and irresistible. No one dared to look at him in the eye and say no. He told me he should take up selling encyclopedias.

I was suspicious. Had he developed incontinence and decided to tour the city's plumbing? I followed him to the bathroom, let myself in. He was carefully inspecting the vials of tablets in the medicine cabinet. "Just about through," he wah-wahed at me. "Halcyon. Completes my collection."

He emptied half of the vial into his pocket, flushed

the toilet, and we left.

I scolded him.

"No TV sermon...please," he squawked. "I need the latitude." At least I thought he said latitude. Maybe it was altitude.

* *

I unhooked the wires and wrapped the battery in a torn khaki shirt. Tied tail and sleeves together to form handles and hauled it over my shoulder, rucksack style. It took effort to find some plates of my brain that could still hold a charge. I was like the battery. Sea waters had seeped in, surf had soaked junctions and splices in brine, and twice each day the pull of the moon set in motion a rotting away. The rum helped of course, and when I could get it the sleep. It was a spiral. Being exhausted made me anxious and the anxiety pushed sleep further away so I grew exhausted.

I was tempted by Hofstadter's stash. I had taken the jar at the lawyer's invitation, he and I were cleaning out Hofstadter's home. Mostly crap, stuff the lawyer sent off to the Salvation Army.

"Would you like to keep something?" We stood among dozens of packing boxes.

"He left me a house." The man meant to be generous, I knew, generous and intimate, but only for the moment, and I regretted not accommodating him.

"Just a keepsake. To remind you of your friendship?"

"All my friendships were hard," Hofstadter told me once. "All of them needed an interpreter. And all my loves were complicated by hate."

I dug around in the boxes, there was nothing I wanted, ashtrays, books on astronomy, history, Buddha, death and dying. Then I remembered the plastic jar and retrieved it from the medicine cabinet. The lawyer read Sugar Substitute, crayoned in black. "I'll keep these," I said, and the lawyer looked on puzzled.

Mostly Phenobarbital, but also pretty little capsules stamped in tiny, legible letters. Ativan and Halcyon. I spilled them on the card table in the living room and arranged them by color. They were a collection, they were my stamps. But collections increase. This was assembled to diminish. Spend them one at a time and buy sleep, at the end of which you are out of currency, you are broke. It was the antidote to the Ant and the Grasshopper. That hit me with a pang. Not that I wished Hofstadter was here, I wouldn't do that to him, but that he could enjoy the joke.

I struggled with my pack to the north point. The beast remained in its pen. I wrestled the battery in, it didn't want to return, took steel wool to the bolts and brackets, scraped rust free, oiled the seating and fitted it neatly. Then I mounted the metal chair. Words were painted in black gloss across the dash. I had to look at them for several minutes to read them, I don't know why, I just didn't recognize them right off. They made up a message, and it was addressed to me:

WARNING.

DO NOT OPERATE MACHINERY IF DROWSY OR ILL.

Good advice. I laughed, not aloud, for that hurt, but in my head. Good advice, but I wasn't able to take it. Drowsy or ill covered my waking hours. I slapped my cheeks and stretched my eyes wide.

I turned the key in the ignition, put my thumb to the starter button, and the monster gave out a great roar, I'd stuck a pin in its ass. A roar that bloomed inside the tin cage, Godlike. Better than that, manlike, a man sound. I'd been listening to God's sounds for months—they're boring, surf rubbing against gravel, wind in the thin leaves, I'd been listening to all those puny sounds and going mad. Here was a machine waking, coughing up hawkers of oil and grease. It shook the hairs from your head. There were two levers between my legs—to steer the two cat tracks—and two pedals on the floor. A perpendicular lever at my left elbow for transmission shift, a second lever and a great bulb-topped handle to the right. I got down from my seat, opened both doors of the shed wide as they'd go, and turned around. The yellow beast rumbled in neutral. Was it preparing to charge? I was the one who rescued it, set it free like a genie from a bottle. Would it run me flat and rule the island until the next dupe came along? Hard as I looked, I couldn't tell what it was thinking.

Back in the saddle, I found the handle for engine speed. The flywheel engaged and we rolled an inch backward, the tread crunched against the rear wall. The tin house squealed, it had no give. The beast, with me nervously astride, edged out through the doors. The left pedal decelerated, the other braked. I was right about steering. I revved the engine. Lungers of diesel fuel ballooned up and got lost in the dust of the stars, the only cloud in the sky.

For practice I drove a circle around the shed. Of course—it wasn't a coincidence. The cleared perimeter was exactly the width of the dozer's blade, someone had mowed down the growth. I fiddled with the last lever, the one with the ball handle. Back and forth moved the blade up and down, right and left changed pitch.

I steered down the grade, over the river rock and up the other side. No stopping this. In half an hour I bladed a space large enough for a small house. Vine and branch yielded in its path, they uprooted with the softest popping sound, not a complaint, and lay like soldiers on a beach. This was something I could do. This wasn't half-bad, undoing God's work, remaking the world. Of course, that's what God would have said about making it in the first place. So long as you had the right tools, not half-bad.

CHAPTER 9.

The trouble started when Tommy was eight. Bullshit, I can hear Hofstadter's voice. The trouble started long ago, you weren't paying attention.

"You're not paying attention. You don't like to examine life up close, Mooney. The close-in shots make you uncomfortable. You can't concentrate on what's important."

"So what?" I answered.

"So," he said. He squinted as if I just shot off a flashbulb. You could tell he was in one of those moods.

The way I remember, the trouble started when Tommy was eight. He was a fanciful kid, not especially good in school, but not bad either, kind of a dreamy kid that goes along at his own pace. I wanted him to be good in reading and baseball, but I wasn't, and while Reba's smart as a whip it takes two to tango. He's who he was. Drawing was what he liked mostly, drawing. He'd filled up coloring books, then sketch pads, we couldn't keep him in paper. One Christmas Reba bought one of these enormous frames stores use to hold wrapping paper. She loaded it with a roll of cheap white stock. It was just the ticket, Tommy had it in his room and he stayed in there for hours. He did these long drawings without end.

I don't mean he had talent. The pictures made no sense. When I asked him what one was, he told me they're not pictures after all, it's a book, but what I'd call them really, they were more designs. Even his art teacher, I mean the kid was in the third grade it wasn't as if this was graduate school, but even his art teacher didn't understand it.

He drew since I could remember, and it began to reach frenzy level when he was maybe seven or eight. Hours in his room, we never saw him. I told Reba, maybe that roll of paper isn't such a good idea, but she says people will be what they are. About the same time Tommy got the idea he wanted a dog. We explained about allergies. Still, whenever he saw some breed on the street he rattled off its characteristics. The beagle was originally bred on the continent of Europe for speed and hunting. It has long legs for the brush and a keen sense of smell. Where he got all this I don't know, but he could tell you what breed worked sheep and what dogs hung around the courts of the Tsars.

Another thing. He didn't have many friends in school. In fact, he didn't have any, and we were a little worried. I was the scrawny kid in the corner, but you hope your kid will do everything right and I figured Reba and I, perfect marriage and all, we had a shot at it. So when Tommy came home and announced he wanted to invite a friend over, we were pleased. The friend was named Jeremy—there were six kids in his class named

Jeremy—but Tommy said that's not what to call him, he had a nickname. Understand, Stacey was now two years old, we were parents with twenty seasons in the majors, we didn't know anything about it, what we expected from childhood was that it would be just that, childhood. We told Tommy, great, invite Jeremy over, I'll cook out and Reba will do a strawberry shortcake.

Jeremy showed up. It was a weekday and I was minutes back from the Clerk's office. About this time I was new on the job, trying to make a good impression and not knowing what in hell to do, so maybe I was a little tense. Jeremy showed up, and I admit I was disappointed. He was a creepy-looking kid, no neck and glasses, who didn't seem interested in sports or TV or anything, and my fear was what any parent would fear. That Jeremy was just like Tommy. Just like me. But at least it was something. They went off, and Reba was cooking away and called them for dinner.

"Dog," Tommy said to him, "you can sit with us at the table. Right over there."

Jeremy took the seat across from Tommy, by the baby's chair.

"What do you call him?" Reba asked. She was eye-ing me.

"Dog. I call him Dog." We looked to Jeremy, to make sure he's not insulted. He stuck out his tongue and panted.

Everyone tore through the hamburgers and baked beans. When dessert was served Reba asked, "Jeremy, would you like ice cream on your shortcake?" The kid said yes, please. Tommy interrupted.

"If you want ice cream, you have to do a trick." Reba protested, but Jeremy stopped her.

"No, it's all right. I've learned one." He hopped off his chair, lay down on the floor and rolled over. Then he kneeled with his hands up like paws. "The time," he announced, "is now six fifty-four and forty seconds."

"OK," said Tommy. "You get dessert."

"That's a nice trick," Reba told him. "How did you learn to do that?"

Jeremy displayed his wrist. "It's a digital Swatch. I snuck a look when I was rolling over."

Reba didn't think anything of this. When I brought it up in bed she told me not to worry.

Reba was a funny blend. She passed in our little burg for a flower child, although ours didn't do acid or hit the road with the Dead, they were a milder version, and she was always encouraging Tommy to be himself and not to worry about what the popular kids think. Just be yourself, do what *you* want to do, what *you* think is right. She meant it. My take was, that's great advice until what they want is not what we want. I fretted about it but she seemed so wise, I tended to listen to her. Her reassurance went a long way. But her telling me not to worry about Tommy and Dog was like telling a polar bear not to go swimming, the water's too cold. I worried all the time. About Reba, about Tommy, and now, for the two years since she'd been born and the nine months before, about Stacey. I worried about money, I worried about the job. Running cases hadn't produced steady income, and with city employment, every two weeks they gave you a check. I told the Clerk in the interview, it's a job I would die for, although what I meant, but I didn't yet know it, was, it's a job that would kill me. With nothing to do, you lived convinced they'd discover the whole scam and do away with the slot. You forgot they were in on it. This was discouraging, but not remarkable. Remarkable was that every two weeks, they handed you this check.

To make matters worse, at the start of Tommy's dog period, I screwed up with the Clerk herself. It happened maybe two months after the cookout with Jeremy. I regularly had coffee in the employees' lounge, once midmorning and again in the afternoon. In the morning the air was fresh and breakfasty. Carafes of boiling water, regular and decaf, stand on the coils, you helped yourself and put a quarter in the Seattle World's Fair mug. There were times someone had made a cup of cocoa or heated up a cinnamon bun, the aromas were pleasant and people talked about the weekend and about football games they'd seen on the television.

The afternoon was a different matter. The bottom inch of coffee would smell of scorching. Dishes from lunch stacked in the sink. They usually involved tomato sauce, and a watery red soup splashed around the plates. Someone who always brought his lunch and let other people wash up was Canges.

I went to see the Clerk. I told her it is not merely messy. The kitchen reflects on the mind-set of the workers. At first I thought she was showing interest, she listened and her eyes closed behind thick lenses, but when I finished, she said, Is that it? I hadn't mentioned Canges by name, I kept my comments on a professional level. It was clear the Clerk didn't care. Canges learned of it, I am sure, and that set off the feud between us. I wished I had my words back. Later, at my first annual review in May, I brought it up again, I was going to apologize for being meticulous, I'd rehearsed it, although of course I'm not meticulous, just easily nauseated, and she stopped me. You'll have to get used to it, Mooney. Many of life's unpleasantries are beyond our control.

The same week as the annual review were the parent-teacher conferences. Reba and I went together. I cruised in without a care. What could they say about a child in the third grade? Everyone was coming to hear that his kid gets along well with others, doesn't bother his neighbor, hasn't wet his pants. What else is there to third grade?

We waited while the parents ahead of us were at the desk nodding agreeably. It looked like what I expected. We entered and told her our names. Tommy's parents, Mrs. Sonderman said and smiled. Then asked us to wait. It's that awful feeling, the hygienist tells your X-rays, hmm, I better have the dentist look at you. Mrs. Sonderman went down the hall and returned with a woman she introduced as Doctor so and so. Doctor so and so was the school social worker, though why a doctor was not explained.

Mrs. Sonderman had a loose-leaf notebook in front of her, the size of maybe a baked lasagna, with a page for each kid. Opened to Mooney. They told us they are concerned about Tommy. Very softly, you could tell this was their sympathetic mode. For one thing, his relationship with Jeremy, did we know about it? I laughed it off, told them not to worry, kids will be kids. Reba, of all people, was sitting on the edge of the chair gnawing her lower lip. How's that for the old switcheroo? I was defending our son against the onslaught of the child-eating cows and Reba was grim death.

"They just play at this dog thing," I told them. "It's just a game."

They asked if we knew about the art project and we told them sure, Tommy said he had an art project and he and Dog, I used the nickname to show I didn't take it seriously, it was just a game, he and Dog were doing it together.

Have you seen it? they asked, and we said no, we didn't know it was finished, and Mrs. Sonderman walked to the closet and got out a hefty scroll of Tommy's wrapping paper. She pinned one end to the corkboard by the door and began to unwind. The mural reached across two walls of the classroom, probably forty feet, and the Doctor and Reba were putting colored pushpins into the blackboard frames. Finally they got to the end and came back to the desk.

It was hard to identify. It couldn't mean anything, mostly Tommy's scrawls and designs. It was another world, you got that right off. They used pencil and crayon, but also poster paints and the part of the world in paint could drive you over. The sky is green and the trees are red, and as you look at it you realize each color seems like it's been opened up, sliced into, and it's bleeding another color. At the bottom are strewn a few recognizable objects. Body parts: lots of legs and arms, but here and there heads, torsos, fingers.

In several panels, an airplane flies high above. It's one of those old-fashioned biplanes, outdoor seating one behind the other, yellow traced in black. You can't miss it. Different attitudes, but not shooting, not a combatant. It might be scouting the scene. At the very end in the corner it's been signed, in black crayon:

Canine Ser. No. 156641, Pilot

Canine Ser. No. 183779, Co-Pilot

"That's a potful of work," I said. It was the truth, it must have taken weeks to do. "You can't call these kids lazy."

Mrs. Sonderman and the Doctor exchanged looks. Reba was trying to steal a look for herself. I was wondering whose side she was on.

"Do you want to hear the title, Mr. Mooney?"

"Sure."

"'Revolution of the Underclass.' Tom and Jeremy wrote it on the back."

There followed a lot of talk of significance, whether this or that was significant. The signatures, the caption. The fact that Tommy saw himself as an observer, in the airplane. It was a nice idea, I must say it appealed to me. There was bloody hell going on below and you had this pretty machine and you could stay out of it and watch, fly around and watch. The best seats in the house. It appealed to me, all but the flying. I'm no good on heights.

The Doctor wanted us to authorize regular sessions for her with Tommy. Chats, she said, nothing more than chats. For an assessment. She produced a form that needed our approval. Reba said to me what do I think, and I said, sure that's fine, how could it hurt? That's what I said, but underneath I was scared, you had to be. Reba asked if we'd hear about the chats. The Doctor took this as a stumper of a question, feigned thought, and finally came out with, Yes, if that's in Tommy's interest. I'm telling about this as if the four of us were sitting around having tea, and until about this point it was more of a conversation than a street fight, but when she told me Yes, if it's in Tommy's interest, things started to come apart. Mrs. Sonderman's loose-leaf was across the room, pages have fluttered off the rings during flight. The kind, syrupy tone in their voices had dried up. By the end Reba was leading me out and the Doctor was crying and hiding behind Mrs. Sonderman, mostly I would guess because of what I had to say. The chats, I should add, were off.

I consulted about this disruption with Hofstadter. He had two broken panes in his basement window, and I'd volunteered to fix them. The rains were causing mildew. Hofstadter was hopeless with tools, and I've always fiddled with fix-ups and machines. Cutting glass to fit, scraping out old paint and puttying are satisfying tasks, they give you a sense of order. I was up on the ladder and I told him about the conference with Mrs. Sonderman.

"She means well, Mooney. Don't be upset with her." Hofstadter was dressed in his uniform. He never varied. Khaki pants, khaki work shirt, black military boots laced to the shin. Today, against the draft in the basement that comes in through the window, he wore a gray cardigan sweater buttoned to the top.

"How could it not be in Tommy's interest to tell his parents about those talks?"

"We don't know. We have to guess what's in his interest."

"But they don't know either, do they?"

"No. They don't either. You simply need to trust your instincts."

"I don't have any instincts about this." He chewed

his lip to show agreement.

"Besides, I just want what will make him happy." He didn't answer right away. He waited. I laid the putty in the frames, tapped in the first pane, was blading off the excess.

"I'm not sure you should keep saying that." I was up on the ladder, only a couple of steps, my limit, or beyond since I'm beginning to shake. The basement had a low ceiling, and most of the work I could do from here.

"Why not?"

"Well, to start with it's not true. We all want complicated things, and happiness is just our word for having our way."

"You're saying happiness is overrated."

"I'm saying it's meaningless. It's arrogance itself. It's laughable. It is the discussion between two squares of toilet paper, their goals for the future. The one says, I have it in mind to clean a sable brush. I'll soak up the delicate colors from the tip of a famous watercolorist. A seascape, I think. The second says, yes, that's a noble ambition, but don't you think we should insist they call us bathroom tissue? So much more delicate.

"Talk about your vanities."

I didn't share this conversation with Reba. She was suspicious of Hofstadter to start with, and this wouldn't have endeared him to her.

* *

She and I talked about Tommy all the time. Stayed up and talked and then I would lie awake. One night I slipped into his room to see him asleep—when they were little I used to do that all the time, watch them sleep—so I slipped in and he wasn't there. It was eleven o'clock at night and he wasn't there. We called the cops, I know it sounds dramatic but he was maybe ten years old at the time, we called the cops and in minutes a patrolman called from a Dunkin' Doughnuts downtown saying Jeremy and Tommy were on their way home in a squad car. They'd violated the curfew ordinance but the cops were only giving them a talking to and were bringing them home. Eleven o'clock on a school night and he went out the window for a pecan twist.

Reba by this time was pretty upset. She'd moved beyond the just-a-phase phase. Tommy was stealing all our time from Stacey, she said, who was then three or four and managed to avoid most of this, sitting on the floor quietly looking through word books. Tommy might have stolen time, and it sure wasn't doing Stacey any harm, maybe just the opposite, maybe the less time the better, but Reba didn't want to hear that. The dog thing was still going strong, and worse. Jeremy and he talked to each other in a private code, you heard them on the telephone and his gym teacher wrote us about it. I wrote back kids-are-kids, but I couldn't ignore it.

The telephone rang during dinner and I answered and told Jeremy to hold on. Tommy picked up in the kitchen and said, casual as can be, "Cricktow bullum maloosa," came back and finished his tuna casserole, and I asked what was that, and he said, easy as punch, I told him I was at dinner, I'll have to call back. Reba asked what language is that and he told her it's more of a dialect. It's Collie, they're learning it because Dog, Jeremy, doesn't have a dog but he's saving up and when he has his own place, that's what he wants, a collie.

"What do you want?" I asked Tommy, and wished I

hadn't, because I could just see his eyes widen, all with Reba's allergies and Stacey more so, or we would have one.

Tommy knew this. When the subject first came up, Reba explained about allergies. "Well, then." Tommy said. "You must be allergic to me as well."

When I asked him What do you want it was as if he had been waiting backstage at "The Tonight Show" just to appear on camera and field this question.

"An English spaniel. They're cheerful dogs with a sense of humor. While retaining the field characteristics that have made them the choice of sportsmen, they're good with children and noisy with intruders. They make excellent house pets and lifelong companions."

Later that night, close to midnight, I heard a voice and got out of bed. Tommy was on the phone to Jeremy and they were discussing whether his parents were coming around. As soon as he heard the floor creak under my foot he went into the language, into Collie.

It's a ransom game, raising kids. They're like the guy who comes into the bank and says I've got a bomb taped to my chest, give me all your money or we're all going sky high. You stare at him and you stare at the front of his shirt, wishing you had x-ray vision, and you just can't tell. That's the scary part, you can't tell.

Reba and I talked it over. And over and over. My nerves were frayed. At work Canges had started in with my nameplate, every day I came in, letters were added or scrambled and it read YO NEMO and LOONEY TOONEY and A LEMON. I didn't know what the Clerk would think about me, about anything, it was not a good time.

Reba argued it could be worse. That was one of her

winning cards in life, it could be worse. For his eleventh birthday, Reba and I went to a kennel and picked out a spaniel. Not a pup. This one was two years old, housebroken, trained the woman said to gun or voice. I had to admit it was a cute dog, and I made separate trips, one to take Reba home and a second to pick the dog up in a special carrying box, all's so it won't trigger allergies.

Tommy was thrilled. He woke that day and announced he was now known as Tom. Tom was just thrilled. I couldn't remember seeing him so happy as he was that day. Reba and I explained about outdoors, how the dog would live outdoors, and Tommy would have to care for it, pick up after it and watch its water and food and exercise.

He and Jeremy built a humongous doghouse out of plywood. He's my kid, he knows how to use a hammer and nails. One room, maybe six by six by four high, with a shelf bracketed into it, like a loft in a condo. The first night, Tom and Jeremy slept in it. Swami—he had it named before we got home—Swami and Tom on the floor and Jeremy on the shelf in a sleeping bag. We thought that was cute, we thought this was a terrific present, maybe we've done something right. But Tommy didn't come in. I don't mean ever, he came in for meals and to use the bathroom. But more and more he stayed out in that doghouse. With the chill of September, they tore off the roof and insulated the whole interior with scraps they scrounged from a construction site. It's fine, he told us. Swami gives off lots of heat, and it's cozy.

He hasn't named him Swami, he told us. That's his title, his position. Swami is involved in the religious life of the dog order. His actual name we can't pronounce, because, naturally, it's in Spaniel. I didn't ask Tom whether he spoke Spaniel. There's good and bad to all this: while Tom began to smell like Swami, not dirty or anything, but doggy, and we didn't see too much of him, he and Jeremy stopped speaking in code.

And some bad. One, Swami kept getting out. He didn't roam far, he seemed to know where he lived. But I would drive home in that damn traffic after a day of wrangling with Canges and there, a block away from our house, that dog would be standing in the middle of the street. I'd get Tommy to chase him down, he'd tell me not to worry, the dog needs to wander to clear his mind. Sure, I said. But he gets to the highway—we had a busy four-lane maybe half a mile from us—he gets to the highway it will clear more than his mind. Swami, Tom told me straight and serious, Swami possesses magical powers. He cannot be injured by the war machines of humans. I don't know where he got this stuff.

"You've got to keep that dog locked up." I can hear myself saying it. Like a threat. Or like the judge, sending a nonsupport off for thirty days. "That dog may have secret magical powers, but the truck that hits him won't be in on the secret."

I went to the Builders' Depot that weekend for a double roll of fencing wire and a rented post-hole digger. Tom and Jeremy and I built a dog run. A pretty good job, too, although the boys bitched the whole time. It's a prison, they said. How would you like to live in a prison? Still, we did a good job, and I got a kick out of doing it together, a family project. It didn't mean anything. Swami was out of it as much as he was in. They didn't want him locked up.

Still, those were good days. You pay for all the good ones, but those were good ones. Reba seemed to think maybe I had done the right thing, maybe this dog was the answer, keeping him outside, and it helped take the stress off for once. When you're worried about things like kids or the office it's hard to be romantic, and I had gone a long time without paying attention to her. The booze didn't help, about the time of the Revolution of the Underclass I started on the booze maybe a little too heavy and that doesn't help your love life. Those months after Tom's eleventh birthday were good times, Stacey happy like she ought to be, not a care, Tommy growing up and speaking English not Collie, and Reba thinking maybe what I promised her was true. Maybe I'd keep a regular job with a regular paycheck and our kids would get raised in one piece and the marriage would turn out to have been, just as I'd said, damn close to perfect.

CHAPTER 10.

The next night—or was it the next? With nothing between them, they lined up like barbershop mirrors—I was back on the bulldozer, fortified with half a loaf of packaged bread from the freezer and a bottle of rum to work until dawn. Nights seemed to be shortening, would they die out as the days had? Still, I preferred the dark, soft and easy on the eyes. The sand fleas made a brief appearance at dusk, and whether it was the noise or the greasy diesel exhaust, or because my flesh had become sharp to the taste, aged and rancid, they let me be.

I rode that bulldozer hard. Hours at a time. By the third night I stopped thinking lever, pedals, up-down, back-front, and it moved under my feet. I might have plowed through the time, but kidneys sloshed about my hips like bags of warmed ice and brought me down. I got off the dozer about midnight, stood to pee in the starlit clearing that I myself had just cut. It was a wonderful feeling. The ugly scar on the earth was my own. I stood frozen and unable. Who was there? Just my own ghosts, a boys' choir of ghosts surrounded me. I walked into the brush, far enough to hide, and delivered my water. A process of elimination. It's a little crazy, since how good are they at ghosting if you can lose them in the bushes? Like God in the Garden of Eden. He is looking for that couple and He calls, Where are you hiding? This is God, after all, the omnipotent and all-seeing, the God of the Baltimore Catechism. It doesn't give you a lot of confidence He's keeping track.

The cut grew on its own. I merely guided it down, like a sheet you toss on a bed and pull evenly to the edges, a nice feeling. The two corners were tucked at right angles before I knew it. Since the island was long and skinny, without intending I carved a straight edge perpendicular to its length. I like geometry. Reba used to say it was gender-based. Lines beget science, circles art. Women doodle in circles, men in lines. Except artists, artists use it all. She was explaining Tommy's murals to me.

Once the corners were laid, the sides of rectangle grew naturally as the clearing rolled south. I fashioned stakes from cut willows and eyeballed them in a line. I had put four large spools of packing twine on my shopping list. What could Isaac have thought, the man is going to open a retail store?

One night working away I heard music. Faint, like a radio left on at the house, except I had no radio. When I stopped to listen the music stopped. The encounter with the hermit of the shed had made me cynical, and I sat and thought. It's me, I realized. Humming a kid's tune. Into the Forest. Appropriate. The twine, tied by a half-hitch across the notched stakes, chalked an uncertain white line into the starlight. I considered reshooting my survey in the sunlight, but the nights were cool and dry, and blurred the world. I'd bet that among nocturnal animals—field mice, owls and such—there's a low rate of suicide. People favor the day, they like certainty, but I'm on the other side. In the twinkling light you couldn't be sure of things, that floating white line might be something else, the center line of some two-lane that led the hell out of here.

* *

"Into the Forest." Why would I remember that tune? Five notes, and all the time I sat on the bulldozer I was singing "Into the Forest" as though I was one of the dwarfs, maybe Dopey.

The tough times for our son seemed to be over. He and Swami lived outside, and we were graced only on occasion with a prediction or preference from the magical mystical dog. And just as we hit that little glide of downhill peace Reba and I encountered our own bumps in the road. I don't know how it happened, because I adored her, had since we met, and while I hadn't been exactly a success, she had stuck by me, and remained one of these people who lived her own life, not another's.

The first pothole came the day of Stacey's recital. For one thing, I thought five years old was too young to be giving a recital. For another, I was worried about the office. The mayor was up for reelection and he was talking about City Hall efficiency, itself a contradiction but in an election year the voters want promises and paradox, so every department was ordered to examine redundancy. When the mayor talked redundancy, his staff talked cuts, and on the Clerk's desk—I knew because I fetched it from the typing pool—was a list of all the hires, ranked in order from most recent on down, and the name of what white male incompetent do you think headed the rest? By this time my old profession had grown competitive, younger people were running cases, I saw them daily, asking innocently for files, but who knew better than me? Kids in law school, kids of lawyers, lawyers themselves. The field was overcrowded. I needed this job.

Weekends Reba and I strategized about how to demonstrate that I was not redundant. It was a stretch. Before we could hit on a plan, the mayor's opponent turned up a scandal—City Hall employees fixing neighbors' traffic tickets—and the firings that came as a response produced the very efficiencies the mayor sought. His quick action got him reelected. The story had an Old Testament ring to it, a victory for humility and stupidity over competence. God ranks humility right up there next to cleanliness. You've got to wonder about His values.

My job was safe, no need to worry. But then there rarely is. Need has nothing to do with it, there's no need for smallpox or mosquitoes or famine either.

Stace had been hammering away at her recital piece on the spinet for weeks now. "Into the Forest." Da da dum, di di dum, Da dum di do dum.. Left and right hand in unison, or so the sheet music said, until the last climactic chord. This recital was on a Saturday afternoon, and to relax, some time after lunch, I fixed myself a drink and maybe a second. Off we went, me driving, Reba in a red peasant dress she'd made herself. She designed it and sewed it and the identical dress for Stace, and to see them together knocked me out. Reba was a perfect eight. She cut her black hair like a helmet around her face, and Stace was her double except for the bangs. Stace preferred bangs especially for the piano so hair doesn't fall in her eyes. I clicked off a couple of Kodaks on the timer of the four of us, five including Elizabeth. You'd have thought it was a magazine ad. Stace and Tommy strapped themselves in the back seat, Elizabeth too, Stace's doll, without whom she went nowhere, not kindergarten, not baths, nowhere.

At Miss Tutweiler's studio the parents filed in. The kids sat up front around a giant black grand, it looked poised to eat you if you come too close. Already I'm worried. Stace was five years old, for Godsake, and this piano was a huge piece of machinery and none too stable. When the kids played it the lid shook ominously and the whole thing, get this, stood on three legs. Miss Tutweiler handed out programs that went on forever, but it soon became clear we wouldn't be there overnight since most of the pieces were short. The students went in order of advancement, the newest first. By the bottom of the program, kids would be playing real music, Chopin, Brahms, that sort of thing. Stacey was batting fourth. Cleanup.

Miss Tutweiler announced that a parent should introduce his kid. Reba whispered to me, you, and I nodded. Stace was sitting in the front row, directly beneath the open maw of the Yamaha. Her feet swung free inches above the floor and she was giving Elizabeth the Heimlich maneuver. As to the whereabouts of my brain there was, as they say in cop shows, no reliable evidence. The third kid wrapped up "The Barnyard," right hand only, I realized Stace was the first of the two-handers, and I was on. Miss Tutweiler said, Mr. Mooney. I walked to the front of the room, I turned and I blanked.

Blank. I couldn't remember who I was. I stood there and I heard the kids start to laugh, Tommy first. Still I did not remember what in hell I was supposed to do. Miss Tutweiler slinked over and pointed to a line on the program and I squinted and said, "Bobby Ratcliff 'Cossack's Dance'," and that got a roar of laughter because that was the one after Stace. I was not Mr. Ratcliff. Miss Tutweiler was back pointing and thank God, there was my daughter's name, and I got it out and added "Into the Forest" and took my seat.

The laughter didn't die down for three pieces. No one paid attention as Stace slogged through "Into the Forest," the first time losing her concentration and playing a bunch of wrong notes and the second time in broken rhythms, much worse than she'd done it at home. I had to sit next to Reba, whose body was wound, like sitting next to a murderer at sentencing you could feel the tension, sit and listen to "Circus Clown," "The First Robin," Clementi's "Sonatina in F," first part, and I don't know what else. Twice more that afternoon, the sun's rays long and sleepy through the window and feet shuffling on the grit of the bare wood floor, someone broke the silence right before a piece was announced, someone murmured "Bobby Ratcliff 'Cossack's Dance'," and it got a roar. The world's greatest wisecrack. One of those times it was Tommy. And through it all, Stace sat in the front row. You could see the drops of water run down her cheek, off her chin, and splat onto Elizabeth's hair, combed and in a bow for the big day. You could see, honest to God, where the pink bow was growing dark.

It was a horror. Later I figured out what happened: I forgot the movie mode. I could handle situations if I ran them through my mind first, like a movie. Then, in rehearsal, I figured out what I was supposed to say and how I was supposed to feel. But I hadn't run the reel through, I was just sitting there thinking about Stace swinging her feet from the chair and hugging the breath out of Elizabeth, and I hadn't run it through. The recital ended in about five days and Reba took the keys from me and led the family back to the car. I walked with Stace. Sorry, Dorothy, I told her. That's a family joke. I wanted to name her Dorothy after Judy Garland in that movie. It was one of those compromises, Reba wanted Stacey.

She didn't say anything. Reba saw to it that the doors were closed and the seatbelts were fastened, Elizabeth's too, got behind the wheel, and I got in the suicide seat. The car rolled away moderate as could be from Miss Tutweiler's, and then Reba let me have it.

"At least you ought to consider your children," was how it ended up, which was I thought a low blow. "Consider them next time before you drink yourself into oblivion."

"That's hardly fair. I got stage fright. It could happen to anyone."

"To anyone who has drunk eight ounces of bourbon."

"You're measuring?"

"Someone should."

"Elizabeth says," Stacey piped up from the back seat. "Elizabeth says you should stop fighting."

I was not ready for this female conspiracy. Three of them against me, two were blood family and one a doll.

I spun in my seat.

"Tell Elizabeth to mind her own God damn business."

Stace looked as if I had hit her. I wanted my words back, wanted to say I'm sorry, but Reba didn't give me a chance.

"Len. She's a bloody child. For heaven's sake watch your language."

"What about yours? What about bloody?"

"Bloody isn't cursing. It's an expression."

I still owed Stace an apology. It never came. "Tell Elizabeth we aren't fighting. We're having a difference of opinion. We're discussing weights and measures. How much is eight ounces. Your mother and I don't fight." At this Tommy snorted. Snuk, snuk.

I didn't let it pass. "What in hell is that supposed to mean, Mr. Bobby Ratcliff?"

"You fight all the time," he said triumphantly.

"The hell we do." My words produced another snort.

"Is that a lie or an omission?" I had just had a conversation with Tommy about telling the truth, and it was coming back at me. He'd been cutting class and never mentioning it to us, and my thesis—every parent's thesis which he ends up eating daily with his cornflakes—was that an omission was just like a lie.

"Are you in on this?" I asked Reba. "Are you satisfied with this?"

"Len, you're missing the point. The point is you should watch your drinking."

"I do watch it. You should watch the road. That light was red."

"No it wasn't," Reba said and glanced in the rear-view mirror. Fact is, it had already turned green but the glance told me she wasn't sure, and there was no way for her to prove it now.

"Green all the way," said Tommy.

"It's a fine state when parents don't stick together disciplining their children." A crack the width of a screwdriver blade started in my forehead just above the eyes and spread to each temple. Maybe it was the booze wearing off but I didn't think so, I really hadn't had that much. Eight ounces is a lot, I really don't think I had eight ounces.

"We're not talking about the children," Reba said like a schoolteacher. "We're talking about you."

"All the way," said Tommy and Stace giggled.

"Why don't you pull over," I said. "Just pull over here and I'll get out."

Tommy was now singing. "All the way. All the way. Light green all the way." The melody was "Into the Forest."

"That's enough." I said, half turning, and something in my face must have been fierce because he quieted down.

But not for long. We went five or six blocks and he struck up a conversation with Stace. "Swami thinks that in time the humans will kill themselves off. There won't need to be a revolution because if humans fight in their own families eventually they'll fight each other."

"You tell Swami to keep his predictions to himself. Otherwise you know what happens to opinionated dogs?"

"What happens?"

"Dog food, that's what."

Tommy snorted again. Snuk. It had become his favorite word. "That's ridiculous. You must be thinking of horses. Dogs wouldn't eat dog food made from dogs. That's cannibalism. Dogs are highly civilized."

"Listen," I said. I don't know how to stop being so angry. I am in a car going home with the people I love most in the world. The only people. "Don't think that dog can't disappear one day. Don't think some truck can't come around a curve too fast one day and poof. He's history."

"He's history," Tommy said, stubborn as me, his voice going up in the air like a chin, "he's history, so am I."

"That might suit all three of us." What I meant was Swami, him and me. Later I thought about this remark. You could see how Tommy might have misunderstood it. But it was out.

"Leonard, quit. This is so childish." That crevice had passed through the temples and was circling around to the back of my head. A split running in old wood. The top of my skull could fall off.

"First I'm a drunk, now I'm a child. Well, the Lord looks after us both." I opened the door and unclipped the seatbelt and everyone screamed. Reba jammed on the brakes and I sort of hopped out as the car was coming to a stop. I meant to wait for it to stop but my timing was off and I stumbled out and fell, tore my good pair of wool slacks at the knee. I was feeling foolish as can be, but there was no going back.

I got up, picking gravel out of my palms. Reba was looking at me as if I'd escaped from the mental ward. I slammed the car door and began to walk the other way. After a few minutes I heard her drive off. I turned and walked on home, the fresh air clearing some fog, and embarrassment replacing the headache as number one on the discomfort hit parade. The entire walk, I swear, I was singing to myself. Light green all the way.

* *

Night after night you'd notice the moon. It bloated and shrank, showed up at different times, and if you were given to caring, you could tell about time and seasons. One night in particular, it was coming out of the sea to my right humpbacked and off balance. Nobody makes much of God's mistakes. He gets away with a lot, who is there to forgive His sins? There was a broken path of light on the water, the punctured moon might wobble down it like a bowling ball and smack into my island. The moon is supposed to be cool, to have no heat, but from where I sat you couldn't tell.

I did three rows through berry bush and palm. Then I took lunch: four slices of bread, just the crust since I'd clawed out the center and tossed it to the crab. Washed down the meal with rum. I'd lugged a case up to the north end so I wouldn't run out. All I needed to carry then was a few bites and a jug of water. I sat chewing and watching the pebbled ocean surface. I didn't much like it. It had no path of light any more, just liquid. Liquid must be the mother state. Solid doesn't change, gas blows away. Liquid has everything you need to make a world. If the first soup had been brewed in granite, this planet would have been a flop. Maybe that's what all those stars are, God's flops. It took him a potful of tries to get it right. Although seeing us farting around makes you realize He didn't stop with us, He's still trying to get it right. On probation. If He'd gone to work for the Clerk, He would have had a review in thirty days, but as it is He has forever.

I peered down the string to align the long edge of the clearing. My field was straight at the top and now on the sides, perhaps forty feet in width and as yet unknown in length. I studied the bramble at its boundary and could see nothing. Black. When the brain loses oxygen, I read somewhere, colors go first. Everything turns black and white. Then, from the outside in, vision itself. Life gets framed in a black circle, like the closing shot of an old cartoon. So what you see in your last seconds is Your-Name-Here, The End, and Porky Pig in the middle, tha-tha-tha-that's all folks. People off themselves by walking into the sea. Not me. All that closeness. I'm claustrophobic, that wouldn't suit me. And no tall buildings. Nothing bloody, close or high. Pills for me, I think. The brain losing oxygen, the only movie turning black and white, like the end of *The Wizard of Oz*. And Porky Pig in the last frame.

I worked until my eyes closed. Then I lay down and slept, right there where I'd cleared, on the sandy soil still warm from the day. Just the amount of sun I could tolerate, the coffee-colored dirt creamy with sand, all stamped with the reassuring wavelets from the tractor treads. I awoke and made my way back to the house. My little project, my garden of empty, was steadily marching south. Perhaps when I reached the grove by the back stairs where C. Aubrey sat, I would blade him under, blade the house from its foundation. Move it all into the ocean, I could hear the groans of protest as the flimsy boards came loose, the nails that thought they could sit forever in their wooden dens and rust into flakes, all sprung as the dozer scuffed the entire heap, all creation, onto the beach. Down to the outgoing tide. The crab would rejoice, Emancipation Proclamation. Pro clams and crabs, Crabonia's Fourth of July. And I would be left with this odd-shaped letter, a backwards J done in outline.

The nights looked the same. Only the moon and my sculpture changed. One afternoon some damn weekend sailor moored his boat in the bay. He put his field glasses to my shoreline and when he saw me, or thought he did, he waved and hallooed, stuck his head down the gangway and called below. I ran out to the pier and shook the pitchfork at him. By then his wife was up on deck. They made anchorage and sat there all afternoon. I watched them drink drinks, I could hear the ice, imagined them talking, that chummy way couples do, trying to find in my pitchfork a meaning other than the obvious one. At midnight I walked up to the north shed to start the tractor. Of all things, the noise of the diesel sent him packing. I watched his silhouette, these prissy running lights red and green putt-putting into the black horizon. Looked like a Christmas sled someone stuck on a suburban roof, sliding into oblivion, good riddance to bad rubbish. After he left, lonely for him, I lowered the blade.

I'd bet that the people who want to save tropical rain forests have never had the chance to knock them down. In the dark, with sad bleak stars leaking out of the sky, the engine singing a night song, it was the end of days. And the fumes, the gluey rich fumes of machine. Better than booze. I fixed the blade at ground level and mowed down vine and fern.

Desolate, hopeless, wonderful. I sat on that iron seat, holes punched in it and cast in the shape of a heart, I sat there without thought. Every so often my brain dropped by, curious, like an old man watching construction at a plywood cutout, and if I noticed it hanging about, I fed it word ladders. I changed TREE into SAND

TREE
THEE
THEM
THEN
THIN
CHIN
CAIN
PAIN
PAID
SAID
SAND

and I was satisfied with the outcome. It was close to perfect except THIN and CHIN didn't belong. I worked other word ladders as the machine ground away. I changed DREAD into HEART, five-letter puzzles were tough, and GOD to END, and FEAR TO BEAR. For this last one, in order to get in PUER and RUBE, I rang through fifteen steps. Maybe I would gather shells and spell out my ladders. People would see them from the sky, people flying with their families for Christmas holiday, they would take pictures to put in their album. A field of words migrating letter by letter. They would fly over and wonder what dismal soul is signaling with a child's game.

I finished at dawn and motored back to the shed. Day brought with it the need to feed the beast. The powers that be had thoughtfully left behind a half-dozen drums of diesel fuel and the tools of supply. A rude sawhorse, two-by-twos nailed into X's and joined with a braced beam. I hoisted a barrel onto the crotches of the horse and attached a length of rubber hose. The way they'd designed the shed, I first thought they had forgotten to finish the floor. But the partial pad had a purpose—when the cat was driven off, onto the sand, its fuel tank was lower than the bunghole. Once I figured it out, all you needed do was wrestle the drum onto the sawhorse, uncap it and fix the tubing, and fuel gurgled downhill into the tank. Feeding the beast.

I gathered up crap from the shed—two quart containers for motor oil and a couple of empty bottles—and walked back to the house. Isaac would haul off trash when he left provisions. Otherwise I would drown in my own garbage.

Dog-tired but not wanting to go to bed, I sat outside talking to C. Aubrey until the sun heated up. It must have been about summertime by then, because the light of the sun was unbearable even hidden as it was behind the house. My eyes hurt to think of it. I told C. Aubrey about the visitors on the sailboat and how I wasn't able to take a leak, which was funny in a way. I started to laugh that dry and cracked laugh, all those ghosts gathered in the woods balcony-style and staring down on me. Funny, because they were of course *my* ghosts and if I couldn't scatter them at least I ought to be on good enough terms to piss in front of them. Not funny, too, and as I sat there having a last drink before what I hoped would be bedtime, perhaps enough sleep to loosen the tin strip that bound my forehead, and noiselessly laughing and talking to this face on a tree, I felt the warm pee of tears streaming down my face, just streaming down.

CHAPTER 11.

When it happened, the next pothole, I was in a good mood. The Clerk had reamed out Canges in front of everybody. Her office overlooked the bullpen, where we worked, a large open space painted apple green. The bullpen was filled with glass-topped tables where law clerks and worker bees spread papers, opened up court boxes, and looked through pleadings. The men wore short sleeves and rayon ties that cleaned up nicely. Men and women alike favored strong toilet water and from the folders came a single smell, a spice pressboard gardenia oleander citrus. In the folders were the angry words of grievances and petitions. We sorted through papers, and as time moved heavy we gave those papers the importance kids give to baseball cards. The only thing in the room you knew was alive, the only thing that moved for sure, was the clock. Every so often, rarer still as the day wore on, the minute hand clicked to a new dot like a bug chasing warm sun.

This day the Clerk saw Canges stroll in and she

nailed him. Not that he didn't deserve it. Canges moved files around the building, that was a job he coveted and no one could take it from him. But whenever he loaded up the two-handled cart with file boxes and wandered off, the joke was, he's out with a dolly. He would go to Juvenile to visit the court steno with the great chest. He would drop in at Probation, the redhead needed him to try her coffee cake, they would jaw half an hour. People teased him when he came back, Canges, did you get any apple turnover? Not me, I didn't say a thing because he didn't take it from me. But the others did, and Canges just beamed, you could tell he was proud of the way he was.

This time he'd been off at Superior, where appeals went when they left Municipal, if anyone appealed, which they rarely did, since mostly they'd been so dicked over at Municipal Court they just wanted out. But every once in a while a collection company lost a case, the Legal Aid lawyer tore up the track so they couldn't railroad people through, or the Public Defender took time off from polishing his résumé. And the judge listened. A new tune on the jukebox, and the judge ruled for the defendant. In collection cases, a win for the defendant was like a no-hitter. Maybe a couple a year. But the collection company, to show that no young punk from Legal Aid could screw with them, would appeal. It wasn't the lousy price of the dinette set, believe me.

Canges had been missing without checking out for most of the afternoon, and the Clerk was looking for him and steaming. Someone let slip, as a matter of fact I did, that perhaps he was still down at Superior. Our Clerk called the Superior clerk—they were buddies if you could imagine our Clerk with a buddy instead of a

Rottweiler—and out of the bag jumped the cat. The clerk at Superior didn't like sex either, it must be a requirement of the job, and when Canges was on the prowl, no one misjudged that his real passion was coffee cake. Canges slinked back, the Clerk was waiting for him, the door open, pacing her office, and she let him have it. Alley-catting, is what she said. For the rest of the day, I let go an occasional meow and everyone in the bullpen broke up. I invented a running gag, but because of what happened next, I forgot to make it run.

What happened next: I was driving home savoring the good day. That's all I was thinking about. If I ever saw him, I don't know it.

When I came into the house Reba and Stace were there, agitated, and Reba told me Tommy was out looking for the dog, we always said *the* dog so we didn't confuse it with the human one. Tommy'd been gone since noon Reba said, and she was worried. She has a great sixth sense. Not too shabby on the other five, Reba is, she is someone who spends a lot of time on the senses. She had a premonition, and her fears filled up the bottom of my lungs so the breath only reached the shoulders. Just then the door kicked open and our firstborn appeared, covered in blood. Oh my God, one of us said, maybe both, he's been hit. He was carrying Swami, who oddly had no blood on him. No blood and his coat was lustrous but the way the dog's head was lolling over the crook of Tommy's elbow, you knew he was gone, there was not a chance in the world he was alive.

I set down the drink I'd poured, and Reba shrieked and said, "Dear God, Tommy, what's happened?" although we knew, I did. Tommy gave me a look I'll never forget. I went to see if I could help and he shuffled me this queen of spades, knife-edge look.

"Why didn't you stop?"

I swear I didn't know what he was talking about. My stomach heaved and I thought to myself I've hit the dog, I've killed Swami. But then I figured, no that couldn't be right. I hadn't had a drink at work, if I had hit the dog I would have heard it.

"Why didn't you stop?" he asked again, not really a question, and you could see in his eyes he was wishing for his own car so he could run over me.

"Where? What are you talking about?"

"You drove right past us. A million miles an hour. Swami was still breathing and I called out and yelled and you never stopped. Just when you turned off the highway. Why didn't you stop?"

"Tommy," I said. I knew he didn't like to be called that but I forgot myself, he'd been Tommy for twelve years and Tom for less than one. "Tommy, I didn't see you. If I'd seen you..."

Reba was there with a towel. She wiped the blood from his face and tried to take the dog out of his arms, but he held on. Are you all right, she wanted to know, and how did you get so much blood on you. The dog, I swear, didn't have a drop, his coat looked silky, ready for a show, and except for the flopping head and the milk-glass eyes, you would have thought nothing was wrong, you would have thought it'd make a good magazine cover if we could only get the kid to smile.

I stood indicted for the death of Swami. Beyond a reasonable doubt. In Tommy's world of runes and sly intelligence, the power of an evil will triumphed. I wish

I could have my words back, and I know he thought those words unlatched the gate on the dog run, led Swami past the end of our street, past the fences and scents and pfitzers he knew to the four-lane, gripped the wheel of the car or truck—no one ever came forward—and swerved it to clip the priest of his secret society.

He and Dog buried Swami. In violation of the municipal ordinance about dead animal disposal, they buried the corpse in the northeast corner of our yard. We'd already turned out our lights, but from our bedroom window Reba and I heard the ritual, words spoken over the hole in the ground in Collie or Spaniel, it was hard to tell.

Reba felt that would be the end of it. This would bring a natural closure. We would discuss loss as a family, love and loss, how they come together, and talking would heal things. Talking heals only two things, Hofstadter told me—this from a man who paid to play—and both cures are temporary. One is the hope of the listener that perhaps he is not inadequate. The inadequacy of a shrink, he said, refreshes itself daily.

Two is silence.

These discussions didn't last. We had discussions at the dinner table, Reba and I, occasionally Stace chimed in, until as Hofstadter would say we confirmed our inadequacy, and then we stopped. A week later, Tommy asked from nowhere. "Why do adults always lie about things?"

"What do you mean?" Reba took the podium on behalf of adults.

Tommy sniffed. You could see him weighing whether it was worth the effort to tell us. "'You'll get over it,'" he said at last. "Things like that. The dentist tells you it won't hurt. What's the purpose?"

Reba looked at me. "They want to save you the pain," I said. It was a question I'd thought about.

"But it doesn't help," he explained. You could tell Tommy was hoping I'd change things. I'd tell him I'd be an exception and tell the truth, and we both knew I couldn't do that. It's not something you want to admit, but I couldn't change things.

The respectful period of mourning was followed by a respectful period of sullenness, but we never heard another word. Tom continued to draw on the roll of paper, but his pictures were different. They became normal size, even small, and technical. Full of gears and measurements and pulleys. Gone were the gathering storms of poster paint, the battles between clouds of red and black and yellow. He got interested in mechanical drawing, with compasses and T-squares, and he produced blueprints of phantasmal machines. One, for example, was a death ray, you use it if some bully cuts in line. You hook this gizmo to the wall at the head of the line. It came in a specially designed case, disguised as the facade of the building. If you're at McDonald's the case looks like the golden arches—how you install it without being seen Tom hadn't perfected, he told me he was still working on that—and then you manipulate its gears with a remote control from your position in line. The rifle emerges from the case, takes a sighting, and pops the guy. While everyone is examining the body the rifle withdraws into its camouflage. The drawings show this accordion flange coming out of the top of a shopping center ATM, right in the center of that convex mirror that's there for your protection. The cover is no bigger than the diameter of the rifle so the rifle's hidden. Like "Candid Camera."

Reba and I decided it was over, the canine era was done and the next era had to be better no matter what, and of course we were wrong. I told Hofstadter, I've had enough of this, and he said, That's what you think.

Just deciding it was over, the canine era of our lives, Reba and I were doing better. There was no more talk of layoffs. It looked like we might be out of the forest. One night a man we'd never met appeared at our door. Maybe a year after they buried Swami. A large man, black bushy eyebrows and a sad bovine look, wearing a uniform—turned out he drove for United Parcel. I answered the door, figuring we're getting a package. When he said who he was, Jeremy's father, it took me a moment to think, oh of course, Dog, but I didn't say it.

We invited him in and I made a pot of coffee and we sat in the living room. Reba served him a cup and saucer and his hands were too large. He'd have done better with a mug. Stace clicked off the TV and disappeared. Dog's father waited until we were settled, the skim milk and sugar went around unused, he was perched on the end of the easy chair trying to figure out how the cup and saucer fit together and we were sitting on the sofa waiting for him to tell us why he'd come. He's worried, he said at last, about our sons. They ditch school all the time and he thinks they're headed for trouble. I told him about boys being boys, and he said trouble, this latest incident just shows it. He wasn't putting any blame on our boy, it wasn't a question of blame. What incident, I said, and he looked at me like I'm a dunce.

"The CD player."

"What about a CD player?" Reba asked.

"The boys broke into a car in the school parking lot and stole a CD player. You mean you don't know?"

"I don't think it was Tom," I said.

"Who?"

"Tom. Our son."

"I don't know him as Tom," Dog's father said. "I know him as Prince."

"Well, that's it, then. You have the wrong kid."

He gave this large, wet sigh.

"Listen, Mr. Mooney. All I know is if that's your kid..." and he pointed to Stace and Swami and Tommy in front of the Spanish moss, the shoe-store picture sitting on the Kimball spinet, payments still being made and Stace having quit soon after "Into the Forest," "...if that's your kid, he's the one. He and Jeremy never go anywhere apart. They're always together, and Jeremy got suspended from school for breaking into a car and stealing a CD player, and if your kid didn't it's because mine didn't rat on your kid, it's because they're thicker than thieves and just as mum."

"Tommy hasn't mentioned this to me," Reba said, her voice mellow to signal to Jeremy's father she understands. Understands him better than he does himself. Reba has rapport, more than she needs. She can instantly take the point of view of someone she's never met before. "You can be sure we'll ask him about this."

"Whose car?" I don't know why I asked. What difference?

"The shop teacher," he said. "Nice man."

"I'm not sure you have the right kid," I told him.

Frankly I was a little scared, and what you do when you're being attacked is circle the wagons. Jeremy's father shot me a look from under his storm-cloud brows. I could tell he was chewing about whether or not to take me on. Reba distracted us and broke the clinch.

"You can be sure we'll have a heart-to-heart."

"Thanks, Mrs. Mooney. You know what I'm saying. This isn't a question of blame." He put the cup on the saucer, till now he had one in each hand, and clinked the set onto the table. He had a big paunch, and leaning over from the edge of his seat took his breath. I quickly put my cup down too, the two chimes sounded the end of the visit.

He was at the door, slipping into his UPS jacket. "I worry," he told Reba. "His mother and I worry. Between this and the pot, I don't know what to do."

"What pot?"

I was glad Reba said it. If we were going to look like the parents in the voodoo trance, I was glad it wasn't me, because I was always doing things like that.

"They use pot, Mrs. Mooney. They smoke every day. It's one reason they cut school so much, they go off to that park in back of the projects and smoke."

"What are you talking about?"

"They smoke dope, Mr. Mooney."

"Hold on. That's against the law. Do you know I work for the Clerk of the Municipal Court?"

"Mr. Mooney," his expression turned more tired. He had those big eyelids top and bottom that made it look as if sleep never came, just piled up in folds around his lids. "Mr. Mooney, I've caught 'em in our garage. The stash, the roaches. I took a day off from work and trailed them to the park. That's why I'm worried."

A little gasp came out of Reba. I told him it's ridiculous. Pot costs money, Tommy gets this meager allowance.

"They rip off things. Basketballs from the school gym. Spare tires and radios from unlocked cars in the park."

We were standing in the front hall. When Reba saw my hand go to his chest she opened the door.

"Possession of marijuana is against the law, mister." I sounded like Sergeant Friday. "Maybe you got the wrong kid, maybe it's this Prince. We know our kid. He's no druggie. For godsake, he's thirteen."

I was leaning now on the hand, I admit that, talking in a normal tone of voice but assertive. The way the Clerk would talk when she was telling you off. I wasn't shouting, but I wasn't not shouting either. As it happens I was thinking of popping this guy in his fat cow face.

"You don't have to shout, Mr. Mooney. I'm only telling you what I know."

I explained how he was mistaking assertiveness for noise. I do remember that. Whatever happened next makes no difference. Dog's father was out the door, and Reba was upset at what I said and what the neighbors heard and, too or maybe mostly, the case against Tommy. She thought I owed Dog's father an apology, and perhaps I did, and she brought it up again, later, after our conversation with Tommy, because of course Dog's father had everything dead on and Tommy never once denied it, not a thing. But what the hell good are apologies? You tell me that. What good do words do, words that people say?

There followed the heart-to-hearts. Reba was concerned with the stealing more than the pot, she'd smoked dope in her youth and I did minor shoplifting as a kid, so we made a one-two punch of gee, I know how you feel. These talks were usually held around the family dinner table, Stace laconically sliding green beans around the plate until she could bolt, Tommy shrugging through our sympathies. I came off sounding like the narrator in one of those Army films, the evils that lie in wait in foreign ports.

Once or twice I brought the lecture to Tommy's room. It was usually protected by a sound from his stereo that science should harness to dissolve kidney stones. He liked this group, Pink Floyd, and he played it loud enough to pick up Grammy votes on Mars. On his door Tommy'd hung a diamond-shaped sign that said, Danger High Voltage Electricity, he lifted it from some local power station, a stunt I thought endearing when he did it at ten but which I now saw as toes on the slippery slope. I went up the stairs, knocked on that tinned door and got no response. I opened it gingerly, showing my respect for enemy territory. He was on the bed thumbing through a Pink Floyd fan magazine. I sat on the end of the bed, talked in soft tones to encourage him to turn down the volume. He nodded once or twice, even occasionally took his eyes from the page to shoot me a glare. On a good day, it was like confession when you were a kid. The priest talks, all you need do is bide time. Eventually you're sprung. On a bad day, we outshouted the music, we might have been auditioning.

I told him it was weird. Of all the classes, shop class. That was something I would enjoy, woodworking, and I would hope he'd enjoy it too. He had made that great doghouse, I reminded him, but it was the wrong thing to say. He looked at me through the thick film of his eyes, and I saw the picture of him holding Swami, like it'd been popped into a shoe store frame, Stanley's Shoes Cure the Blues.

That was our most civilized talk. The rest of them were more like a tennis match with us bashing words across the net, each as hard as you can hit. Here's a highlight tape:

—where I'm coming from

—on the wrong bus

—your drug of choice

—leads to another

—stepping on my space

—we have rights too

—where I'm coming from

"What did you say to make him so angry?" Reba asked when I came downstairs to pour myself a drink.

"He wasn't angry."

"What made him slam the door like that?"

"*He* didn't slam the door."

"Maybe I'll go talk to him."

I laid out my hand to point the way. She went upstairs to tell him she understood how he felt, and maybe she did. The first sip of bourbon was enough, it was into my veins, into the long muscles that held up my head, I felt them give. Stretched out on the sofa and relaxed, let them let go of that dead stone weight, they'd had a hard day. One word floated down the staircase. It was Tommy's voice, I heard nothing else of their conversation, and this one word floated down like a piece of ash. You know the way when you start a fire sometimes the newspaper flakes and a piece floats free of the flue and butterflies its way around the room? I heard him say just the one word.

History.

CHAPTER 12.

Look sharp feel sharp be sharp. The blade of the cat shaved the earth. In the light of a thumbnail moon, the rectangle now stretched most of the island's shaft, straight, forty feet across and swept clean of life. In the middle of one night I shut down the engine and looked through the trees. Not twenty yards away stood the profile of C. Aubrey Smith.

I went into the house, found one of the books Isaac had brought me, built a fire and sat in the one comfortable chair to read. The lines started to swim like fish in a tank. I had had nothing to eat and the rum was catching up to me. I tossed the book onto the fire. The glue of the spine caught first and the whole gadget went up in a flash. Book burning's gotten itself a bad name.

Outside, on the corner of the space, the bulldozer needed housing and feeding. Instead I walked on the beach. The Boston Whaler thunked against the wooden pier, anxious to get underway. I had forgotten about it, and its creaking nagged at me. I went down the dock thinking to board it, but one foot on the aluminum seat and the boat squirreled and shied away. It didn't want passengers. A first arc of light split the horizon, it hurt to look at, and an annoying wind lifted grains of sand and stuck them into my hair and ears. A snake the size of a broken shoelace moved to hide under a brown palm frond. Should I get back on my machine and drive a scoopful of sand, the snake included, into the sea? When was St. Patrick's Day? Patrick had driven out the snakes, but I'd guess they were missed. Who wants to live without his demons?

I went back to the house and lay down on the scruffed yellow sofa in the living room. This dream got hold of me, and even though I was aware of being in a dream it didn't help, I was still scared. There was frost on the inside of the window, a window somewhere here on the island, maybe the watchman's lost window. Tongues of frost, thick at the bottom and spiking up like stalagmites. And inside I could see Reba and the kids. It was like one of those telephone company ads, a happy Christmas scene, everyone gathered around a dining room table. Except me. I was looking in, and while I knew I could will myself out of the dream, I could do anything but join them. The rap of my knuckles on the glass made no sound. I'd lost my voice and had no wand. I stood pressed to the glass, and the heat of my body began to melt the frost. The sound came back, like someone had found the volume knob, and I started tapping on the window to get their attention, but it was too late. I tap-tap-tapped in this frigging dream and they looked up to see who was at the window, but it was too late, they melted away. They were trapped in the frost, and when it melted, so did they.

When I awoke the crab had run itself smack into a corner, scrambling to get out. He drummed against the wood like a blind man, his claws were scrabbling click-clack in a frenzy. I stomped over. He circled tighter into the baseboard and an inch up the walls as if to climb them. Fell over on his back, flipped upright and went at it again in a renewed fit. It infuriated me, the stupidity of that motion, so futile, and I picked him up, went to the front screen and tossed him discus-style high and out toward the dunes. Up 'til then I'd been afraid to touch him, I don't know whether they bite or how strong those pincers are, but I flung him into the gray.

The dream had ended, but not the anxiety. I poured a drink and sat down listening to my boom-box heart. In my pockets I found little bits of seaweed, brown crackling shreds, I must have picked them up on the walk. Also a tiny cowry shell wrapped in tissue paper. I sat at the bare pine table in the living room and arranged them. Why had I collected them? I put them in rows. They had a stale, gummy smell. The shell I put back in my pocket.

* *

It's funny about St. Patrick's Day, most Irishmen hate it. Not the day so much, but the priest-nun stories and the phonies. I looked forward to it, and I got ready for the dumb Paddy jokes that Canges always threw at me. The last one, before I split with Alice, the last one was a classic. Ten of us from the office went out to a place with green beer on tap, and they insisted on picking up my tab. Anyone named Mooney is king on St. Patrick's Day. Canges was trying to get my goat, but I'd watched the late talk shows the night before, so I was ready for him. "You don't see people named Canges getting a parade for themselves. Maybe a canned ham," and that got a laugh around. Some of them wanted to keep it going, the bars were full and everyone's drinking, so we had a couple of shots of Bushmill's, the drink of choice, and my gang was cozying up to two women from Motor Vehicle wearing green corsages.

By this time I'd had a few drinks myself. I slipped away from the pack and, I know I shouldn't have, I looked up Mrs. Segura. Unannounced. She lived in the projects. Her address was on the court summons and I had it in mind. At first she wouldn't let me in, but I told her my name again, and soon I was inside her little apartment, a pot of something spicy boiling on the stove and us standing there talking. Or I was. I didn't want to do anything, I just wanted to talk. This apartment was dingy, everything bought on the cheap and no welcome mats with masters of the hunt, but it was cozy. A red dinette set in the middle of the room. On the kitchen counter—I wandered in to see the kitchen and she didn't stop me—on the counter was this tin shrine, like a make-believe town, and a candle was burning in front. She'd just put the dishes away from dinner. Smells great, I said, thinking maybe she'd ask if I was hungry, but she didn't, she just looked away.

What about the refrigerator, I said, and she said maybe she can get the money back from Tino and bring her payments current. Who's Tino, I asked, and she told me her son took the money, he lives at the far end of the projects with his family and when he ran out of money he took hers, he knows where she hides it, inside the flour sack.

"You ought to change the hiding place."

"No," she said. "Is OK. He needed the money." She gave me this look as if I understood. I asked her if they'd set a date for her trial, and whether I could be of any help, and she said, no it's all right but she certainly appreciates my asking. Well, I said, it's my job in the Clerk's Office to make sure justice is done. Now, that's a load, but she watched me with those black eyes, her arms were folded across her terrific chest, you couldn't tell whether she was on to me or just scared, and she nodded and said that's an important job. It is, I said. Our system is based on justice, we're a country not of men but of laws. It's important that justice be done regardless of race, creed or national origin. I swear to God I said that, and I suppose I believe it, but there aren't many places you can make that speech. I felt terrific. She agreed and I left. That's all there was to it.

* *

I unwrapped the cowry and placed it carefully on the sand. Rain had gathered in long logs across the horizon, waiting to fall, and the sea and sky were flat, the color of body-shop primer. I could not remember the last time it had rained. Everything I passed on my walk had a name, claw of crab, derelict plank, yellow kelp, clump of tar. The stuff that grew had names I didn't know. What if I went around unnaming everything? Two-by-four, sawed unevenly at the end and discarded. I picked up the lumber, maybe a yard long, and carried it at my side. It was too clumsy for a walking stick. Gray-white gulls pecked away at the sand in front of me, high-stepping out of the incoming waves and running back to their crab holes as water pulled back. The birds kept a fixed distance, they gave me the same margin they gave the surf.

The sound was constant, water slapping water in a reshuffle. I lifted the two-by-four to shoulder height and carried it ready. One gull had stayed behind, worrying a crab hole, and had let the margin slip. God help me, I don't know why, but I let the board fly. Its squared edge caught the bird perfectly at the neck and smashed him into the sand. The wings gave a shudder that caught no air and then were still.

I retrieved what was left. A handful of flesh. There was nothing to it. Factory-installed beads stuck into the sides of the head went from black to pale as I watched, like a dead television screen. Two gray feathers came off the underwing and fluttered to the ground. The bones, you could tell from the runty mass, were fragile, little twigs. It was astonishing, how it lay in my hand with no more weight than a sandwich. Its feet were gnarled and precise, tooled to be tucked under in flight. As the feathers went out the wing they folded over each other and reduced in size, so the smallest ones outboard and rear were perfect miniatures. The beak had the hardness of shell. I carried it for ten or twenty steps, moved to put the thing back together again. Then I dropped it to the bubbling sand and sat in an edge of foam.

Somehow I had come loose from the planet. I'd been knocked off, like some cup you left on top of the car before you pulled out and forgot and pretty soon, splat, the coffee had spilled on the pavement and all you saw in the rearview mirror was the white cup sucked along in the draft of the car, except I was the cup. That's how it seemed, and that's why, I suppose, I sat there next to the dead bird, shaking slightly like an idling engine.

When I looked up I saw Hofstadter staring at me. I knew right off this was—what?—a hallucination? a daydream? He sat on what looked like a bale of cotton. His face was blurred and unfinished, but it was Hofstadter all right, he had a singular shape, thin and defiant, no one like him. White, tufty hair cropped boot-camp style, long fingers stained tobacco-brown. He lit the cigarette in his lips, spit out a loose flake of tobacco with that peculiar Thoo he always did. Inhaled so deep you could see the smoke reach his shoulders, make them sink with pleasure. Then he let the smoke out and looked me over carefully.

"How are you enjoying the house?"

"It suits me," I said. He nodded. Hofstadter was never much given to small talk.

"You've taken to dressing like me." I looked down. Our costumes were identical, high black boots, the khaki pants and shirt, except he wore a watch with a steel band. I shrugged. After all, who was he to complain? It's not as if the combination of clothes you choose to wear is trademarked. Besides, he was dead.

"Looks like rain," I said, and he squinted up at the sky. "Rain makes me anxious."

He nodded his head slowly. "Most things do."

"Feel like a quick game?" I asked. I'd found a chess set in the closet. It was missing some pieces but it would do.

He shook his head. "We don't concentrate well."

"Tell me about the afterlife. What's it like?"

"The afterlife?" He laughed. "Pretty much like this."

"No difference?"

He took another drag. "Not much. No tuberculars.

Nobody dies of TB anymore." I smiled.

"Don't give it any thought," he went on. "We all get the heaven we deserve. Isn't that enough? In mine, there are worms. Worms galore at the grave site."

He jumped down from the cotton bale, stepped on his cigarette and pushed it into the sand, disappeared.

* *

Hofstadter had taught me chess, although I couldn't keep up with him. He beat me easily, so we invented ways to even up the match. First we handicapped him by taking away pieces, but the result was that when I won, I'd beaten a cripple. Then we tried a game where I could line my pieces up at the start wherever I wanted. That's not chess, I'd complain, and he'd say, well, the object is to achieve conflict. Conflict, you must push up against something.

Once we'd decided to disregard the rules we were on our way to finding a balance. I hit on the idea of reverse chess. The object was to lose, the other side had to take an offered piece, and he who lost his king first lost the game. It appealed to me, clearing the board of clutter so the blanks popped up like urban renewal.

We named our invention Ssech, which was chess reversed. A race toward oblivion. Oddly, I was quite good at it and at last we'd found something where I could give him a run.

* *

I thought nothing of his visit. I was taken with my own circumstance, killing the bird was so foreign I soon believed someone else had done it. Back down the beach I couldn't see the corpse. Perhaps the tide had already taken it, perhaps it had flown away. The open ceiling weighed low, and I felt pushed down, not merely by my solitude. The beach was the floor of a small room, overheated, no windows for air. I stooped down and fetched a conch shell in front of me. It smelled of death. If you can hear the sea, what unknown world can you sniff? I unbuttoned my shirt and stuck it in, next to my flesh, walked on. Soon I had a dozen shells jostling against my skin. I parted the thin line of brush, stood on my long strip of earth, and emptied the shells. They fell, chipping against each other. The rains had started, and my hair, the shirt itself were dripping water. I collected five more shirt-loads in the rain. A use would reveal itself.

I went back, fixed a drink, and set about gathering once again, this time at the north end of my rectangle. The clouds banked in long, low layers. They would be here for a while. This morning's rain—was it morning? without the sun it was hard to tell—this rain was light, not unpleasant on my face. The new weather suited my mood. It was brooding, not light or dark, not youth or old age. The sky went on forever, it made no promises. I'd read a poem in high school about how the earth will end in fire or ice. My money's on an eternal light drizzle.

The shell collection lay in piles at each end of the space. Conch and snail-like things, but mostly clamshells. Concave side down, the clams would work best. Signage seemed to be their only function, signage and design.

I considered lining the space, but I didn't have near enough shells. Looking down the length of my clearing, I realized I'd built an airstrip. That was exactly its dimensions. I set to work, and by the time I was ready for a drink and some food, I had fashioned one pile into giant numbers, Seventeen, at the end of the strip. I've seen numbers on runways, they seem arbitrary, and the digits seven and one appeal to me. They are straightforward and guileless.

After a meal I napped. When I woke the light had disappeared and the rains increased. I went out again, to the near side of the strip. The water was beginning to pool across the earth, and crabs darted from puddle to puddle. Was the paroled prisoner among them? Did he bear me a grudge? The north pile produced a second number, seventy-one.

* *

What happened was, Tommy simply left. No note, no negotiation you change this I'll do that, no reason, no nothing. He and Dog. They hit the road. One night they were gone, Dog hijacked his father's car, and they left it in St. Louis, parked in front of a precinct house with the keys on the dash and a Texaco credit card in the glove compartment. A full tank of gas, fresh and dewy from the carwash. The receipt showed they got the works, liquid wax, underbody wash, and trunk vacuum, and gave twenty percent off your next wash.

Dog's father hired a private detective and we split the cost for a month. But the detective turned up nothing. Two sixteen-year-olds, gone. Gone, done, dont, dint, hint, hunt, hurt. No reason, at least none that I could figure. Sure, we'd had words, but no single incident. Maybe a week before he and I had a garden-variety fight, the usual this-is-our-house-and-you'll-do-as-we-say fight. I tossed his water pipe, the rock star posters, and the sign saying High Voltage into the garbage and he said he could have us arrested. It's an illegal taking of property in violation of the due process clause of the Constitution. But that was no more a blisterer than most of our conversations. It wasn't the Pink Floyd concert, because he didn't know about that. No one did. After he went, I was ashamed of what I did, and I told no one, not even Reba.

Pink Floyd was Tommy's favorite group. Tommy's sixteenth birthday was coming and it happens that, the week after, Pink Floyd was giving a concert in the Veterans' Auditorium. Our little city didn't often get big rock groups, and Tommy was racing around, crazy to go, and there were no tickets. I'd used every connection at City Hall, and I didn't have any. Connections.

A batch of floor seats went on sale at the door and Tommy wanted to camp out and we said no way, José. He was really pissed at this. The night before I set the alarm and got up at three and drove out to the Auditorium. It was a cold March morning, and I put my office clothes in a satchel to change, and dressed instead for the Arctic. Kids were strewn around in sleeping bags and in tents, it looked like the end of the world was coming. I brought a thermos of coffee and some blankets and a folding chair, and I sat there and watch a grubby sun come up and light this bedraggled band of kids who were smoking, banging their hands together, using the Sanolets while their friends saved their place in line.

I got the tickets OK, five in a primo location. I was planning on springing it as a surprise, but especially on Tommy since he and I had been having a tough time of it. Reba planned on a special meal, and we told Tommy to invite Dog for dinner and I figured I'd announce over dinner that all of us, the whole family and Dog, would all go. I made sure I was home in plenty of time, and Reba wrapped her father's watch for him, sixteen is, she said, a special birthday.

They didn't show. We ate the steaks and the strawberry shortcake, Reba, Stace and I, and Reba was philosophical, she said you know boys, at this age families aren't their priority, and she wrapped a big slice of cake for each of them in Saran. It was all I could do to chew down the steak. We got ready for bed and still he wasn't home. Afterward, I put the tickets in my sock drawer and waited for the right time to give them to him.

And I never did. The concert came and went. I don't mean I forgot, I just never gave him the tickets and eventually I snuck them into the garbage.

But that's not what drove him out of the house, because he didn't know about it. Whatever drove him out we never learned, because he just disappeared and we never heard from him. Not never, once, but as good as never. A couple months after he took off, we got a postcard from Indianapolis. He wrote on it. "That P.I. was pathetic—leave off trying to find me, I'm doing fine and it just costs me bus tickets. Tom." On the other side was a picture of the Marion County (Ind.) courthouse.

We posted messages on the lost children networks. Police stations help you do that, as there are a lot of parents out there looking for their kids, looking to say, I don't know what. If they had some magic words, you'd have thought they would have spoken them before. We posted messages in case Tommy wanted to make contact or needed money, but we never heard. Reba had this intuition that he was in touch with Stace, and while her intuitions are usually on the mark, you can't expect Stace to rat on her brother. We asked, but we didn't push it.

Someone told us that the worst thing that can happen to a parent is burying a child, and I can't prove it but I think that whoever told us was wrong. I think not burying a child is worse.

CHAPTER 13.

Who told it to us was the counselor, a sixtyish woman with a bulb of Brillo-gray hair and loads of sensitivity, who when she wanted to know about sex—they are given to asking that kind of thing—said marital relations. Are you both comfortable with your marital relations? I thought to give her a hard time and talk about my in-laws, but she was deadly earnest, and besides, I was rooting for her.

Not Reba. Reba had made up her mind. "I have great sympathy for you," Reba told her, and she said thank you, Mrs. Mooney. Reba was helping the counselor counsel and slipping her that I-know-what-you're-going-through look, we are soldiers together in the unending war against male stupidity, but Reba was not rooting for her. Reba had decided to split.

The counselor told us the worst thing that can happen to a parent is to bury a child, most marriages don't survive it, and in a sense, she said, we've had to bury Tommy. Metaphorically. Reba gave her the sorority nod, Amen sister, Great White Squaw speakum truth, and said that's not all of it. If Leonard and I could have gone through this together, I would have been prepared to work on the marriage, but you have to understand. Leonard is a Nineteen Fifties man. And the counselor nodded back, Amen, like the secret handshake. I was beginning to feel like I was at testimonial dinner and I'd made a tactical error by dressing as a shrimp cocktail.

It was maybe two years after Tommy disappeared, less, and in a manner of speaking we *had* gone through it together. I hadn't skipped out anywhere, I was right there, going through it day and night. But I had to tell the counselor, like I'd told Reba, mostly I go through it alone. Mostly when I dream about Swami struck down on the highway and the Revolt of the Underclasses and Pink Floyd, I dream my dreams alone. So for my money a lot of this bobbing heads and clucking tongues, everyone pitch in and help each other do what's expected, was just talk.

I told her that, and she and Reba exchanged yet another significant look, they understood each other perfectly they oozed with understanding, and if there was a stamp in the counseling game that says Process This File, Transfer to Monroe County, the counselor was pressing it back and forth on the ink pad in her brain.

Three sessions were required by law, your docket fee covered the cost, and any more were extra. The counselor was bulking up on compassion, just getting warm. We lasted through the three and I was ready to ante up for another set, when Reba said, no, what's done is done.

Tom disappeared, boarded that train of drugs, freedom and hostility that toured the country at the time, maybe it's still in business and I'm just out of children, stopping in the smallest town and luring away the youth. I wish I knew why. One postcard, then never wrote again. Despite what she said, I think Reba blamed me for it. It's only human to blame someone, so at first I blamed God, then Reba, then I gave up and accepted her point of view. She knows about things like this. It was the final stress between us. They say when the parents divorce the kids have trouble. Here, when the kids had trouble the parents divorced.

Reba joined a support group of women whose kids had skipped. She came back from those meetings, Wednesday nights at the Presbyterian church, her eyes glistening with insight. She wanted to stay up past midnight and talk about awareness and realization, and I don't mean to be harsh, but I was wondering about Indianapolis, worried whether we'd chased him from St. Louis and if he'd continue in a straight line and whether I should get my tail to Indy to see what I could see.

Hofstadter told me by all means, go. He was no expert, he seemed to have children himself, long since estranged, and if he knew how it happened or how to fix it he didn't say. "Go," he told me. "Get on an airplane."

"I hate airplanes. I'm terrified of airplanes, some day the earth will rise up and smite me like some Biblical story or it will fall away forever." After all, gravity is only a law and laws are made to be broken, that's what Municipal Court is about.

Hofstadter had come down to the courthouse to watch a trial, sometimes there would be a good one and I'd recommend it, and we were having lunch in the cafeteria in the subbasement. The special on Tuesdays was meat loaf and creamed corn, we were eating the identical meal except I had tea and he had coffee. We sat there holding tight to our trays and contemplated the airplane sensation. We both looked to the window expecting to see the world, but two floors below ground, we got an air shaft. I could visualize an airplane gone awry, a farm and a road spinning and tilting like they were caught in a tornado.

"What if," I asked, "you were some reluctant angel, some dropout who couldn't quite get the hang of gliding and landing? There must be one or two like that."

"Desk jobs," Hofstadter said. "They end up earth-bound or cloud-bound but not in the air."

Hofstadter took a tile of meat loaf on his fork, slathered it with gravy, and pointed it at me.

"I have a great idea for an airline," he says. "You know how they're always giving coupons to get you to come back or fly more. They have the dignity of toothpaste companies, they must be so hard up. The airline I propose has a different gimmick. In order to get a discount on my airline, all you have to do is cry. Can't you see it? The stew comes on the PA and says, OK, you have to buckle up and watch the film about oxygen masks, but first, I want you to think about something sad. Think about the life you've wasted, about your son with the cleft palate, your mother who died alone. Pretty soon, everyone is bawling. She passes around these tissues, with the headsets, and pretty soon you're at 30,000 feet en route Dulles."

* *

Off to Indianapolis, the last sighting. I logged in for indefinite vacation time, I had only two weeks coming, any longer it would be a leave of absence. Swallowed my terror and boarded an airplane. Before I went, the private investigator gave me some tips: find out where the kids hang, he told me, ask cops, priests, other kids. Especially, he said, especially other kids dealing dope.

I checked into a Holiday Inn south of town and rented an economy car. Depressing, your knees hit the wheel and every car on the road pushed you around. I wouldn't be able to find a kid dealing if he wore a badge and a change-belt, so I tried a priest and I asked the kid who served my breakfast, two over easy toast and coffee two-ninety-nine. The kid slinked away as if I was a leper, and the priest was beyond hope, he told me where the CYO met.

The cops helped. For seven days I cruised the malls, the video parlors, three safe houses. Not a nibble. It was tough duty, asking about your own son as if you'd misplaced him, you put him down somewhere with your sunglasses and you couldn't remember where. I carried the Stanley's Shoes photo, and some of the kids told me nice dog, they really took to Swami. But nobody'd seen Tommy. They hit me up for spare change, they'd made me for a mark, chatting me up about the dog or how tough it must be to lose your kid, and I knew it was bought sympathy but I didn't care. Every morning at the front desk I broke a twenty into singles and during the day I gave them out.

At night I came home and ate at the H.I. bar atop the hotel. It had been built to rotate and provide a panoramic view of southeast Indianapolis, but it was broken. Before TV and bed I took the elevator down to the lower level and swam in the indoor pool. It was more of a tub, the length of three overhead strokes and I'm no swimmer, cast out of a plastic that made you shudder to touch, it felt like the skin of a corpse. I had a few drinks and the Businessman's Special and sloshed around in the eerie light of the pool. Several of the kids told me give up the search, he doesn't want to be found, and others told me Chicago. Indy has no action, if he was here he was passing through, that's all anyone does in Indy, and now he must be in Chicago.

A week of Businessman's Specials and I went home. Nothing came of it. Mostly I remember walking up and down in that pool, a green that dentists used to have on their machinery before they had decorators, pacing up and down in this yellow-bulbed basement pool like a cage. I didn't go to Chicago.

Instead I went home and did a workbook.

Someone in Reba's group self-published them. The relationships workbook. What we do well together, what my partner does well for me. What I do well for my partner. Even as I filled in the blanks, I knew I was not heading for a high mark in the course.

One day we walked in to show the counselor our stuff, it was the only time I got more stuff than Reeb. She was aces at the workbook, except for this one time. The question was, What does your spouse bring you? I'd written crappy answers, what you'd expect, joy, love, happiness, that sort of thing, and Brillo Lady looked at me as if I'd brought in a dog turd. But Reba had printed one sentence on the page. Reba's writing was like her, precise, straight up and down, no nonsense. She'd written, "I can't think of an answer." She couldn't think of an answer, and Brillo Lady looked at me as if I was behind the curve.

The exercises were not a complete loss. One thing they did was focus me on Stace, since one asked you to list the things you did with your children, and that was where I came up with the idea for a dollhouse.

This was not what Reba had in mind. The purpose of the workbook was to reexamine, she told me, her and my relationship. Tommy's disappearance was symptomatic of other troubles, her relationship to me was subordinate and inferior, and we needed to establish greater parity. This is not my fault, she explained, but both of ours, we are prisoners of our environment and we've allowed stereotypes to push us around. But she no longer intended to let it happen, she intended to liberate both of us.

That's why I focused on this dollhouse. I needed something to do. Whatever Reba was saying I didn't have answers for, and it hit me that this was something Stace would love, a dollhouse built to scale for Elizabeth.

I drew the plans first, measuring the wall in Stace's room while she was at the movies with her friends, sketching it out, sneaking the plywood and paint in through the cellar door. I posted the sketch on my wall down under the stairs and computed the dimensions. Elizabeth measured out at eight inches, which made a scale of one to seven and gave each room an eighteen-inch ceiling. I decided on a two-story house with a basement, a washer and dryer in the basement, a sun room of glass, though I substituted sheet plastic from a modeling store, and each story about twenty inches deep otherwise you can't reach the back wall. A power jig would have been terrific, but I had good hand tools and with a coping saw, a modeling knife for the balsa wood, and a little gimlet, I was able to get the thing pretty well assembled. I designed the house to be modular, so I could get it upstairs, otherwise I would have built the famous boat in the cellar that you can't sail out. The simple joints were tacked in place by three-quarter-inch brads, set screws to hold the floor brackets and furring strips across the back as a horizontal brace. Then, at the corners, I rigged this series of dowels, so that each floor nested on top of the other. I put carpet in the living and dining room, wall-to-wall, and linoleum in the kitchen. Then, the coup de grace, I hinged a facade onto the living room, so you could open and close the entire room, and within the facade built a little colonial door. I even went to the Radio Shack and got a doorbell. The only trouble was it was out of scale, no one made a one-to-seven electric doorbell.

All the while Reba and Stace knew I was working on something but I'd covered it in blue plastic and they weren't particularly interested. Reba found out when we progressed to Chapter Six, What I'd Like to Do With the Family, and the way it worked was, you completed a chapter on your own, then you and your spouse compared workbooks. I wasn't very good at it, first of all each chapter was a few questions then a lot of space you were supposed to fill up with words. They said feelings, but you knew they wanted words.

So this time I filled up the space with a sketch. I drew in the dollhouse, complete with hinged front panel and washer-dryer. At first Reba was amused, she was charmed.

"What's this?" she said smiling.

I told her. I explained it was almost ready for launching, but I still wanted to get wallpaper and do some painting, then maybe Stace would do the furnishings. You'd have thought I explained how I wanted Stace to donate her body to science. Reba's face fell a mile, and though she wouldn't tell me why, I could see she was disappointed. Not quite disappointed but not charmed anymore either.

Later, during counseling, Reba told this story. How she saw this drawing and heard my plans and how sad it made her. Our daughter, she told the counselor, was *twelve*, and I was building her a dollhouse. It embarrassed me, the way she said it.

One Saturday when Stace was at a basketball game, I decided I was done. I brought the dollhouse floor by floor upstairs and did my assembly. The dowels, the cross-braces. It fit together like a Mercedes. I'd spent a lot of time on the measurements. I looked around and got Elizabeth from the back of the shelf in Stace's closet and stood her against the wall in the living room. Closed the door and the facade, so you couldn't see inside.

I could hardly wait for her to get home. Reba brought her back, Reba'd gone to the game too, and I told them to get ready for a great unveiling. We went up to the room and Stace gave it a look.

"*What* is *that*?" She almost screamed it, and I realized how imposing the whole apparatus was, in that little bedroom it looked twice as large as it did in our basement. I explained it. Then I got us all to lie down on the floor, that's the best way to present it, I'd already tried this out, lie down on the floor and push the doorbell. Ding dong, it had a two-note chime. That got a laugh. Reba too. They didn't expect that. OK, now open the door, and they peered in. And then open the facade and there was Elizabeth, leaning against the upstairs banister, the way Loretta Young used to open that old TV show. No matter what the counselor thought, it was a terrific presentation.

Stace didn't know what to say. I was sure she was just overwhelmed, it was massive against that wall and now that I saw the three stories pieced together I didn't think the foundation was such a good idea, it just made the whole assembly larger. Maybe it overwhelmed her. Reba kissed my cheek and held my hand all the while I was explaining to Stace about its features: how the spindles for the bannister were turned, and carpeting the stairs, and where I tried to electrify it for lights but to hide the wires you needed tools I didn't have. Stace was biting her lower lip. Overall I considered it an unqualified success.

Not Reba. She told the counselor that Stace hadn't played dolls in years, and maybe that's true but you know how that is, kids come in and out of hobbies and maybe Stace's simply needed a boost. The counselor asked me about putting those drawings into the workbook and do I think in retrospect I used the sketches instead of my feelings. She hedged her questions that way, gave you an out, in retrospect do you think this or that, as if retrospect were a town somewhere you could go back to and try again. I told her about my movie theory, how you could protect yourself. All that stuff in us, that inevitably puts us down because someone dies or moves away or runs off to Italy, all that stuff only worked when it bounces off. I told her about light—a beam is invisible until it strikes an object. So, you take away the reflective surfaces, presto, no more sorrow.

She said that it was interesting I used drawings instead of words, did I have difficulty finding words for feelings, and I said no. I didn't tell her what I thought, I didn't see that it would do any good, you'd have to see the trustworthy look on her face to know that she had the answer and she desperately wanted me to guess it on my own. But what I think is, words are like gravestones, the feelings are long dead in your heart and that's when you put the words on top of them.

The counselor turned out to be not much help. Like the private investigator. They were looking for the Lost Atlantis. She said all I needed was to be myself. I knew she meant well, but what a dumb thing to say. My son had disappeared, a counselor whose entire clientele is divorcing—you can tell how much fun she is having—meets me twice and says I'm clinically depressed, and I'm in counseling because my wife has joined a group that has convinced her that I belong in a museum. The last of the century's American man, endangered but resilient. More and more at work I feel stepped on. I am the astronaut without a space ship, it is hard to tell if I am falling or the stars are simply moving away. I am unable to cope with reality, except that reality is all I have, adrift and alone. Some masters in social work tells me to be myself, and whenever I consider her suggestion seriously, which I do—I am game for anything at this point—an inner voice tells me that her advice is wrong, it is tempting fate.

The counseling did nothing but burn up our scrip.

We were through the three sessions, a month or two passed and Reba said not much, went religiously to her Wednesday night *bundt* meetings. It was the times. She was reading the feminist writers and I thought at first she'd be pleased to find kindred souls, but it made her angrier. One night over a pork loin roast, Stace and I looking forward to grilled zuccini, Reeb announced she has decided to move across town, close to the university. Reba waited until I'd carved the meat, and I'd complimented her on it, the roast was done just right and the skin was crisp when you sliced it. She wanted to get a degree in counseling. She thought at fifteen Stace was old enough to decide for herself where she should live.

It was inconceivable to me. We are a family. It was inconceivable that she would sacrifice convention for personal happiness. There's a lot on the table, I said, as always eloquent on these issues. This catches us unawares. But it certainly didn't catch Reba, and from the spiral Stace's fork made in her apple sauce, a swirling spiral, each curve tighter like in the movies to show someone getting dizzy, I realized she was in on it. I told Stace to take her time, to think about where she wanted to be. She didn't say a thing. I told her I love her and her mother does too (I'd never said it that way before, her mother) and whatever she decides is great with me, which was bunk because I really wanted her to stay, sitting there I was already too lonesome to bear and Reba hadn't begun to pack. I was clocking the odds and I figured to be the favorite. After all, Stace wanted to stay with her friends, to be with them in high school, and she'd have to switch schools if she switched to the other side of town. More than the favorite, I was a dead cinch.

You decide, I told her. You decide, Dorothy. I figured Reba may be going but the family address was staying, Stace's books and records, a built-in doll house complete to three stories and a working doorbell. She won't find that cross town. Still, I should have said something.

About two days later I was walking down for breakfast and on the stairs I heard them laughing in the kitchen. And I just knew. I knew Stace had decided to go live with her mother. I'd always thought of Stace in pigtails, although she never wore them. She always wore her hair short like her mom. In pigtails, wanting to come back to Kansas to Aunt Em and Ray Bolger. You could have knocked me over.

CHAPTER 14.

Early morning the rains dried up. Single drops plipping from leaf and shingle made a soft static in the quiet. The air changed too, it began to swell and stir with the smell of pooling water. The weather wasn't through. The sky was still loaded, a single wooly cloud tented my house and sent spidery virga down. If neatness counted, like it does in contests, God would have trimmed the shaggy ends. You'd be surprised how often He's not on the job.

I brewed a pot of coffee and drank it cup by cup at the kitchen table. Hofstadter's jug of Sugar Substitute sat centered on the white porcelain top, and this day I picked it up, spilled the pills onto the table, and sorted them. The whites held a commanding lead. I had not had a day's sleep in too long. First I would take a walk, then knock down a couple of whites. It would even up the sides a little, and I could test if they were for snoozing.

I went out to inspect my patch of space. The numbers on the near end glistened like a newly painted car, metallic on top and color below. The force of rain had washed the shells bone clean, and their edges had sunk into the earth. The soil was so sandy that the puddles were already leaching in, the strip would dry in a few hours. Yellow-green shoots appeared here and there. Maybe I'd take the blade to it again and plow them under. Fuel was low, but I had no plans for a drive.

It was not unpleasant out there, picking up the occasional branch and watching shoelace snakes and thumbnail frogs scurry out of my path. My garden. It was as if I had simply died. I had died and my tasks in the world went happily on, someone else opened the files, assigned the cases of missed installments and tenant deposits. The dentist cleaned some other teeth twice a year, but me, I was gone, my garbage wasn't there for landfill. Mrs. Segura would have to worry about her refrigerator without me.

While I walked I began singing the *Agnus Dei* part of the mass. It's my favorite part, and I sang it to the tune of "Into the Forest." *Agnus Dei, qui tollis peccata mundi, miserere nobis*. You had to repeat the last notes of "Into the Forest" to make the *miserere* part fit, and even then there was a *bis* left over.

I met Reba at a party, one of those no-host tumbles where people gather in the kitchen and talk on and on about their lives. She wore a white blouse open at the neck and a black velvet skirt, and I fell in love with her right then. Her collarbone sticks out—for some reason that's what I brought up, that's what we discussed. Her skin had the softness of life, the resilience. Where has that gone? I bent down to pull a root and saw my rough and deadened hands. I could feel flesh hanging on my bones, it was bruised and in the way. I touched my hair, to my nicked fingers it was brittle and without sheen. What had happened? When had the green stalk that grew in me disappeared? We were supposed to prop each other up, poles to a tepee. But, to tell the truth, I didn't like the leaning. It gave me vertigo.

For the move Reba packed up her stuff in cartons from the liquor store. Afterward the dividers lay around the basement until Alice's brief occupation. Alice lined them up with the trash cans, three dozen accordion dividers, twelve bottles to the case. If there was a message in Reba's selection of the source for the boxes, she never said a thing. They were not my brands. Her friends from the support group helped her move. By the time I came home from work they were all gone, her clothes, Stace, the friends, the boxes. All that was left were Reba and the accordion dividers. She stayed behind to say goodbye. She kissed my cheek, then shook my hand and instructed me to take care of myself. Like a doctor might, seriously meaning it, though she neglected to put in the details.

"Leonard, I'm really sorry about this," she said. "I'm sorry about the children, and I'm sorry I'm not a better lover to you and that you can't have just one drink and that you can't help worrying about the world. But mostly, I'm sorry for myself and at least that will stop."

I felt odd, standing on our driveway shaking hands with my wife. Ex, I guess.

Hofstadter was his usual quirky self on the subject. He recommended two books to me, made me write down the titles.

"There's one rule," he said. "I want you to read one

during the day and one after dinner."

I thought they would be about divorce or marriage or something on the subject. But they weren't. They were just stories. After I'd finished—it takes me forever to read a book—we discussed them. He asked me to tell him the story. I could tell him pretty well about the first, but nothing about the other. Nothing, not even the names of the people.

I stopped drinking. It seemed to matter so to Reeb, so I stopped. You're a great one, Hofstadter said. Nobody can say you don't learn, but nobody can say it does any good. You'll be helping old ladies cross the street in hell.

I took up membership in a gym. First I got bored with calisthenics, then with sobriety. They are overrated. Somebody at work, this lady from Licensing, took me under her wing. She is newly divorced, she told me, although I found out it was five years earlier, and she wanted me to join *her* group, it would really help. They were learning how to deal with loss. That's the last thing I needed. I didn't need to learn. I'd become good at it on my own. Besides, I had no one left to lose.

We grocery shopped together. She was sure, left to myself, I'd develop scurvy. I took instruction on basic food groups and the significance of carbohydrates and something else, nothing I retained. She cooked me dinner once or twice and we went to the movies and she was full of advice. Look on the bright side, she kept reminding me. There must be things you like about being single. That's a place to start. Write them down, the five things in your life that are better.

I made a list of the blessings. Reba has to worry about Stace's adolescence, I don't. Of course, Stace has never been a major problem. Two, no one will tell me now that it was my second or third drink, as if somehow that news, which it is not, news, would sap my desire instead of my pleasure. There again, having gone dry at the time, that was a small gain. I'll no longer face the interminable requests about the light sockets or the fence latch, although I enjoy fixing things and I'm good at it. Reba would ask you questions in the movies, as if maybe you had directed it and knew whether that was the girl's brother from the first scene, so I put that down as number four. And the interminable menstrual cycles, and the paraphernalia, and the silent scoldings that I took to be within the pull of the moon. It is hard, living with a woman, the constant hectoring of life's lessons.

I made up this list and the lady from Licensing went over it and said, How about sex? I must have looked startled, and she laughed and explained, no, I meant on the list. That embarrassed me too, I wasn't interested in sex with her, for one thing she had a strong resemblance to Edward G. Robinson and I had been fighting off the suspicion she was packing heat, like Rocco in *Key Largo*. I was relieved to find out she didn't mean with her, but I wasn't about to tell her about me and Reba. Fact is, in bed I missed Reba like an amputated limb, but there was one offsetting benefit. Reba liked to snuggle close. She was affectionate, snugging in like a puppy in a brood. Alice was a relief that way. She went at it like putting away the groceries and afterward she'd announce, okay, now let's sleep.

So the lady from Licensing was, I suppose, my exit person. Except I took a long time to exit. It was a long fall, when you fall out of the sky there's nothing to fear because there's only sky below. Of course, you don't know it at the time, you think the earth is coming up to smack you. Eventually, you forget your fear of heights and forget that you're falling. After Reeb left it was years before I met Alice, and all that time I was simply passing through the air. I didn't bump into a single soul.

* *

The rectangle was restored, cleaned and squared away. I dragged a couple of the larger branches back to the house to cut and stow as firewood. *Agnus Dei*. Lamb of God, who forgives the sins of the world, have mercy upon us. If I trimmed it to *me*, what's the Latin for me? Have mercy on just me, it fit the tune better. *Miserere me*. Besides, what do I care about those other people? The less mercy for them the more for me. Perhaps I would have Isaac bring me a fresh leg of lamb to roast, some new potatoes, mint jelly, perhaps I'll put that on my list.

I popped a couple of the football-shaped pills, poured myself a glass of rum, and sat out back shooting the breeze with C. Aubrey. I wanted sleep. We changed LAMB to NULL in nine steps. It was a good way to relax, at least until the sand gnats found me. They drove me inside. I went upstairs and flopped naked onto the bed. I dreamed, but I could remember only the flies. The flies circled closer and their buzzing was louder and louder. I slept soundly and for most of the day, but when I awoke that circling was all I remembered and I was in a sweat. The flies were so real, their noise in my ear, around and again. I sat upright on the mattress and saw the wet imprint of my body. Like a corpse chalked on the sidewalk. Still there was buzzing, louder than flies, it seemed right over my head and it reached from the dream over into the wakening. Louder, the way you hear more when your ears pop. Woozy from the rum and unsteady between sleep and waking, I pulled on a pair of trousers and ran barefoot outside. If the buzzing was real, it was coming now from the back of the house.

I went through the screen door and looked up. A tiny airplane with a single engine was angling down toward my clearing. Its nose was high and in the windshield glare, plastic reflecting a plastic light, you couldn't say whether there was anyone inside. The airplane descended evenly and disappeared behind the growth. Someone had landed.

CHAPTER 15.

Is it malaria that, once you've been bitten, comes back at you for the rest of your life? Disappears for months or years and then suddenly you find sweat slipping down your brow, you're shaking with chills, and your heart, that you'd long forgotten, left in the garage to beat its regular beats, is stumbling down a long flight of stairs?

I rushed to an opening in the trees edging the runway. The airplane rolled to the far end of the strip, turned menacingly toward me, and taxied back the full length. The engine ran up for a half minute. I thought most likely they've made a mistake, most likely they are going to take off again, but the engine scuffed and died. The door on the far side opened and a man got out. He was about six feet, dark oily hair, fit and mean—you could tell from his brow and the twitch of his shoulders. He scowled at the sky. His jeans were blanched white and bulged at the knees, he wore a T-shirt with the name of some product I didn't know, and on his feet Mexican huaraches. I made out the retreads on the bottom as he spun in his seat and let himself down to the mucky earth.

I stepped back a few paces. Squinted through the line of brush that bordered the space. From the near side the other door opened and a kid hopped down, younger than the first. Somehow not a threat, slight for one thing, and finer. Short blond hair streaked and lightened by the sun, something frail in the frame. Wore a denim shirt cut off at the shoulders and under the flopping tail tan shorts. Sandals of blue braided rope.

I stood wondering whether to make a run for the toolshed, and while I wondered the two of them did a curious thing. They walked to the edge of the runway, pulled out some of the debris I had piled there, vines and branches, and used it to decorate the airplane. Draped leaves over the fuselage and wings. Then they stood back to inspect their work, the taller one in charge and deciding where more was needed, the blond one doing most of the work. Only when they were satisfied did they turn, together, and walk directly at me.

I was sure I hadn't been seen, they ignored my presence. Still, it was too late to retreat, and I had no defenses. You knew from the way the tall one moved he wasn't about to be run off with a pitchfork. They both walked easily, as if the island was theirs. Especially the tall one, a swagger, and when he was fifty paces away called to me.

"You build that runway?"

I didn't answer. I stood frozen in the trees, the plate of my chest heaving up and down. Then, walking dead at me, he asked again.

"That's some dumb ass job, matey. Don't you know

the numbers are supposed to correlate to magnetic course? Compass headings? There's no compass heading seven one zero."

I started to yell back, I was going to yell so what, but the eerie sound of my voice shut me up. I hadn't heard it in months. Thin and high, it belonged to someone else.

He shook his head and parted the fronds of two low palms so he and his pal could pass through. He was close enough now he didn't have to shout. "Some fucking runway." His hands flopped at his side, like he might draw on the sheriff anytime now, and the way his arms hung, loose and ready, you could tell he wasn't worried about me.

Finally they glanced up, now close enough to see me face to face.

"Jesus," said the skinny one. "Look at you." And only then did I realize it was a woman. Really a girl, a long-limbed girl with hardly any figure, hips like a boy, legs and arms deeply tanned. Her hair, white up close, white gold against the freckled gold of her forehead, had been mowed recently by a clipper, it was cut short even for a young boy. When she got near you wondered how you could have missed her, she was leggy and unmistakably female. Two brass studs in the lobe of the left ear. Through the bulb of a perfect nostril, she showed the tiny arc of a silver ring.

"Wow," said the man. "Look at you." For a good ten seconds that's what the two of them did. I hadn't seen another person since Isaac had left me on this island, so I watched too. People are oddities, all you need is a few months outside their company if you need proof. His eyes were set deep into shadows so you couldn't see what he was thinking, and there were fleshy erosion lines running from the wings of his nose down to the mouth's corners. Angry lines. They made it hard to guess at his age. He wore a heavy gold necklace, one of those Greek-looking designs, and a doubled bracelet to match. Each piece must have weighed a half-pound. He reached into the back pocket of his jeans and pulled out a cold chisel. Watched me watch it and began cleaning his nails.

"Look, pal. We're sorry to intrude on your little hermit's den here, but the visibility's lousy. We need to put down awhile. We'll be off soon as the cover lifts."

I cleared my throat and tried speaking. Wished I'd had Hofstadter's wand.

"It's the start of the rainy season."

"What are you, the weatherman? What's that supposed to mean?" Up close you could see into the eye sockets. Muddy, flitting eyes, winged mites that didn't alight long enough for anyone to take a swat.

"Just that it might not lift."

He bit at a hangnail, spat out the tag, curled his fingers to inspect the work. The chisel edge gleamed where a grinding wheel had rubbed the blade. He looked past me, past C. Aubrey, toward the house. I was scared. When he shifted his glance, he bobbed his head, like a boxer feinting. Even when he looked beyond you, like he was checking for reinforcements did you have any pals? He was watching you.

"So. Just that it might not lift. Well matey. We just might not be off then." He thumb-tacked his look on me.

"You're going to spend the night?"

"You guessed it, old man. We're going to spend the night."

I had to give up something, so I gave up words. "My name is Leonard."

He nodded his head, like I had guessed and guessed right.

"C'mon," he said over his shoulder, and walked by me toward the house. The girl came up behind him.

"Don't mind him," she said. "He has no manners."

I'd been watching him like a snake, so this was my first notice of her. Stuck on that perfect body was an unresolved face. It wasn't quite finished, but it looked to be just fine because of the soft eyes. She stuck out her hand.

"My name's Arden, and that's Michael." She had a pleasant and reassuring accent, it had a tang, later I found out she was Australian. The eyes, sea green and cheerful, looked right up at you. "Michael's been flying around in the shit, low ceilings and zero visibility. It tends to make him unsociable."

I shook her hand. It was warm, you could feel the blood in it, and softer than anything I could remember.

"We'll be no trouble. We're light eaters, and we have our own grub. Some wine too." I'm sure she kept talking because of my stare. I'd stopped looking at her. The face I saw reflected in her eyes was foreign and thin, I couldn't make out what was wrong.

"Not to worry, Leonard. This slop will lift. We don't need much clearance, we like it low to the deck. We'll cook our own dinner and shag out anywhere, a couch, the floor. Disappear in the morning. Don't worry, Leonard." She said it a second time because she could see of course that I did.

Michael stopped at the back stairs and called.

"There's just you here?"

"Just me."

"Telephone? CB?" I shook my head.

He shrugged as if I'd proved his point about my lunacy, then went in. Michael carried a zippered duffle with him, and when I got to the house he was in the first floor bedroom, right under mine, tossing clothes onto the small bed. I ignored him. I went into the bathroom and searched around. A few daggers of the broken mirror were still there, behind the bowl.

I found the largest piece. Carefully I propped it against a faucet. Bent to find myself. And started exactly as Arden had, when she'd come through the foliage and found me. In the wobbling triangle of glass, a red-eyed skull peered suspiciously, reluctantly out. He squinted, stretched his eyes, opened his mouth in a soundless howl, snarled to show yellow teeth in the maw of a boiled face. A scraggy white beard, lips blistered and split, the hair thin and haphazard. Whoever it was had clearly lost track of time, maybe some other measurements as well. No doubting why they took me as mad.

I walked back into the living room to see Michael heading out the front door. He carried a square of wood wrapped with fishing line in one hand, and a stone the size of an apple in the other. At the line's end hung three bare hooks.

"Your fridge represents severe trouble," he said walking away. He treated you that way, talked while he walked away from you.

"Unhealthy. Cholesterol, toxins, devoid of riboflavin and niacin. You need to watch what you eat, matey, or your dick'll fall off."

I looked about for the girl. She was not in the house. I went out back and walked toward the airplane. Snow white with red stripes across the rudder and wings, and small, tip to rudder no longer than a car. A single engine, and a two-bladed propeller that might be made of wood. The plane sat on two fat tires under either wing and on a third wheel under the tail, so that on even ground, its nose pointed into the air, like that of an obedient dog. From its near door, one long leg stuck out as a counterweight. Inside Arden was rummaging around. She hopped down.

"Veggies," she said to me and hoisted two net bags over her head. "We never travel without." She handed them to me. "You get started. Scrape the carrots gently, and wash the potatoes but don't peel. All the goodies are in the peel. We'll fry the onions separately with the fish, if he gets a fish, and I'll be back with some wine."

Her words went so quickly I had no time to reply. I stood watching. They both spoke so fast and competent, it left me breathless. She came back out of the plane with two bottles crooked in her arm, took me by the elbow and turned me toward the house.

"You carry all this food with you?"

"We often bivouac. Just like the Girl Guides. B stands for bivouac and be ready. What else? Barbituates. We'll land on a beach, camp and cook right there." She spoke proudly. "Even then, Michael emphasizes presentation."

We reached the cleared space behind the house where you could see down the shore. Michael had stripped to his underwear and he was kneeling at the water's edge. He had tied the rock in a nested knot three feet up from the end of the line. Now he rummaged about, opened shells and cut the innards out to bait the hook. He stepped into the surf, waded out beyond the low breakers, and began to twirl the rock around his head lasso-style. Three turns, a fourth, each on a longer radius, and let the whole tackle fly. I followed her indoors.

"Land on a beach?"

We stood side by side at the sink. I was scraping carrots, as I'd been told.

"There are miles and miles of them. No houses, just long stretches of sand. The 185 has balloon tires, can put down damn near anywhere. We were looking for a deserted beach when we came upon your airfield. With the rains, the sand softens, and your little strip seemed far the better choice."

I asked no more questions. Instead, I slipped out back and tried speaking. My voice continued to startle me, tentative and squeaky, and I realized all my chats with C. Aubrey had been silent. Words wouldn't move out of the way before the next words came along. My tongue hadn't done much in a while and had become stone-weighted. It clanged around in the mouth. It was like that movie of the hunchback and the beautiful woman, where he's up in the belfry ringing the bells but he can't hear them because he's deaf.

Michael returned as we were cleaning up, carrying his jeans and homemade tackle in one hand. In the other, strung through the gills, four small fish. He tossed the fish into the sink.

"Grunts, mostly," he explained, "and one sienna. Usually if you find one mackerel there's a school."

The tail of one fish flopped in a death twitch, and I stepped back. Michael rummaged about the kitchen drawers. "Tools, mate. You need good tools in this world. Secret of my success. Be a love, Arden, get my knife and a pair of dry trousers."

She left through the back door. Levering his cold chisel by the blade he conked each of the fish on the head. No more flopping. Then he inspected the stew pot we had started and sniffed critically into the fry pan.

"Not too much butter," he scolded the onions. "Need those arteries clean. So, matey, tell me about your strip. Who's it for? You fly?"

I shrugged. There was something ominous in his presence. I was wishing she'd return.

"Speak up, hermit. We expecting anyone?" I shook my head.

"You're sure?" He asked amiably enough and tossed the chisel in half turns, catching it first by the blade then the handle. He could do it without looking.

"Yes." My voice slithered away under his question like one of those little snakes after the rains.

"Do be sure," he said. Then he came close, maybe six inches from my face, and repeated those words. Do be sure. He flipped the chisel and centered its edge against my breastbone. Leaned on it. Then with the heel of his hand chucked the stub end. The force knocked me back.

"Do be sure," he said kindly. "Wouldn't want to do you like I did those grunts."

Arden walked in and handed him a knife. One of those spring-loaded things. He put it to his face, snapped out the blade like a punk in a movie, and turned to clean the fish.

The blow had opened a half-inch slit across my chest. A dark spot, sticky black on the khaki, was seeping into the front of my shirt. I went upstairs to put on a fresh shirt. I didn't want her to see.

When I came downstairs, Arden was setting the table for dinner. She'd found frayed rattan place mats in the upper cabinets—I'd never looked—and she'd lit two hurricane candles. Michael fiddled with what looked like a toy telephone and a little computer. No bigger than a book.

"C'mere." I went over to look. On the screen was a lighted map of the Caribbean, I could tell from Florida's limp member, and weather was swirling around it.

"How's that? Tomorrow's forecast, courtesy of those assholes in the old U.S. who pay their taxes."

"I pay my taxes," I said. It was hard to get words off my fear-thick tongue before the next ones came along. Michael looked at me as if again I'd proved his point.

Arden finished setting the table around him. It looked like someone's house, china and glasses from a fitted picnic basket they took off the plane. The dinner was terrific. I had forgotten about food, good food. Michael stripped the flesh of the fish free of the bone and scrambled it in among peppers sliced paper thin and curling onions. It was chewy and full of sea-flavor. He'd brought fresh lemons and limes, and had cut them into quarter-earth wedges and fried them in too. Michael talked as if we were old friends. He was sure I could get a vegetable garden going out back, lots of sun and the soil hadn't been used. This soil isn't glaciated, he told us, deficient in minerals so you can't plant it every year.

Plant, then compost, Michael instructed the forkfuls of food as he devoured them. I wanted to agree with him.

"Michael worked as a chef," Arden announced. "Some of Houston's best restaurants." She looked over for him to continue, but he kept stoking in the food. On the whole, they were good company, especially compared to what I'd had. Except he was nasty to the limit and about as trustworthy as a chain saw.

Arden talked about the spirit of the beings we were eating. She said if we were conscious of our food we would take away its real virtues, what was good about the grunt and the onion, not only what tasted good. Ingest their experiences.

"What if it's an evil onion?"

Michael laughed. "He's right." He speared a veggie. "How do we know that's not a nasty onion? One who sneaks about fucking his fellow tubers?"

"You'd know," she said to me sincere as a priest. "You are in touch, Leonard. Living alone has done that for you."

Michael didn't pay her much mind. He mumbled through a mouthful, "She's fuckin' nuts."

I looked hard at the plate. I didn't want to disappoint her, but I couldn't get the first impression of that onion.

"So," Michael asked. "If you don't fly why'd you build a runway?"

"I didn't know that's what it was when I started." I had my voice back. When I went upstairs to put a plaster over the cut, I had practiced.

"Well matey, that's very thoughtful. Very thoughtful. We appreciate thoughtful people. But you better muck it up a bit. It sticks out from the air, you can see it miles away. A strip not on the charts—that's suspicious, you'll end up with unwanted visitors. Someone like us."

"Muck it up how?"

He shoveled in a load of fish and potato. "For one thing, take those dumb ass numbers off. And throw some cuttings around. Change the shape from the air, less conspicuous."

"If I'd had cuttings on it, you wouldn't have been able to land."

"Right," he said. "Right, Leonard. Excellent point. I'll have to think that through."

After dinner she and I were in the kitchen, doing up the dishes. I felt odd, my mind kept going back to what I'd seen in the mirror—an unfinished shape. Like one of those clay dolls you'd see in a museum, something a caveman fired in an oven of stones. Hollowed, no sex, the whole figure red-baked as the earth it came from. Maybe a hole at the back, where the potter blew into it to form it, a mouthpiece hole that makes a lonesome sound when the wind blows across it. Michael came in.

"Get my gym bag, will you?" She had a plate in her hand, wiping it round about with a towel. She turned it to dry the underside.

"Be a love," he said softly, "and do it now." In a normal voice, sweet. And as the word Now finished his arm lashed out. A cable on a mad winch, but with perfect accuracy. The open hand smacked against the side of her head. Casual, precise. Whap. Arden's cheek turned red and the blow knocked the smallest squeak of pain from her. By her sideburn, his watchband had opened a short line of red. She started to say something, but caught herself and left by the back door.

The blow sounded like halving a melon, and turned my stomach. There's no excuse for cruelty, life is tough enough without it. I didn't know what kitchen job he'd held but I'd bet it involved a cleaver.

She returned with the bag and I was happy to see her. He and I had stopped staring at each other. I'd decided to keep to myself the old saw about not hitting ladies. For one thing, his mother had probably told him. For another, my ribs continued to serve me and I didn't fancy them chiseled into barbecue lengths.

The bag, it turned out, held his stash. He rolled a joint and passed it around. I took a puff or two so as not to seem unfriendly, then went into the kitchen and put away the dinner things. I don't like the idea much, not since it took Tommy.

Arden sat on the battered couch sketching. I perched at the far end and watched. She did a cat, starting from the corner of the ear, down the back and out the tail, all in a single line. The way she drew, she might have stopped at the tip of the tail, and there would have been no mistaking what it was. That's how good it was, a single line. Then she did an elephant, smaller than the cat and dense, no motion, then a kangaroo. She drew easily, the pencil never left the page and the drawing just appeared out of the paper.

"I told you we'd be no trouble," she said mid-elephant. I had to smile, though it cracked my lips. I'm parlor-sitting with a man who greets everything in his path, a host or a green pepper, by dicing it up, and she insists on reassuring me.

We did a second joint. I was thinking how good it was to have guests, except for my terror.

"All right," she said at once. "Everyone outside."

I'd thought myself unaffected by the dope, but we'd gone through a lot of wine. I was dizzy and weightless. The outside air was soft from the rains, and stars seemed to be on the verge of breaking out. It was like someone else's sky. We walked among the little dunes. There she had us lie down in the saw grass, in a kind of linked circle, her head on my stomach, mine on Michael's, Michael's head on her. We watched the sky. I know it sounds weird, but we watched the sky for I don't know how long. It was peaceful, after I got used to having my head on Michael's stomach, which I didn't.

She broke the silence. Now reach down, she told us, and feel the face of the head resting on you. Imagine you're blind and you have to study this face. You wouldn't have thought Michael would go in for this, but just like she was the kindergarten teacher, Michael's fingers were on my nose, my forehead. Could he smother me, I wondered, with a single hand? When he didn't, at least at the moment, I relaxed.

My fingers had not moved, they rested still on Arden's brow. I ventured them out, down the fragile bridge of her nose. Her skin was supple and the temperature of the air. You could feel its color. Her hair was cut shorter than any woman I'd known and soft as fur. How dark could skin get, how white hair? I let my fingers slide to the rim of bone beneath the eyebrow, across the soft jelly of the eye. Through the clouds patches of star disappeared and appeared like a rash. My fingers traced the line of her jaw. When they wandered to her mouth, it opened. Slowly. Still, I started. Michael might hear my breath, he might easily kill me. My index finger moved across the rim and swell of her lip, touched the perfect ridge of her front teeth. The edge was dry in the midst of that moistness. I could hear my heart.

She spoke. Her words sounded through my fingers. I could hear her words in the air and in the hollows of her bone.

"The scientists who run the Hubble telescope leave the camera lens focused on far stars. The lens is open for hours, sometimes a full day. It gathers light. The stars are so distant it takes billions of years for their shining, no matter how brilliant, how intense, to reach us. The light must be gathered gradually.

"That is what we are. We are a ground array of telescopes patiently gathering light."

We lay still. Michael's breath raised and lowered my head. It was he who broke it up.

"Sorry mateys. This sand'll freeze my ass. I'm to bed."

When I failed to move immediately he cocked his middle finger and flicked it across the tip of my nose. It hurt like hell. I yelled and got up. I hoped she might stay, but she got up too, brushed off and followed him inside.

I needed to give them space, so I began to walk the length of the runway. Walking fifty paces ahead of me was Hofstadter. I called but he kept moving off. I knew he'd heard me. It was all the more troublesome because he was my own invention. Not like the Hermit. I had willed Hofstadter's ghost up and now he ignored me. At the far end of the strip, I picked up the shells that made out the numbers and scattered them into the bush.

By the time I came back to the house, their door was closed. I had this sudden fear, what if they were making love, what if they do later and I have to listen to them the entire night. I returned. Their light was out and all was quiet. I lay, basting in anger and something else I couldn't tell, maybe just excitement, and tried to sleep.

* *

Again a buzzing awakened me, this time without the flies and without the dreams. Something in the sound told me before I was out of bed that it was their airplane, and it was departing. I looked out the window, but I faced the ocean and could catch no sight of them. They were gone.

Downstairs I checked the skies. Their machine had disappeared into the mothering clouds. The drone too. I was the better for their leaving. Michael had a menacing way, he fed on people. When you could catch sight of his eyes deep in their caves you caught a carelessness I've seen before. In Criminal, when they're waiting to call arraignments or dispositions, a roomful of sullen petulant types who read the floor and mumble through sentencing. We didn't get hardened felons, these are city ordinances, parking tickets, drunk and disorderly, that kind of thing. But Michael, you could tell, brooded the same way. I was better off with him gone—the last thing I needed in my life was misgivings based in reality.

I opened the refrigerator. They had made me a present of half a dozen eggs, three oranges, and, pasted to a baguette with one of those yellow paper stickums, a brand new five hundred dollar bill. I'd never seen one, it looked phony. "Thanks for the tie-down," said the note. It was her hand, finely scrolled, no signature.

I scrambled up two of the eggs with a slice of canned ham. Angry and relieved, I ate the batch in a rush.

In the living room, propped askew on the flimsy

mantel, another gift. She had left me the drawing. To the little menagerie she'd added a parrot, just the head, and a spider in a web, each done in the finest point. And in the upper right corner, a quick portrait of a man. Around the head a halo, like you see on religious paintings where the one being martyred looks unrealistically peaceful. Her drawing had a face of baked-in lines and a single emotion, weedy, uneven hair and a fried and lonely look in his eye. If you didn't know, you'd have said she made him up, she couldn't have found a face so godforsaken, but I knew. I recognized him from my peek at the mirror. It was one hell of a likeness.

CHAPTER 16.

I slinked into the drizzling morning with a job in mind. How can they fly without seeing? Perhaps above, perhaps you break through clouds and emerge into a bright blue world. That would be one of the few blessings of flying, take off in mist and get yourself reborn into a world above like a movie, like Alice through the looking glass. That part of it appeals to me, I'd like flying if you could do it without the need for altitude. I suppose speed is another benefit, but I can't say I'm ever in a rush.

I fetched fallen branches from the sides of the strip and scattered them about haphazardly, to camouflage the straight edges that I'd cut with such care. The rains stopped and started ten times as I worked, sullen rains from clouds you could have reached from a stepladder. The feel of water washing down my face was familiar and annoying.

I was in high spirits when I started. But the rain soon sogged my shirt and trousers, and I slipped into a funk. I couldn't imagine what had put me down so, I'd lived months on the island without joy or sadness. The place had a limited stock of them, just as it had a short shelf of spices. You can get on fine without marjoram or thyme or cayenne.

By the time I finished, whatever use the strip had served for Michael disappeared in the clutter, and now it looked like trash. A blank in a blank. If you were blind you wouldn't see the blanks. A bulldozer would make a great gift for a blind man. Beats a seeing-eye dog, no scooping up, no special seats on the bus and you travel wherever you please. Still the rain kept falling.

* *

I went to see Reba. Secretly, in the evening, I saw them from the street. She was getting out of a sad gray car with vanity plates: LRN2ACHV. I swear. A tall, scrawny man unfolded himself out the driver's side and took her arm. She had a frozen smile. He looked vacant. It was a mistake, this peeking into their world, but I couldn't help it.

I heard from Stace that they were moving.

"Mom's lease comes up for renewal at the end of the month, and Derek wants us to move in with him. He's got a nice house, three bedrooms, air hockey, and everything." It was a Saturday, Stace came by to see how I'm doing. I'm doing lousy. There was nothing to eat in the refrigerator, and I wished the hell I had shopped because she would stay for lunch if I had. I offered to open a can of soup, nuke a potpie.

"So who is Derek?"

"Dad, don't you know? Mom's been dating Derek for maybe two months."

"Scruffy-looking, gray Honda?" Stace nodded.

"She works fast, Dorothy."

"I guess. You didn't know?"

"She doesn't confide in me. I'm O-O-P. Out of the picture." Stace considered this and I could see the spark of her mother's new freedom flit by her eyes.

"This is her first romance?"

"I guess. She had an exit person, a real creep. Nothing serious. Derek's an improvement."

"An exit person?"

"Someone to help you bridge the last relationship." Stace glanced up, saw in my face she was talking about me. "Derek's an improvement."

"So where'd they meet?"

"He's in her sensitivity class."

"Sensitivity, great. Someone named Derek probably needs classes. How about sincerity class, has he signed up for that? Next semester? How about introductory nobility of the spirit?"

She ignored me. She'd agreed to stay. "Just the chicken pie, no soup." I set the table for the two of us.

"What kind of name is that, Derek? Sounds like something from a construction crew. Or a great movie, John Derek and Jeannie Crain in *Road Builders*."

She'd made up her mind not to laugh. We changed the subject, talked about women's basketball and why it's the superior game. The microwave beeps. I poured soup for me, minestrone. She broke up the crust on the potpie and crumbled it into the white gravy. I popped us each a cold Mountain Dew.

"So tell me. He's around a lot, this Derek?"

"I guess."

"You like him?"

"He's OK. Tries to be funny."

"Tell me."

"He's cute. Funny cute, or tries to be. Know what I mean?"

"No." I need details.

"Rags on me. When he calls? 'Hello, is this Stacey Mooney? Do you date older men? I'm a good-looking Gemini into Mozart, museums and macrobiotics.'"

"Cute like that?"

"Like that." She fished out a white cube of potato.

"They go on dates? You see him when he comes over to pick her up?" Stace was too smart. She saw where this was going.

"Dad…"

"He hangs around, does he? He's there for dinner? What's he like for breakfast? Is he a cornflakes man? Wheaties, I'll bet he's a Wheaties man."

"Dad. I'm not going to do this."

And she didn't. She picked out the potato and pimientos from the pie and left the rest. It's too hot, she told me.

She and her mother moved in with Derek. He was a high-school principal. Stace got her own room, her own TV and privacy, except every other weekend when a brat of a stepbrother came for his father's visitation. Stace had all the lingo: support, modification of orders, visitation.

It hit me hard. A man who thinks that life consists of telling people what to do when the bell rings. Defective people at that, adolescents. The week after they moved in I was sitting and brooding on it. I had begun dinner with several Jim Beam old-fashioneds—

the first two made to formula, muddling the bitters and a splash of soda among the sugar, then the ice, then the bourbon stirred thoroughly into the pinkish syrup. There is great anticipation in the properly made drink. Later I skipped the bitters, the sugar made it too sweet. I sat in front of Dan Rather's earnest face with my glass full of whiskey. I had neglected the fruit, and it occurred to me my dinner lacked nutritional balance. I got up and retrieved the orange half and the jar of maraschino cherries to the table. By eight o'clock Rather had disappeared and something unintelligible was on. A black family in bright cotton sweaters was sitting in a living room discussing an upcoming dance and the audience laughed every five seconds. I got in the Plymouth and headed into the night.

A lined rain was falling. I had Derek's address from Stacey, my twice-a-month visitations were to start there. If I timed my trips properly, Derek's ex and I could free our schedules the same days, visit the zoo together. I parked across the street from the house, turned off the lights. Inside, on the first floor, lamps and a television set gleamed out to advertise this as a happy home. I stared at the blue light a long time hoping Reba would feel my presence. She would sense me—ESP, tuned through years of intimacy to the same frequency, would alert her to my presence, my need. She would slip on a coat, no, better she'd tent it over her head, come outside, recognize the car. She would say nothing, just get in and come back with me. Stace would follow the next day, simply coming to our house after school ends. She'd thump upstairs, flop on her bed, happy to be there. Spend the afternoon playing with her dollhouse.

Reba would never return to this neighborhood. Whatever clothes she had left behind in the principal's house I would replace. A shopping spree in New York City, a small corner suite at the Plaza, one night of theater and a romantic dinner, and we fly back home penniless and in love.

Nothing happened. My bladder shrank in the cold. I got out, realized I'd forgotten to bring a coat. Rain trickled down my neck. I walked toward the lighted window, reached the pfitzers planted neatly in a row under it. Inside Reba and Derek sat on reclining chairs, they sat parallel watching television. I was confused—one, are they watching television or am I? On their screen a young couple in spangles skated around a rink. Two, Reba could not abide sports. I moved around to watch with them, I watched the skaters pirouette and glide, and maybe fifteen feet from Derek's shoulder, I unzipped and pissed on the healthy and pruned pfitzers of my rival. In the rain there was no new sound to alarm them. I closed up, walked back to where I could see their faces. She was absolutely without expression. Perhaps he'd drugged her and that was why she stayed.

I stood in the rain, I don't know how long. Next door a porch light came on, the front door opened, someone left. I made for the concrete walk, strolled through the rain toward my car. Nasty weather, I called to a woman in yellow plastic, called it out heartily.

I went home, soaking wet. The damn car heater didn't work and I could feel a chill coming on. I swallowed a handful of cold capsules and put on the water for tea, but it took too long to boil. Waiting, I poured another bourbon. I was feeling a little groggy by this time, and I knew I ought to go to bed. Instead I changed into some dry things, called Hofstadter. He didn't want company. Is this urgent? he asked, and I said no. He's watching TV, he said. Olympic figure skating, pairs.

When the water boiled I made a hot toddy and turned on the set. All that skating made me furious. I got back in the Plymouth. This time I was going to ring the bell. But when I got there the first floor was dark. Just dark, and a single light burned upstairs. I got out and stood in the rain. I figured, what the hell, my clothes are already wet, but they weren't, I forgot about the change.

The light went off. It was in the corner room and it went off. I stood fixing the dark house in my sight and the rain that ran down my face tasted of salt.

When the cops picked me up they said I was howling. Like a dog. The neighbor thought it *was* a dog and called around, but then someone looked out at the street and there I was. I honestly don't remember. I remember the Come out, you bastard, and fight like a man, and how that moved to howling I do not know.

Hofstadter fetched me at the precinct house and took me home. Didn't have to bail me out or anything, just took me home. He convinced them not to charge me, to let me sleep it off. He could be very persuasive, Hofstadter, especially then when he had a voice. They told me they were prepared to book me for D&D, that was their term for it, and peeping. When they said that, I heard it wrong, thought they meant peeing, and I couldn't believe there was an ordinance against that, but no, peeping as in Tom. That was all I needed, a new court file crossing Canges's desk entitled the People versus Leonard Mooney.

"She's gone, Mooney." Hofstadter turned his advocacy on me. "Face up to it and let her go. You can stand outside her house panting or barking or even retrieving a stick, but it isn't going to help. She's gone, get over her."

We were in my kitchen. He had agreed to one drink if I would swap him the car keys until the morning.

"Yeah. Listen, I *am* over her. I just want to whip his ass."

"Right," Hofstadter said. "Whip his ass. It's a good thing he's a heavy sleeper. Her too, she probably could have taken you out. In your next life, Mooney, you'll come back as an actor. The only question is whether they'll credit you for all this time toward the pension."

Peeping Tom, that's a good one. Not that I haven't had that fantasy. I bet everyone has, even Derek, it's universal. In mine, I am looking through a window, watching commonplace stuff. A man leafs through a newspaper, paying no attention. He rubs his eye. A woman passes through the room and speaks. She touches the drapes. The man responds. What is my fascination? The house is my own. I am spying on myself. Why would I care about someone else's life?

* *

The airstrip was gone, stir in rubble and debris and it disappears. The sight dismayed me, never mind that I was the one who did it. I went to the house, tossed down a football pill, three points, and walked out front. The aluminum Whaler was rubbing against the pier, making this insistent, animal sound. It was annoying, it would interrupt my sleep. I untied the frayed cord that held the boat to the pier and set the thing adrift. For a while it stayed where it was, nuzzling the wood and disinclined to leave me, but the tide caught it and it drifted out beyond the puny waves.

My visitors had moved the chaise lounge out to the dunes. I lay down on it. The gray sky had begun to crack apart in cream-colored seams. I closed my eyes.

I was in that zone between sleep and wakefulness. Who makes a pill to let you stay there? Whatever I had swallowed kicked in, and I felt a gradual release. As if someone loosened the tin band I wore around my head several turns, and with that a warmth leaked down my face, down across my body. Eyes still closed, I sensed a form hovering nearby. It reached out and touched my forehead. This was not like coming upon Hofstadter, that I knew was an imagining. This was tangible. I opened my eyes and realized that the sun had come out. The boat was nowhere to be seen.

Water stretched back to the retina of the sky. Maybe we are stuck in a gargantuan eyeball, maybe we are looking at it as it is looking over us. Is the world any better off for describing itself? Me, I prefer the explanation of a large inverted bowl sitting atop four tortoises. That does me just fine.

She couldn't be much over twenty and he, he was probably Tommy's age. What if they'd met Tommy, what if they knew him, what if they were in business together? Did he still call himself Tommy, and did Dog call himself Dog? Were they here in this ocean? In some other one? Were they alive? I watched the sky and hoped they would fly down from it.

* *

I lay there and got my money's worth out of the pill.

Really Hofstadter's, he'd bought it or stolen it. They don't make them big enough. Or maybe they do, and these are stale and running out of steam. Toward the end I went to see Hofstadter. Just before he reupped at the hospital for the last time. I told him he looked good. He put his wand to his throat.

"Yeah," he croaked through the metal box. "For a corpse…No energy." His voice was metallic and filled with feeling. It could have been old or young, man or woman.

"The hell with energy. What do you want to do?"

"Dictionary." You could tell it hurt to talk.

"Dictionary? You want to look something up? I'll do it, what's the word?"

"Moribund." Then he cracked a smile like his face just broke and laughed with the huff of a barkless dog.

I asked about hospital life. He grimaced.

"Every morning. They stick you. Then questions. What day? Who the president?" He rested. "What the hell. I care. President!"

I thought he'd gone to sleep, but he had another gripe.

"Then. Chaplain. Do I want. Pray!" He winked at me. I could just see the chaplain—he'd do better in the morgue.

"I'll talk to him," I said. Hofstadter waved me off. His backhand was attached to a plastic tube, and he couldn't give it the old down-the-liner. "I'll talk to him. If prayer worked, every horse race would be an eight-way tie."

That cracked him another smile. He asked about Alice.

I had come around to a view of Alice exactly the

opposite of why we married in the first place. She was fleshy, willing, friendly, and at first I would dive into her like a pool of water. It was cooling, I don't mean sex but the effect, cooling, I could feel the anger cooling. When you dive in, the water never complains. But the very liquid mass now had begun to repel. I know, it's unfair, it's not her fault and I'm a beast, but I'll let you in on a little secret. We're all beasts.

I figured it out and after that I began to be repelled. The pendulous breasts, the nails done to a rounded point and polished like a new year model Ford Truck, the lipstick applied just so. I'm sure she regarded them as skillfully maintained, skillfully presented. But the more I saw of them and her, unrelentingly available and eager, the less desire I felt. Alice, the hot-blooded keeper of Miramonte castle, became my saltpeter.

I didn't say any of this to Hofstadter. I told him everything was hunky-dory. But somehow I think maybe he knew and that's why he left me this island. It was a way station. Don't get mad, don't get even, just get out.

* *

Nothing but sea and sky. How did the magazines make it look so alluring? Writers concocting stories to make you think they've got the drop on it.

Then I did an odd thing. First I pulled myself out of the chaise. I had dozed so long red ribs showed across the back of my legs where the plastic webbing had stuck. The dark had come back, there was no moon or stars, the rains were gathering for another go at it. I'd spent the day mucking up the airstrip, no straight lines and not enough space to land clear of branches and debris. And what I did was clean it off again. CLEAN to

CLEAR in twenty steps. I picked up every leaf, and by the time I was through there was not a stone larger than a beer can on the whole expanse. I can't say why, it was an empty-headed thing, having spent an entire day doing the opposite. Though days were something I had to burn.

CHAPTER 17.

I phoned Reba's new number. My Saturday was coming, every second week was my Saturday, and I needed to arrange to pick up Stace. I was greatly heartened by the male voice on the answering machine. For us scavengers who fly high enough carrion is everywhere.

"*Allo allo. Zees ees la maison du Monsieur Derek et fils, et aussi Les Mademoiselles Reba et fille. Sil vous plait, leave a message, mes amis, at le beep, and nous returnez le call tout de suite. Merci beaucoup.*"

Stace rang back. I didn't need to pick her up. She'd be downtown in the morning, Derek had a tenkay first thing.

"What's a tenkay?" I asked. Maybe it's some operation on the male reproductive system. With any luck it's the medical term for surgical removal of the cock.

"A race. Ten kilometers. Derek runs. He's getting ready for the state iron man."

"Iron man?" My euphoria began to slip away. I might have to call the answering machine for a refresher fix.

"Run, bike and swim. Ten kilometers each, except one-kay in the pool. He's in the over forty-fives."

"Really. I'm surprised. Over forty-fives."

"Yes."

"You're sure he's in the over forty-fives?"

"You didn't think he was that old?"

"Old? Oh, I thought you meant I.Q."

The receiver groaned.

"Da-ad. You should take up running. Or an aerobics class. You could use the exercise." Right. Derek and I down the home stretch. You'll recognize me, I'm the miler carrying the scissors.

We met for lunch at the Malt Shop. I had a cheeseburger and black coffee. Stace got a double order of fries and a diet Coke.

"That cheese goes right to the arteries," she said in a scold.

"Thanks, Doctor Kildare."

"Who's he?"

"Never mind." Everything this day seemed to point at my mortality.

"Besides," I chided her, "that plate of fries isn't exactly on the Surgeon General's list."

"It's different. I'm a kid. Men your age should be more careful. Do you get an annual prostate check?"

"Listen, Dorothy. Let's leave my prostate off the lunch table, if you don't mind." She shrugged, examined a fry bloodied in ketchup. "How did Derek do this morning?"

"OK. Fifty-sixth overall, but third in his class."

"So how does that bode for the iron man?"

"Actually not so hot."

"Is it possible he's rusting?"

Stace ignored the shot. "Derek clocks the competition and compares. From his journals? Very scientific. Running is his best event. If he's to do well he's got to finish higher there. Cut down his time."

"Why doesn't he call a cab?"

"Ha ha. I meant it, Dad, about the exercise. You could use it. You never know, you might meet someone in those classes."

"Thanks."

"It's not healthy for a man to live alone."

"Stace, my love life is my love life. I don't grill you about yours." She shot me a name-rank-serial number glare.

"Lots of luck," she said.

The fries were gone. She pondered dessert. Ordered a single scoop of vanilla ice cream. She was embarrassed to ask, so I did it for her.

"I'll have the same, but do me a favor. Microwave mine on low for exactly twenty seconds and put a little pond of maple syrup on the top." The waitress wrote down my order, she took this seriously. Mine too, said Stace as if this is a new concept, she's never heard of it but she's willing to give it a try.

"Tell me about the journals."

"What journals?"

"Journals. You said Derek could tell about the competition from journals."

"Oh yeah. Well, Derek keeps these journals. Way back, to when he was in high school. He ran the quarter mile and the relay. Has medals. Every time he runs or swims or bowls, he puts how he did in these journals, who he beat, who beat him. We have them in the kitchen. You can read them."

"I can? I'll be over this evening."

"I don't mean you. I mean while we're waiting for dinner to be ready, for the timer to go off. Or sometimes he'll read them to us and tell us about it."

"You're putting me on."

"No. Honest."

"What does your mother think of that?"

"I don't know. I don't think she minds."

The waitress came. Stemmed china cups each with a blind yellow eye. She asked if that's how we like it and I gave her thumbs up. Stace stirred her ice cream into a single soupy consistency, dipped the spoon and licked it. She went through hers, I swapped dishes with her, and she started through mine.

"So, your mother seems to like this guy?" I said this cautiously. Anyone with a brain could see the answer I was looking for.

"I guess."

"And all this adolescent crap with the races and the journals." I figured to save the answering machine message for a better time. "She seems to like that too?"

"I guess." Stace licked a gooey drop from the back of her spoon. "She says athletic men make good lovers."

"Stacey! For God's sake, how old are you?"

"I'm twelve, Dad." She looked at me the way Reba did, as if I would never know any better. "Twelve. I know about these things. You'll have to face up to it." One of her mother's expressions.

"No I won't."

"No you won't what?"

"Have to face up to it. I may not be able to change it, but I sure as hell don't have to face up to it." Reeb would tell me that. I would tell her about some kid the courts picked up from his parents, cigarette burns on his arms, and she would tell me about facing up to those people in the world.

Later we walked through downtown, got her a book for school from the library, looked in the shop windows. I drove her home—not home, to Derek's. She remarked how I seemed to know the route. I said nothing. Derek was outside, moving a lawn sprinkler. I hesitated to get out of the car. Would a neighbor recognize me as the midnight coyote? Had they been showing mug shots around the neighborhood of established peepers? I had no choice. If I didn't get out to meet him he'd think I was a coward. Accurate, but demeaning.

His looks, not bent over just standing alone, surprised me. He was tall, over six feet, and he had one of those knobby Adam's apples. Meaty hands with big knuckles, fingers that would get stuck in a pop bottle. He was positioning an arc sprinkler as if he was Strategic Air Command, adjusting its spray. I had installed an underground system in our lawn.

"You ought to put one in," I told him.

"What's that?" He wiped his hand on his running shorts to shake mine. With that Adam's apple, it's a beauty, win the apple prize at the county fair, you'd expect him to have a deep voice but it wasn't, it was yodeling but assured. Perfect for telling kids to shape up, and this is their last chance, stuff like that. A teachy voice.

"A sprinkler system. You ought to put in one of those automatic kinds."

"Yeah. Good idea." You could tell he didn't think so. "Hey, thanks for dropping Stacey off." That was an odd thing to say, even belligerent, given as how she's my daughter. I let it pass.

"She's a great girl. I want you to know, Len. She's a great girl." I nodded. I was thinking of slugging him. He was still in his jogging suit, skimpy little rayon pants and a sleeveless shirt with a plastic number square pinned to it. Prudential Life 1473 June Jog. How long would it take you to shower and change? I noticed I still had his hand in mine. I dropped it, I considered its provenance and I dropped it like a toad. This hand has been diddling my wife. Was he thinking the same thing?

"You have children?" Why was I asking this question? He was almost a foot taller than I and if I threw a punch, it would have to be up and away. I'd feel silly hitting him in the chest, any punch would have to travel on an upward and uncertain course.

"Two boys. Derek Junior's in grad school studying public accounting. And Chip is right here in town. At my school. Just pulled down high eleven-fifties in his junior boards."

"Did he?"

"Sure did," Derek said. Stace was standing there knowing exactly what was happening, but she couldn't figure how to head it off. Me either.

"Did he pull those down?"

"Sure did. Now, we'd like him to pull them up a little. He's a great sprinter and lots of top places are after him."

"They're after him?"

"Sure are. And if he pulls them up, he's got a shot to

get in anywhere. Duke, Stanford, the little Ivies."

"If he pulls them up?"

"Right. Not much. Just a notch or so."

"Well, he should start by not pulling them down."

"What?"

"He should stop pulling them down. He just pulled them down. He keeps pulling them down, he'll have further to pull them up."

Stace said she was going inside. I decided to stand my ground on this one. Derek looked confused. He took advantage of the break to change direction.

"Great comfort, sons."

"Sure are."

"I mean…I didn't mean sons. Kids." If you'd given him the benefit of the doubt you'd have seen how hard he was trying. I didn't have to give him anything. I'd given enough.

"Kids. Sure are."

"Too bad about your kid. Tommy, I mean."

Out of his mouth the word enraged me. I left off thinking about the punch. I contemplated getting in my car and driving over him.

"Why is that?" Time had passed since he'd spoken and he realized he had made an error.

"Well, you know." He studied the dial on the sprinkler. It let you set the pattern of the watering, a long rectangle, a quarter-circle. "You know. Gone off like that and not a word." Did this man live a Prudential Life?

"Oh no. We hear." Why was I doing this? Why didn't I get in the car and run up this four-foot pruned hill, thick green lawn fertilized every other week in the growing season according to the instructions on the package, weeded and edged, run over the bastard, back and forth, tire treads tracing a satisfying and parallel route across his blue track shirt with the white piping.

"You hear?"

"Oh yes. I hear. Mail comes to the house. Tommy is fine. He lives in Green Bay, Wisconsin. He's the traveling secretary for the Packers. It's a dream job. He's getting his GED at night."

"He is?"

"Absolutely. Rents a duplex right on the lake. Sailing in the summer and in the winter, ice boating, skating parties. High school just didn't interest him, nothing in it. He's doing it by mail. Then he's thinking of starting his own firm."

"He is?"

"Yeah. But first he may do college. Not four years, something less."

"Less?"

"Telescoped, you know? Accelerated, get his degree in a couple of years. Maybe the little Ivies."

I know it was a dumb thing to do, I know it now and I knew every bit of it then, while I was doing it, but I couldn't help myself. I smiled and turned and I walked down the hill, over the part he'd watered and over the dry parking strip that he'd get to next. I got in the car and started it up, and he was standing there, the dripping sprinkler in his left hand—was that the hand?—and I started up the engine and holding my teeth together hard as I could I rolled away.

I was freshening up my first drink, it was maybe five o'clock or a little earlier, when the phone went off. At least I'd gotten her to call.

"Leonard."

"Hi, Baby. What's up?"

"Leonard. I want you to have these days with Stacey."

"Yeah. Well, it's in the decree."

"I *want* you to have them. This relationship is important for her maturation, and I want her to know her father." She was stealing them from me, I could tell. She was giving them to me and telling me how important they were to her, to *her* for Christ sake, and that was the way she would steal them from me.

"Good," I said. "I'm glad that you're glad."

"But I think you should just pick her up and drop her off and not visit our home."

"I *live* in our home."

"You know what I mean. I don't think you should stand around chatting with Derek. It does something to you."

"What does it do to you?"

"Stop it. What you told him, about Tommy. That's not funny. That's sick. Hurtful. I didn't know what to think, but it's sick."

"Sick isn't all bad." That was a lame line, but it was all I could come up with. It was better than saying something stupid, which I said in about a minute.

"Ice boating. I can't believe it, Leonard, except I can." I didn't say anything. Fact is, I was smiling.

"Leonard, do yourself a favor. Get some help. Go see someone."

"Thanks, Reeb. I was thinking of putting in for some sensitivity training."

"That's not what I mean."

"Can I enroll? My scores are in the high eleven fifties. Or do I need to take self-awareness as a prerequisite? Is that an advanced course, first you need to take self-awareness with a grade of at least C? And public accounting?"

"Leonard, you're not making sense. You sound like you're drinking. I am not going to have this fight if you're drinking."

"Then we may have found a permanent peace. Peace in our time."

"Leonard, I'm serious, think about it. Ask your friend Hofstadter. He's seeing someone. Maybe you could see him too."

"Hofstadter!" It was like hearing Derek mention Tommy. "Hofstadter! Hofstadter's dying, for Christ sake. Hofstadter's dying of cancer." If there was an argument here, it was ending. Falling out of the sky.

"Hofstadter's doctor might see you."

"Well I can't. I can't plan that far ahead. I may be leaving the country."

"What?"

"I may be leaving the country." Here's that Olympic-sized stupid thing and I was hearing myself speak it. "I won't be able to take up a long-term relationship with Hofstadter's doctor."

"Where are you going?"

"Too early to say. I'll let you know, though."

Reba was silent for a while. I couldn't tell, it may have just been exasperation. Then she said, "Leonard, I'm worried about you. I can't say why, but I am."

I could say. I knew. Why was it a mystery to her? I was falling out of the sky. That's what I wanted to tell her, I wanted to tell her I am falling out of the sky and there's no one to catch me, you used to be here to catch me and you're gone and that man's hand is on the sprinkler, that sprinkler that sits on the lawn with bugs and chemicals and dog shit, and you shouldn't let him put that hand on you. But I didn't. I didn't say much more, maybe anything, and Reba gave this little sigh and the conversation was over.

* *

Of course I *did* leave the country, but that came years later and Reba would have had no reason to put the two together. I didn't, actually, until I was standing in the kitchen, looking out at the boring ocean. I was standing there dreaming at the blank that is sea and sky, and I heard the plane overhead. I don't know how long you could hear that drone, probably from far away. I suddenly realized it was *my* drone, my plane, coming in to the island. I rushed out to greet it. Again it was on its last run to the strip, low over the trees out the back window.

"They're here," I called to C. Aubrey and waited. It landed to the north, turned and taxied back. It turned again, to face north. I could make out through the branches that the number on the tail had been repainted and the stripes were now blue. But it was my plane. Michael's face scowled at the space ahead, the hollows of his eyes were covered by a wraparound metallic lens. His mouth clamped down in determination and anger. The engine revved, and the damn thing ran up the other way. God, I felt it like a slap on the head. It lifted off and cleared the trees at the far end. Leaned into the wind and angled up. Why would they do that, touch down, turn around and take off again? I was a little relieved—the sight of Michael had squeezed the bulb of my bladder—but mostly I was crushed. It wasn't as if I got a lot of visitors.

I was about to tell C. Aubrey. I had taken to speaking out loud to him to keep my voice in practice. I was turning to say something to him when the fronds of the palm break parted and easy as the breeze Arden strolled through.

CHAPTER 18.

Strolled through the brush, walked straight and unafraid at me, she might have pushed aside those branches to save my life. I was thrilled to see her. Also not. For one thing, I had reason to worry. Where was Michael gone to, and what would he do to me when he came back? She wore a halter made of a blue bandana print and cut-off denim shorts, the same rope sandals. There was no mistaking her for a boy this time. Sunglasses, a floppy straw hat with a madras band. Loose, as if she didn't know it was there stuck to her hand, she carried a satchel with a commercial logo printed on its side. She noticed me staring at it.

"Nike," she said. "Just do it."

"What?"

"Just do it. That's their advert. Dear God, Leonard, how long have you been kipped out here?"

"I don't know," I said. I should have given her an answer, it wouldn't have mattered. I simply couldn't think at the moment.

She walked up a foot in front of me, licked the end

of her index finger and wrote on my cheek. Hi, I sensed the wet letters. Her fingertip was soft and plump, but electric too, you could feel its shape pressing its own nest into my cheek. And warmth, like her fingers had been sunning themselves on a rock. It was the kindest touch since Provo when the estate agent had shaken hands.

"Hi." Close up, I could see the band of freckles under her tan. They ran across the bridge of her nose, the lightest flakes sprinkled about.

"Hi," I answered.

"Michael's gone off for a meeting. Dropped me here. He's a regular St. Nicholas."

I started to respond but I was afraid my voice would break. It was hard to get words out of the way before the next ones came along. My tongue clanged around in the mouth and couldn't do much. C. Aubrey and I didn't do much small talk.

"It was this or a deserted beach. I told him I'd prefer company for the day. We avoid the big cities." She went in and I followed to the kitchen. She unpacked bags of food from her satchel and arranged them into the refrigerator.

"Don't panic"—she read my eyes—"he'll be back for me. Hopes to make it by dinnertime if the ceilings hold. I've brought fresh fruit and vegetables. Limes. I'll fix a salad for lunch and for dinner we'll search out mussels."

She stood fussing at the counter. Her hair was straw white, could it have grown lighter? From the back she had a boy's silhouette above the waist, and when she moved her arms, the blades of her shoulders flashed through the skin. Her hips flared out, breathtakingly female. Looking at the way the denim creased and fit around her, reminded me of things I had forgotten. She turned and I could tell she knew how I'd been watching.

"I hope that's all right, my falling into your lap like this. It's rude, to barge in as we've done, but I hope it's all right."

"Of course." I was genuine but I couldn't get my voice to sound it. I used to be good at making my voice sincere, it didn't matter what I was thinking. "I don't have any plans I can't change." She smiled at that and slid past me into the room she and Michael had used before. "I'm fagged," she said. "We've been scud running since before dawn. I'll take a nap and maybe a swim before lunch."

"Good," I told her but the door had already closed.

I hung around while she slept. Fixed the leak in the hot water knob on the sink and arranged to reputty a cracked pane upstairs. Stuff I should have done months before but hadn't got around to. I tried to puzzle out my tug on seeing her. When the plane landed, I'd been pleased for the company, even though it was both of them. Michael would undertake an organ transplant without the replacement organ. When she stayed behind, you'd think I'd got what I wanted. But having her so close made me uncomfortable.

Soon all the panes in the window had new putty. I began to wonder if she would ever get up. Finally, the midday sun stashed in the back of the drawer, she rose.

Again she'd arrived with the provisions of a greengrocer. Michael is big on fresh fruits and vegetables, she told me. Very interested in health, is Michael.

She put things into a salad. That little delicate lettuce, the yellow-green kind, banana and figs. She had a package of soft rolls, bakery-new and speckled with bits of seed. I set their paper napkins on the table, I had mostly used a dish towel, and even spoons. She cleared and served pound cake from cellophane bags, with canned pears. She'd found little cups in the topmost cupboard, ramekins she called them. We sat and ate dessert.

"Don't you worry about your figure?" What a dopey thing to say.

"No. I don't pay it much mind."

"Well, you are what you eat."

"I don't think so," she dug up bits of cake, tilted her cup to get at them better. Her spoon went ching ching against the china, like a bird scratching the dirt. "I don't think I'm composed of mango and croutons and standing rib roast. I am composed of mercy, appetite, beauty and dominion." She looked up and drilled my eyes. "You too."

I had no answer for that. It was a great announcement and it made me feel important. I asked her if she wanted a drink and she said no, so I didn't have one either although I had a thirst. We sat at the table and talked. She told me about the Australian surf, and hitchhiking around the world. Isn't that dangerous, I asked, thinking of my own children, and she said no, not if you're careful. I figured if she could say it, maybe it was true. Arden was something of a dingbat—she told me if you trust people they'd do right by you—but I didn't want to argue. All the while she drew little [illegible]ures on a sketchpad. Noses, fifty different noses, trees, a conch shell, and stuff that was around. She told me about Michael's business, what they do in their little plane.

Michael started as an ordinary consumer, and when I scrinched my nose because I didn't understand, she said, a smoker. He found it harder and harder to get good boo, she called marijuana boo. He was living in Houston, and he'd bought some boo when he was in Mexico so he already had a source. Low down, she said, but a source. And he invented this scheme. He bought a Mazatlan condo and a jeep, put them both in a phony name. Advertised in the Houston paper to rent out the condo for a week's vacation, at a price under the market. Drive my car to Mexico and use my townhouse. He booked up in no time, it was a good deal. The tourists drove down. His man in Mazatlan would swap gas tanks and put in one that concealed fifty kilos of marijuana. The tourists then drove back to Houston, Michael would sell what they delivered at street prices. By the next ad he was up twenty grand.

Arden met him in Belize. He had bought an airplane to improve the lines of distribution. They stayed out of trouble by restricting the cargo to grass and by flying the middle leg. That's all we do, she explained. The middle leg. Mexico to the Bahamas.

"You don't have to be greedy. Hard drugs pay more, but they're trouble. With boo, people get caught flying at either end. For one thing, growers are amateurs. And there's too much hardware in the States. We pick up in Quintana Roo, Merida, Cancun, refuel in the Caymans, and dump in the Bahamas. Mexico is a breeze and so far in the Caymans they don't seem to care. But the

Bahamas can be tight. That's why finding you is so lucky. You're an alternate field just where we need one. Where the going can get tough."

"I don't want in this."

"Not to worry, Leonard. Michael is smart. He won't be here long. That's another of our secrets, how he stays safe. Keeps mixing the signals. Two months ago he liked the idea of traveling with a female, but he'll drop that too. The airplane, the numbers, me, he'll change it all."

"What happens next? To the boo?" It sounded silly when I said it.

She shrugged. "Not our concern. It gets in. Sometimes a mother ship, off-loaded by speedboats. Sometimes they find a mule willing to take in a suitcase on a cruise ship. Every so often they magnet a waterproof locker to the hull of the Love Boat. Divers remove it in Lauderdale. Different ways in."

"Why do you do it?"

Arden let slip an easy smile. Shrugged.

"Good dope, good sex." She shot me a look and caught me embarrassed. "And it's a rush. Gliding thirty feet over the water where the radar can't find you, putting down on beaches, on little Mexican strips lit by stars. Beats Brisbane."

Her words sent a shiver through me. A tiny plane flitting across the seas. Hofstadter and I had debated what we'd prefer if we were passengers in a plane that was going down, slow or gradual. I was trimming his hair with electric clippers. If the tail falls off, it will plunge like a stone. Or one engine goes out and you have a long, helical descent into the sea.

"That has to be better," I had argued. "At least you

have time to reflect, you have some hope."

"Hope is overrated. I would opt for fewer moments of abject terror, where there's no control or reflection. Only the certainty of that very short stop."

Hofstadter's description had given me the same shudder. "No," I told him. "You'd want the chance to think about your life. Isn't it supposed to pass before you?"

"You want a chance to think about your life, Mooney? You want one, you got it." He began to laugh, silently, little puffs of air coming out of the pumping shoulders. Like that smoker they used to have in Times Square, doughnuts of smoke popping silently from the billboard. "Don't worry about your life passing before you," Hofstadter said when he finished the puffs. "It already has."

"Is he a good pilot?" I asked Arden.

She rose and began to rinse off the dishes.

"Actually, he doesn't have a license. Doesn't want to be traced. But he certainly knows how everything works."

My forehead pulled into a frown. She caught it right away. "You don't have to worry about me, Leonard. My dad does that."

"Where's he now, your dad?"

She looked at me as if I might rat on her if she told. "In Brisbane."

"And he worries?"

She nodded. "It's his way of holding on."

"Maybe he sees you making mistakes."

That drew a smile. "I'm sure he does. They're bleeding obvious."

"And when you're making a mess of it, he worries."

"And he knows better? Give it up, Leonard. Give it fucking up." It hit me that she was only a few years older than Stacey.

She hung the dishtowel over the metal rod inside the center cupboard and stacked the cups in the rack to dry. "Come," she said. "We'll walk on the beach."

The surf was enormous. It looked two stories high and it rolled at us layered in white and black shelves. Rains sputtered about. Arden found a clump of mussels on the far rocks, where the island turned and headed north, and cut a handful free with Michael's spring-loaded knife. "We'll steam them up for dinner." She stuck her nose in their midst and sniffed deeply.

I grimaced. They looked unappetizing.

"You ought to be careful about this pot business. There's no going back on your acts."

She listened to this and bowed her head slightly. Like the start of a curtsy, a small thank you for your crapped-out advice.

"'Our acts our angels are.' Have you never heard that? No? It's from a hymn." And she began to sing, this tiny voice batting around in the gravely hiss of the surf. When she sang, the muscle between her eyebrows knit into a dart of concentration.

"Are you religious?" I asked when the song stopped. She surprised me, this girl-woman, how beautiful her voice was.

"Do you mean church? Balls, no."

The water was shuffling on top of itself, with the sound of a million grains of rice pouring into a tin silo. Mist settled on top of the waves.

"There'll be no flying tonight," she said, almost to herself. "We won't see Michael until the morning." That frightened me. He needed to come back. He was responsible for her, not me. The wind picked up and made a high sound off the water.

"Come," she said, loud into the whistle. "Let's swim."

She slipped her top over her head. She had small, ramekin breasts, and unmarked, golden skin. She stood, waiting for me. Then thumbed down her shorts and underpants in a single motion. I had yet to catch my breath, I could hardly decline for lack of it, though in truth I had no interest in swimming, and when still I stood there, looking over her head so as not to look at her, she turned and dashed into the surf. I thought I'd never see her again. She was beneath a wave, her perfect hips flashed, and then her feet, pressed in a steeple, followed and they too disappeared. The seas kept rolling in, you would think they were piling up to crush that slender body, and I grew anxious. I've lost her, I'd say, and Michael? Would he just shrug? Or would he dice me into a chopped salad.

I shed my shirt, pretending to be about to go after her, when she appeared, two or three tiers farther out, and waved. People ask themselves all the time, at least I do, is it real or am I imagining this? But they don't mean it. Standing on that beach—had I seen her body in front of me? her tanned skin, marked only by the knot-eyes of her nipples and navel, and the honey-brown tuft of hair—hardly enough colors to distinguish air from water, none left over for Arden?—I had this feeling *these* were my delusions, not the ones I'd been living with. These, the surf and the sky and the golden girl bobbing about.

After longer than I wished, she was running toward me. My shirt was in my hand, and I put it around her. It was wet through. She was laughing.

"You're very beautiful."

"Yes?" That pleased her, and her words came between breaths. "It is not their shape but their use, that they are humans."

"Who said that?"

"I did. Is someone else here?" She glanced back and I laughed. I was embarrassed by her nakedness, even under my shirt. The nice thing was she knew it and didn't tease me.

She picked up her clothes and the sinister clump of mussels and we walked back to the house. My arm was around her and she was shivering. By the time we reached the porch so was I, I was shivering and holding on for myself.

Arden took a shower and got into warm things. The folded knife had fallen from the pocket of her cutoffs and lay on the floor. Seeing it gave me an idea that I didn't do. I put it behind me. Instead, I lit some yellowed newspaper in the hearth and heaped on pine logs and driftwood. The fire crackled and spit colored flames, red-orange in the seams of the wood, and blues and yellows from the salts of the sea. Arden came out and put on a pot of water. We would have tea before dinner, she instructed.

"You know," I said. We were standing in the living room. "You really ought to let your hair grow."

Whatever I said hit the alarm.

"Listen, Leonard. Back the fuck off. My father is

right to worry, Michael is a bad influence, dealing is dangerous. Even, I swim too far out. Now this? I don't need it. Michael will torch this place in a minute, don't think he won't"

"Sorry," I said. I was, too. "I only meant..." I didn't want to finish.

"I know what you meant. I ought to let my hair grow, a nice hairdo would soften the face. Pity, isn't it, how she won't try a nice pageboy. And those studs and the nose ring. Just back the fuck off." She picked up the teapot and flung it. It bounced off the splashboard and into the sink.

I went outside and checked the generator. I'd lubricated it and set the brushes only weeks before, but I did again. When I came back she was fixing dinner.

"Can I help?" I asked.

"Sure," she said. The aluminum teapot was back on a burner and had up a head of steam. You'd have thought no words had passed between us.

On the broom closet door hung a stash of dried peppers, and Arden pulled one off. She handed me a yellow onion—"Michael doesn't take off without fuel and onions"—and we stood at the sink together. She popped the mussels in fresh water to breathe out the sand and steamed them for appetizers. Her favorite, she said, but they were too dark and sea-tasting for me. "You have to be careful," she told me as she downed the last. "A bad mollusk can do you in."

"Where'd you learn about cooking?"

"From Michael. He's really into seeing people enjoy themselves."

We emptied a tin of corned beef and boiled it with

a head of cabbage she'd brought from the plane. The way humans eat. She asked me how I got here and I talked about Hofstadter and his putting me in his will, and working for the courts and Canges. I even told her about Mrs. Segura. The food made me talky, the way whiskey does the rummy, I just opened up. Rains drummed against the house, it sounded like a sandstorm, we might have been lost in the Sahara.

I did the dishes. Afterward, she rummaged in the linen closet and found the shoebox of chess pieces. Missing a black rook and a white pawn. Asked if I played.

We set up the board with a wooden spool and a toothpaste top to fill out the set. They worked fine. She beat me two games, but they were close. Then I taught her Ssech. She didn't much care for it.

"Where will Michael spend the night?" I asked. She raised her brow as if who knows?

"Does he get jealous?"

"Why Leonard, are you thinking of making your move?" That embarrassed me again. She was younger than Stace. That was exactly what I'd been thinking, but Michael wouldn't shrug at that. I poured myself a drink and sat on the porch. I didn't get it. Was she a ward or a forbidden lover? I couldn't tell.

When I came in, she was sketching seabirds. I sat and watched. She went on about dust. How most of the dust in the universe works in unity, but some motes drift off and swirl about, lost for eons. Some motes join together, form a brain, and discover reason. But they're still lost and need to return to unity. Good vibratory patterns will do it. My stomach had vibratory patterns from the mussels. It was all ditzy stuff, and if she hadn't been so good at drawing or I hadn't been lost in the universe, I wouldn't have paid any mind. She stuck her arm at a funny angle to shade the gull feathers. I moved over on the cruddy daybed couch to see. She could draw like anything.

Finally, she turned in. I wasn't tired so I sat up and watched the fire. Through that flimsy door she lay between my sheets, that unmarked body, those eyes closed and unguarded. Her eyes were remarkable. You know how if you look at most people, you see the same thing. Canges, for example, or Michael, in their eyes they're suspicious, alert and ready to feed. In hers wasn't any of that. In hers you saw yourself. Mange-bitten and dismal, but yourself, like it was on polished stone.

What I didn't do but thought about? While she was showering? I thought to carve a hole in the boards upstairs. Her knife sat on the floor, and her room was just below mine. All I needed to do was slice a crack through the caulking that held the boards together, there was no subfloor or insulation or anything. I would have had time to clean up the shavings. Her body was so beautiful, that was all, and too I wanted to see her sleeping. That's what I thought of, how it would be to see her sleeping.

In the middle of the night, restless and wide awake, I went downstairs. I'd decided to try to sleep when she did, when it was dark. But I'd gotten used to the night, there wasn't so much to see. For a second thing, I was agitated—all that humanity and good food. It brought on a natural anxiety that it couldn't last.

Two sheets of sketched seabirds lay on the kitchen table. They were like pages from a parts catalogue. Some drawings were large, full detail you could see the feathers under the wing, flexed and holding air. Others were no more than a quick vee. Quietly I opened her door. If she'd been undressed or anything, I was ready to shut it fast. At least I told myself that. But she wasn't—she was sound asleep in a white T-shirt, the sheet pulled to her chest. She looked about ten. I sat down on the edge of her bed. Her eyes moved beneath the closed lids, slithered around, and her nostrils twitched like they had hold of a soft perfume in the air. I went back upstairs. I was proud that I hadn't carved that hole, I felt good about myself. Another sensation, equally strong. I wished I had.

I slept eventually. Like a dead man, except that for the first time in a while I dreamed. For a long time with my drinking, my dreams had all died, but this night I was visited by a vivid, life-size movie.

In it, Tommy is on the floor of his room. He is drawing on a huge roll of brown butcher paper. Its edges are crenellated, like a castle wall. Looking at the chaotic drawing, I can't see him. The paper has coiled around him and it guards him, flattens out in front where he's drawing. And as I watch, he chalks in the sea. White and cerulean chalk, blue-green poster paint, black grease pencil. I stick around, waiting for him to sketch some people swimming in the water, a dog barking on the beach. I mention to him how it would give scale, but he doesn't hear. Maybe a family, I say to help, maybe a kid flying a kite. But he keeps chalking in wave after wave, layered, some giant's deck of cards, shuffle, cut and deal a zillion hands of foam.

CHAPTER 19.

Alice received the news of my departure with equanimity. She and I had stopped sleeping together, we simply lost interest, forgot about it, and by this time the doormats had been successfully coordinated and all the valences hung. Alice received the news without rancor or emotion or even blinking. She told me a divorce for people at our stage should be simple and if I like, if I am eager to get underway, she would handle it. I told her I like. I need not be concerned about the property I've received from Hofstadter, she said, inheritances are not considered spousal property in our state and so we should have no difficulty splitting up our assets. That's very good to hear, I responded. Alice is a good sport, she was since that very first day at Miramonte. She offered to list the house and handle the sale for half the usual commission, and I readily agreed.

There was more stress at work. The files of the Surrogate's Court are open to the public, and after I gave notice Canges got hold of Hofstadter's will. Pretty soon he put it about that I'd come into a fortune. No one knew what the actual values were, but everyone assumed that an inheritance meant a large inheritance. The Clerk called me in.

"You're leaving us, Mooney." It was not a question, but a declaration. The Clerk was seated at her busy desk, peering over the top of a pair of glasses. Even sitting, the Clerk had authority, she might have been a bishop announcing my excommunication. My impulse, which I fought away, was to deny everything and repent.

"Yes, a week from tomorrow."

"I hear you've come into money."

I shrugged. If I spoke, it would be to apologize, so I just shrugged.

"Wealth without labor," she held up her index finger and shook it at the ceiling of her office, maybe at God, "is a mixed blessing. There are dangers. Don't let yourself wander down that road, it leads to uselessness." What made her think I had any more of the journey to go?

"I would wish you well, Mooney, but I don't believe it will do you any good." I nodded, was dismissed.

With the vacation I had coming I could have gone immediately. Mrs. Segura's case was set for hearing, so instead I stayed on an extra week. The finance company had filed a motion for summary judgment. Assisted by a Spanish-speaking woman at Legal Aid, Mrs. Segura answered the complaint, but now the company maintained she admitted that payments hadn't been made in months, there was no need for a trial, and they wanted their refrigerator back. It was one of thirty motions for summary judgment this finance company had set during a fifteen-minute period at two forty-five on a Wednesday afternoon. I telephoned her the night before.

"Make sure you're in court. You never know what will happen, and you want to be there."

"*Claro que sí*," she answered. "I understand."

I pulled the jackets for the court hearings. I found hers, and, slouching low in the desk chair, straightened the fasteners and slid the finance company's motion off the clips and into the wastebasket. I stuck the jacket back with the others, and the runner carried away the batch of them in a shopping cart for the hearing.

That afternoon, I made it over to her courtroom. A random few were waiting, courtrooms always look like an old Greyhound terminal, there were arraignments scheduled for three and probation hearings for three-thirty. Mixed with the misdemeanants—isn't that the best title? just beats the shit out of them and makes them watch their shoes?—was the usual litter of hangers-on, retired folk, family. On cold or stormy days the homeless came to get out of the weather and if they didn't smell too bad we let them stay. A couple of lawyers in slope-heeled loafers.

Mrs. Segura arrived at quarter of three on the nose. The judge had begun to call the cases, his watch was fast and you went by his watch. I couldn't maneuver to sit by her without being conspicuous, but I watched her. Her face was a Madonna's, she had this perfect and dark profile and while she seemed to comprehend nothing around her, from the set of her mouth you sensed it didn't matter. The judge was entering summary judgments one after the other in a tired voice, bam, bam, he could have been throwing out junk mail. When he called her case she stood up. She was the only defendant to appear. It stopped him, he was caught in the headlights of her eyes.

"Mrs. Segura?"

"Yes, Judge." She said *judge* funny, her J was a cross between W and a guttural growl. Whudge.

"You're here? Let the record reflect that the defendant Isabel Segura is in court. Are you represented?"

"Huh?"

"Do you have a lawyer?'

"No Judge. No lawyer." She turned to look at me and I was filled with a terror that she was going to mention my name. But the judge wasn't watching.

"Do you have anything to say about this motion, Mrs. Segura?"

"Yes Judge. I need my refrigerator." The finance company lawyer snorted, and the court reporter laughed mostly silently, but the judge, I could tell, Mrs. Segura had smitten him too.

"Well," he said and he tilted his glasses forward and opened the manila jacket. "Let's see what this is all about. Summary judgment on an installment note. Where's the motion?"

The finance company lawyer jumped up.

"There's no motion in here," said the judge.

"We filed it, your honor. I have here a certificate of mailing showing it was filed and a copy was sent to the defendant at her last known address."

"That may be as it is, young man. But there's no motion in the jacket. I'm going to put this case over. You'll have to refile and get yourself a hearing date."

"Your honor," said the lawyer.

"No your-honoring now. That's it. Now look, son, winning twenty-nine motions out of thirty isn't a bad batting average." The lawyer sat down.

"Mrs. Segura, thank you for coming in. You can go. And for now you can keep your refrigerator."

I caught up with her in the hall.

"You were great, Isabel. You keep doing that, showing up and fighting. I can't be here much longer, but if you keep fighting them, you may just win."

She looked at me funny, a little smile in her eyes. "You rootin' for me?"

"I'm rootin' for you."

"But you with them."

"Still, I'm rootin' for you." She smiled this time on her lips. Then she took her pinky finger and reached up. I'm short, sixty-seven inches if each one shows up and works hard, but she was shorter. She reached up and touched the tip of my nose.

Later I was at my desk in the bullpen. I was thinking of her touch, thinking that maybe it would help if we all called them Whudges. Nobody would have to be afraid of them. From across the room, Canges saw me smiling. "Ah," he said in his announcer's voice, "Mooney is dreaming of his nights in Sonora. Or maybe his nights in Señora?"

I ignored him. For one thing, I don't like vulgar jokes. Canges wouldn't quit.

"I tell you, ladies and gents. I saw the two of them in the hall." He was declaiming this, so everyone in the bullpen could hear. "Quite a touching scene. Touching. Literally. Leonard is not going to go hungry. I think our Leonard has plans to be dining on Mexican taco soon.

Watch out, Leonard. Don't get *la tourista*."

This brought the usual laugh.

I kept my eye on the file, I didn't have much time left in the office. Sure enough, two days later the identical motion came through the mails. Mrs. Segura was back in the system, her refrigerator was again in the cross-hairs of the finance company.

Cases go by in bunches, like bananas. We don't do a single of anything. That gave me the idea. Every so often, to clear the shelves, the Clerk orders us to flip through and assemble the cases where there's been no activity for a couple years. Then we prepare orders to dismiss them for the chief judge to sign. The Clerk does it all, but the chief judge backs her up. It's called For Want of Prosecution, and it's legal, there's a rule and all. Instead of waiting for the Clerk to initiate it, I did. No one would ever complain, because these cases are just swept aside, it's like housecleaning, and no one would ever suspect that anyone in the Clerk's office except the Clerk herself initiated anything. So I stayed late one day, went through the shelves and picked out two dozen cases where there had been no activity. Then I typed up orders to dismiss for each of them. There was nothing to that, all you did was photocopy a form and fill in the name and number of the case. They were all alike, fish in a school. Except I stuck in the Segura case.

No one had to con a judge. I felt good about that, I didn't want to con a judge. I left the stack on Canges's desk. The elves and the shoemaker, while he was off at a topless bar, someone did his work for him. And the next morning, Canges took the bait. I watched him crate up the stack, note the numbers, and send the packet off to Motion Term. I would have loved to be around when they investigated why an active case has been dismissed, when they found Canges's initials on the folder. I'd fly back from the islands. But all leave-takings involve a loss, Reba told me that about our divorce, and I had to lose the opportunity to see Canges roasted on a spit. By midday all twenty-five orders were back, to be stuck in the jackets. The case of E-Z Finance against Mrs. Segura had been dismissed.

I dropped in on her that night. She was wearing a black dress and around her neck a little silver cross. Most women her age have lines at the neck, but her skin was taut and perfect. On the television set a sitcom was playing at high volume and we sat at the gray dinette table, watching and talking. Loud, above the laugh track. I asked about her son, and she said he hadn't been bothering her lately. I was saving my news. I asked what he does, and that confused her because apparently he doesn't do anything. He hangs out with his family and his girlfriend, he drinks beer, and every so often he steals money from her. I complimented the cross she was wearing and she told me she was a religious woman. *Muy réligioso*. She picked it off her chest and held it out to me. I reached out and let the chain drape over my hand. My knuckles grazed her throat. The silver was warm from her skin.

Then I told her about the case. "It may not last. The finance company might figure out what happened and come back after you. But they've got dozens of cases. Chances are you won't hear from them again."

I gave her a copy of the signed order of dismissal and told her to keep it with her valuable papers. I know that's dumb, she had no valuable papers, but it's what I said. She nodded her head and folded the paper into thirds. Carefully, each fold straight on the line of the other and she sharpened the edge by pressing her thumbnail to it.

"So," she said and Velcroed those flat black eyes on mine. "Do you want to fuck me?"

Well, the thing of it is, I did. Of course I did. But I didn't. Not after the way she put it and especially not after what Canges said. I was thinking that if I did somehow it would show, Canges would be all over me the next day at the office. Later, when it was too late, I remembered. There was no next day. I was off to the island.

* *

Soon after sunup I was awakened by the bird-squeal of a door, rusted hinges on the back shed, the clanging as it closed. I dressed and went down to find Arden. She was not in the house. I poured a mug of the coffee she'd brewed and went to look for her. Outside rain dripped from every leaf and eave, and the morning sun, white and uninterrupted as we hadn't seen for days, lit up the world like the bright end of a carwash. I followed a whooshing sound out to the strip. Arden had fetched Hofstadter's large garage broom and was pushing sheets of water across the slick marl. Water rolled from hollow to hollow, and before it could come to rest she chased it down, rooted it from the pool it was forming and rolled it into the tangled growth at the edge. She wore her denim shorts and a faded pink knit shirt. Her bare feet had printed a petal pattern in the earth.

When I reached her she stopped and, a little breathless, explained. "I thought I'd just brush off the excess. Then the heat of the day will dry it off. As it is he can't put down here."

"There are worse things," I said.

She smiled. "Promises, promises." I couldn't tell whether she was teasing. I took the broom from her hand and laid it down. I thought to kiss her, but instead, I turned her toward the north.

She asked me questions on the way, twice like a little kid where are we going. "This," I said when we got there, "this is an improvement on the broom." I threw open the doors of the shed.

"Golly Miss Molly!" she yelled. "Can you make it go?"

I took the seat of the machine and hoisted her up beside me. There was just enough room for her to stand. The cat fired on the first try and I backed into the sun. Then I gave a quick lecture on levers and pedals. Pulled on the handbrake, inched around and pushed her into the iron seat. I was standing behind, holding on to her shoulders. "The airport, please. And step on it."

She jammed the gas levers so hard I went off the back, but I clambered on again at the gully. The cat raced, she gave a war whoop and drove out, straight line, both tracks fueled to full stop. You had to turn the cat by manipulating each tread, there's no wheel, but Arden couldn't have cared less about turns. Top speed, maybe ten, down the road the cat had made for itself, up the far side and onto the strip.

Once she lowered the blade, you'd have thought she would slow down. Nothing doing. Water and mud sloshed around, crabs from the barracks, the underground population must have thought it was Pearl Harbor Day for crustaceans. You couldn't make yourself heard over the noise. I leaned over and turned the key in its slot.

"Listen, don't take off the clay. We're only just above sea level."

"Roger," she cried, cranking it up.

By the time we finished peeling off a skin, the sun was high and steamy. Large blisters of the rectangle were drying to a coffee color. The pooled water lay in shallows. Tan speckles covered her face, mine also I suppose, she had mud in her hair, in her ears, flecking her eyebrows. We put the cat away and walked the length back toward the house.

"You should get cleaned up," I told her. I wished we had more land to bulldoze. God, I could have scraped all the way to Key West if there'd only been earth to move.

"You too. We'll use nature's bath." I knew she meant for us to take a swim, but I don't swim. Or not well. Her shirt had dime-sized bleach marks on the sleeve. I hadn't thought much of sex since I came here, it had just left my life. Sex and touch and doing kind deeds, they had disappeared like a magazine subscription you let run out. Once it was gone it was gone. Ever since she'd landed I had thought of not much else. But in my mind's eye, it was Michael, not me, who was making love to her. What would Hofstadter's shrink say about that, where your own fantasies cast someone else in the leading role and you don't get an audition?

We were standing on the beach that led to the house. She unfastened the single button at the neck of her shirt and stripped it off.

"These will need laundering," she said, casual as if she were making an inventory. I began to undress, realized I was reacting to her presence, slowed down. She stood naked in front of me. Her skin was the color of a statue, a lion, I could not find breath enough to touch her. Everywhere that she hadn't been covered she was splattered with mud. I summoned my courage, undid my belt and lowered my trousers. Looking on her, on her beauty had visibly affected me. I don't know what expression percolated to my face, I can't imagine a suitable one. She could see I was embarrassed.

"I'm very flattered," she said softly. Then placed the palms of her hands against my chest and, balancing carefully on them, leaned forward and kissed me, the lightest kiss, on the lips. Two little doughnuts of flesh that grazed each other.

"Life, Leonard. Life." My eyes were still closed from the kiss. "You'll like it."

And she took my hand and walked with me into the surf. We held hands the whole time. The sun was brand spanking new, and the water had more colors than I've ever seen, maybe fifty kinds of blue. Cream and white and ivory, a dozen greens. We ducked under the rolling waves, they were gentle and no higher than my head. The storms early that week had kicked up the surf, had passed on, someone else's headache. We ducked into the water, swam and played and it felt like we were being born.

As we walked back a sparrow landed in the dune grasses. She ran ahead. I gathered the clothing we'd scattered and held it to my chest. She reappeared with two slices of bread, rubbing her palms together to break them up. Then she scattered the crumbs. The bird started right in.

We stood naked, a foot apart. "Birds are returning spirits. This is the aura of someone you know. Maybe your friend."

"Hofstadter? I don't think so. His style is more crab."

"Maybe a friend who's still alive. Or maybe Hofstadter, spirits can take different shapes."

I gave the bird a serious look. It had no pockets to stash a pack of Camels. "No," I said. "No nicotine stains, no Hofstadter."

Arden nodded at this as truth.

She walked to the house and went right into the shower. I put the clothes down in a lump and followed. The shower curtain was open, it didn't bother her. I stood, waiting my turn, and watched. Voiceless. If Judgment Day started right then and they began calling the roll for attendance I could not have said Here.

I took my shower next. As I walked out, drying myself, I glanced into her room. She lay in bed, the sheet pulled about her. I can't say whether she moved when I went by, but if she did it was to inch back, to make room.

"When Stace was a kid," I said. I swear, that's what came to me.

"When Stace was a kid she used to be scared of grasshoppers." Don't ask me why. Arden let me off the hook. She didn't say a thing. We dressed and made a pot of noodles for lunch, which I overcooked and burned the sauce as I went on about grasshoppers and Tommy's dog and who knows what else.

How many times have I made love in my life? How many do I remember? Where have they gone? What have become of the rest?

CHAPTER 20.

I slept. I hadn't had a drink in a while, but I slept anyway. When I awoke, Arden was fussing about with the laptop and phone. She wore a white sleeveless blouse with Mexican needlework doodled about the collar.

"Do you know, I can find anyone listed in a U.S. telephone directory?" she asked.

"Who are you looking for?"

"That's just it, isn't it? I don't know anyone. I've looked up Michael's parents. Watch, I'll bet I can find you."

I didn't say anything.

"Or Reba. Want to?"

"No," I said. "I know where she is."

I went into the kitchen, opened a tin and made chicken sandwiches. We ate two apiece and drank Modelo Negro beer cold out of the bottle.

"I've been thinking," she said. "When we leave, simply park your bulldozer in the middle of the strip."

"Why do that?"

"To keep unwanted visitors away. Your runway is

difficult enough. Foreshortened no one will risk it, there's not enough length divided in half. And no one will try to steer around it."

"But I want you to come back."

"Leonard," she had Reba's Leonard down pat. "Leonard, do as I say. You're a sitting duck out here. A lot of people in this line of work would love to find a private strip six hundred nautical miles off the coast of Florida. Some of them are not quite as civilized as Michael. And don't be misled. He is barely our side of the Bronze Age."

I didn't say a thing. But my wince gave me away and she smiled the way you do when the needle goes in, to show you don't mind. After lunch she announced she wanted to cut my hair, make me presentable. She had me carry one of the straight-backed chairs from the kitchen outside to the flat stretch of sand between the porch and the dunes. She brought a sheet and tools from her toilet kit, a comb, a pair of scissors.

I sat, she spread the sheet over me professionally, tucked it at the neck, and began to trim. Slid the fingers of her left hand across my scalp to grasp and measure and snipped with the right. "You have nice hair," she said. "How do you want it?"

"Like yours."

"Sorry. That needs electric clippers. I'll do what I can."

The sun was bright and a breeze came off the water. Hair fell away in white locks, when had it turned? Her hands went over my head, gently holding and cutting. I saw into the armhole of her sleeve, how her muscle flexed, how the breast moved. She fixed her eyes on her work.

"You're a trusting one," she said. Her body moved around me. I could close my eyes and know where she was from the airy scent of her shadow.

I wanted not to talk. "Yes?"

"You've a right to be. Trusting. I know what I'm doing. Used to cut my brothers' hair. I like it. I'm in charge."

The snipping was irregular, like a clock with its own rhythm. At first it made me flinch. The comb was trying to make a part, but from her tiny pout I could tell it was failing. Wisps of hair lit on my lower lip. She moved her thumb lightly to clear them, then blew. I was a mouse to her snake.

"Don't go away," she said and went inside. Returned carrying a bowl of hot water, soap, and a razor. She used a washcloth to swirl the soap into a lather, and shaved my neck in front where it joined the beard and in back a straight line at the base of the skull. Then she trimmed the remaining beard, scrutinizing and clucking all the while the scissors snipped away.

I kept thinking of the Hunchback. He takes care of the bells in the cathedral tower, and when he screws up they whip him in the square, and this beautiful woman brings him water. Was she redheaded or did I just imagine that? It's an old movie, black and white, so how would I know about the red hair? The old Hunchback is this God-forgiven cripple and he spaz-talks, his tongue is the size of a pear and it sticks in his mouth. A young woman with long curls brings him water and sponges off his brow. I asked Did she know the movie, and she said, sure, it's a Disney, isn't it? I said no, because that just couldn't be. The one I was thinking of couldn't be a Disney.

Sooner than I wanted we were finished. She rubbed my scalp, scrubbed the shaved parts with the warm cloth. She stepped back and removed the sheet with a flourish. "Olé." She insisted I go in to see the result. Arden had rehung the mirror in the bathroom. Looking in it I saw an ordinary man. Grizzled and boiled in the sun, but for the most part sane, like the people you found in the grocery line. A man who could pass, you might ask him for directions, no visible traces of madness save a slender rim of red about the eye and, of course, the halo.

We walked along the beaches. I had lived on this island for months, maybe longer, and I had never walked the beaches. How the waves shaped the land. Every cove seemed the kind you see in magazines with the slim couple swimming, she in a one-piece white bathing suit.

"Where do you suppose they get their colors?" I must have sounded like a schoolboy, but I'd never noticed them before. You could talk that way with Arden, she was a little goo-goo herself.

"You know about that from physics," she said.

"Tell me."

"What we see is merely what's reflected back. If everything is reflected and nothing absorbed, we see white. If everything is absorbed, black. White and black, both voids. Only when some of the rays are reflected do we see color."

I really liked to hear her talk.

"So I'm seeing color and generating color."

"You are in the universe, Leonard. Even a dumb rock spinning in space is a unit of matter and a unit of energy. It transforms one into the other. You are no less."

"That's nice," I said. "To be floating around the universe as a unit of energy."

"It is more than nice. You inhabit a body and a

spiritual realm at the same time. You are a numinous substance in the ebb and flow of the earthly sphere."

What she was saying was not exactly Catechism, but I must say it made me feel perky all the same. Nice was enough for me. Like belonging to a special club, and no greens fees. A numinous substance in the ebb and flow of the earthly sphere. Walking barefoot along a beach with this dingbat, it was easy to believe.

We fetched Hofstadter's fishing gear from the shed. I had never taken it out, had no interest in it or the sea, but she was excited and we scrounged up the rod and a small latched tackle box that jangled with hooks and swivels and weights. On the floor of the living room closet I'd seen an ancient reel frozen with rust. She told me the names of the parts. I broke it down on the kitchen table, steel-wooled the obvious stuff and lubricated the gears. Soon it was humming. Arden rigged the line with a bait hook and gray sinkers the shape of a pyramid, and in the lavender of the afternoon we went out and stood knee deep in the surf. The sand sank away below my feet, I felt like a tree that had grown there. I gave an awkward heave.

"No, no." The sinkers didn't make it past the waves. "It's all in the timing. And the hands."

She thumbed back the bailing guard and poised the weights behind her, then with an easy flick of the rod cast the line thirty yards from where we stood, beyond the swells. The rig plunked into the glassy surface.

"Wow. Where'd you learn to cast like that?"

"Australia, mate." She was pleased with herself. "We're surrounded by the stuff. Water, about which we say, since fish pee in it, you want to make sure you never take it without whiskey."

We fooled around for an hour without a bite. Whenever we got bored, Arden switched baits. She started with little sand crabs she'd dug up on shore, stuck live on the nasty hook without a moment's compassion, then some awful bottled stuff we found in the tackle box. Nothing. We scrounged up a quahog. Arden opened a jackknife to scrape its insides, then ran the hook twice through the tough part, a long string the consistency of a rubber band. That did the trick. On her second try she hooked up sharply. The line ran out but she stopped it, cranked in and landed a flopping fish. Great glee, running backward out of the surf to bring it to air, then fussed around getting it unhooked.

"Leonard, get a priest. In the tackle box. It's suffocating." The fish made her tender where the crabs and the clam were chum. Go figure what fires our mercies. I found a sap in the box, a foot-long wooden bat weighted with lead in the end. Arden dispatched the fish with a single downward blow.

"That's a jack," she said. "They school. Get the line back in." In a matter of minutes we had two more. That was all she wanted.

She cleaned them on the beach, slick as can be filleted two steaks from each fish and threw the leavings back into the surf. Recycling, she said. Their souls go up to be caught again in heaven, their innards remain below. Food for our food.

The sun was a hand's width above the horizon, hurting our eyes. We walked back toward the house to the drone of an engine. As we stood watching, an airplane flew low above. Low and slow, as if it was going to land. It wasn't Michael, this showed two engines, its underside was painted the tan of my trousers. Arden said its name, it's an Aztec. She frowned and looked mean at it, tried to scowl it away. The plane made a right-angle turn a mile beyond the island's point, flew a short straight leg and then a second bank at us again, and descended toward the strip. It looked for all the world that he was going to set down. The line the chisel had made on my chest began to throb, and I thought of Arden's words, I should have taken her advice and parked that bulldozer. Blocked them all, Michael too.

The Aztec gradually lost altitude, following the same line that Michael had used to land. Then it hovered at tree line, flew the entire strip fifteen feet above the ground, and when it reached the north end climbed back into the sky.

I looked at her. "Good riddance."

"No such luck. He's taken its measure," she said. "He's figuring whether the strip is long enough, dry enough."

"What did he decide?"

She frowned. Wait and see. I walked back to the house carrying the rod and four of the fish steaks. Adrenaline and fear tingled the skin of my cheeks like bay rum. This was how I would fight him off if he returned, fish steaks and pitchfork. Two days before it wouldn't have mattered, I would have signed over the deed. You start to care about anything, it comes with hurt. You can't help it, if you want to keep something you stand a chance of losing it, they come together. Like a razor and razor blades. Smart packaging.

I wrapped the fish and she stacked them in the

refrigerator, both of us silent and listening. Sure enough, I was at the kitchen sink, soaping the strange scent of blood off my hands, when the hum returned overhead. Engines slow, now I recognized the sound. A slight pitch change as he made the first turn, then the second. I walked out the back stairs. C. Aubrey watched me and didn't make a sound, sat there trying not to be noticed. A lot of help your friends are.

The twin was slowing even more. Softening up, hanging on to the air. "Full flaps," Arden said at my side. "He's putting down." For a kid once removed from a kid who wasn't a pilot she seemed to know this stuff. The Aztec lowered itself behind the trees. It was down. We heard the airplane reach the far end, turn around and taxi back toward the house. When he got there, fifty feet from where we stood, he turned again and revved the engines. Maybe he was going to leave. Maybe he just wanted to see if he could do it, and now he was going to leave. Before I could advance this notion, the engines died. I walked the ten steps back to the tool locker and took out the pitchfork.

"Are you going to stack hay at a time like this?"

I didn't answer. She sounded assured, but standing next to me she was nervous as I was. If not when she spoke then a moment later, I felt her tremble when a squat man, maybe my height and easily twice as wide, walked through the palm break. He was wearing black cotton trousers, highly polished cowboy boots, the expensive kind you see on stockbrokers, and a white tropical shirt buttoned at the wrists. The shirt wasn't tucked in, it draped evenly over his paunch. His hair was clipped close, like Nancy's friend Sluggo, the black spots of a stubble as if he hadn't had it shaved in two days, and his neck was wide as a thigh. It entered his shoulders in folds, maybe he could extend it to catch a passing mosquito. We stood there looking at each other. He was watching the pitchfork in my hand, I was holding on at the ferrule, Arden and I must have looked like that painting. Below his overhanging shirt, tucked into a wide leather belt worn about his crotch, how did I not notice it before, was a pistol. Not a revolver, this thing clearly could not revolve. Square, black, and about the size of a medium pizza.

We stood sheriff and bad guy, it looked like a tie until I notice the pistol, still I stood there waiting for an opening line when, of all things, came the sound of a second airplane. Arden and I looked up, he didn't. "Michael," she said. I was relieved. The chiseled line on my breastbone pulsed anew, fresh-minted acids dripped into my rumbling stomach, but still I was relieved. More so when our visitor said the same thing.

"Michael."

"You know him?"

He pursed his lips. He wasn't talking while the flavor lasts. Finally he spoke.

"He is my partner." The man had a thick foreign accent I couldn't place, east of France and west of Korea. I reversed the pitchfork, planted its tines in the soil, and came forward with my hand out. His expression didn't change. I stopped. We stood frozen until Michael's plane landed, turned, ran up the engine and shut down. Michael came through the break.

"Fat Man. Enough room?"

"Two hundred feet to spare. Just like you said."

Fat Man kept his eyes on Arden and me, unsure of what we might do.

"That's Arden, Fat Man. That's my punch."

The newcomer looked at us, decided Michael meant the girl. "Good day, Arden." He dipped in a slight bow.

"And next to the punch, that's the crazy fuckin' hermit."

"Good day, hermit." Again the courtly nod.

"Arden," Michael called. He hadn't reached us yet. "There's Tecata in the ice chest, tap me one will you? And tie it down? I've had a tough fuckin' day."

"Listen," I said to Michael and they all did. "Listen, you should watch your language." The tone was how I would talk to Tommy. But Michael didn't take offense. He glanced over his shoulder, as if maybe his language was coming loose from its moorings, it needed watching. He turned back to me, mystified. He might have been seeing me for the first time.

"Here," Michael spoke up and tossed what looked to be a canister to Arden. She snared it one-handed. "Peel off three for the hermit. Landing fees."

He had thrown her a roll of American money. She undid the rubber band, one of those wide ones the kids used to keep on their soccer shin guards, and unrolled three bills. Handed them to me. Three thousand dollars. They added fear to my fear, but I balled them up and stuck them in my pocket.

The motion broke the stalemate. "Fat Man will be staying the night," Michael announced. "We brought pork chops, steaks. Red wine and artichokes."

Arden told him of the fish we caught. "You eat fish, Fat Man? Sure, that'll do. Meat's frozen in the Igloo, it'll keep."

There was a tension, suddenly I had Bogart's role in *Key Largo* and I couldn't for the life of me remember what happened to him at the end of the movie. I had to think he did better than Eddie Robinson, but I wished I could remember. We went into the house. Just do as he says, Arden whispered to me, but so far he hadn't said anything.

They moved right in. Fat Man was rude like Michael but at the same time gracious, his glance told you he knew you were scared of him. Not Michael. Michael had this attitude that he doesn't care what you think, he's in business for himself. Truth is, I admire it, if you had it you could live in the midst of people and never worry about them, what the Clerk thought, or Canges or who was laughing at you.

Fat Man walked around the living room. He examined every ash tray, every shelf. He passed close to me and I smelled motor oil and tobacco on his clothes, he might be a bus driver, a mechanic. The effort he took in speaking his few words made his eyes blink. In the one closet he found the stack of games. He took out a dandelion yellow cardboard box and dumped dominoes onto a card table. Sat with a grunt, dealt out two hands face up, and began to play them both.

If I put the towel out for Isaac, what then? They'd probably understand that as a signal, and if not they would know once Isaac landed. I could see a red line chisel-width on his beautiful skin. Better to wait? I couldn't tell. I decided to muddle through dinner and see what developed.

* *

Michael showered. Maybe my hair and Arden's were

in the drain, maybe Michael would detect our tandem showers by spooning out samples and sending them to the lab.

Arden and I unloaded the beer and food from the plane. Chose four cold cans by the ice packs and cracked them. Michael drank one off, folded it, tossed it to the floor, and opened a second. Fat Man sat across from him, and wordlessly each set up a line of the tiles. As it grew dark, Arden began dinner. The smell of browning onions filled the house. I hung out by her, listening to the static of the fry pan and the occasional click of tiles from the living room. They were playing for high stakes, I saw piles of dollars on the table. She cooked the fish steaks rare, she said that was best, and drowned them in lime juice.

When the food was ready we served them around their game and pulled up chairs to watch. For minutes no one spoke.

"Nice hairdo," Michael said to his plate. I didn't respond.

"You, hermit. Did you hear me? I said, nice hairdo."

"Thanks." I was forcing down a forkful of fish.

"You must have one devoted barber. To make the trip way the fuck out here to cut your hair."

I drank some beer. Studied the printing on the can. Hecho en Mexico. Michael finished his, crushed the can and tossed it into the corner.

"Put your empties in the trash," Fat Man said. Michael ignored him.

"Don't you hear me, hermit? You must have one devoted barber."

"Arden cut it."

"Is that right? Well, she's quite a girl, is Arden. Isn't she?"

"Leave it, Michael." Arden spoke evenly, but you knew it was a reprimand. I wanted to take a leak but I thought if I stood up he'd order me to stay.

"Quite a girl. What do you think, Fat Man? Isn't she quite a girl." He reached to his back pocket, took out the chisel, clunked it onto the table. "Did you ever notice, Leonard? Her breasts taste like the sea. Salty but nice. Ever notice that?"

Fat Man burped. "Sorry," he said.

"No need to apologize," said Arden. "Nature's call."

"Ever notice that, hermit?"

Arden went on. "When I was a kid we used to have contests."

"Contests?" Fat Man rose for another beer. "What contests?" he asked from the kitchen.

"Burping. My oldest brother could rattle the windows." Then she forced a burp, a good one, and Fat Man laughed admiringly. "We wanted him to play the Opera House in Sydney." She did a second, but without force. Fat Man laughed. He tried soundlessly, looking like he might gag, and Arden imitated his bulging cheeks.

"That's enough. It makes me sick," Michael said.

"He would do it when the teacher's back was turned."

Fat Man tried again and, failing again, downed his beer in one slug. "I am not shitting," Michael said. He picked up the chisel and held it to the table blade down. "That's disgusting. It makes me sick."

And Fat Man burped. He and Arden laughed.

"Sorry, Michael," he said looking to Arden. "Nature's call."

I offered to do up the dishes. I was happy to get to the sink. I would have emptied their bed pans.

"I'll take the couch," Fat Man said. "I don't want to throw you two out of your bed."

"No problem," Michael told him. "You've had a long night. She and I will sleep outside, bags and a tent."

"You sure?" Fat Man seemed senior to Michael but he bowed to his temper. He didn't want any favors.

"Absolutely. If the weather turns we'll put the hermit on the couch. Besides, it's a pretty night. Nothing like a good pounce under the stars."

I was scrubbing the fry pan when Fat Man entered the bedroom. In minutes I heard his snore. Michael and Arden went to see to the airplanes, I wasn't sure what they were doing, but Michael's voice floated back angry and martial. I thought she might need me, and I hung about putting things away in the kitchen until they came back.

"Michael," I had never said his name before, wished I had something else to call him. "You need to know this. I don't like all this traffic."

"You don't like? You like and don't like, too, hermit?"

"I don't mind your landing here a few times, but now this other plane. I'm not running an airport." Arden shot me a quick glance I couldn't read, maybe to warn me off.

He looked surprised. Losing at dominoes or maybe the beer had put him in a foul mood, though from what I'd seen he might not have another.

"Listen up, asshole. You're not running, period. You got no choice in the matter. I'm in charge of the operation. At the moment that includes your little pissant island."

He pulled his chisel and began to clean his nails on the corner of its blade. I'm sure it was meant to frighten me but he needn't have done it. I was already scared.

"I'm just worried about the owners. From Provo? They're out here when I least expect it. Or they send the local constable. That's why I built the strip, for them. If they find someone's plane on it I don't know what they'll do. Once they saw smoke from the chimney and they had the cops check it out. They forgot the house had a fireplace."

Michael's lips turned in. "Is that right?" he asked. I had said the magic four-letter word. Turn safe to cops. "Well, you stop worrying, Leonard. You leave the worrying to me." He flicked the chisel around and again leaned it lightly on my breastbone. I prepared myself for another notch. He waited till I opened my eyes. Split a gleamy smile, flipped the chisel again so he held it by the blade, and wristed the tool so the handle tapped hard against my skull.

He turned and hauled Arden by the forearm the back way, into the dark.

I waited till he was gone to rub the knot on my head. Then I went out the front. The hurt put tears in my eyes. I could tap the rum, but if they found it they would drink it. Serve me up for happy hour.

Up the beach a hundred yards, just where I expected to find him, was Hofstadter's ghost, sitting on the back rest of a bus-stop bench. No doubt it was Hofstadter but his features had begun to fade. Where his outline met the foliage, you could see through to the trees.

"So," I said. "How's it going?"

He looked at me, disappointed. "Tell me, Mooney.

What do you make of your grudge with Canges?" That was an odd thing to say. I hadn't thought of Canges in weeks.

"Hell I don't know. We just don't get along."

Hofstadter nodded and rubbed his lips as if he knew better. The thing about Canges is he doesn't care what people think of him. It drives me crazy. I need everyone to like me, and someone with that attitude isn't in the game. I have this technique, it involves the sincerity look and using their first names all the time. People like Canges don't respond to it. So his attitude not only makes me envious. It prevents me from achieving my goal.

My answer didn't seem to suit Hofstadter. He spit out a flake of tobacco, *thoo*.

"You know how Tommy's doing?"

"No, I said. How?"

"He's having a tough time of it."

That pissed me off. Here's some damn kid pinging me on the skull with a chisel, and the ghost of my pal is needling me. I didn't need him to tell me that. I'm ashamed enough of my failures. Which I also kept to myself, but Hofstadter picked up on it.

"Stop," he said.

"Stop what?"

"Stop being ashamed of your failures."

"I'm not," I told him. He looked at me, gave that backhanded wave and began to shimmy away.

"Oh yeah," he said as an afterthought. "I'm on to why you're sleeping nighttimes and why you stopped drinking." It was true. Ever since Arden. I hadn't had a drink in three days.

"Yeah, why?"

"You think you might have a chance to screw her. But it won't work."

"Why not?"

"For one thing, you're impotent."

"I wouldn't be so sure," I told him. The subject had been on my mind. The ghost wasn't through.

"For a second, you can't decide whether she's your daughter or your lover." He was fading into the scrub. I realized he had his old voice back. "I'll give you a clue. She's neither." By now he had disappeared, and his last sentence came from the air.

"Anyway, nice to see you sober."

I went back, climbed the stairs and dozed. What could I do? Arden needed to look out for herself.

* *

In the middle of the night, in that marshy spot between fears and dreams, a scraping noise brought me to the dormer window. Arden, dressed only in panties that were white in the moonless night, was dragging the chaise lounge across the dunes. "There," I heard her say. Michael walked from behind the house into my view. He carried a bottle by its neck, wine by its shape, and he too wore only underwear. She aligned the lounge so it lay along my line of sight. I stepped back from the window so they wouldn't see me. Carelessly, he stripped off his pants and stepped out of them. Then he walked over to her and stripped hers. There was something bullying in what he did, something to show how he didn't care about her, even this last piece of clothing. He placed her down on the lounge, arranged her limbs, and calmly stretched his length on top of her. One of her hands reached slowly over her head and grasped the top bar of the chaise frame. It exposed her bare armpit. Her other hand rested on his back.

I moved back to the window. Over his shoulder her eyes found mine. Hers were steady and open, and even from my distance, especially from my distance, full of sadness. The two of them looked like a cheap porn flick, except beyond there was this disappearing blue line, a single line that flashed with the boom and whoosh of the surf. I watched. In the gathered light of the stars he began the foolish moves of coupling. There was nothing obscene about it. It was a casual act, I remember thinking that, how casual. How silly. Are there life throes as well as death? Surely this must be it. All the time his body twitching, his pale hips pinned in by the white fence posts of her knees, all that time her eyes held onto mine.

CHAPTER 21.

By noon the next day, the last can of Tecata had been mashed into a tin butterfly and tossed into the corner with its buddies. Fat Man and Michael sat and ticked dominoes one against another. The only words that passed between them were about weather. They spoke of winds and stagnant fronts and countervailing lows. Fat Man had a theory to explain the system that had roosted on top of us, and Michael listened to it in a grudge, his face announcing that he took the declining barometer personally. When they disagreed Fat Man dialed up weather maps on the computer and swiveled the screen toward Michael in triumph. Every once in a while Michael would look over at me and I'd brace, expecting to be told to go out and rout the clouds.

Fat Man explained the predicament. His twin needed the winds to north or south, right down the centerline is the way he put it. The soggier the strip, the more favorable the winds had to be.

"Does that come as a surprise?" Michael spat at

him. "Couldn't we have expected that? Trade winds tend to be westerly."

Fat Man fixed his jaw in frustration. "Don't be impertinent, Michael. What we expect means nothing now. We do not get the right blow," he said, rolling the R from his throat like the enemy in a war movie, "we stay put." He meant it to end the discussion. Michael waited until Fat Man's eyes were elsewhere and shot him an insolent glare.

We were gathered in the living room, it was a little family reunion. The two men sat at the card table bent over their game, I lay on the couch looking at a magazine that had come off the plane. About flying, aerobatics. The pictures made me woozy.

Arden had brought a ladder-back chair from the kitchen and was sewing a button on a blouse. Michael told her there was a case of wine in the Aztec, she should get off her butt and fetch it. I moved to help, but he fixed me with a look and ordered me to stay put. He seemed to know something about Arden and me that I didn't.

"You go by yourself," he said and she pushed back her chair. I was left with the two of them, unprotected.

"So," Fat Man said looking toward the kitchen. "You're taking her on the next one?"

"Sure."

"I'm opposed. It is unorthodox. She brings nothing."

I perked up at this, lifting my shoulders. Michael noticed right off.

"Big word, captain," he said to Fat Man but watched me. "Unorthodox. What does that mean?"

"It means if she's not a help she's a hinder. She has

no function. Leave her behind."

I couldn't tell whether Michael was considering Fat Man's suggestion or deciding what pattern to scrimshaw on the inside of my skull, which is where he was staring. Me, I sat still and tried to look like I had never heard of sex.

The kitchen screen slammed. Arden came in shouldering a box of oversized bottles, four in all, of a California zinfandel.

"That's what you fly around to drink?" Michael said, unhappy. "You'll poison me on that wine, Fat Man, I'll die of rotgut on this piece of birdshit in the middle of the sea."

Fat Man ignored him. Michael pulled a bottle out of the case, unscrewed the top and filled a water glass halfway. He took a swallow and pruned up his face.

"Poison," he said. "I wouldn't rub it on a horse."

"I like it," Fat Man answered. "It has a nice nose."

"I don't understand this man. He makes a hundred grand on a single score and carries dishwater as his wine. Hermit. What you got to drink?"

"I'm out." There were three bottles of rum in the cabinet above the stove, but when my guests left that had to last me until Isaac could pick up an order and return. If Michael found them he might remove my kidneys. I had a choice between sobriety and death. It is not as easy as it sounds. Besides, I figured the drunker they got the longer they'd stay.

"You got a source of supply?"

"An outboard passing to Mayaguana. I have to signal him in. Comes at best once a week."

Michael let it drop. I finished the magazine and

went back to the start.

Fat Man arranged the dominoes on the table. They made a rhythmic tick. He stirred them about. "Explain it to me again," Michael asked him across the table. "This one makes me nervous."

"It is easy," Fat Man said, flattening out his stacks of money. "You have no cause for concern." He pushed his thumbnail to the edges of his bills to square off the piles.

"First we do a reconnaissance run. Clear the area. If we find a fleet of fishing boats camped on our site, we need to figure new coordinates.

"If not, if the site's clear, we are all set. The decoy is ready. At the agreed time, he takes off, climbs to three thousand five. He has filed a flight plan that shows him returning to his home airstrip. Drug dealers do not file flight plans. He does some practice maneuvers. They watch him on the screen. We come in south of Cuba, then down to the deck for the run north. We enter the air defense zone on the Gulf side, under the radar. Fifty feet AGL. We rendezvous at a predetermined fix, and when he sees us below him he lets us know. Flashes his landing light. He descends, all the while they're watching his blip on the screen, it's the only one they see.

"Why is he coming down? they wonder. He might be spotting tuna schools, airplanes are hired to do that. Or sightseeing or practicing engine out. There is nothing illegal in descending. So he descends. We have an agreed frequency, we are listening for him. On his count, we pass the same altitude, he turns off his transponder, we turn ours on. He dives to the deck and we climb. On the screen they have been watching only one plane, one transponder. Even if for a split second there are two blips, what are they to surmise? It must be an echo. It must be the same guy. He goes home low, we go at altitude. Cross the coast at the Everglades, where no one sees us, land at Flamingo."

"And the decoy?"

"He comes in behind us. He has taken off and landed there, no sweat. We get off the plane, we are two regular guys. Texans, in from Brownsville."

"You? You're a Texan?"

"Brownsville. We got fishing rods, tennis racquets, a half-gallon of Jim Beam. We book into a motel one night. We go fishing, two regular guys who like to fish. We take our time. Tour the Everglades, we rent a boat and, if God is good to us, we catch some redfish. We unload later, perhaps a rendezvous in the panhandle."

I smiled at the flaw in the plan: Fat Man with a tennis racquet. Fat Man could get a racquet to fire bullets. But they didn't ask me.

Michael sat thoughtfully. He took up an empty beer can by his chair, wiggled it impatiently and peered into its hole, maybe it had been filled by divine intervention.

"Hermit, you got anything to drink?"

I repeated my story. I didn't do it easily, a clammy dew broke out on my upper lip. Why hadn't I told him the truth? What difference how drunk they got?

"In your plane?"

"Mine got the range," said Fat Man.

"What about the punch?"

"I told you what I think. But it is up to you. Leave her here, bring her along. *Das macht nichts.*"

I walked outside by C. Aubrey, plucked a few blades of saw grass and tossed them in the air. They blew down true east. Michael was watching from the back door.

"Stay away from those airplanes, asshole. You got fast hands. You may want to keep them attached to the arms."

I wandered north toward the shed. The wind blew across carrying spray and the fresh spit of rain. When I got to the end I looked out into an asphalt sea. What if I had kept the Boston Whaler? Would I have the nerve to chance it? I was glad it was gone, the question had floated off with it. The agony of trying to decide, making a run for it. I'd paid no attention—what direction had Isaac come from, how would one find land? When were high seas too high? I'd probably never have gotten it out of the bay, I never learned how to use the damn thing. We'd capsize and they'd fish us out and bring us back to dry. Michael would cold-chisel a heart and arrow in my chest. I was prepared to risk death but not pain.

Up at the point I went to work on the cat. I'd hoped by now Isaac would have brought me new plugs but he had missed those items two shopping lists running. The engine had been misfiring and I was sure cleaning the points, even with the tools I had, would do until the plugs came.

I was bent over the engine with a circle wrench, absorbed in the job. The gaps were fouled but they were cleaning up nicely. I had left both doors open for light. The sudden voice booming into that tin box made me twitch.

"What is the signal?" The wrench jumped from my hand and clanged on the engine block.

"Damn," I said, my heart racing. "You scared me."

Fat Man stood blocking the bright light. He asked

his question a second time and took a half-step in. I could make out only his silhouette, but its bulk and its closing on me didn't do anything to calm my nerves.

"What signal?"

"You said someone supplies you, comes by once a week, but you have to signal him. What is the signal?"

"Ah. A white towel."

"Where?"

"Out the upper window. At the house."

"Nothing to do with this?" He tapped the frame of the bulldozer and it chimed. Only then did I realize he was holding his pistol.

"Nothing."

"So. What are you doing?"

"It's been running rough."

His head bobbed like a coconut on the sea.

"You are not thinking of driving off?" With the light behind him I couldn't see his face.

"Yeah. Actually, I thought I'd drive to Washington, D.C., the FBI building, and ask to see J. Edgar Hoover."

"Hoover is dead."

"No kidding? Whaddya know. There goes my reward." He gave a grunt.

"You sleep on the couch tonight, Hermit. You stay off the second floor."

"Sure. Fine."

He grunted again, turned, and went back to the house.

I spent the rest of the day at the north shed. Even after the light had dimmed to shadows. I changed the oil, cleaned off the engine, and wiped the grease from my hands. By the time I returned, one of the bottles of pink wine had been emptied and stood lodged in the corner in the midst of mashed cans. Michael, fully clothed, was asleep on the couch. Arden and Fat Man were bent over the card table at a game of Chinese checkers. I opened my hands to ask where he wanted me.

"I am sleeping upstairs. In your bed, Mister Hermit. Leave Michael be. One of you take the downstairs bed, one outside. And I warn you, you too, lady. No funny stuff tonight. I do not care what happens between the two of you but he is a jealous man and I need him thinking about the tasks at hand. We will be locating waypoints at fifty feet off the deck and I need a navigator who is sober."

I nodded, went outside. The chaise was where they had left it. Up behind the dunes were a pair of sleeping bags on foam pads. I got in one, hers I hoped, lay down and watched the sky. There were a few stars. Mostly there were these huge eraser marks, where the stars had been rubbed out, that chased each other around the sky.

I closed my eyes. I don't get it, I said to myself.

—What's that? Hofstadter asked.

—Fat Man and Michael are convinced we're looking to hop into bed together.

—So? If it wasn't for penmanship that thesis gets an A plus.

Hofstadter could always get a rise from me.

—Tell me, he said out of nowhere. I was almost asleep.

—When the Sister said you must be mistaken about your mother, what did you say?

—Me? I said I didn't know what to do.

—And?

—And she said you must pray to God. And I said, God is either a heathen or an indolent lout.

That amused old Hofstadter. He gave that snorty laugh as if he was about to cough up a lung. By then I'd looked up the words.

* *

I slept into the morning. A wind had blown off the rains and a filmy sun sat on the roof of the house. Breakfast was long over. Arden was nowhere to be seen. If I didn't ask for her Michael would think I'd been with her, if I did he'd think it was a cover. I said nothing—made myself some toast and heated up the coffee, and found a place in the living room where the men were again sitting, the dominoes face down and idle. All the dollar bills had migrated to Fat Man's stack, and the game had ended for lack of currency. A fresh liter of wine, its top unscrewed, stood on the floor by Michael's chair.

"You must have something better than this piss." Michael put his hand to the bottle as if he would shove it over. He had long, narrow fingers and on the last of his left hand he wore a gold signet ring. Delicate hands, I wondered if he came from people that worried about him. He stood up and went into the kitchen. Cabinet doors opened, slammed shut in frustration. He was getting warm.

"Hey, look here." The carburetor that pumped blood behind my eyes upped its rate. Would he cut me open over three quarts of rum?

"Hermit, what the hell is this?"

He was rattling something, on his way in. My breastbone started to throb and he was shoving a white plastic jar under my nose. He had found the Sugar Substitute. "Touchdown, Fat Man. The hermit's stash. We got ourselves a hermit with a habit."

Michael leaned over and grabbed me by the armpit. You could tell from his fingers he'd studied ways to hurt people. His grip closed, it was so painful I stood up, or he pulled me up, and at the same time I had no strength in my legs. The pain made my arm stop feeling, shot through my shoulder and my head. Fat Man said something to him and he let me go.

I sank to the couch. A pulse beat on my lips. Michael spilled the pills out on the table. Stood over them with keen eyes, like he meant to down them in order. Fat Man moved fast. He used the score pad as a sorting blade and corralled the pills into groups, assigned values to each, like chips. Halcion worth two, the Valium one. Michael read their names aloud. They got to the end, and Fat Man dealt him the leftover, like you would gristle to a patient dog. Michael placed it on his tongue and washed it down with an inch of the zin. The game of dominoes resumed.

I walked out to the beach. Winds kicked at the water, its surface was covered in little white pimples that sprayed as they burst. Where the hell was Hofstadter's ghost when I needed him? Doubtless gone on. Think about it, they can get into the cineplex free, there are better things for ghosts to do than hang around. Otherwise we'd be overpopulated with them. Of course, Hofstadter's particular ghost hadn't been much help.

I studied the ocean. Once to every man and nation, goes the hymn. Once to every man and nation comes the moment to decide. That's not what I sang, though. I sang, Light Green All the Way. Arden was walking toward me in her denim shorts, a sweater of raw silk against the chill. Her skin was dark as wood.

I hadn't been alone with her since our rendezvous over Michael's shoulder, and I didn't know what to say.

"I was worried for you."

She gave me a smile of the mildest scold. As if she was about to correct my grammar. "You were jealous, not worried. But your imagination is worse than reality."

"Did I imagine something?"

"You imagined it makes a difference. You must bear in mind that it's only a body."

"Only a body. I'll try to remember that, only a body. Still, it comes in handy when you need an insurance physical."

She laughed and put her hand to my cheek. It was a dilemma. I wasn't supposed to worry about her, but I was prepared to say anything to keep her hand there.

"This job Fat Man is planning," I said. She nodded.

"All the safety catches are off. This involves U.S. Customs, spy planes. If you're caught with them, they'll send you away too."

"Is that the worst that can happen?" She could act like a kid when she wanted to. I guess it wasn't acting.

"Yes, yes. That's the worst, you'll spend days and nights alone, off in a cell by yourself. No one around." She smiled again and I realized she was smiling at how the prisoner described prison. "Or worse."

"Worse than the worst?"

"Worse. You could get hurt. Killed."

"And death? You disapprove?"

"Yes I disapprove. For God's sake, Arden, you're so

young." I almost added, to sound less like a father, beautiful. Here I was arguing for life, a fragile position given that I was at best a recent convert. Nothing like impending death to get your mind off suicide. Let Michael carve my lungs out. Maybe I could stop her from doing something stupid like disappearing. A girl like that in a lockup, I couldn't think of it. I envisioned this nice couple flying from Brisbane to Indianapolis, I could see them pacing up and down in the Holiday Inn pool.

"I don't want to put you off by caring..."

"You can care," she said. "You just can't expect to take over my life."

"It's your life I'm talking about. One stupid move will have you hanging out with the deceased."

She turned to look out at the horizon. The toasted skin of her shoulders showed through the weave of the sweater. "Listen," she whispered at a level even with the hiss of the unfolding water. "Listen to this. I love to say it."

She recited in a voice soft as the surf.

"'At the ends of the universe is a blood red cord that ties life to death, man to woman, will to destiny. Let the knot of that red sash, which cradles the hips of the goddess, bind in me the ends of life and dream. I am an old man with more than my share of hopes and misgivings. Let my thoughts lie together in peace. At my death let the bubbles of blood on my lips taste as sweet as berries. Give me not words of consolation, give me magic, the fire of one beyond the borders of enchantment. Give me the spell of living well.'"

Then she turned, leaned and spread her fingertips against my chest to bear her weight, as she had done before, and kissed my lips.

I looked up, startled. I sensed someone else on the beach, and what with the slim population of our island, odds were six-to-five pick-'em Michael was coming to whip me into a froth of blood berries.

But it wasn't. It was Fat Man, happy as a pig at the trough and oblivious to us. He wore knee-length shorts and a black T-shirt. He looked like a man in a barrel, except it was all him. He was carrying a long pole with a dish at its end. Perched on his head was a set of large, bug-like earphones. He studied the ground in front of him, and the way he walked, steadily, you couldn't tell the wine he'd put away that morning. Around his waist he had one of those webbed pouches, the kind tourists use so nobody picks their pockets, and he kept tugging at it to stay up. He didn't notice us until he was twenty feet away. Then he rose up with a start and took off the headset.

"Look look," he called, excited. He pulled at his pocket and Arden and I watched his hand open with a magician's slowness on two pieces of metal. One was a cigarette lighter, a Zippo, the Marine Corps globe and eagle on its side. The other was oxidized beyond recognition.

"A watch," he said. "It's a watch."

Arden seemed to like him. "Signs of intelligent life," she said and he nodded. She reminded me a lot of Reba, she was positive about things.

"No pirate treasure?"

Fat Man grinned at her. "Not yet, lady. But keep your finger crossed."

She took her two index fingers and crossed them in front of her, the sign to ward off a vampire. He smiled broadly, back to a gold molar the size of a marble.

We strolled along with him as he swept the metal detector across the sand. Even though we couldn't hear, it was fun.

"One needs a hypothesis to be effective." Between pings Fat Man explained himself. "The high water mark. That is my theory. The high water mark would always remain the same, so if you wanted to bury something and find it again that would establish one of the coordinates."

"Makes sense," I said but with the headset on he didn't notice.

"Where's Michael?" Arden asked and then tugged at his sleeve so he watched her lips.

"He is asleep, lady. Michael drinks because he loses at gaming and because he is afraid." Fat Man stopped, listened, started again. "Fear is not an asset in our business. If these matters make him afraid he might perhaps contemplate a different vocation."

"What's to be afraid of?" I asked and Arden dug me in the ribs. Fat Man kept on.

"If he is afraid, he will simply die sooner. I have seen it happen. You must spit in the eye of death. Death must fear you, not the other way around."

Arden shouted at him. "Yes. Exactly. I've been telling Leonard the same thing." He nodded to show he heard her, then held up a hand. Moved it to press an earpiece close, swept his dish over a patch several times, and marked a spot with his toe. He unclipped the ear pieces so they rested on his shoulders. Arden repeated her words.

"She is right. Listen to the lady, Mister Hermit, she is absolutely right."

He sank to his knees, a garden trowel in one hand and its diggings in the other, sorting through. Arden and I stood and watched. Our hands touched by accident, the round part at the edge of each hand. I left mine there and so did she.

"Aha," Fat Man grunted dramatically. "Here we are." He held up a verdigris coin. "Science is wonderful, no?" He rubbed the sand from the coin and corrosion came off with it. Scraped at it with his thumbnail and held it up for us to see. A penny, you could make out the date. 1970. The year Tommy was born. We began our search again, three abreast.

"Science," Fat Man said again, happily.

"Science has done us in," said Arden.

"No no, Miss. Don't say that. Science lets us fly airplanes."

"Tell me this," Arden took his arm. She had won him over, you could see it. "Tell me this. Why do people prefer science and darkness when they could be dancing beams of light?"

"I do not know, Miss." Fat Man stopped. He handed the coin to Arden. "You keep this. For good luck." I swallowed my thought. It was too obvious to utter: here she is, flying around the skies with someone who may be licensed as a psycho but not as a pilot, she's going to need more than a green penny. Then he took my hand in his, red and meaty, placed the Zippo in it, and closed my fingers. "Good luck to you also, Hermit. You should take care of her," he said to me. "She is a special lady."

It seemed the right time. "Fat Man," I said the name as respectfully as I could. "Fat Man, leave her behind. A trip like this she's just a nuisance. Takes up space, and you both would be less visible without her. Leave her behind."

He puckered his lips. Perhaps I'd fed him a sourball, had overstepped my bounds. His face showed no uncertainty, although maybe his people are different, maybe where he comes from when you are unsure you look people straight in the eye.

"That is not for me to say, my friend. I would like to help you out. But that is not for me to decide. You should take it up with Michael." I thought to myself I would. I meant it, too.

I was disappointed that he would do no more. But mostly I was pleased with the way we talked, like old comrades. It was odd, walking along with this man and discussing plans for the future, the way married people do late at night.

The three of us walked along for another hour. Every so often, Fat Man would mark a spot, lower himself down and spade at the sand, but the only other echo he found was a two-inch bolt. What was it doing there, a foot deep into the pebble and shell? Did it hold down this island to some secret strut that trailed to the ocean's floor? I touched the lighter, it sank heavy and rounded in my pants pocket. Perhaps it had been Hofstadter's. Perhaps he had used it on Camel after Camel, dragging in deep in that way he had, the pleasure in the smoke seeping pure into his eyes.

Fat Man dug himself into mellowness, or so I figured. As he scrounged for this last bolt, the gulls circled closer. Maybe they thought Fat Man was working a crab hole, maybe the smell of the damp sand excited them, whatever it was every successive pass they came closer. Fat Man unearthed the bolt, and as he stood to show us his find, a gull dive-bombed him. Pulled out only feet off his head, scrawking and flapping so hard I felt the push of its wing on my cheek. When you're locked away on an island, the touch of a bird's wing can drive you mad. Fat Man must have felt it too, touched by the draft, that's what set him off. He unzipped his pouch and rummaged around. Pulled out that vicious-looking pistol. He pulled at it so it gave a loud click, then raised it to eye level. I wasn't sure what he was doing, and Blam, it went off. Blam blam blam. He fired into the flock of gulls, haphazard as if he didn't give a shit. Birds wheeled and screeched and flapped away, crazy as he was. They were gone in seconds and we stood in this eerie center of dead space. He hadn't hit anything. Still, the noise of it. You've got to be crazy to fire at some bird you don't know, who hasn't done a thing to you. I felt I might get sick.

Overhead, trace clouds slipped by. Their shadows spotted the beach and made it look unhealthy. Fat Man put away his pistol, readjusted his headset and we walked on without saying anything. All that bang-bang had changed the mood. At the end of the shelf, where the mangroves came down and prevented our passing, Fat Man lowered the headset to his shoulders, we turned and walked back toward the house. Maybe Michael would sleep through the day, maybe he'd get himself reversed. Or maybe Fat Man would fly off the end of the island into the sea and Arden and I would stuff the drunken bully in the oven, pour ourselves tall rum sodas, and play two-handed dominoes into the night. The spell of living well.

Once Fat Man had quit his treasure hunt we moved along quickly. We passed the dock and took the path to the house, walking now where the surface was white and crusted. It was nearing evening, the sun was about to douse itself into the warped sea and the sand fleas would soon be out.

We were twenty yards from the house. Fat Man leaned over and scooped a handful of dry sand. He held it out and slowly let the grains flow to the ground. When we looked at him blankly he scooped a second handful, walked down to the hard sand and scuffed a straight line. Scuffed a single barb for an arrow. Standing at the top of the line he let the grains of sand fall. They blew in a line right into the groove. The wind had shifted to the north. Right down the centerline.

CHAPTER 22.

They told me Reba was on the phone. Happily it wasn't Canges who told me, seeing as how there was no privacy in the bullpen. Canges was a great listener-in, and he would have asked solicitously whether everything was OK at home, ardent to find out it was not. I already knew that it wasn't, that was my first thought. Reba never called me at work and if she called something was wrong.

"It can't be the case," I told her.

"Well, it was a police car and the assistant principal said they took him to the station."

"But it can't technically be an arrest. He's a minor. In Juvenile they call it a detention."

"Leonard, will you please get a grip? What difference what it's called? Don't you want to know what it's for?"

The truth is, of course, I didn't. But it wouldn't matter, when people ask you Don't you want to know, you're going to. What I wanted didn't matter a fig.

"Possession of methamphetamine. They caught him with a sugar cube laced with the stuff."

Cuffs of concrete tightened around my wrist and the matching necklace pushed down on my rib cage. I asked her which station and she told me. She was on her way over.

"And listen to this. How they caught him? He took it out in class. He was telling his buddies, right in front of the teacher, how you can make it in chemistry lab. The assistant principal said, 'I didn't have any choice, Mrs. Mooney. The teacher brings him down to me and says it was like show-and-tell up there, and when I ask your son does he have anything to say, he answers, yeah, can I have the speedball back. I didn't have any choice.'"

"What did you say?"

"Well, I told him I could see his point of view. I can. Do you want to know what class?"

The way she asked she gave it away. I was wishing it was one of those old-time radio quiz shows, where they call you up and tell you the category for the question, and you decide how much to bet. I would have bet the house on this answer.

"Shop class."

Reba was impressed. "How did you know?"

Two days later Reba, Tommy and I were in Juvenile Court. Its courtroom was at the opposite end of a block-long hall from where I worked, I knew the clerk, in fact he volunteered to put us first on the docket, to get us out of there. It was nice to have some pull. We were sitting behind the two-foot grille that separates the lawyers and bailiffs and judges from the great unwashed, we may dispense equal justice in our business, the grille proclaimed, so long as all you slobs behind the rail keep in mind it's our business. Reba and I were sitting together and Tommy was in the same pew slouched against the far wall.

Have you thought of what you're going to say, Reba asked him, and he answered what difference.

"It'll make a difference," I told him.

"I'll tell you one thing I don't want," he said as an afterthought. It was the most words we'd heard from him since this started. "I don't want you wailing and whining and telling the judge how he's our little boy and he used to be a nice kid and we don't know where we've gone wrong. None of that Orphan Annie crap. It's useless."

This wasn't the time for an argument, but he was wrong on this one. "I don't think it's useless. I happen to work here, this is something I may know about. The book on this judge is she'll listen, particularly since it's a first offense and you don't have any kind of record. If she'll listen, then it's worth saying something."

"Holy shit. You've already started."

I didn't know what he meant—you know how kids say you don't have a clue? I really didn't—but I didn't get the chance to find out because the clerk was asking us to please rise and the judge was bustling through the door as if she just had a few minutes for this, she was on her way to somewhere important. Once she settled in, she took her time. They called our case and we entered through the swinging gate and sat at the defendant's table facing the bench. The judge scanned the file, I'd checked it out, it had the police report and a half-page social worker's interview. The judge was a tough-looking lady, she had a face like a cartoon eagle. Her mouth was in the shape of McDonald's golden arch and her beak came down over the chin. Teeny glasses that she slid into focus up and down her nose, on the city's salary she couldn't afford ones that fit. She finished reading the papers. Nodded and the DA spoke, they used a special DA for Juvenile. The DA put no spin on it, hardly mentioning Tommy whether he was a choirboy or a committed thug. The judge asked Tommy does he have anything to say. To which sitting in his seat, his legs sprawled out, he gave a Nah, just like that. When she asked us, Reba rose and spoke, that's what we'd agreed, and Reeb said the usual things, but moving, I thought.

The judge instructed Tommy to stand up, and he did, though he let it be known standing was painful for him, his legs would barely support him, and we were standing beside him. Then she talked to him as if she'd known him for years.

"Tommy. I've got good news for you. There's nothing I can do to you. If you're intent on screwing up your life, there's nothing I can do, nothing the DA can do. Even your parents, who are here because they're concerned that you might." I snuck a look. Tommy's head was pulled back and in, as if he was worried she might smack him.

"I can make you uncomfortable, even unhappy. I can put you in a jail cell, and the next time you show up here I will. I promise. But I can't make your decisions. Only you can. So relax. We don't use electroshock or hypnosis. You still get to decide.

"I will tell you this. You want to be free from drugs, free to walk the streets, then you might get on a different road. But I can't help you get there, I can't even tell you something you don't know. You know all this."

Tommy mumbled something, whether or not the judge heard I couldn't say. I don't think it was something you memorize in civics class, but she didn't seem to care. She'd said her piece. She suspended sentence, imposed costs, and banged down the gavel. The clerk told us how to pay the costs, and we were gone. Two weeks later, so was Tommy.

At dinner that night, Tommy told Stace about it. In his version the judge was a pal, she doesn't bullshit you, just does her job. Where they'd formed this bond I didn't know. He mentioned casually he was thinking of taking the judge's advice. Reba and I looked at each other, we were pleased. It just showed how clueless we were, we were pleased. After he left, he went over to see Dog, Stace explained what he meant. He meant the judge had at least one good idea, told him maybe it was time to hit the road.

There's a part of all this that I've kept to myself. Like the Pink Floyd tickets. I simply don't have a good explanation. When we were standing there, you could tell Tommy was nervous. Scared. I felt him trembling, he wasn't a criminal, he was a kid. Our hands were hanging down, Reba was on one side and I was on the other, his and my hands were hanging down inches apart. And they touched. Right at the round part on the heel, the meaty part. Instinctively I pulled my hand away. I wish I hadn't done that. I wish I had taken his hand in mine and held it, the way Arden took mine when we walked into the water. I wish that every day since it happened.

* *

I heard their voices in the kitchen, civil and short with information. Arden and Fat Man spoke quietly, as if they knew I was sleeping. A few words about winds and toast snuck through thewallboards, who takes milk with their coffee. Outside was nearly black, the first flaws of gray were spidering the glass of my window. I might have slept, too, but the screen door banged a half-dozen times, shoes clumped down the back stairs and up again and in.

The tempo of the conversation rose to anger. At Michael's voice I pulled up the sheet and stretched it over my head. Arden's words came through distinctly, "No, no, I don't want to," and then a murmur from Michael. It was that fearsome quiet before he'd smacked her. Next came a low wail, my sheet was too thin to muffle it. A chair must have fallen over, because I jumped.

I lay still and listening. There was nothing. Got up, pulled on khakis and boots and went out. The morning had cracked yellow and pink across the sky, and the light came through the kitchen window jolly as an animated short subject. Arden sat at the table before a coffee mug. Tracks of her tears gleamed on her cheeks.

"What's wrong?"

"Nothing," she said. It was a kid's answer. I waited. She wiped her nose with the back of her hand.

"I want out," she said. I waited some more and she went on.

"You were right, it *is* dangerous. At first they didn't need me, but now they say they do."

"Why?"

"It doesn't matter," she said, so I waited again.

"At first they were going to use just the one plane. But now they want to have the 185 as a backup, in case the Aztec is hot. So I'm supposed to stay with it until the job's over."

She looked up at me, but I was saved from answering. The two men came back.

"Move it," said Michael. "Take the recon run with Fat Man." For a sinking moment, I thought he meant me.

"Come on, move it." He went to put the death grip to her armpit, but she didn't wait. She was on her feet.

"Aren't you going?" I asked him.

"Tomorrow's the job. Today Fat Man'll fly reconnaissance, clear the area. The punch will assist, I'm staying here to watch you." He glared at me as if he read my thoughts.

They went out the door and I followed. I waited until the men were occupied with the Aztec. Fat Man lay under a wing checking its brakes and Michael looked on.

"I'm sorry," I said to Arden. "I've done what I can."

"Done?" she spun on me. She had a low boiling point. "You haven't done squat."

"I asked them not to take you."

"That's not doing, that's talking. Doing is doing."

She had me going. I thought she wanted me to back off. I told her, but she wasn't having any.

"That's too easy. If you care about something, what should it matter what I want? Besides, I'm just a kid. What the hell do I know?"

Michael came back to get her. She called over her shoulder.

"Another thing, hermit. That game. Ssech. It's fucked. It's backward."

He clamped her armpit and half threw her up on the wing. When he pinched you there your whole side went numb, and Arden stumbled into the airplane. As soon as the door slammed, Fat Man cranked the first engine.

I didn't wait to see them off and be left with Michael to while away the time. Instead I cut into the brush and bushwhacked for a while. After the plane rolled by I cut to the edge of the strip and followed it toward the north end.

I needed a plan. There was nothing in the shed to suggest one, just some oilcans and a major absence of rum. I considered working my way back to the house to signal Isaac, but by the time he came it would be too late, and besides if Fat Man had told Michael about the signal, I would have long since been diced into a gazpacho.

I sat on the seat of the bulldozer thinking on Arden's words and wishing I'd brought one of the remaining bottles. The sun worked itself halfway up a desperate sky. Too much planning gets you into trouble. You're sitting on the bus, here comes a fellow to take the open seat next to yours so you inch over into the space and he passes you up. And the next fellow, the one who's skinny and doesn't mind the narrow seat, he's wearing a hood over his skull face and carrying a scythe.

Midday I worked my way back to the house and peered in the kitchen window. Michael sat at the table in front of a bowl of cold cereal. He wore jeans, no shoes, and a sweatshirt with its arms ripped off. He hadn't combed his hair, and slick and misdirected it added a lunacy to his menace. His head was propped on his fists and the way he was scowling, those Cheerios were in trouble.

I did a few chores, pinned some shingles back on and nailed a board that had sprung on the front steps, mostly just put in an appearance. But he paid me no mind. Then I walked back to the shed and opened the bulldozer's hood to clean the engine.

It gave me the idea. I knew about car motors. Airplanes had ones very much the same, really simpler so they didn't break down. It was a gamble—I'd be staking my supplies, which were already at a Leningrad low. I finished up on the dozer, there was really nothing left to do, stuck a few tools in my back pocket and waited.

Before sunset, I made another appearance at the house. I figured Michael would be climbing the walls. He wasn't quite—he was sitting in the living room playing solitaire on the coffee table. Hofstadter's jar sat by his arm. From the seconds it took him to focus on my arrival I figured he'd hit the Substitute once or twice.

"I just remembered," I said. "I think there may be some rum in a top cabinet."

I went through the charade of moving a chair to the counter, climbing up and down slamming cabinet doors.

"Sure enough," I said. "A last bottle."

He came at me so fast he scrambled a winning hand of patience, grabbed the bottle from me and cracked the seal.

"You want a glass?" I asked. Michael didn't answer. I came in carrying two, but his glare let me know that this lion intended to eat the whole zebra. Back in the kitchen, I made a couple of cheese sandwiches and stuck them and a second bottle in my shirt. Then took off for the north end.

That was the longest wait of all. I forced myself to leave the bottle capped until the job was over, otherwise I'd screw it up for sure. If Michael found me, there'd be no excuse.

The sun had set when I walked back. All the lights were on, and through the window I saw Michael on the day-bed couch, a leg sprawled on the floor. He looked asleep. I wasn't about to test him for doneness with a toothpick. Reeb used to do that with a cake, test it then frost it and let the kids lick the beaters. Here I wouldn't be the beaters, I would be the egg in the mix.

Through the break Michael's plane sat with its nose sticking up to sniff the wind. I went to its far side, took a screwdriver from my pocket and removed the cowling. The engine showed itself, though in the moonless night I couldn't see what was what. My heart was pumping so hard I could feel my eyelids. Sure you're scared, but everyone is. Arden with Fat Man, Tommy in Indianapolis, Stacey with her bugs, Stace was always scared of bugs that fly. Just belly up and do the job.

Inside I heard the toilet flush. Oh shit, I thought, and then flinched because it would have struck Hofstadter as a funny remark. Oh shit, I whispered, to make the giggle go away without coming out. I reached in and found the wires coming out of the plugs, followed them down with my hand to the distributor, and pulled off the cap.

Bang. The back screen door slammed. I froze. Slowly I raised my head and peered behind the propeller. Michael stood on the back steps, staring at the sky. Slowly as I could manage, I lowered myself to the sand.

I lay there waiting for the end to come. I figured I'd never hear him, the ground was soft, he'd be on me, come around the airplane, he'd find the cowling missing and me prostrate by the far wheel, and he'd calmly put the chisel to the nape of my neck and with a single thump remove skull from stalk. I lay there for as long as I could, I bet half an hour, hoping to hear the screen door close again or even his footsteps by my neck. There was nothing. Eventually I raised up. He was nowhere to be seen.

I screwed the cowling back, stuck the distributor cap in my pocket and made for the shed.

* *

The cheese sandwiches were the best anyone's ever eaten, and the rum made it a great party. Except for company I had everything I needed. My blood was racing so from the theft, the rum took a while to edge into the stream.

But it did. In the middle of the night, I mounted the bulldozer, drove out and turned it on its house. On the first pass its blade clipped the front corner and the shed sagged with a whining little creak. I realized that the distributor cap was a lousy choice: they'd discover it missing and come get me. I should have been more subtle. Rage and hope swelled in my throat, mixed with the rum they had a sour, digested taste. I pointed the machine at the drooping flank ahead of me and pushed the throttles to full stop.

It didn't take long. Sides of corrugated aluminum lay at the bottom of the gully, while the incoming surf tried to cover up what I'd done. Drifting in the foam were two saw horses, half a dozen emptied motor oil cans, and the two drums that had held fuel. Oily rags swam about the channel bleeding rainbows into the seas.

At some point I lay on the sand and slept. The greasy rainbows were in my dreams. I was awakened occasionally by a sharp thirst and the remorse that sat on my chest. Remorse for Arden's leaving, for Reba's and Tommy's and Stace's leaving, for mine too. At the end of my sleep, Hofstadter was coughing like an engine that wouldn't catch.

Finally the engine caught, and gave off a buzz that turned into a hum, and then into an airplane. I sat up. In the first light, Fat Man's Aztec was one hundred feet off the sea, lining up the length of the island. It lowered itself below the palms, landed, and taxied back toward the house.

The engines kept humming, and I knew it was readying to fly again. I leapt to my feet, ran down the gully and up the other side. By the time I made the runway the twin was sitting at the far end facing me, its engines singing to burst. Run-up before take-off, I recognized the procedure by now. I sprinted down the center of the strip waving my arms like a man swimming up the waterfall.

Fat Man came off the brakes and the airplane jumped at me. They must have been counting that I would flinch—they kept coming. Me too, I swam at them. The gap between us disappeared. When it was inches from too late—did they think I'd get airborne first?—the plane lifted off and over my head. Its wind pressed down on my hair and blew against my cheek. Michael's visored face showed in the windscreen and Fat Man lifted a hand goodbye.

The plane roared over me and disappeared into the first light. I was alone. I thought to cry, but when I put fingers to my eye, there was only sand to brush away.

CHAPTER 23.

On the back stairs sat Arden. My face gave a big, goofy smile, my first in a long time, and the muscles ached to do it. She might have been an apparition, there's no occupancy limit, but she stood and pulled at the seat of her shorts. It was not the gesture of a ghost.

"I thought you left."

"I did. I'm back."

"Where to?"

"Fat Man took me on the reconnaissance. It was fun."

"Not for Michael." That drew a tough-on-him wrinkle from the nostrils.

"They've gone?"

"Gone for good." She didn't mean it in the moral sense. "To pull their job and then to the States."

"And they put you here?"

She nodded. Held a piece of paper in her hand.

"They left me behind. The 185 wouldn't start, so they just left it behind. Fat Man never'd wanted to take me in the first place."

"What's that?" I pointed to the paper and she looked it as if it was a surprise, glanced to see it between her finger and thumb.

"The 185."

"The plane?"

"Yeah. Michael's left it behind." I peered through the branches. In the new light I could make out smears of snow-white metal where Michael's square aircraft remained parked.

"Why?"

"He's through with it. Maybe it's hot and it won't start. He's abandoned it." She spoke breathlessly—I wasn't sure how she felt. "And," holding the paper out, "he's signed the airplane over to me."

We went inside and I brewed a pot of coffee. I didn't know what to think. Had she really been marooned here, this child-woman, and an airplane? My island could only support so much clutter.

"Will they be coming back?" I began to realize the horror of my fortune.

"They're after a big score. He's graduated to Fat Man's league, he won't be back for me." She smiled. Smiling made her look like some old pal you hadn't seen for years, some comforting pal who thought everything you did was terrific. I thought to tell her that.

"What will you do with the airplane?" She shrugged. What I meant was, how do you get out of here? This was about eight minutes after I'd thought I was deserted, after I'd decided that loneliness would crush my body like a truck.

"Do you know how to fly the thing?"

"Not exactly."

"I would have guessed that exactly is how you want to fly it."

She smiled. "What I mean is, I know a lot of basic stuff. I don't know what I don't know. I can navigate off the fixes, find Provo or Nassau. When we were on long legs, Michael taught me controls, steering that's easy—and I can probably get it up in the air. Getting it down, that's different."

"That can't be much of a problem. It comes down by itself."

Arden laughed. "Worse comes to worse, there's a book in the seat pocket. It lays out all the procedures, checklist style. I've seen Michael use it. Even emergencies." She didn't want to haggle over the future.

"And you? He was through with you, too?"

She tucked the edge of her lip under her front teeth in thought. Then nodded. "Apparently. It's an effective way of breaking it off, don't you think?"

She'd been up really early, so she went in to nap. I walked out back to discuss the matter with C. Aubrey. Hofstadter was there, leaning against the tree, his ass in C. Aubrey's face. He was down to smudges now, no more than the exhaust from an untuned pickup. It was clear he was in a disappearing mode.

"What are you doing out here?" Hofstadter asked.

"Me? I came to talk to the tree."

Hofstadter nodded. "Does he give you advice?"

That surprised me. I never took Hofstadter for stupid. "No, of course not. He's just a tree. Besides, why would I need advice?"

"No reason. Just that you've driven off everything

you ever loved."

"Driven off. That's bullshit. I haven't driven off anyone." At this Hofstadter pretended to look around. Picked up the frond of a palm and peered under it.

"You mean they're here? They're just hiding?"

He was beginning to get under my skin. At some point you'd expect him to act responsibly.

"Listen, smart ass. Not a day goes by I don't think of Reba and Stace. That I don't worry about Tommy. Especially after what you said."

That didn't impress him. You could tell by the way he thumbed at his lip. Hofstadter was hard to bullshit even when he was alive. I changed the approach.

"Look. I've had a tough time of it. I thought they'd all gone off."

"You wanted them gone."

"Not the girl."

"Not until she returned."

He was backing me into a corner. "You don't understand. You've forgotten what it's like. Every time one of them leaves, you die a little."

"That's not dying, Mooney. You've got it backwards. That's living."

I wanted him to stay. "Have you noticed?" I asked quickly. "I've stopped the booze. Mostly." I could tell he knew about the bender last night, but to his credit he kept it to himself.

"So I heard." And what was left of him shrugged. "Well, who knows? Maybe there's hope. Trouble is," and he kind of got down from the tree and started to move off. "Trouble is, where I'm going, hope is contraband. You can only bring over stuff for home consumption.

Post-its, crescent wrench, peanut butter. Soooo," and here he gave me a preliminary fade, out and in, "so I'm leaving mine with you."

He cupped his hands together like he'd caught a grasshopper. I went over to see, and when I got there he threw out his hands, a magician launching a dove. Nothing came out, and the traces that were Hofstadter disappeared. Or moved. He didn't show well in direct sun. I thought I saw him gliding down the airstrip.

I wasn't about to let him off so easy. I shouted after him, "What's done is done." That stopped him and he turned.

"You're an eloquent bastard, Mooney. Life on this island has given you the tongue of the poet."

"Still, what's done is done. You can't change the past."

"Nor the future," Hofstadter retorted. "What does that leave?" He gave me the old squint.

"What's that supposed to mean?"

He grunted. He was in one of his moods. I could see it in the cock of his head. He turned to go. Next to him, moving away—a second cloud of exhaust—was the Hunchback. He and the Hunchback had their arms around each other, like drinking buddies, and Hofstader's hand was resting on the very hump.

I sat outside and thought a while. You had to. If I got anywhere I don't remember. The screen door squeaked behind me and Arden bounced down the steps.

"Food, Leonard, food. Follow me."

Michael and Fat Man had jettisoned excess weight—they didn't figure to need provisions for a while—and they'd left brown sacks all over the strip.

Packets of food were still cool from the food locker. Arden and I carried the sacks into the house and she inventoried our trove across the kitchen counters. We might have plundered a ship on the rocks. Six ears of corn, snap beans, a crate of eggs, plastic bags of fruit. She chopped up the fruit, mango and oranges, and tossed them in a salad bowl. I fried two omelets, browned them and folded in a soft Italian cheese. We ate out on the screened porch and watched the sky light up. It was a great breakfast. I didn't know what the hell I was going to do with her, let alone the airplane, but I ate all the food.

We sat on the porch, side by side. She talked about Brisbane, growing up, and I told her of Reba and the kids and what has passed for my life.

"Why do you talk about it with such..."

"Such what?" I couldn't think what she was going to say.

"Sorrow. Why do you talk about it with such sorrow?" It was an odd thing to ask, I didn't have an answer. I guess because it made me sad.

"You think it's a happy story?"

"I don't think stories are happy or sad, I think they just are. People are happy or sad, but only for a moment, and then they change. Your kids sound great, Leonard. Tommy sounds like a kindred soul."

I had to put this down to her age. Still, she would see it from the kid's point of view. All the while I was wondering, will she go back with Isaac if I ask her. I knew this wasn't going to last, so it seemed to me better to move on it rather than have it move on you.

She thought of something, leapt to her feet and

raced up the beach.

I cleaned up from breakfast. I was just finishing the fry pan when I heard the bulldozer. She drove it to the middle of the strip and shut down there, like she'd told me to do. In a funny way, I was touched. Worried, too, but touched.

She came in a girlish skip into the house. "Are you sure?" I asked her. "They may come back."

"They may."

"And if they do, won't they be angry we blocked their way?"

"Furious."

I didn't find this easy. She was nesting in. I liked having a companion who wasn't a vegetable or an illusion. But she couldn't stay. I knew that. I must be thirty years older, she wouldn't want to stay.

"And what will become of my little construction job? If it's not an airstrip, what is it?"

"Why…it's a meditation garden. When you want to be alone, you'll go out and sit on the bulldozer to think things through."

"I don't want to be alone." That was out before I'd had time to think, but she didn't pick up on it.

She bit her lip. "I know, then. We build a tennis court. I know how, I've done that at home. We'll wet it down and roll it with these great push-pull cylinder things that are painted green and one fills with water. We'll get your man—what is his name?"

"Isaac."

"—your man Isaac to bring us nets and tape and posts, and perhaps an umpire's chair with a striped umbrella, and you and I will play tennis on the sand."

"Will we? I'd like that."

"We will. We'll wear whites, I'll shop for a tennis dress with lace panties and you will have long trousers, and your man Isaac will call the score in a clipped Bahamian accent, advantage Mr. Hermit—what is your last name?"

I told her.

"Perfect. Advantage Mr. Mooney. Game and set Mr. Mooney, he leads one set to nil. After the match the three of us will sit on the porch. Isaac will drape his blazer over a chair and we'll sip iced mint tea and discuss points of strategy."

The days were like that. We walked about and she taught me the names of everything that grew there. That's how I came to know C. Aubrey was a Norfolk pine, I wouldn't have known a Norfolk pine from a Carolina wren but Arden did, and she found both there and called them by name to their faces.

Arden very much liked names. The words themselves don't matter, but it's a game, isn't it, knowing stuff like that? The first man who ate a pomegranate after calling it that still had seeds between his teeth. It doesn't build anything or move life anywhere, it's rather like the news. You can do without it, and most times it gets in the way, but it doesn't offend and it keeps you in touch with the human race, if you're so inclined.

The naming and the fishing got us easily through the days. When my craving for a drink was about to send me off the deep end, a dose of anxiety over Arden neutralized it. She bunked downstairs, and I bunked up. The nights were tough. I wasn't used to sleep or sobriety. I paced the house and walked the beach and every so often I mounted the bulldozer intending to move it. Instead I'd sit and think about our day—get used to pleasure, Arden would tell me, it won't bite—and maybe peek in on her asleep, and I'd get through to the dawn.

Why was I anxious? I wanted her around and I didn't. And I didn't know whether we would sleep together. She was so casual about sex, and I couldn't read Hofstadter on the subject. My own cravings were just returning, peeking through like Alice's crocuses in spring, an event she got excited about and I recall as disappointing.

Afternoons we would get out the fishing rod and stand to our knees together in the sizzling water to catch dinner. My casting was improving, but I couldn't match the lazy way she flipped the little pyramid sinker that pulled line out past the waves, plunking and settling. Or match her for knowing when to strike. Don't poke about, she would tell me. Sense it. Be that crab on the hook and you'll know when you're nibbled on. We caught little fish, jack and grunts, maybe a pound each. Dinner size. She knew their names, too, and she'd speak to them about the voyage on which their souls were embarking and their next appearance on earth, before she deftly bonked out their lights. Good eating, but little fish.

We talked. It was odd. When I spoke of my family I saw not the people but cutouts where they had been. As a kid, Stace had these paper-doll books, you'd push out the doll and it left behind a gray cardboard outline. That's how I'd come to think of them.

Arden was interested in Tommy. Especially his paintings. Numinous worlds, she said when I described them, worlds of their own. We were standing in a warm surf and there was no action. I would have suggested quitting though it was pleasant there, the bubble and foam comforting, and Arden in her cotton sweatshirt with the sleeves pushed past her elbows like a teenager.

"You talk about him as if he's both a tragedy and a great success. You're half-right, he's a success."

"He is?" I wasn't about to take her word, though I wished I could, I wished she didn't have those studs in her nose.

"Yes. He has a lot of you in him. You are related etheric beings. He's out in the world and you're here, hiding behind booze and isolation. Inside you both lie the clarity and contentment you seek." She flung a cast beyond the swells and handed me the rod. I began a slow retrieve.

I meant to ask what Tommy had of me in him, but just as she finished her sentence, I felt a twang on the line. The pole angled over deeply, and the line on the reel sang out against the drag. "Hit him," she shouted, and I didn't know what she meant. "Hit him," she was pantomiming a jerk on the rod, so I jerked it. "Again, again," and I did.

The angle the line made into the water flattened when the fish ran from the blind tug, then increased as he dove. It was twilight, and in the red water the weight of the fish was deep and jagged. He flopped against the line, you could feel his head horsing and his body curling into a C-clamp. I looked over to Arden to see if she wanted to take the rod. Her eyes glistened. Her eyes fixed on the vee where the line went into the water. "That's a nice fish," she said to herself, pleased. When the fish ran to the deep the reel couldn't keep up with the pull and I took three grudging steps farther into the ocean. With the rod butt stuck in my belly I cranked with my left hand and pumped the shaft with my right. The muscle in my forearm began to ache. She came around and put her fingers on the points of my hipbone.

"Don't let him pull me out to sea."

"No," she was watching closely. She held on lightly, as if she was a fighting chair and we had forgotten to buckle the strap. It didn't help but I liked it just the same.

"He'll tire himself. Let him. Don't fight when he's fighting. Let him fight the rod." I cranked and did as she said.

The line came to rest, snagged I thought, and heavy on the bottom. I pulled gently to dislodge it, but Arden said no, he's just resting, and he was. The line began to move again, outward. I would have tossed it all in if she hadn't been there. When the fish let me I recovered line. Once, just beyond the waves, he surfaced. Burst a little plomp on the evening water, silver and pink, and dove again.

"*Pargo*," I heard in her breath behind me, and I thought maybe she was cursing the fish. I reeled in against the weight. Now he was closer, yards beyond the surf and her voice quieted with concern.

"You can't pull against the waves. If you do you'll lose him. When the wash is going out, let him go."

The fish was tiring. I timed the swells. When they moved the seas to shore, I took in line. We brought him gingerly through the breaking surf. A last wave caught him and tossed him into us, the water to our knees. We walked the flopping thing, dead but for his gasp, back up the beach.

From the fight I'd thought he'd be the size of a

dinghy, but he was only two feet long and, beached and put away, weighed maybe twenty pounds. Pink and fleshy, he had taken the hook between two dentines that could punch holes in a car door. Red snapper, Arden said, *pargo*. One of the great eating fishes and if I'd chance it, she would prepare it for me the way Michael did. I was going to say, Hang it by its heels, but I let it go. Michael was gone. And Arden had been after me to give up grudges. She said they weighed only on the people who carried them.

Arden slid one hand under the gills and lifted the fish between us. Then she shook my hand as if we might be taking a picture on a tourist pier. I wished we had, I wished we'd had a picture and I'd send it to the Clerk, and on the back I'd write, Dear Canges, Drop dead.

Arden cleaned the fish with Michael's knife and cut large steaks from its sides. I carried them to the house. She went down to the rocks. Mussels, she told me, for appetizers.

I wrapped the slabs of fish in newspaper and shelved them lengthwise in the refrigerator. When I went back to the beach, she had her clump of mussels and was stripping down to swim. I watched from the beach, she didn't seem to mind. There was not a line on her body. She swam way out, to where the lavender waters were smooth and groomed, like a golf course. Then she turned tail up and dove. The white bouy of her buttocks, then the points of her feet. Had she bottomed out? When she surfaced she swam parallel to the shore, around the point so I couldn't see her anymore, and finally, when I'd thought about God knows what, came swimming back. The way she stroked the water I wished it was me, the way each arm cocked at its own angle, an angle she made up, held over the black pudding-skin, and then slid magically in without a splash. She could make it to China.

Twenty yards from shore she stopped. Surf rolled behind her, still you could tell she was listening. I heard it too, the bumblebee drone of an airplane. Could they land around the cat? On the beach? Had they changed their minds and come back for her? For me? I saw the airplane, high, each wing lit with a single dot. It passed off to the north. It wasn't them at all, it was someone else.

Arden showered. I built a fire and made iced tea. Fat Man had left lemons and I cut two across the girth and down through into quarters. There was a tea strainer in the drawer, and I squeezed the juice through it to catch the pulp and seeds. One of the seeds had begun to sprout a tiny green tail. I stacked cracked ice in a large water glass, like a cocktail shaker in a David Niven movie. We sat and watched the fire and drank our tea like highballs.

While the fish was baking I brought potatoes and a cutting board into the living room so we could sit together. I peeled and she chopped. I was thinking—actually I was thinking nothing. Just the way it was, I was stuck between events and designs and I was thinking nothing. It was a perfect time, I don't know that I'd ever had one like it

She got up to see about the fish and came back holding the distributor cap. I'd left it on the counter.

"Leonard, what's this?"

"It's a distributor cap."

"What does it do?" She had the expression of one of

those young county attorneys zeroing in on exactly where you were when the light turned red.

"It distributes the current to the plugs so they fire in order."

"Where did it come from?"

"I'll tell you after dinner." I meant it, too. I wasn't ashamed of what I'd done—I simply wanted to enjoy dinner without all that talk of motives and relationships. They're hard to digest.

Arden set the table, she'd found cloth napkins in the uppermost cabinet. I'd never noticed them, blue cloth napkins shot with hollyhocks, and the frayed straw place mats. You have to know that she had parents who cared about her. You could tell from the way she folded those napkins. She thought about other people's feelings and you knew someone had taken the trouble to teach her about them and folding linen napkins and manners. I wondered what her parents thought of her life. I didn't like to think Arden had walked out on them. Maybe she sends them trinkets when she travels, souvenir serapes from Mexico and little marimbas painted with a scene of Mount Sugarloaf, not just postcards.

I told her a story about Indianapolis, maybe my only memory except for strolls in that grim basement pool. When you're there, Indianapolis, all over the place you see signs for Hoosiers. The Hoosier Bar, Hoosier Motors, Go Hoosiers. I asked people what it meant, and no one knew. The fellow who checked in my rental car at the airport said there were a bunch of theories and they ranged from the name for a guy who's good with his fists, to an abbreviation for Who's there? but no one knew. I asked him, It bother you to be called something and you don't even know what you are? No, he said, it didn't.

When the mussels were ready she brought them into the living room and sat cross-legged on the floor. I ate three. Fact is, I didn't really like them. Arden ate the rest, must have been more than a dozen, prying them out of their black cocoons where they sat like eyes, like some secret flesh.

"That's just the way I fancy them," she said to me between slurps, "steamed with salt and onion."

CHAPTER 24.

The fish was delicious. I sharked through it. Up to my fins in food, I only noticed her toward the end. Her hands were folded in her lap. The meal sat upon her plate, a few bites around the edges.

"What's wrong?"

"I don't know."

She had the slightest moustache of dew on her lip.

"I think I'll lie down."

She pushed back her chair and staggered to her feet, as if I'd spiked the punch. What do people think when the first palsy jumps their hand? That wasn't me, someone must have tweaked a string or goosed the puppeteer. She moved unsteadily to the hall and into the downstairs bedroom. The plates sat bored and joyless, waiting for someone to feed. I finished my food, thought to eat hers but covered it instead with a plastic sack and stuck it in the refrigerator.

I did up the pans. There was a low groan, like a sound in the plumbing. I shut down the taps and heard it again. I went to find her in the darkened room. She was doubled over on the bed, holding her gut.

"I don't think I'm well, Leonard."

What the hell was I thinking? How would I care for her if she was sick? And she was. I ran upstairs, tore the white sheet from the bed and hung it from the window. A signal with an exclamation point. I hadn't summoned Isaac for weeks. I'd lost track of what day it was and had forgotten what direction he came from. When I got back down Arden was trying to pull herself out of the bed.

"Toilet."

I got her to the bowl in time. The vomit was black, blue-black like the inside of the mussel shells, and I thought to myself, that's the answer. She'll get rid of the mussels. She did, she retched again and again, her forehead pressed engine hot against my palm. That must do it, that must be the last of it, and each time I thought it was, her insides clenched and she opened up to rid herself of whatever was wrong.

I moistened a washcloth and wiped down her face, got her to rinse her mouth with tiny sips of water. In the midst of it, my own stomach started its pangs, which I put off as a sympathetic reaction. I needed not to get sick, not until she was better. Even in the dark her hair was white, straw stitched with silver. Relieved that she was over the worst, I changed her into stuff from my drawer, clean cotton boxer shorts and a T-shirt, and arranged her back in bed. Her eyes were rheumy, and she seemed to have no substance. All feathers, the mass of the body of a bird after the soul flies, and I pulled the sheet to her chin.

It was the longest night of my life. Arden lay in a cool sweat, shivering and asking for blankets. I got out the entire supply of the house. That failed to warm her, so I took off my shirt and lay on top of her. She submerged and rose in this film of being awake, floating inches above and dapping again to the surface, never really with me. Whatever it was, something kept her above the line. Some tiny, ice-thin tension, her consciousness floated like a water bug.

She would start, thinking she had more to disgorge, and I would grip her around the waist and walk her to the toilet. Her stomach by then was knotting against itself, there could be nothing wrung. The last time we took our tour, I placed her in bed.

"Leonard."

"Yes."

"My feet. I have no feeling in my feet."

I reached down. They were cold and the skin felt as if it was stretched over clay.

"I'm scared," she said.

"Me too."

"Will you be my angel now?"

I smiled. It had nothing behind it, a phony baloney wince that tacked the lips up into the cheeks. Fact is, I was sweating from the rock in my stomach and that say-cheese was the best I could summon.

"It's time for angel to appear." You had to lean in to hear her words. Her breath was sour and faint, her eyes were wandering, and she talked in a whisper. "Angels come in a crisis. When life seems not to be moving." All I could do was hold on, there was nothing to fix. She dozed for a minute, then came back in that midnight voice.

"Life doesn't stop, though. That's an illusion. Life moves forward. Will you be my angel now?"

"I don't know how."

"It's easy. You know how acrobats on the high wire? when they start to fall? reach way over with their fingers tipped?" I nodded. The muscles of her throat were tired from vomiting and the sound came out small and far away.

"What they're doing...they are reaching out to touch their angel. Fingertips...when you teeter..."

My hands were on her feet. For all the world I thought of that fish, that red snapper, pulled from its favorite easy chair into a sea of unfriendly air and how quickly the light went out of it.

More than once I raced through the first floor hoping they'd left behind the cell phone. I tried the old movie routine, just imagine yourself watching all this and you'll be free of it. But it didn't work.

We lay coupled in quiet. I looked on her face and realized what was missing. It wasn't her fault, it's just that I'd lived with a real woman, and Arden wasn't quite a real woman yet. She was trying. When a man loves a real woman, he wants to bring her his faults and have her make them over. He wants her to change them into a refreshed youth, into the courage he used to have. I figured that out in the night, waiting for Arden's breath to die down like a bad wind. Once it seemed to stop and my heart shrank in my chest like a walnut. I used to do that with Reeb, but my will ticked away, I couldn't go on bringing her that stuff. People only have so much tolerance, and if I kept bringing stuff in by the carload, she would have bolted.

Thinking Arden was asleep, I rose.

"Why didn't the airplane start?"

"Because I took out the distributor cap." She smiled. I don't know why I hesitated to tell her. I wasn't sorry I'd done it and if you care you have to do something. Even if it pissed her off. Besides, she was too weak to complain.

In the kitchen I filled a saucepan with water, put it on the burner and stuck in the last bottle of rum. Then I ran up to the strip to where she'd parked the bulldozer. The keys were in it. I got it underway and drove to the end by the house. Fast as it would go, Arden-style, throttle levers to full stop. I bladed all the extra wood by the house, the stacks of scruff and debris from the strip, down to the beach. One ugly mess, my height. I dumped heated rum on the pile and threw in a match. With a shoosh, flames leapt into the night. Across the bay, peering as I could, there was not a light to be made out, not a ship's bulb or the glow of a running light.

Back inside the bedroom we could hear the popping of the flames. Someone would see it as a signal fire and not an accident. Strong young women Arden's age didn't die from eating a bad mussel in the Caribbean. I lay down at the foot of the bed and slept in patches. My own skin was clammy with nausea and I envied her the vomiting. My hand was on her foot, where the smooth shin of her leg joined the ankle.

"Leonard."

She spoke softly and I couldn't tell how long I'd been asleep.

"My hands. The one is tingly."

"That's a good sign. Maybe that's a sign of healing."

"But the other. I can't feel the other."

I grabbed the hand she waved above the sheet. It too

was cool. She can't be right about angels. If that's what we need to recover our balance it won't work. Most of the time we don't know we're faltering. You couldn't miss Arden's signs. Others, Tommy, when they're getting ready to go it's gradual, it sneaks up on you. But illness is easy, you couldn't have seen her and missed it. The eyes belonged to someone else. They had sunk deeper into their sockets, the lids fluttered like the wiring had gone wrong, and her words came out wrong.

Outside day was cracking through the shell of the sky. The loneliness of the new light made me realize no one was coming to help. I had to get her out. The fire had burned out and a thin rope of smoke rose from the soot. I had no choice.

The 185 sat with its nose stuck in the air and a chip on its shoulder. Come on, M. Looney, it was thinking. Come on, I dare you.

I answered back. "You're just a machine, and I'm good with machines."

It said nothing, just sat there looking superior. "You bastard. Even bent over with cramps, terrified, I can make you work. The lists, all I have to do is find them and follow them."

Its door was unlocked and the single key lay on top of the instrument panel. Two seats up front, a tiny bench that might hold two more in back. Could Arden lie down there, would she be safe? Could I get up in the air and find a city? First, I suppose, find land, then a city? And how to get it down again?

I installed the cap, and checked the map compartment for the lists she'd mentioned. Air sickness bags, a pad with notes about weather and winds.

Nothing else. Maybe I wouldn't find them. Maybe a merciful saint had hidden the checklists, to save me for better things on this earth. A door pocket on the passenger's side held only tissues, a Spanish-English dictionary, and a gauzy green scarf. I started to root for the theory of divine intervention. In the other door's pocket were a wooden dipstick smelling of gasoline, a log book, and—my heart sank—a dozen pages coated in plastic, held together by a single ring. I took the pages back to the house. So much for the power of prayer.

Arden was sleeping. I turned on the hall light and lay angled across the foot of her bed so I could scan the pages by the yellow bulb. The few mussels I'd eaten were gathering in my stomach like the Sioux at Little Big Horn. Armed with spears.

Checklists, just as she'd said. I took them into the bathroom and sat on the can. Two sets of lists, Normal Procedures on white pages, Emergency Procedures on red. I couldn't bring myself to look at the red, we would simply need luck. In the Normal was a list for each step, or so I hoped, of a journey. Preflight, Taking Off, En Route Climb, Descent, and Landing. That happiest of topics, Shutting Down the Airplane. In logical order. How hard could this be? So long as I never had to look down, and so long as the guy who wrote these lists had pulled an A in the course, I'd be fine.

Here was a text on how to stay alive. Not my favorite subject. I thought of those dry conversations with Hofstadter, choosing your last moments. A plunge from several thousand feet into the ocean wouldn't have been my first pick. I had always favored pills, they offered a perfect way, an easy and uninterruptible sleep. You want your last moments to be safe and sound. No condemned man orders a last meal of tripe and Brussels sprouts, to see if maybe he's developing sophisticated tastes.

I read through the checklists. Half the terms didn't mean anything. REGULATE MIXTURE. Would Arden know how it was to be regulated and which knob did it? How to set elevator and rudder flaps for takeoff, what were the flight instruments? The tasks fell into two main categories. There were the ones you had to adjust or set or fix, and then a bunch of others you only had to check. I drew a thin, mental line through each item that said CHECK. We'd have to trust Arden's angels. Some concepts I understood, the instructions on throttle and airspeeds, and if we could simply find the throttle I figured I could do that part. Thankfully the checklists didn't address the emotional stuff, crashing or falling, you'd never know from them that they were suggesting anything unnatural. Just keep looking up.

The sky was clear but gusty, the weather might be changing. I carried Arden, wrapped in two blankets, out the back door and through the palm break. The 185 shone tinny in the dawn. It perched on its tail wheel, looking up innocent as a cat watching a bird. She wanted in the front right seat, by me, so I loaded her through the door and strapped both the waist belt and the shoulder cinch around the padded form of her. She was limp, I had to check to make sure I had buckled something in there besides the blankets.

I ducked under the wing and pulled the chocks that secured the wheels. Then I swung myself into the pilot's left seat.

God, it was small. I handed the checklists to Arden.

Then I sat back and found myself angled backward and looking at the sky.

"How do you see where you're going?"

"When it gets up speed, the tail lifts up and you'll be level. Until then you usually make S turns."

"S turns."

"But on this short runway, Michael said no. Can't afford to give up runway. Just go straight."

The time had come. Arden moved the plastic cards close to bring them into focus. I studied the panel and she helped me guess at the switches and knobs before me.

"Are you afraid?" she asked. The breath from her mouth made a sound.

"Terrified."

"Just remember. Fear isn't pain. It's just the weak little brother. You can conquer fear." I was going over the names of dials.

"Maybe so. But you know how family is. Maybe pain is just down the block, waiting to kick the Bejeezus out of whoever takes on his weak little brother." She barely smiled. I wanted her conscious for as long as she could make it. I needed the company.

Between her hit-and-miss memory and the checklist, we put a name to most of the switches. Pedals control the rudder, they were working, yoke turns for right and left and pulls and pushes for up and down. It seemed to make sense. In the hands of someone who knew what to do the damned thing might even fly.

We went to the first entry:

STARTING ENGINE

1. Mixture- RICH

2. Propeller- HIGH RPM

3. Carburetor Heat- COLD

That stopped me. Arden seemed pretty sure that it already was cold and there was nothing we could do to heat it up.

4. Throttle- PUMP ONCE, or as much as six times if engine is hot
5. Propeller area- CLEAR
6. Master switch- ON
7. Ignition switch- START (release when engine starts)

The engine faked, cranked and fired. Really fired. Its combustion shook the whole cigar tube. The wings trembled in the wash. God help me, would it fly early? Now was the time to back out, not fifty feet above the ground or spread over the rocks at the end of the island like so much aluminum siding. Here is piled M. Looney, mourned by C. Aubrey Smith and survived by the imaginary hermit of the shed. Remembered in Christ by a single crab, who at the wake described to his family how he once roomed with the main course. That mound you see by the grave marker is caused by the hump on his back.

We could shut down and wait for Isaac. I could stand on the beach and signal a boat if one passed, call to it or swim out. I could drive this airplane out on the beach and set it on fire. There must be a better way to get Arden somewhere fast, one that did not involve leaving the surface of the earth. Then I released the brakes.

We practiced taxiing. I would need a good head of speed, Arden told me twice and so did the checklist procedure for short field. Twenty degrees of flaps and maximum speed. I zig-zagged up and down the lower half of the strip to see how taxiing worked. The airplane rested on its tail, and its nose-high slant gave you a view of the tops of the trees that were waiting for you. The only way to see where you were was by driving a constant S. But to get up to speed on a short and soft runway, we'd need to grit it out and hope we were pointed, as the checklist instructed, straight down the centerline. There was no mention of what to do without a centerline.

"Are you with me?" She nodded. Her eyes had sunk deeper still, I thought whoever was in there was taking a last look around the room before giving the key back to the front desk.

"You know that thing you quoted me? Magic, the spell of living well?"

She nodded.

"Say that again."

She started, her words mush and the spaces between them disappearing. Still, as I'm zigging and zagging, she got through most of it.

"So. What's it called? Where's it from?"

Her mouth gave up the smallest smile.

"The Egyptian Book of the Dead."

"Great."

I motored the airplane to the very edge of the runway and pulled the yoke to get it headed the other way. Nothing happened—the yoke turned the plane in the air, not on the ground, I had to gas it and use the rudder pedals. We got our U, trimming fern fronds with the wing as the plane rotated. Arden read off the entries for BEFORE TAKEOFF and we did whatever we could find. Some of the dashboard items were labeled, a great comfort. We never did locate the magnetos or the carburetor heat, but those were both CHECK items, and with any luck, they didn't need checking. Next topic on the list, unavoidable unless you skipped to the end, Tying up the Airplane, was SHORT FIELD TAKEOFF.

We went over the eight items a last time. Arden pushed the flap lever to the notch that read twenty degrees. I stood on the brakes and pushed the throttle in as far as it would go. The airplane shook against its restraint, and the engine raced with a full, impatient sound. I kept my eye on the edge of the strip—that's how I'd decided to make sure we were going straight, eye-balling a uniform distance from what I hoped was the straight edge of the clearing—and took my feet off the brakes. The machine lurched forward, the ground began to plod by below. In fifty feet the tail came up, just as Arden had promised, and we had a perfect view of the large palms at the end of the strip accelerating toward us. By now it was too late to do anything but skinny down and hope we could lift off the ground. Otherwise I had picked out the two trees we would aim between. If we hit hard enough, the wings would come off and the fuselage would slide down the gully that led to the shed, end up on the rocks that anchored our island to the sea. Most small airplane crashes end in fire, Arden said. The tanks are usually full of fuel.

The brush line came at me faster and faster. Let it fly by itself, Arden had warned me, don't pull the nose up too fast or we'll stall and crash. We were in the air, barely. A wall of fern and palm raced at us, you could see each leaf, great fidelity, depth of field. Especially at eye level. I shut my eyes and heard a whish, the cutting of soft branches. When I opened them again, we were twenty feet in the air, and vines and browned palm leaves were blowing off the spinning tires.

And then we were over the ocean. I let go a howl, I have an idea of why those Indians whooped going into battle and it isn't from courage. Slowly at first, we climbed above the water. It stretched below, concrete hard and black in the morning sun. Don't look down. The plane took a nauseating dip. Arden had pushed up the flaps lever, and when they retracted we sunk.

"Don't do that again," I yelled at her. Sick or not.

"No need. Only need to do it once."

"And warn me next time."

"No next time."

She shouted the procedures for en route climb. I hadn't expected the noise, it didn't add to my peace of mind. The plane climbed to a thousand feet and I said that was plenty. She insisted, no, go higher. There was some rule about altitude and direction, at what level you were supposed to fly, but she didn't know it. Altitude, she insisted, was safety. I thought the argument not worth having. I would be as dead falling from one thousand feet as four, and I had no plans for spending time it would take to get there. We climbed. Next on the list was Cruise. Arden called off her instructions, we discussed what they meant, and I complied with the ones where we had a legitimate guess. So far, I said to her, we've made every light.

"You know what we forgot?"

My heart went out the window, began its fall to the sea.

"What?"

"You're supposed to check the winds. Take off

upwind. I forgot to tell you."

"I'm not going back to try it again. That will have to do."

We turned to a compass heading she guessed for us. Turning was easy, except for the terror. My hands had soldered to the yoke and each time I wanted to use them I had to stare them loose. Our plan was to get near enough and high enough so we could sight Nassau, fly to it and raise the airfield on the radio.

Something she had said bothered me.

"Arden."

"Yes?"

"What you said about crashes? Fuel?"

"Yes?"

"How much gas do we have?"

"I don't know. The rule is you fill up whenever you land."

I searched wildly about the panel. I had noticed fuel gauges when Arden and I first went over the instruments, but they had disappeared. Finally, by keeping my finger on each window and reading them across the two gauges reappeared. One for each tank. Over an arc that went from a healthy green through beige to an ominous red, two needles flickered. Bounced around with every air bump, wiggling like grass in a high wind. You couldn't tell with any precision but our fuel seemed to register between the hash marks for half and empty.

"How much gas do we need to get to Nassau?"

"Don't know."

"And the last time Michael flew this plane. Where did he refuel it?"

"Don't know. Not sure he did."

I looked below us. The ocean flashed a single unfriendly surface. As I watched, a small, cabined power boat crossed directly under our path. I could make out a U-shaped deck behind, the white vee of the wake. I knew I should stop staring. What height suggests is, it might up and disappear, and the sensation of that, that eclipse, is dizzying. Dizzying and a drug, but I couldn't take my eyes away. The solace of that boat, it didn't know we were there. Off in the corner I saw our shadow. Tiny, a black shadow far off to the left, a ghost of us skimming the top of the water. The sight of something of me—let alone insubstantial or unreal, that didn't help—the sight of my shadow in a tin tube skimming along the water, startling mullet and snapper, seas below deep as a canyon and filled with God knows what, was too much. I had taken only a hurried piece of bread for breakfast, and when I looked down at that shadow, the heel of bread congealed and rose up fast. Headed north to freedom. I swallowed it a second time.

Arden was dozing, the blankets were hooded over her head and her lips had fallen apart. The brown of her tanned face had an odd cast to it, it was like a primer coat that had dried and evaporated, as if she was just paint on skin. I began to hum. "Into the Forest." At high altitude you can force your ears open by pressing your tongue to the roof of the mouth. It makes a nice, private chamber and in there I sang, Light green all the way. I had to sing it in my head. My mouth was dry as carpet.

I checked the compass again. There was something she'd said about needing to adjust it, but it was sealed, it had no knobs on it. Maybe that was some other instrument. I tried to keep centered on a heading of two-eighty, north by northwest, like the movie, but every time the airplane jostled it mushed about. Two-eighty was, she'd thought, a course to intersect the Bahamas. As soon as we were within range we planned to announce ourselves on an emergency radio frequency. What the frequency was and how you raised them, I realized when I saw how she slept, how she seemed dead to the world, she had neglected to tell me.

I thought of Tommy. Tommy in that sunny biplane swooping above the cruelty and battle of his drawing, the yellow form traced in black. I put the crayon in my mind and drew the outline of the airplane. I don't mean I thought about a drawing of an airplane, I mean some detachable part of me with stand-away eyes and stomach and panic went outside and walked around the wing and the wheel, then around the other side, down to the tail and back. Even the propeller. What had Tommy done for the propeller, was that outlined too? I couldn't remember. The way you would expect to draw a whirling propeller was a circle, maybe a bunch of faint, concentric circles, like you see in cartoons. How had Tommy done it? It really mattered to me, but, thirty-five hundred fluctuating feet above the planet where I'd spent my happiest days, also some unhappy ones though they began to take on a silver glow, it really mattered to me but I couldn't remember.

CHAPTER 25.

Pain's little brother turned out to be no schoolyard sissy. He could fight his own fights. The needles on the fuel gauges were still bouncing in tandem, as if they had rehearsed their act and their exit. But the dance was calming down. When I first looked, on a good bounce the little red points flickered to midway, but now they failed to clear the hash mark to the short side of one-quarter. We were over a mothering expanse of ocean, yet the way Arden had described it, we were supposed to be seeing a line of islands like the wizard's yellow-brick road. All that water, and my mouth gone from dry to moonscape. Ahead on the horizon, highlighted by the sunshine behind me, rose a towering fleet of clouds, their bases at our level and their bubbling tops stretching up farther than I could bear to think. Loud on the buzzing intercom was the sound of a lunatic in our own cockpit singing at the top of his lungs—and in Latin. I couldn't seem to turn him down.

Once she found that groove of sleep, Arden didn't

want to snap out of it. I heard my voice, full of a father's anger. "Arden, for God's sake get up." You could see some movement behind the eyelid, but it wasn't quite consciousness. Some time about here, we are flying about and I am on this constant verge of peeing and there is nothing, I am the coyote in a Roadrunner cartoon, there is nothing below me, I realize this is ending. If I'd wanted to sleep with Arden, and I had, it was too late. I had and I hadn't—she dropped in on me like a gift, and with gifts you can't negotiate. Gifts fall from the sky. What we did or didn't do and whether she was there for a day or a year or a life wasn't the point. Isn't that the thing about Reba too? Isn't that the thing about love?

My hands had welded to the yoke and now they refused to come loose. I stared the fingers of the right hand off, one by one they came, then the thumb. The hand moved uncertainly toward Arden, found her shoulder. "Up, wake up."

She opened her eyes. I was so happy to see those pupils that I didn't recognize the reflection in them, I didn't catch the jeopardy until she inhaled to form a shout. Her alarm made me look outside. The ominous line of clouds had tilted to the right, so it cut the windshield almost perpendicular. When I had shaken her, the weight of my fear remained behind in one hand, and I'd steered the airplane on its side.

We careened off in a deep decline and instinctively I jerked the wheel to the right. My weight doubled in the seat below me and with a nauseating yaw the airplane righted itself. The acid of adrenaline pricked my forehead and lips, my shoulder blades shivered under a fresh coat of sweat.

"Hey," she grinned. "That was something."

I had no answer. I was chewing on stomach. But at least the nose dive had brought her back. "Arden, listen. We've been up for half an hour and I don't see those islands. Are you sure of the heading?"

She gave a little grimace.

"And the fuel. There are no gas stations up here. I'm not sure we know where we are."

She looked out. "Over the ocean," she said softly.

"The frequency. Didn't you say there's a frequency for emergencies. We need help."

She leaned over. There were four panels showing liquid crystal numbers before us, and she dialed one expertly.

"That's it. Someone will be listening."

"Now what?"

She slid off again toward sleep.

"Arden, for God's sake, wake up." I moved to shake her again. And again when my right hand came loose the left dragged the plane into a curve. It was as if the only way I could go straight was to have these two forces, you wouldn't know they were both me, pulling for all their worth in opposite directions. I steered the yoke even and tried again, this time watching to make sure the horizon stayed put.

She yawned, hunched her shoulders under the blankets.

"Now what?"

"I'm not sure."

"Arden!"

"I think that's all there is to it. Michael rarely used the radio, and then only with his friends. You push that little button on the wheel to talk. Then they talk back."

The button was at my thumb. Time to broadcast, and I go speechless. Here I was four thousand feet over an ungodly ocean. Sharks were looking up smiling, here comes dinner: the chef's special, the breakfast burrito, crunchy metal on the outside and delicious ground round inside. I didn't know which way to go, how to get down, and a new issue about forty city blocks ahead was coming at me, what happened when that dark soup got to us? It was all I could do to push and talk.

"Hello," I said gingerly. "Is anyone there?"

There was silence. We hadn't counted on being ignored.

"You have to let it go," Arden said.

"What?"

"The button. You push on it then you let it go to listen?"

"You certain? That sounds screwy. If the button turns it on…?"

"Leonard. I'm sure."

I tried it again. Nothing.

I don't know where I expected the voice to come from, but sure as hell not above, like God Almighty in some school play. I looked up to make certain: the Lord of Hosts was announcing himself out of a two-inch speaker in the cabin roof.

"American Heavy eight four two, aircraft on emergency frequency say again please."

I looked over at Arden. She clamped her lips in achievement.

"Hello," I ventured again. "We may need some help finding a place to land."

"Aircraft on emergency. Say call sign and location."

I assumed that was me. American was an airline. I hadn't reckoned on troubling someone who had passengers to look after, sites of interest to point out.

"Hi. I don't know my call sign. Is it in here somewhere?"

"Is this a joke? Mister, you're on the emergency frequency. This better not be a joke."

Ohmygod. What if he leaves me?

"No sir, no joke. Please. We're trying to find Nassau and I have a very sick woman aboard and I'm needing some help."

"Say your call sign."

"I don't know it. No one gave me one."

"Say location."

"I don't know that either."

"Listen Mister…" American Heavy was losing patience. Arden muttered something. I leaned over to hear her small words, then passed them on.

"We left Penniel Key about forty minutes ago. We've been flying a heading of…" and she gave me the rest of the words a second time between pauses "…two eight zero. We're hoping to raise Nassau."

"Unidentified aircraft, Nassau bound. Are you declaring an emergency?"

"I don't think I have to declare it. It's here."

"Say name of pilot."

"Well, my name is Leonard Mooney. But I'm not exactly a pilot."

There was a long silence while I listened to the stupidity of my statement crackling back like radar. The emotionless voice came on again overhead. "Stand by,

Leonard. American Heavy eight four two relaying your message to Nassau Control."

"Thank you."

"Leonard."

"Yes sir?"

"You're not a pilot?"

"No, sir."

"You're a student pilot?"

"No, sir."

"But you've flown a plane before?"

"No sir. *In* a plane. "

"Leonard. Listen to me. Keep the throttle in all the way. Keep your wings straight and level. And keep out of the clouds."

This was no more than Arden had told me, but the voice seemed so well-intentioned that I thanked him and we waited for Nassau Control. It wasn't long.

"Mr. Mooney." It was a Carib voice, sing-song, black and British.

"Here."

"Mr. Mooney, my name is Hodges. What type of aircraft are you?"

Arden had dozed back asleep. I thought I knew the answer and tried it, a 185. I got color and number on board, but he asked me a lot of things I couldn't answer. He didn't seem upset by any of my don't-knows, except fuel remaining. I had the impression he wanted that tidbit. But he couldn't call on the next kid in class. All he had was me.

"Mr. Mooney, please pay close attention. Look to the stack of radio equipment. At its very bottom you will see an instrument with several knobs, an unlit bulb, and four numbers displayed in white." I looked. There it was.

"Got it."

"Turn the dials under each of the windows so the numbers read 4345." I did what he said. "Now find the button marked ID and depress it." I did. The bulb lit yellow. We flew across five seconds of silence. A long trip, during which I kept my thumb on the button hoping for the down elevator. The gray cloud-wall was so close I could see water leaking out its bottom.

"We have you on our screen," Hodges said. I felt like Alexander Graham Bell raising Watson. "You are at three thousand nine, four six nautical miles south and east of Nassau, relative bearing zero one five degrees."

"Mr. Hodges? I don't mean to be ungrateful, but none of that means anything to me. I'm glad you found me, but I'm much more concerned with the vice versa."

"We agree, Mr. Mooney. You see an instrument on your panel that looks like a compass? Directly in front of you." I had noticed it before, when Arden and I studied the dashboard, and she had determined to use the floating compass attached to the roof. "To its lower right you will find a small adjustment knob. Turn it so that it reads two four five on top." I figured that out. I'm not bad with machines. "And notice, Mr. Mooney, that instrument should correspond with your magnetic compass. The one hanging in front of the windscreen. Whenever it gets out of line, you should correct it. Now, Mr. Mooney, using that instrument turn your airplane in a shallow bank to the right so that two six eight comes up to the top. Very gentle, very shallow."

I did. That must have been why we didn't know where we were. We'd been following course on an instrument that was off. It was probably one of those CHECK items. My small pleasure dissipated when I looked up to see how he'd pointed us. Dead ahead boiled the row of clouds, you could make out the dark mud of movement.

"I want you to fly straight on that heading."

"If I do that, I'll be in the middle of the storm in minutes."

"We'll get you under. Now I want you to begin to lose altitude."

"How do I do that?" There was a silence. Maybe Hodges was consulting the expert on losing altitude.

"Gently pull back the throttle. Do you know which is the throttle? Good. Gently back, I will keep an eye on your altitude. When you reach two thousand three hundred feet, I will tell you gently to push in the throttle."

I did as Hodges said. With the knob back, the plane began to sink. Instinctively I pushed it forward.

"We don't show you descending."

I had chickened out. The idea of being down was appealing, but the going down, that was frightening. I pulled back the knob again. Sure enough, the airplane lost altitude but not all at once. Hodges seemed to know what he was about.

"You are doing fine, Mr. Mooney. You must avoid those clouds and maintain visual contact." With what? I thought to ask, but I didn't have the chance. "What is the nature of the illness of your passenger?"

"Food poisoning," I said. "Bad mussels." He came back quickly, asking for symptoms. With each answer his voice disappeared, returned. I realized he was broadcasting my answers and was being prompted with the next question. Couldn't it wait? When I mentioned the loss of feeling in Arden's hands, his voice pulled its belt in a notch.

Hodges had dropped us to an altitude just below the rain clouds. We flew under the canopy, a tattered bottom of black fringe, and its closeness made me dizzy with fright. Just as the plane's shadow had done, it gave you a sense of distance. Distance and idiocy, this was not a place a sane man would want to be. I had the briefest glimpse of a bright green splotch in the sea. A fried egg griddling dead ahead. It was quick, like those ads they stick in between movie frames to get you to buy popcorn. The flash of a fairway, vivid colors. That's how I knew I'd seen it, the colors, and when I closed my eyes, it was inked on the eyelids.

Quick as it appeared, it vanished. So did everything, sea, sky all grayed out. The airplane started bucking, like driving a car at high speed over parking bumpers. I was too scared to throw up. Rains sheeted over the windshield, so thick we were blind. I told Hodges. His voice, until now shelf-solid, developed a doo-op bass of panic. My instinct was to brake and pull over to the side. Can airplanes fly in the rain?

"Listen carefully, Mr. Mooney. On the instrument panel in front of you, right in the center, you will see a round gauge that shows the outline of an airplane against a blue background. Do you have it?"

"Yes."

"I want you to watch that airplane. Always keep that airplane straight across the horizon. Don't give in to thinking you know better. Do you understand?"

"Yes." The motor was loud in my ears but the singing of the Mass had stopped. I watched the gauge. The airplane on it was stable but the horizon moved every time we banked. The blue of its sky wasn't real, it was like a glazed bowl, flat and empty.

Every two seconds, Hodges was at me. Slight bank left, pinch back the throttle, touch the left pedal. When he didn't have instructions he would ask how I was doing. I told him, Fine. Indeed I was. The turbulence had eased. The toy airplane on the dial balanced on the horizon straight up, and once I waggled its wings to make sure the gauge wasn't broken. With nothing to look at, flying was a video game, I began to enjoy the day. I figured it was my last. And the manipulation of controls and instruments. I can get machines to behave, and I had in my hands a truly magical one.

"Do not give in to an impulse that you are askew," Hodges warned again. "You are the airplane on that blue horizon, maintain that attitude straight across no matter what. And resist the temptation to make the airplane go up or down. You are in fact descending at a proper rate. Leave the yoke where it is, don't pull or push at it." I watched the horizon on the dash. Arden had shown me another dial that tells you whether you're gaining or losing altitude, and I glanced at that too. I had too much to watch, how the hell was I going to see the ground?

"We have you six miles from the strip. We will soon pick you up with glasses. You're doing fine."

Fine must have been the secret word, and we were the duck. The airplane gave a sudden and deep drop, bounced at the end of the string. Arden groaned.

Then cooed. "Ohh. Look at that."

I did. Outside the windscreen the rain had thinned, and we saw a length of Parker's pen-blue sea and a sparkling green island shaped like a guano splat. A city in its midst, and to the north of that, down the nose of the airplane, a white concrete strip. Hodges had brought us in right on the runway.

Following his words, I bled off the throttle and Arden rallied to put down the flaps. The ground moved up at us, and the concrete lined itself up to slide under our wheels. Hodges seemed to like what we were doing. Pools of water dotted the strip. Lights and numbers passed below, then yard after yard of delicious concrete, and still we weren't down. I suddenly panicked—we were too high. I didn't want to miss this landing and be directed to the next available island. I pointed the nose down and dove for the runway.

"No no," Hodges yelled at me. "Too fast."

I pulled back on the yoke as we dipped above the concrete, but I'd already screwed it up. The plane acted as if we'd hit an air mattress and bounced back two stories off the pavement. "Let it fall, let go," I heard him yell, and I wished he'd used another word.

I closed my eyes and willed my hands from the wheel. We smacked the ground and porpoised high into the air. A second hit, this time with the tail scraping on the bounce up. On the third hit the tires stuck. I couldn't hear what Hodges was saying. The airplane slowed, and for a split second hope opened my eyes. We began to swerve, each wobble wider than the last, and the plane spun around. Did several rotations on the wet pavement. For an interminable time we were skidding backwards. But slowing, slowing. A last swerve turned us around to face forward just as the runway disappeared and the wheels thudded into soft ground. We stopped. No motion, nothing. You can't imagine what a good feeling nothing is. We were down.

Arden leaned over, put her lips, dry and barked, to my cheek, and murmured some words. I don't know what they were, it didn't matter. I opened my door and, I swear, ten hands reached in. One pair switched off switches, one undid belts, one lifted me, bodily though not harshly, from my seat. The lineup, I realized later, included narcs and local police and paramedics, as well as a bunch of hangar jockeys who thought this a dandy stunt and who had contributed their wisdom to the collective effort to get some amateur from four thousand feet back to soft asphalt. I was aware of a siren nearby, then speeding off, but it wasn't until my rescuers had seated me in some terminal office and I asked for her that I realized they'd packaged Arden off to the hospital.

There was a lot of paper to be pushed. Just like the Clerk would have handled it, the Clerk would do fine in Nassau. Forms and inquiry reports, an affidavit saying I had nothing to declare. The serious stuff was about the former owner of the plane. I told them what I knew, which did not include his last name. They corroborated my story about the island with a call to the estate agent in Provo. Then they checked the house title and ordered a copy of Hofstadter's will to be faxed from back home. I hope it was Canges who got the request. We're confirming the identity of Leonard Mooney of Penniel Cay, a routine police investigation concerning a beautiful woman and a rogue airplane.

I was doing fine in all this. My hands were shaking

and I was so drowsy I was afraid I'd fall asleep and insult the interrogators, but to most eyes I was fine. The cops told me Arden's condition was a botulism you could die from, but she'd thrown most of it up and now they'd shoot her full of something and she'd be out of the hospital in a day or two. Maybe it was when they heard themselves called a dirty name, but as we were talking those three mussels in my stomach achieved fission or fusion, and my gut was ripping open. I got up to find a toilet and I never made it. The floor was coming at me. It was just as Hofstadter and I feared about leaving the surface of the earth. The floor was coming up fast, but happily I started my dive from only five feet seven.

CHAPTER 26.

For a few days I moseyed in and out. Arden told me, Relax and enjoy it. She argued for the unconscious over the conscious. Being unconscious, she maintained, improved the quality of your witness.

Sure enough, while I was sick the most wondrous things happened. Also loathsome. My stomach turned inside out, I was running uncontrolled at both ends and sweating while I shivered, but whether it was the fever or the medicine they gave me or the dizziness from tottering at the edge, not some tinny melancholy but the real live edge, something brought on these delicious visions. It was a dream chute, I would slide for a long time, except for the cramps in my gut, the stabbing throat, and the bed pans. I could see why people prefer sleep to waking. I kept coming in and out like a home movie with a large budget, and on the way I passed through some great scenes.

Arden starred in many of them. She was sporting a new, white-gold haircut, the camera had shot her against a background of dreadful and lifeless blue. Turned out, those weren't completely hallucinations. She'd been released, and had come to sit with me daily.

Also Tommy. An older Tommy, subdued and nervous, a Tommy whose face was a cross between his and mine. Serious-mouthed and adult. By one sideburn a jagged scar lightning-bolted out of his scalp and ran from his black hairline for two inches, the skin shiny like a balloon stretched to the point of breaking. It was a mark the world had put on him. Every once in a while I dreamed a figure I knew to be him, the stubble of a beard and Reba's eyes, observing me as if I was under glass and then I saw him and Arden from above, they were looking down on some generic sick person in a hospital bed.

I was watching all this from this cheap ceiling fixture with space for a single bulb, and I was the bulb. I was low wattage, though not the long-lasting kind, just the opposite, and I saw the world without shadow. Pity roamed the room eating up light. There below lay old Mooney, a sight too sorry to laugh over and too clownish to cry about, pale as ashes and deathly still. Outside the sheet, his hands turned palm up the way saints' hands do in those preposterous statues. Some martyr from the Middle Ages is being riddled with arrows, and he looks sad, not about the arrows, he doesn't mind those, and he turns up his hands like his real problem is he is carved from stone and someone is about to pass him the turkey platter. Side by side in two straight chairs by the bed were Arden and Tommy. Sometimes the Hunchback came and sat the vigil with them. Once he took Tommy's hand and [illegible] it. You could sense the concern in their bent spines, the way their shoulders gathered at the neck.

Another vision that was weird. I was sitting on a beach and someone was lying with his head in my lap. They say in dreams the only person whose identity you can count on is yourself. I looked down and the person was me. With one difference. The face was covered with powdery snow. How would you handle that? What if it was your father? Would you brush it off or blow on it or let it melt? I didn't do anything, I wasn't sure I could make the snow disappear and I was afraid to try.

I know about pity—it's blind, deaf and dumb. It's a wild pig let loose on the landscape and it eats up everything in its path, love included. And self-pity is the biggest pig of all.

One day I came to and I knew I was there, more or less, to stay. My first reaction was disappointment. I mean, where the hell was I? At least on the island I wasn't in anyone's way. Now I'd escaped without wanting to, and I wasn't at all sure I liked the results. For one thing, my throat felt like I'd swallowed a conch shell.

Bustling about in the room was the blackest woman I'd ever seen. She was shaped like a snowman and she wore a robin's-egg blue cardigan over a white uniform. Not quite over—it lay in scalloped folds on the deck made by her considerable rear end. She must have seen me wake up angry and swallowing hard, for she brought me a little paper cup of ice chips.

"Welcome, Mr. Mooney," she sang. She had great diction. "You have been one sick puppy." That was such a funny thing to say, here I am just off the bus from the land of the dreamy dreams, next stop last stop, everybody off, and she's cracking wise. I couldn't help myself—I went to laugh but I had no voice. Only a knife point where the voice had been, and my mind raced in horror to Hofstadter. But the soreness was from the tubes they stick down your throat for oxygen. I suppose I should be thankful for it.

Between the visions, like commercials, Nurse Enid Mowbrey appeared for sixty-second spots. Enid Mowbrey was the pitchman for reality, the way Bob Hope was for Buicks. On her second visit she marched in carrying a pair of scissors. She opened the window, reached out, and grabbed a stalk of branch-high vine. Snipped off a skinny sprig, loaded with buds. She stuck it in a plastic pitcher with water and left it on the swinging table that was supposed to hold my meals.

"You are wanting a spot of color, Mr. Mooney. It cheers the spirit." I didn't need anything of the kind, and two, this was a nondescript twig with gray buds, no color to be seen. I told her as much.

"You *are* the Gloomy Gus, Mr. Mooney, living out there by yourself. I've heard about your life. What is the matter with you?"

"I like my life," I fibbed.

"Well," said Enid Mowbrey. "Enid Mowbrey is on this case."

I skunked down under the sheet.

"Look here," she said. "You see that?" She pointed the scissors at the stick in the pitcher. At the crotch of a bud was a webby-looking thing. "When the butterfly emerges from that cocoon, there's no going back. You too, Mr. Mooney. You will not crawl around like a caterpillar any more. We shall sing Amen as you flutter about the room on speckled wings. You'll just have to get used to that."

Another woman telling me what I'll have to get used to.

Enid Mowbrey scowled at me and shook her scissors. Me, I skunked down a little more and snoozed.

Maybe an hour later Arden showed up. She *had* been to the barber and her hair was freshly mowed. It was like pruning a plant, she said, the cut invigorated her. Under her putty tan, the color was returning to her skin.

She has a surprise, a visitor, she told me, but it must wait until I'm stronger. Is it good, I asked, and she said, you'll see. I don't know why, I was sure it was about Tommy. I figured I dreamed up Arden's new haircut and it came to pass so maybe I'd dreamed up Tommy too, and my heart began to pound so hard I lost control of my bowels.

They cleaned me up and Arden came back and I was about to guess my surprise but they brought in an enormous crinkly thing and plopped it on my bed. Of all things it was a gift basket from Alice, somehow she'd heard of my hospital stay and had sent this gift basket the size of an easy chair. It was wrapped in gold cellophane, and inside were pears and marmalade and walnuts and filberts, a tin of biscuits and one of butter cookies, several cheeses, a jar of candied gherkins, champagne from New Jersey, butterscotch drops, and a paper-wrapped bottle of rose hip jam.

How did she find out, I asked, and Arden told me we'd been on the television. The press had got hold of the story of the man who had never flown a plane before bringing in this girl and they'd played it at the end of the national news. We've heard from everyone, Arden said happily, here's Reba's number and Stace called and now Alice has sent this basket. Not everyone, but she was so tickled I kept the thought to myself.

There was a telephone by the bed and I asked Arden to pass it over. I was staring at a slip of paper where Arden had written Reba's number and it was growing damp from the sweat of my palm.

"You want to wait until you're better?" she asked, and I said I'm as good as I'm going to get.

The long ring, the long pause.

"*Bon giorno. You got Il Direttore Derecchio e su moglie Reba. We out on da canals, pooshin da gondola. You hear-a da beep, you leave-a da numba, we call-a you back. Arrivederci.*"

I hung up. Arden and I sat. I told her maybe when I called Stace I'd tell her Arden and I would come for a visit in Oregon. How would she like that?

She let a smile crack her lips and gaped at me the longest while. Finally she spoke.

"Well. You have to ask Stacey. You can't just go and present me, something they have to cart around."

This was a hell of a place I'd flown to. Everyone had ideas about how I could live my life. Still, Arden had been beaten up by the infection and the tubes, she deserved the benefit of the doubt. I figured she'd be happy to have someone plan out her next days. That must have been why the grin. Every once in a while I closed my eyes and when I opened them, Arden was smiling, and I realized I'd been asleep. We talked like an old couple about what's on Atlanta television, the only station on the set. They bead-chained this remote control to the gate of your bed so you could access the essentials.

You could raise and lower the top half of the mattress to sit up, and with the push of a thumb you could get yourself an emergency nurse or Gilligan re-runs.

Our speech had the cadence of a dream, rests and echoes. Arden left unsaid a lot about Oregon—that I should worry about the family I had, not any new members I happened to import from a ragtag island.

Then I asked, knowing she would know. Arden had hitchhiked around the world.

"You speak Italian?"

"A little."

"What's *moglie*?"

She pronounced it right and made me say it after her. You don't speak the G, only Derek does. *Mo-lyeh*, but you swallow your tongue between the syllables.

"That's it," Arden encouraged me. "*Moglie*. It means wife."

Arden had the title to the airplane and she'd found a dealer in Boca Raton to sell it. It's her dowry, she said, it's how she'll pay her hospital bill and have a stake left over. She read stories from the Miami papers at me, and I dozed in and out. When I woke I asked her to start at the beginning and she did.

"It's like Cyrano. The old lover comes and describes the daily goings-on at court." Arden laughed when she told me this, and I realized why. She *was* my old lover, in an odd way, and I was pleased for it.

She rose to leave.

"When do I get to walk around? Get up and walk around?" I ask.

"Maybe tomorrow. Tomorrow if you're strong enough." I'm stronger than ever, I told her, and she looks great. I told her that, too. She did, great.

"If you're so strong, Leonard, and I look so great, let me ask you something."

"Shoot."

"What is that marble-size drop of water on your cheek?"

Ah, it was so. A fat tear had assembled itself in the corner of my eye and was only now tracking its way down.

* *

Restless I picked up the phone. Stace answered on the second ring. Her mother had called when CNN ran the story but Stace hadn't seen it. She only knew we got off some remote island and I was sick and the television was saying I was a hero for saving this young woman. It was great to talk to her and I forgot about being angry that I'd come back. I told her about my idea of having Arden bunk out with her for a while and maybe I'd come too, bring Arden. I wouldn't stay long. The doctors were saying maybe a month of rest and these horse pills. Arden had a close call, they told her, ciguatera poisoning they called it and I remembered the name just in case we ever met face to face. People die from it. I got the same lecture, but I didn't mention it. Stace didn't have to know.

"You won't stay long," she repeats and I know something's up.

"No, just to drop her off."

"How old is this woman?"

"Your age, I guess, maybe younger." Arden had to be younger, and I sensed that was the wrong answer but I hadn't yet heard the question.

"Dad, you haven't changed have you? All those days on the island, at least maybe you'd pick up a suntan."

I needed a hint. She wanted me to guess, no audience participation, but I needed a hint, so I said What.

"Nothing. Only that I haven't seen you in over three years and the first thing you do is ask me to put up some little babe, not a word about missing me, spending time with me. That's all."

"Oh, Stace, I'm sorry." I was, too, but words are parsley on the platter.

"Let me think about it. I'll call." Before I could say a thing, even read the lines she'd given me, she hung up. I was left trying to swallow.

Next was the press. Mrs. Mowbrey told me the press had been waiting to see me, and I said what for.

"They want to put you on the Cable News, Mr. Mooney. People liked the story. You are what passes in these Bahama islands for a celebrity."

That must have been Arden's surprise, but I regretted discovering it because to me it wasn't a good one. I don't like the news and I wished they'd go away.

I got my wish. For one thing, the story cooled while I was unconscious, dreaming up visitors. For another, I didn't help. To the first question—how did it feel to land a plane when I'd never flown one—I said they must have the facts wrong, I'd had a license for years. The second was about saving a life, and I said I'm not at all sure I had. Which of course I'm not. The meeting, three reporters and a video cameraman, dissolved after that, everyone looking to find the name of the crackpot who had dragged them out on a muggy afternoon.

"I don't want to see any more reporters," I told Enid Mowbrey.

"You must deal with that. I have other matters on my

mind. I must see to the Torrington baby." Once you get better around these places they have a tendency to forget you.

* *

A man stuck his polished and mahogany head in the door.

"Mr. Leonard Mooney?" I told him Yes, although I was cautious about another reporter.

"My name is Hodges."

It was like having an old friend come to visit. He wore a see-through blue shirt that hung outside the trousers, short-sleeved. I hugged him from the bed best I could, which is more a tug of the hand and back-patting. All this grabbing upset the table levered over the bed, and he caught Enid Mowbrey's sorrowful twig and pitcher. I warned him because she's a terror, and he laughed and said, "Yes yes Mr. Mooney. We all need terror in our lives, terror and wonder, and our women give it to us." Like we're old vets from the Anzio invasion or something. He put the gray stick back and refilled the pitcher from the tap.

He has, he told me, three children, all in the primary school.

"You look after them," I told him.

"Yes yes. Mrs. Hodges and I do that."

"And don't let any of them fly around in airplanes."

He laughed, thinking I was jokey. "Oh, Mr. Mooney. I don't know about that. If one became a pilot we would be very proud."

I needed to say something about the landing, so I thanked him, which seemed at the time the silliest thing I'd ever said. It embarrassed him, almost a pink blush through the furniture-polish skin, and he wanted no part of it, so I laid off. I asked him whether he'd ever done that before.

"No, Mr. Mooney. I have had fifteen years as a controller and I've handled," here he counted with an index finger on the pinky of the other hand, "no radio, no engine, no fuel and what else? No electrical power, no flaps. You, Mr. Mooney, are my first no pilot." He was a short man, my height, I was glad to see that. Before he left, he fished about in his shirt pocket. "You have won these," he said, and pinned something to the chest of my hospital gown. A little flimsy set of metal wings, and stamped on the shield in its center, Visit the Bahamas.

* *

After the excitement they gave me another shot of something and I took off again to goo-goo land. Tommy showed up, vivid as a dream. He was now a man. He looked more like me, or I like him, but he was missing the craziness. He was calm and handsome, and he spoke softly. He works with his hands, he told me, but that was all the news I can remember. You could see why the news doesn't matter, you never get any real news in dreams.

We talked for hours. At one point my hand wandered up and my fingers touched the scar on his face. It wasn't a bad scar but it's just what a parent fears, you won't be around, your kid will get cut or scalded and here my son had gone and done something and I didn't know what. I wanted to say this, and just as I got close, close enough to collect the breath in my chest, like old Hofstadter with his wand, and coordinate it with my throat which keeps shutting down, Tommy reached up and took hold of my wrist so my fingers stayed on the scar.

We sat there like that for as long as the dream lasted.

He told me where he had been and what had become of Dog, but I don't remember any of the words. Whenever he got to an ugly part, you could see in his eyes the way he switched out of it. He wanted to skip those parts, he was just like I was. While he was saying his story, he leaned forward, still holding my wrist. All the time he had the kindest smile, not laughing, more assuring. Don't worry, Dad, his eyes were saying all the time he was talking. Don't worry, it turns out fine.

This time when I woke, I knew I had imagined Tommy. That was a good sign, telling reality from not, so I figured I must be getting better. Crossing over was easy, except that at the border instead of *tourista*, I picked up my old depression. I don't know what it was that depressed me. The buds on Enid Mowbrey's cut branch were peeking out, tongues of pink with a little yellow in the middle. Also I was thinking what it would look like back on the island, how the slices of cheese were lined up in plastic jackets waiting for me in the refrigerator, the waves on the water.

Another strange thing. I couldn't stop thinking about those flying grasshoppers. The ones that make a racket when you come close? They must have drugged me to have my mind looping the loops, I hadn't thought about flying grasshoppers for years. You know how kids are, there are some things that frighten them and you have to tell them not to be scared. Except of course when they're right, times when they should be scared and there are enough of those. When Stace was a kid, these grasshoppers used to terrify her. They would spring up in front of you and clatter, just as you were about to step on them. We'd walk in the country and I would run off ahead, scattering them and shooing them away. Now Stace was up in Oregon and I'd give any odds the place was chock-a-block full of flying grasshoppers. I'd bet it was the damn grasshopper capital of the world.

CHAPTER 27.

"I'm afraid I spoiled your surprise."

Arden returned bright and early the next day. I was in a fresh gown, my rump was sore from gamma globulin and my stomach was crimping before the bowl of chicken consommé on the bed table.

"Oh?"

"The television people. I don't think I advanced the story. I'm sorry."

"That's fine, Leonard. I didn't think you would like the limelight." I was relieved she wasn't disappointed. I passed on my fifteen seconds of fame, maybe Arden would use them. "My surprise wasn't the television people. It was that you were back on the map, and how the world is welcoming you."

"They are?"

"Everyone is calling."

"Not everyone," I said, and on my words the phone went off. It was a movie moment.

Arden picked it up and chatted away. "He's right here," she said at last, and I didn't know what to think.

It was Stace.

The call triggered in me a mix, like that snack they serve at parties instead of food—you have to pick out the peanuts from the breakfast cereal. Mostly I was relieved. I had meant to beat her to the punch, to call her to tell her I know how she felt. That may not be front-page news everywhere, but it is in our family. But mostly I was relieved.

She started by how she shouldn't have jumped down my throat, and I cut her off. I told her she hadn't jumped down my throat, if she wanted to see how that was done she'd need to meet Arden, who was an Olympic throat jumper. And I told her how I missed her and the things I got to tell Tommy except when I was unconscious. Which I was prepared to recognize as an inferior way of conversing. If you get another chance to grab that hand, you don't think long about it.

Stace said she'd love to put up Arden. Stace sounded as if she'd found herself a clearing in the jungle, no mean feat, and I told her that. She didn't want to take any credit. Mention of the jungle reminded me.

"Stace—I need to ask. Aren't there a lot of woods in Oregon?"

"Woods? You mean forests?"

"Yeah."

"Sure. Why?"

"Well, I was wondering." Don't you have a lot of grasshoppers?"

"Grasshoppers? Dad, are you relapsing?"

"No. I was just wondering."

Just as we were getting chummy she decided to present me with another left hook. "I don't want you to think all is forgiven," she told me. "That I'm not still pissed."

"For what?"

"For quitting. You up and quit on us, so it's about time you come back and start acting like a person."

"Hey, not so fast. I'm a sick man."

"Bullshit, Dad. It's about time."

"Well, I may be coming back but I never said anything about a person. I'm not planning to come back as a person."

"Da-ad," she groaned. It was a reassuring note.

I asked about her boyfriend the carpenter and how her mother was doing, and she filled me in.

"So," said Stace. "I meant to ask. How'd you get her off the island?"

"We flew out," I answered. I tried to be casual, my voice the bored one I imagined test pilots use. But I couldn't help adding, "In a 185."

"Dad," she said about my coming to visit. "Thanks for asking. Thanks for the favor."

"You're doing me the favor, Dorothy."

"Yeah. Well, it works both ways."

Enid Mowbrey wanted me to nap. She was midway through a double shift and in a foul mood. She drew the blinds and put Alice's Alice-sized basket on the window bench where it popped in the breeze from the air conditioner and I nodded off to the hum of the fan and the crackle of yellow cellophane.

* *

When I awoke Enid Mowbrey was rummaging about. "Where did you put my spray of frangipani, Mr. Mooney?" When Hodges knocked over the vase we moved it to the window sill, so I pointed—it was easy to miss—and she went over to inspect.

"Ha," she said, she was Mowbrey of the Yard.

"Ha what?" and she brought it over. I thought she meant the blossoms, but no, her thumbnail pointed to the little webby thing. It'd been sprung and whatever had been inside was now out.

She carefully laid the branch on my bed, though the blossoms shimmered and spilled their yellow pollen, and she began to scour the room. She was on the trail of the escaped prisoner. She searched the corners and around the door jambs, on the night table, in the john. She snuck up on the drapes, simple cotton things Alice would have replaced, and swept her hand across. Then she presented me with a closed fist and slowly opened her fingers.

In the crease of her palm crouched a moth, a puny little thing, the color of a bag you'd pack your lunch in.

"No fluttering about the room on speckled wings?" I asked.

"One of the Lord's creatures," she said. "Beautiful in God's mercy. Say Amen, Mr. Mooney."

"Amen," I said. You have to remember, this was the woman who brought my food and stood me up at the toilet.

She opened the window and freed the moth. It was the puniest moth you'd ever seen, and I was glad of it. I wouldn't needle her again, she'd had her heart set, but still I was glad. No more fables for our time about how the worm turns into a butterfly.

An orderly came to take my order for the evening meal, and I told him no, none of his hospital apple sauce, Arden would be here for dinner, and we'd both have a steak, blood rare, and French fries, I'm ravenous, and one for Nurse Mowbrey and one for him. He said he would see what he could do.

Alone again I took the phone and placed the call. I might have called Alice to thank her for the butter cookies but I didn't. You have to go with your heart. I got the man himself, the principal of a thousand voices.

"You have reached the principle principal."

"Derek? Leonard Mooney."

"Leonard Mooney. We thought you were among the dead."

"Well I was, but I'm back. How are the times?"

"What?"

"The times."

"What times?"

"For the tenkay, races, stuff like that. Going down I hope?" There was a silence.

"Listen, asshole. I don't have to take anything from you. We heard all about that howling episode. 'Come out and fight.' That was you."

"That was me."

"Yeah? Well, you ought to be ashamed."

I didn't know what he wanted me to say. I am?

"I am," I said. It seemed to set him back.

"Do you want Reba?" The way he asked, it was a gopher ball of a line, Canges would knock it out of the park, but I let it go.

"Is she there?"

"I'll put her on."

Reba and I talked. She wanted to hear about the TV stuff, but I was already tired of it. Still we talked, about our lives. She told me she and Derek had gotten married. I was ready for this, so I said, That's great, Babe, you go out and get 'em. I could tell from her voice that she might like the person I had it in mind to become. Or at least she might have, before she met Derek and had to deal with his expectations. She doesn't like to disappoint, Reba, and Derek has his own hopes and plans and she has hers, and she needs to attend to them all.

It sounds crazy but Reba and I understand each other. I'd forgotten to ask Stace for her address and telephone number and Reba got it for me and even suggested that she break the ice with Stace about our popping in on her, make the first call, but I told her no need, the ice had melted. She asked me what I was going to do after Oregon and I said I hadn't a clue and I didn't. Although as she was soon to hear, suddenly I did. I had more than a clue.

Reeb was about to say goodbye, worrying about how her voice sounded, liquid and anxious, what with her husband standing there. She didn't tell me he was there but I was sure. Standing by her shoulder, studying tennis victories from his journals and jogging in place. Her phone was headed for the cradle, when the idea hit me and I screamed.

"Reeb!"

"Yes?"

"Don't hang up yet."

"I won't."

"You know what I'm going to do? After I see Stace?"

"What?"

"After I visit? I'm going to look for Tommy. I'm going

to sell old Hofstadter's house, the island, there'll be enough money to do anything. I'm just going to go look for him and find him."

After that Reba was in tears, and pretty soon I was, but she could afford it and I was woefully short of bodily fluids.

"Well, Babe," I said after a while of this. If you'd been listening in you'd have thought the transatlantic cable had sprung a leak. "What do you think?"

"Oh, Leonard." She said that once more and neither one of us had the breath to say much else. It was like drowning but the opposite, like coming up for the third and last time, this time I'd stay, pop out of wherever I'd been submerged and surface in the land of lung-full beings. Something like that had occurred to me at four thousand feet, before we raised Nassau. The earth looks hard and dangerous from there. You want to keep close to it. You wished the hell you'd never left it and you'd forgive a lot of pettiness, a lot of Cangeses or Dereks, or even Reba's going off with him, if you could only make it back. When a nurse arrived to freshen the I.V., I told her I was dehydrating, she needed to rig the family-sized bag.

No steaks, the kitchen said, but boiled chicken and cling peaches, and maybe the nurse could swing that. Arden had come back, and she said Bugger the peaches, we'll have a party. She took off with something in mind. The nurse pulled me out of bed for a walk around the ward, and by the time we made a lap, Arden had returned toting five large pizzas. The nurses' station went on full alert and Arden rounded up patients and orderlies on the floor. They'd inexplicably housed me in the orthopedic ward, so my neighbors on the floor were all plegics, quads and paras, and pretty soon everyone had gathered in the center hall. I was wheeled in on my bed wearing my wings, most of the other partygoers were on pallets and in wheelchairs, and a few, the shoulder replacements and the arthroscopics, could actually walk. Two cases of Bud arrived on a dolly and Arden sent the beer man back for more. Colostomy bags and bottles were working overtime, but the staff didn't seem to mind, it was a victory party. I stopped Arden dishing a meatball-pepper-extra-cheese.

"Oregon," I said.

"What about it?"

"You're not coming, are you?"

"No."

"I didn't think so. What'll you do?"

She fingered a runaway goober of mozzarella. "I'll come to the States with you. I want to draw the Everglades. And the Grand Canyon."

"You'll need a big pad."

She shot me the look of a pal and took the advice.

What people do at hospital parties is pretty much what they do outside, tell their stories. Each of the quads has a beaut. A gunshot, a hang glider, two water-skiers, and one guy, he got the biggest hand, who was screwing and slid off satin sheets.

We sent word down to Pediatrics for Nurse Mowbrey to join us. She looked in to thank me and shook a finger at me.

"If you are well enough for a party perhaps you need to check out." She wouldn't stay, she was needed by the Torrington baby, and she toddled off with a double slice and a Diet Coke.

I got them to bring out the mammoth gift basket, God help me it looked a little like Alice herself. Had she ever had a gold cellophane dress? And wouldn't you think she'd be filled with perfect pears and marmalades of the world? People brought flowers from their rooms and the physical therapist weaved the stems together, so everyone was wearing leis and floral wreaths. Arden took a laundry pen and drew on people's casts, birds mostly, eagles and flamingos, this for people who live looking up, peeing in a bottle and flat on a board. One guy, the silk-sheet slider, was in a full-body cast, and she drew him life-size on his cast, nude with tiers of muscles and an enormous dork. By the last hour, a nurse was spreading rose-hip jam onto pizza crust, the Jersey champagne had come and gone, and the entire ward was cooking.

The binge triggered a new but brief havoc in my gut. It set me back a few paces. My last evening I was walking around, feeling guilty because of what Nurse Mowbrey had said about checking out. I had heard so much about this Torrington baby I decided to take a look. Enid Mowbrey didn't seem the kind of woman to be thrown by some trifle. So, my ass sticking through the green hospital gown, I wandered down the halls backing to the wall whenever someone came past, to the elevator and down to Pediatrics.

The Torrington baby was born ten weeks premature. At the clerk's office, ten weeks in some lawsuit is a lark. You wouldn't think being a little off schedule you'd miss out on so much. Anyone who thinks he's unprepared for life, he needs a little time to gather himself together, doesn't get it.

I was standing in the ward, seven cribs for seven

preemies, none like the Torrington baby, and Mrs. Mowbrey came to my side. I felt her by me and I sagged into her. Enid Mowbrey didn't flinch, sturdy is the word.

"What are we to do, Mrs. Mowbrey?"

"Whatever do you mean, Mr. Mooney?"

"What are we to do? Will that baby be all right?"

"It is still a baby, Mr. Mooney. It knows enough to move away from pain and toward pleasure. It is one of us."

"Yes?"

"Yes."

"And us?"

"I cannot speak for us, Mr. Mooney. The baby is my patient, not us."

"So," I said. "We'll just have to live with it?"

"That is right, Mr. Mooney. We'll just have to live with it. Compared to what is facing the Torrington baby, that should not be hard."

"You are right, Mrs. Mowbrey. Amen to that."

"Amen."

* *

That night, I was dead asleep chasing dreams with a stick, the telephone rang. Inches from my ear. By the time I lifted the receiver, the caller had gone. There was no one there.

My heart was pumping blood through my ears. It wouldn't slow down. I know it's commonplace, it happens to everyone, like visualizing yourself seconds late at an intersection as a truck rumbles through. It happens all over the world, someone could tell us how often and what the height and age and hobbies of the terrified soul are and how many of them die of a heart attack on the spot. Still, I couldn't catch my breath or quiet myself down.

I rose and walked to the window. The night was lit by so plump a moon it appeared as bogus day. Across the way was a vacant lot. Its soil had been graded, and nuggets of concrete lay about. A hurricane fence surrounded the lot, and on the fence facing me was a large sign that announced the zoning and a phone number. In the blue and sharp light I could make out the pattern of the fence on the ground, the elongated diamonds from the chain link and the dark rectangle that was the shadow of the sign. It was the emptiest sight I'd ever seen. I thought of that rum I'd wasted on the island, the bottle I'd broken that dread-filled night, somehow it had sunk into the soil, and I figured that was the last of drink for me. I was done with it.

Eventually I was sprung. Arden helped me put the house on the market, and even though the estate agent said it would take a while, I was startled by how much she meant to ask. One's own island, she told us, it's a unique venue, which I hadn't realized, I hadn't even realized it was a venue. I didn't mention the airstrip. Or C. Aubrey. People in the world are busy and they don't want to hear about a friend of yours who happens to have knotholes, no matter how strong the bond.

Selling Arden's airplane involved title documents, maintenance logs, airworthiness certificates, a pile of paper that to my surprise Michael kept in good order. The dealer in Boca Raton had a couple of bidders and Arden was pleased with what it would bring. We were both staked to a future, or at least a part of it. You can't be completely staked.

Arden and I boarded the United Airlines. She sat a row ahead and I behind her, by the window. Sitting and waiting was, I thought, a great disadvantage to flying your own plane, assuming you weren't terrified. Maybe I'd ask Stace if she wanted to learn to fly. If I could find him, Tommy too.

I'd given no thought to how to find him. None, although trying seemed so obvious I don't know why I took so long to come up with it. Maybe I'd go back to Indianapolis to pick up the trail or put a picture on telephone poles where the kids hang. Waiting for takeoff, I got this idea. I'd run a large display ad. But it's funny, I must have still been under the drug, because I could see this weird ad, a half-page box with a border:

STANLEY'S SHOES

CURES THE BLUES

MEN WOMEN CHILDREN

with the photograph and my telephone number. I saw that ad running in four or five cities' papers and I saw the Tommy of my visions looking at it, sitting in some YMCA and smiling to himself.

When I understood that I was to try to find Tommy, before I almost dropped the phone on Reba, two other facts hit me. That instant. Not speculation, facts, like you know about death. First, I realized Tommy was alive and walking around somewhere. Second, I knew that when I found him, he'd have this lightning-bolt scar coming out of his scalp.

Men, women and children. Whose idea was that?

The airplane engines ran up and the pilot announced we were number three for takeoff. To kill time I wrote out a ladder. I changed HELL to BACK in eight steps. I looked at the list and laughed. The woman in the aisle seat snuck a sidelong look, here's a guy wearing a pair of kid's pilot wings who laughs at nothing. A loony. She dove into her seat pocket to find the in-flight magazine. I laughed because PANE was in the middle of the ladder, but of course the wrong kind, the kind you look through. Miami, a change to Chicago, then direct to Portland, where Stace would meet me at the baggage carousel.

I thought of old Hofstadter and his dream—the boxes of photographs. I didn't want years in snapshots, years that reveal themselves too late. I wanted mine in small packets, twenty-four hours at a time, each packet stamped with the date and in black ink, Use before the End of the Day. The present isn't so bad. It's where we live and sure as hell where we die. Once you leave off worrying about annihilation, falling out of the sky, you can sit back and enjoy the ride.

The airplane taxied into position. Piloted, I was happy to note, by someone else. Though I felt a kinship with him. With Arden and the passengers too, even the lady who thought I was a lunatic. The airplane roared down the runway. It lifted off, the wheels folded under us with a thunk, and Arden looked back and gave me thumbs-up. We climbed at a roller-coaster angle and banked to the west. Directly below me the long concrete airstrip spun out of sight. The plastic window distorted the edges of my sightline, but I saw the coast. We flew over a boat yard and piers, over tourist ships at port. I looked into the bottomless funnels of their smokestacks. The plane hitched to adjust its bank and the entire island that is New Providence rotated on its roots, lazy-susanned in the sea and slipped behind us, and through all this, it is a curious thing, through all this I felt not a twinge of fear, not the slightest vertigo.

ACKNOWLEDGMENTS

Getting a novel to print is a bit like mushing a sled across the tundra—bleak, toilsome, not possible without help. I am grateful to Alix Beeney, Jody Rein, and as ever to Jaren, for the long tug.

Other novels by Bruce Ducker

BLOODLINES

LEAD US NOT INTO PENN STATION

MARITAL ASSETS

BANKROLL

FAILURE AT THE MISSION TRUST

RULE BY PROXY